THE
SHIKE
STORIES

CROSS SECTIONS

THE
SHIKE STORIES

CROSS SECTIONS

CLY BOEHS

AUTHOR OF *BACK THEN*

LIFFEY PRESS

an imprint of
THE OGHMA PRESS

OGHMA

CREATIVE MEDIA

Bentonville, Arkansas • Los Angeles, California
www.oghmacreative.com

Library of Congress Cataloging-in-Publication Data

Names: Boehs, Cly, author.
Title: Cross Sections/Cly Boehs. | The Shike Stories #1
Description: First Edition. | Bentonville: Liffey, 2021.
Identifiers: LCCN: 2021934730 | ISBN: 978-1-63373-646-7 (hardcover) |
ISBN: 978-1-63373-647-4 (trade paperback) | ISBN: 978-1-63373-648-1 (eBook)
Subjects: BISAC: FICTION/Literary | FICTION/Family Life | FICTION/Religious
LC record available at: https://lccn.loc.gov/2021934730

Liffey Press hardcover edition October, 2021

Jacket art by Carol Bloomgarden
Jacket & Interior Design by Casey W. Cowan
Editing by Gordon Bonnet, Cyndy Prasse Miller, & Amy Cowan

Published by Liffey Press, an imprint of The Oghma Press, a subsidiary of The Oghma Book Group.

To my family with love

Viola Mae Becker Boehs, my mother (1918-2005)
*Taught me resilience, determination, and hopefulness. She was one of the strongest women
I've ever known. Her love of freedom was indomitable.*

Frank Eugene Boehs, my father (1909-2005)
*Taught me the belief in life as it presents itself. He was, at heart, a Buddhist master. He
worked harder and smarter than most men alive.*

Roger Merle Boehs, my brother (1941-2008)
*Taught me what talent is and how it connects with love of discipline and work. He had a
sense of humor and an understanding about the human condition that he brought to every
personal conversation I had with him.*

Jimmy Joe Boehs, my brother (1945-1998)
*Taught me laughter, enthusiasm, Christmas joy, and jazz.
He loved endless talk from day till night.*

Franki Jean Boehs Dennison, my sister (b.1963)
*Teaches me patience, integrity, forgiveness and wholehearted love.
She strives every day to make the world a better place for all of us.*

ACKNOWLEDGEMENTS

THE SHIKE STORIES WERE WRITTEN over many, many years, so the number of people influential in their development is far too many to credit here. The first story was created in a writing circle at Emma's, led by Zee Zahava, in the early nineties which was inspired by a postcard I chose from dozens she offered as prompts to writing. I read that short story, "The Marble Game," in public shortly after it was written, and from there, the young girl narrator simply took wings and flew from one story to the next. I wrote many other works while she was coming to life, but her tales never retreated, only became more urgent to be told. Out of file drawers full of her stories, I gathered those which fit into an arrangement and form that could be read all of a piece.

One of the questions I'm often asked from readers and listeners is if these stories are true. I certainly hope so, but, if by the question—which I think is the intention—the questioners want to know if they are memoir, the answer is no. As I stated in the acknowledgements of Back Then—the novel of short stories that is the overarching narrative about many of the people in The Shike Stories in their later years—I have taken parts of the details and incidents of my family's stories and experiences and used them toward fictional ends. I wish to create a time, place, and atmosphere of my upbringing, not an account or specific rendering of people in my past. Shike and others in her world have taken journeys emanating from their natures and circumstances in this novel.

I am forever indebted to my parents for their encouragement and support through the years of my writing and artmaking. Special gratitude to my sister, Franki Boehs Dennison for her interest, listening, and advice about all my creative endeavors. She, above all others, understands why I write and is attentive to my ongoing accounts of where I am in that process. She has otherworldly patience and amazing social skills. Her love and dialogues with me are cherished deeply.

Many thanks to the expertise and professional guidance of Casey Cowan and Gordon Bonnet of Oghma Creative Media through the entire publication process. The cover to this book is so fine. Special thanks to Carol Bloomgarden and Casey Cowan for their willingness to include me in the designing and its fabulous outcome.

Gordon Bonnet, my writing partner and editor, has seen me through the thick of it countless times. He has heard and read every single story more than once—some, many times, and many which were not included—a prodigious feat. He gave advice always with clarity, skill, and good-naturedness. I trust his editing wholeheartedly. His friendship is a treasure.

I thank the authors, editors, and staff at Oghma for their contributions toward its publication, especially Cyndy Prasse Miller and Amy Cowan for their line editing skills.

My close friend, Nancy Osborn, has read most of these stories, talked to me about them, and offered her expert advice in their development. She is a writer, editor, poet, documentarian, activist, voracious reader, and loving friend—not to mention all the roles she plays as wife, mother, grandmother, and on and on as Renaissance Woman. I rely on her in so many ways—everything from daily health and friendship updates to companionship at opera, live theater and films, the sharing of books, ideas, and, yes, even recipes. There simply aren't words to express my love and appreciation for who she is in my life.

I wish to thank the following for their support during the writing of these stories: Debbie Boehs, Judith Pratt, Jae Sullivan, Anne Furman, Cara Franchi, June Wolfman, The Sheavlys (Scott, Marcia, Jake and Will), Connie Bracco, June Szabo, Elizabeth Wavle-Brown, Donna Stevens, Joan and Ed Ormondroyd, Tonia Saxon, and John Levine—including providing perfect writing space—George Rhoads, Emily Rhoads Johnson, Carrie Turcsik, June

Szabo, Donna Stevens, Leslie Knight, Marjorie Clay, and Marcelle Lapow Tour. My Taoist Tai Chi group of Trumansburg is very special. They inspire me, always, to attempt my best.

I lost two beloved friends recently. Words cannot express their losses in my life. I will be forever grateful to Bob Franchi and Shade Gomez for their friendships and support of my creative endeavors through the years.

THE
SHIKE
STORIES

CROSS SECTIONS

HOLD YOUR HORSES

1.

December, 1941

DADDY STEPS INTO THE LIVING room, looks around, stands without taking off his hat and coat. I run to him and grab his leg. He doesn't reach down like he usually does, picking me up and putting me down with a "You're growin' like a weed." He pats me on the back and says, "Hey, Shypoke, your mother around?" When Daddy calls me Shypoke I know he's thinking about something else. He almost always calls me Shike. Momma told me that Uncle Clifford named me Shypoke. and then everybody started calling me that, and it wasn't long before everybody was running it together, and that's how it got to be Shike. Momma said Shypoke doesn't mean anything except that Uncle Clifford thinks I'm special. But Daddy told me Uncle Clifford must think I don't like to talk and I'm slow as molasses. "But then, it's not you but your Uncle Clifford who's the poke to my way of thinkin'. And the shy part, well, shy… I don't know where he got that idea because neither one of you is bashful by a long shot."

I step back while Daddy takes his hat and coat off and hangs them on the clothes tree by the door. He takes off his shoes real quick, toe-to-heel, toe-to-heel, and puts them together on the shoe tray. I feel a little shudder inside when he walks past me fast toward the kitchen and looks around.

"Momma's in bed," I say and wait.

"In bed? At this hour? Where's Teddy?" Daddy is getting upset. Mom-

ma's been in bed all afternoon, but Daddy is acting like he doesn't know she
ever does this.

"Teddy's next door."

He says to himself, "Well, this's new." To me, he asks, "The Krueger's?"
Why's that?" He looks around the kitchen like he doesn't believe Momma isn't
making supper. Then he walks to the bedroom.

"Darlene?" He steps slow into their bedroom but doesn't close the door.
"Why's Teddy at the Krueger's?"

I hear Momma's voice, a whisper. She sounds like she's been crying. "You
hear the news?"

"Course I heard the news. Why's Teddy next door?"

"I'm, I'm... so dizzy, Vernon. I couldn't hold him proper. He kept kicking me,
and my balance is off. I was afraid to leave him in his crib with Shike while I went
to bed." I hear Daddy take some steps, and he comes through the bedroom door.

"We can't leave him there." His voice is angry but not loud yet.

"Course not," Momma says. "I didn't intend to. Just until you came home."

"Well, I'm going over there now," he says, like he's talking to the living
room and not to Momma. He messes up my hair on top and smiles a little as
he passes me on the way to the coat tree. He is walking very fast. Momma's
talking, but Daddy isn't listening. He grabs his coat but leaves his hat behind.
He leans over and starts putting on his shoes. "We can't leave our kids at the
neighbors, for cryin' out loud." He yanks the strings tight on both of his shoes,
jerking the front door open but standing there a minute, looking at me. "These
people are old. Mrs. Krueger can't take care of a baby!" He talks like Momma's too far away to hear and I'm the one that needs to take care of things
while he's at work. He slams the front door. I don't hear what Momma says. I
only hear her cry soft after Daddy is gone.

I wait at Momma's bedroom door.

"Shike?" she calls. Her voice is hoarse, like she's got a cold.

I run to the bed. She is covered with a quilt she never uses. It's just for show
because it was made by Gramma Dirks and mostly hangs on a rack at the end
of Momma and Daddy's bed. Wedding present. Today it's Momma's blanket.
I pull the footstool around and stand on it so I can see her better.

She rolls on her back. The bed springs make noise. She presses her eyes with her fingers. "You there, honey?" She rolls over on her side, looks at me and reaches out for my hand. Her fingers are wet, but I hold them anyway. She opens her eyes. "You okay, honey?" Her quilt smells like sleep. Her fingers aren't tight around mine, so I let go. I think she doesn't know my hand is there. I turn her hand over and put one of my hands on the bottom and one on the top of hers and press them together.

"Sandwich," I say. She smiles.

"Love sandwich," she says.

We say this sometimes. "You sick again, Momma?"

"Oh, I just don't feel good. It's nothing. Daddy went to get Teddy. I'll get up and put supper together."

I knew she was sick when I was in the living room before Daddy came home. She wasn't taking a nap like she said, with her bedroom door open. I was being quiet, playing with my paper dolls. Shirley Temple is still in the middle of the living room floor standing in her wood base. She's only in her underwear. I can see her through the bedroom door. Her clothes are spread out on the cushions of the couch. Momma wasn't supposed to buy me Shirley Temple, but she said, "Oh what the heck. You live childhood only once." Daddy helped me punch Shirley Temple out of the book, and he cut out her clothes for me. He showed me how to keep her clothes on by folding the tabs over her body. Daddy said something about Shirley Temple and Mennonites, but I didn't hear all he said. When I asked why Shirley Temple and Mennonites don't mix, he didn't answer, just kept cutting with his scissors. But I knew. Mennonites don't go to the movies, but Momma's still in love with them, especially the stars.

When Momma doesn't move from the bed, I look around for her slippers. They are together at the foot of the bed. I go get them.

"Here's your house shoes." I hold them up.

She smiles and slides her legs around and down, sitting up slow with sighs. I move the footstool real fast so she won't stumble on it and fall down.

"Oh my. I am so dizzy. Where is this dizziness coming from?"

"I don't know, Momma."

She reaches over and pats my hand. "It's all right, honey. It's nothing for you to worry about. I'm just a little off today, that's all." She stands up but almost falls. Gramma does this too. I've seen it lots of times, when she grabs a chair or table and waits. "Your Grandma Dirks is dizzy sometimes," Momma's told me. "She's not sick or anything. Just a little airy." Dizzy and airy mean Gramma's getting old. I wonder if Momma's getting old like Gramma.

I stand close to her, then reach over and touch her arm. "I'm okay, honey. Why don't you get started in the kitchen with the dishes and things. I'll be in there in a minute. Everything's sitting on the counter. Daddy can give you a hand." When I get to the door, Momma says, "Hey, diddle, diddle." Her voice is so quiet I almost don't hear her say it. But she's smiling at me.

I smile back and say real loud, "The cat fiddles."

She laughs and says, "...and the cow jumps over the moon! And the little dog laughs to see such a sight... and...."

"The dish runs away with the spoon!" I yell back.

"You go set the dishes and the spoons for me, okay?"

I nod, but I wait until she's standing up and is holding the bed post before I leave to set the table.

———

"YOUR MOTHER UP YET?" DADDY asks as he pushes the front door closed with his foot. He jumps his coat off and lets it fall to the floor. "You wanna pick that up for me, Shike? Lay it over the arm of the sofa." He throws Teddy's blanket toward me. "That too."

I pick up the blanket first and put it on the arm of the sofa like Daddy told me. Then I drag his coat up to the sofa couch, but I can't get it over the arm. It's too heavy. So I pick up Shirley Temple's clothes and put them back with her in the box on the couch. When I push Daddy's coat up on the cushions, I look over and see Daddy's pulling his shoes off toes-to-heels. He doesn't want to walk into the living room with them on, with Momma yelling about no respect. He leaves them side by side in the shoe tray.

Teddy's still bundled up. I can't see his face because Daddy's pulled the string on his bunting so tight the hood covers most of his face. Teddy is crying real loud. He looks like a sack of potatoes that's moving around. Daddy holds the diaper bag out for me. While I drag it to the couch, he holds Teddy on his arm, untying the string around his head. Teddy comes out of his hood screaming bloody murder. I pick up his pacifier that hits the floor. Daddy takes it from me and puts it in his pocket.

"Shhhh, shhhhh," he says to Teddy, bouncing him against his stomach. He walks with him to the bedroom door that he pushes open wide with his foot. "Darlene, Teddy's wet, and there's no supper." He is mad.

"I'm well aware of that, Vernon." Her voice is very tight, like she can hardly say the words. She must've sat down again after I left, because I hear her stand up from the bed. She walks stiff to the door. She stands in the doorway and gives Daddy a mean look. "I don't feel right today. Can't you see that?" She pauses a minute. "You think I'da taken the baby over there if I was okay?"

"Well, okay or not, I don't want Teddy there. Those people're nice, but they're old. Maude Krueger can't take care of a young baby anymore. Where the hell is your head, Darlene?"

Momma waits a minute, brushes her hair back out of her face with her hand. Her eyes look far away, and I want to cry. All at once she sees me and says, "It's okay, Shike, honey. Just go do what I asked you to do."

I feel my face scrunching up, and I start crying even though I don't want to. But I don't cry loud. It's the kind that I can stop if I have to. I run to where she is. I can help her walk.

She touches my head as she walks past me to a dining room chair. She doesn't sit down right away, just leans against it like it's a cane. "Come on, Shike. You be a big girl for me now, okay?"

Daddy walks over to her and tries to hand her Teddy, but she shakes her head. She scoots the chair out and sits down hard. Daddy walks fast to the other side of the dining room table with Teddy bouncing up and down, one of his arms flopping back and forth. He lays Teddy on the dining room table while he takes his bunting off and throws it on the table. He puts the pacifier from his pocket back in Teddy's mouth. Then he starts to take Teddy's jumper off. Teddy isn't crying anymore. He's moving his arms and legs up and down real fast. He smiles at Daddy, then stops his smile, quick. I go over and hold his jumper feet. I think he will stop kicking if I hold his feet. But Daddy bumps against me to let me know I'm in the way. He sits Teddy up and leans him against his stomach while he pulls the jumper out from under him. He holds him up high while I pull the suit off his legs. Teddy makes funny little air-noises, sucking his pacifier. When Daddy lays him back down, his legs are going up and down, up and down.

"Get me a diaper, Shike, will you? And a wet washrag while you're at it." He has Teddy's soggy diaper off when I come back with a clean one, the washrag dripping in my other hand. "Pick the dirty one up off the floor and put it in the bucket in the bathroom." I pick up the smelly diaper by as little as I can and turn my head to the side while I carry it to the bathroom.

"Shike," Daddy says, "It's dragging the floor. C'mon now, you can hold it up proper till you get there. You can wash your hands when you're done. It's not like you didn't have wet diapers yourself when you were little."

I am afraid to lift the diaper too high because then when I walk it might swing against my face, but I do as Daddy wants. I hold it way out away from me.

Momma starts to stand up when I walk past her toward the bathroom. "Let me have that, Shike. I'll take care of it."

I shake my head. I want to help.

I walk fast to the bathroom, lift the bucket's lid, and drop the dirty diaper inside. One corner of it falls over the edge of the bucket and stays there. Momma won't be happy if I don't get it all inside because there are other dirty diapers in the bucket, and they'll smell up the house if I don't get the lid on tight. But I don't want to touch the diaper anymore. I look around for something to poke the corner down with. There's a wire hanger on the doorknob to Momma and Daddy's bedroom. I get it and try to poke the diaper into the bucket with a corner of the hanger. But the diaper won't move. I look inside the bucket to see what's in the way. The bucket is so full that the diaper I want to go inside doesn't have enough room to fall down with the others. I try to push the whole soggy mess with the hanger so I can fit it inside. I gag. The smell of Teddy's poop smears and pee makes my stomach jump, and I think I will throw up. I push down with the hanger real, real hard so I can be done and leave the bathroom. But the hanger slips in my hand, and I start falling head-first toward the bucket, the lid scraping my arm bad as it goes down into the mess up to my elbow. When the bucket tips over, the bottom hits my legs so I move away and stumble, falling on top of Teddy's diapers that've spilled out onto the floor. I push up and try to stand but fall back down onto my stomach, coughing and spitting. I am sick with the smell, and Teddy's diaper mess is all over my face and arms and legs. I think Momma will say my dress is ruined. I am yelling no, no, no and trying to throw everything off of me when Momma walks into the bathroom.

"What in heaven's na…?" she asks but doesn't get all of it out because she looks down at the mess on the floor just before she steps on it.

I start to cry. I can't help it. It just comes out when I see Momma.

"Honey," she says taking little steps back so she won't fall as well. "You hurt?" Momma's stomach is still too big after Teddy's been born. She's fatter than she wants to be.

I can't stop crying so Momma says, "Get up and come here, Shike. I think you're fine, far as I can tell. Let me check." She takes hold of a towel rack for a minute as she walks to the linen closet. "But this is some mess we've got to tend to now."

She opens the closet door and pulls out the mop. "Let's see what we can do. Run some water in the tub. Stop cryin' now, you and I'll get this cleaned up in no time."

Momma is talking too slow. Her words sound funny, smashed together, like they don't have spaces between them. When she sees me looking at her, she says, "I'm fine. I can take care of this. Take off your dress and wash yourself with a wet towel. Here, I'll get one ready for you." She leans the mop against the wall and grabs a towel from another rack and throws it into the sink. Then she reaches way over to turn on the water. She steps very careful up to the faucet and turns down the knob. She doesn't want to fall over the soggy diapers onto the floor. She pushes them to the side with her foot. I take off my dress and drop it on the toilet seat. Momma picks up the wet towel and wrings it out before handing it to me. She leans one arm on the sink while she does this.

The towel feels warm, smells clean, and I rub it all over my face and arms and legs.

"Are your underpants wet?" she asks. "I mean, from the mess?"

I nod.

"Well, put on some clean ones and get yourself another dress... no, wait a minute, Shike." She looks at me like something's my fault. But I see her twist up her mouth a little to say, "Oh, you have to bathe, no sense in putting it off. You stink."

Momma leans over the tub, turns on the faucets too open, too fast, the water splashing her all over. She laughs, wipes her face with her hand while she keeps her balance with her other hand on the rim of the tub. She takes a deep breath and turns the water down, then off, helping me step over the rim into the water that barely covers my legs. After she lathers me and my hair with soap, she says, "Rinse."

While I'm standing on the rug, drying with a clean towel, she tells me, "Oh, put on a pair of Leon's overalls your Aunt Josephine gave us from the farm."

I stand and wait. "Go on, it's okay."

I am running to the drawer where she put them after the last visit to the Ratzlaff farm.

She calls out to me, "I don't have anything else ready for you to put on, except your good wear. Your daddy's work clothes come first."

"Darlene, what's going on?" Daddy is yelling through the bedroom door. I think he might come open the door and yell at us more, but he doesn't. He just tells Momma, "Teddy needs his bottle and—"

Before Daddy is done talking, Momma yells back as loud as she can, "His bottles are made up in the refrigerator, Vernon. Look around a little. You know how to heat one up."

Pretty soon, Daddy is banging pots and pans in the kitchen real, real loud. He slams a cabinet door closed. Then everything gets quiet. I think he's heating one of Teddy's bottles in a pan of water on the stove because he doesn't yell back at Momma anymore.

When I walk into the bathroom in overalls, Momma says, "There, that works. Now, go get that old blue dress I've got hanging in the back of your closet, the one with the rip down the front skirt." She nudges me from the back as she walks me toward the bedroom.

"Momma, I don't want to." I don't want to wear the dress over my overalls. She's going to cover up my overalls, so people won't see I have them on so much.

"For heaven's sakes, why not? You can't be partial to that old thing." Then she turns her head to the side and smiles at me. She goes into the closet herself and slides all my clothes out of the way and pulls the blue dress off its hanger, the hanger swinging off the rack and hitting the bottom of the closet. "I may go to hell for this, but there's so many other things I'm going to hell for, I might as well just add your play clothes to the list." Momma is exaggerating. Exaggerating means she's fibbing but only a little. She told me before when I asked.

"I don't want to wear it, Momma."

"Well, you won't, not like it is, anyhow. Let's spread it out, and I'm thinking if I cut it right here under the gathers, you'll have yourself something to wear under your overalls, like a blouse, whatdaya think?"

I clap my hands.

Momma cuts the skirt off the dress and holds the top up. "It's gonna work. Look at that! A girl's shirt! Give it a try, and if it holds, I'll stitch it later to keep it from unravelin'. Maybe I can cut and hem your overalls while I'm at it. They're a little too long for you. Then you won't have to roll them up so they won't keep fallen down over your shoes."

I undo the overall straps, slip on the shirt and then re-buckle. I could just bust.

"Well, looks like I should get some Good Housekeeping award, don't you think?" Momma picks up the skirt left from the dress and folds it neat. "Go set the table now. I need you to do that for me, okay?"

I start to tell her that I got it partly done already when, all at once, the radio comes on loud from the living room.

Momma stands for a minute and looks at the closed bedroom door. I think she might yell out at Daddy, but she just shakes her head and puts the cut-off skirt on Teddy and my chest-of-drawers.

When I start to go to the kitchen, she says, "No wait, Shike. You gotta pick up these diapers before you leave because I can't lean over to do it."

Momma walks back to the bathroom. I want to scream, but I say okay. I don't know how I'm going to do it without gloves. Momma knows what I'm thinking because she says, "The rubber gloves're in the closet. They'll be too big for you, but they'll work for now." The gloves keep falling off, but I pull one down with my free hand to keep it on when I pick up the diapers. I hold my breath the whole time I put the mess back in the bucket.

When I am finally done, with the lid down tight, I let my breath out in one long sigh.

Momma looks up, sees what I'm doing and laughs. "You might just as well get used to this, Shike, because you're gonna be the one helping me clean up the bucket later. You hold your breath through that chore, you'll pass out for sure." She puts the mop in the bathtub and is wringing it out when I leave. Daddy has turned the radio down low. It is quiet again.

———————

I RUN TO THE KITCHEN and pull a chair next to the cabinet drawers so I can get the plates off the counter. When I crawl up on it, I see Daddy looking at me as he leans over the crib rails to move Teddy back on his side. Then he starts rolling up a towel that he'll put under Teddy's bottle to help hold it to his mouth.

Daddy is happy I am helping Momma, but he says, "Hey, hold your horses there, Shike. Where ya goin' so fast?"

When I stand up on the chair, my legs start to shake.

"Whoa!" Daddy yells. I see him drop the towel and take two hops away from the crib. He runs into the kitchen and stretches for me as I start to fall toward the sink sideways, the chair sliding out from under me. On its way down, it hits Daddy's legs.

"Ow," he yells as he grabs for me but misses. I am hanging by my stomach from the edge of the sink, grabbing the faucet to keep from falling back. It makes a loud groan when it jumps out of its socket. I'm about to slide down when Daddy grabs my overall straps and twists me around against him. I throw my arms around his neck.

He holds me like he does Teddy for a minute. I feel his warm chest through his work clothes. He's wearing a clean shirt and trousers that have been ironed. He keeps these in his locker at work when Momma has them ready, and he puts them on before he comes home. Now he lowers me down to the floor with a little shake. "You know better'n to stand on a chair when you reach for something. What's got into you?"

"Momma told me to set the table," I yell at him. My face is all scrunched up again, and I think I'm going to cry. My legs are still shaking.

Daddy stops me from crying when he says, "It's okay. It's okay," and rubs my back. He leans over the sink and pushes the faucet back in its socket. Then he turns the water on and off. He slaps the front of the sink and sighs. "Some sealer'll fix it, I guess."

He pulls me against his leg while he walks me to the dining room door to check on Teddy in his crib. Teddy's on his back staring at a red ball Daddy's hung from a string, on a stick he's taped to the side of the crib. Teddy tries to hit it for fun, but he misses over and over. Most of the time, he just stares at it and wiggles around and around, making funny noises with air in them.

"I don't want you to do that ever again. You coulda fell down hard." He pushes me toward the table. "You break a leg on top of everything else...." He starts to say more but stops. Teddy's face is turning red. He is making grunting noises. Then he stops and moves around while he looks at the ball some more.

"Darlene," Daddy calls out, walking through the dining room. "Where the tarnation is she?" He looks toward the bedroom. Daddy doesn't wear slippers. He walks around in his stocking-feet.

"She's in the bathroom mopping." I start to tell him what happened with Teddy's diaper bucket but Momma shows up in the dining room door.

"I'm coming. I'm coming. Good Lord, you'd think the world's coming to an end."

Daddy lets go of me and walks toward the living room, walking past Momma like she's not there. He turns up the radio console, goes to his sofa chair, and picks up the newspaper Momma's left for him, like she does every day.

Most times, she has me run out to the driveway and get it, leaving it folded on his chair. Sometimes he comes home in work clothes that are clean, but, other times, when he's still in his uniform that has grease on it, he straightens the towel on the cushion of the sofa chair before he sits down, so he won't get it dirty.

Daddy brings his newspaper up to his face, snapping it open. Then he folds it over again and again, running his fingers along the edges to make a square. He's found something he wants to read.

Teddy starts to cry. The music on the radio is loud because Momma has turned it up again. All at once, President Roosevelt is talking to everybody like he did last night. I hear only some words because Teddy's crying. The president says, *Attack... Islands... damage... lives lost.* There is clapping. Then an announcer gives words faster than I can hear, but I catch, *Churchill... Malaya... war... Japan.*

When Daddy came home after church yesterday, he turned on the radio and listened to the news. Daddy listens now to the news all the time. He doesn't want to leave the living room and the radio. He's worried. While we ate dinner, he talked to Momma at the table about Pearl and bombing and Air Force and landing fields. He said, "no job, for sure" and Grampa Jantz's retirement and changes in the new year.

Momma didn't go to church. She stayed home with me and Teddy. She made fried chicken and then took a nap. She got up before Daddy came home from church.

I put the knives, forks, and spoons with napkins on the table in piles so Momma could spread them out.

We had ice cream Daddy made before church. He spooned it out of the ice cream maker after he took the towel and newspapers off that kept it cold. He pulled the metal can out of the ice and wiped off all the salt before he took off the lid. He told me about how the salt melts the ice so that the mix gets hard inside the container. When he took the dasher out, he laid it on a plate and scraped it himself with a spoon. He let me taste with my fingers. "The biggest treat in a long time," he said, adding to himself with a sigh, "Might be our last for God knows when, if ever again."

"Teddy, Teddy, Teddy. I'm right here." Momma leans over the rails and tickles his stomach. Teddy is kicking his legs and arms out and around. "Okay, okay," she says, running her hand over his diaper quick, then leaning back and looking at me. I know she wants me to help. "How in the world can you have a soggy diaper already? Soggy, soggy, soggy. Soggy could be your middle name."

Momma lifts Teddy out of the crib. "Daddy just chang…. Oh my, I see. You're a very busy boy this evening." She leans against the table for a minute, then walks Teddy over to my red wagon and lays him on the blankets spread out inside. The wagon is Teddy's stroller until we can buy one.

"Shike never had a stroller, and she's turned out just fine," Daddy said to Momma when she told him she wanted one when she and Teddy came home from the hospital.

"You sat up in a wagon," Momma told me when Daddy's back was turned, "just like Teddy will after he's able to sit up by himself." Momma was being snotty to Daddy, but she was talking only to me. "And this little red wagon'll be the stroller for whoever is to follow, maybe for all five or six of you." Momma said this loud enough for Daddy to hear. I knew she was exaggerating. She still wants a stroller, not the wagon anymore.

"Watch your brother for me a minute, Shike. I can't hold him right now." She falls in a chair that's by the table. Teddy is really mad that he's on his back again so soon. He wants to sit up, but he's too little. Momma's told me, "He can hold his head up for a while when I'm holding him, Shike, but he's got a ways to go before he can do it completely on his own, let alone sit up by himself in a wagon."

Momma says to Teddy, "You need to be changed again because this time it's more than just pee in your pants, young man." Teddy doesn't know Momma's talking to him.

All at once, the radio is even louder from the living room. Daddy has turned it up more. The voice is talking real fast. I still can't hear hardly any words over Teddy's crying… but the announcer says something about striking and might and freedom.

"Tend the baby's changin', Shike. This time in the bedroom, will you? Get a diaper and lay it out. I'll come shortly." Momma talks like she's out of breath. She slaps her hand down on the table a little to get me to stop and look at her. "Get the rubber sheet in the bathroom linen closet, okay?"

Daddy has turned the radio up even more. It's louder now than Teddy's screaming.

"For godssakes, Vernon, we can't hear ourselves think," Momma screams at Daddy. "Turn...," she stops talking and just sits and stares at Daddy who is looking at his paper in his sofa chair. She throws her arms up in the air and brings them down on the table. "Goddammit! We get your point!" she yells, but Daddy doesn't turn the radio down.

She shrugs at me and says, "How the hell am I supposed to be doing all of this?"

I'm not sure what she means, so I just pull Teddy in the wagon through the dining room. Maybe she means the supper or maybe she means Teddy's changing, probably both. Daddy is bent over in front of the console in the living room, straining to hear what the announcer is saying.

"I hope he goes deaf, right now! On the spot!" Momma puts her elbow on the table and her hand over her mouth, sitting like that for a minute, then she leans her head in her hand as I pull the wagon to Teddy's and my bedroom. He doesn't sleep in there with me yet, but it's gonna happen sometime "in the near future." Momma calls my bedroom "our bedroom" so I'll get used to the idea of Teddy's moving in with me. I think Momma is crying when I pull the wagon into "our bedroom" and close the door on Daddy's radio news.

"Hoover... everything we got... Red Cross workers," the announcer's voice says through the door. Teddy just won't stop crying. I talk to him to cool him off. His face is red. But suddenly Daddy yanks open the door and walks straight toward Teddy. I jump when he comes through the door. He has a Turkish towel hanging over his shoulder. He grabs Teddy, puts the towel over his arm, and then with Teddy on it, walks with him fast out the bedroom. He almost stumbles over the red wagon.

"Shit," he yells, and, "Tarnation," and gives the wagon a kick. It wobbles but doesn't move. Teddy makes a gaspy sound but stops crying. Daddy bounces him up and down, saying "Ah-ah, ah-ah, ah-ah," in a sing-songy voice as he walks back to the living room and the radio announcer. I walk over and close the door.

I get a diaper out of the dresser. Most times, when I push the drawer closed, the handles rattle, but I can barely hear them because of the radio. "President promises... will be speeding up," the radio says in jerks. I pull the footstool to the edge of the bed and stand on it while I open the diaper. Then I remember what Daddy told me in the kitchen about standing on things and crawl up on top of the bed instead. I turn the diaper so that the pointy part is down toward the edge of the bed and the straight part is at the top. I smooth out the whole shape. Triangle. Momma's taught me. When the triangle is down it's easier for us to change Teddy while we stand by the bed. Momma showed me.

After I finish with the diaper, I step down real careful onto the footstool to get off the bed. From the dining room, I pull the wagon to the living room where Daddy is sitting with Teddy. He's turned down the radio. Dance music is on now. I tell him Momma's gonna change the baby, and I should take him into the bedroom. He looks over at Momma in her chair and shakes his head and keeps patting Teddy's back, holding his head up with his hand while he bounces him a little up and down. I stand and wait. Daddy sighs, finally gets up out of his sofa chair and walks past me and the wagon, shaking his head again. Teddy smells like poop.

Carrying Teddy, he goes to the bathroom and comes back with the rubber sheet that he lays down on the bed, trying to spread it out with one hand while he bends over a little backward to keep Teddy from falling forward. I want to help him spread the sheet, but I can't reach it without stepping onto the footstool. "Give me a hand here, will ya?" Daddy says to me. When I step onto the footstool, he says, "It's all right, I'm right here." Once I get the sheet spread out without wrinkles, he lays Teddy down onto it.

Momma comes into the bedroom and says to Daddy, "I'm better now, Vern. I just needed to collect myself for a minute. I'll take over. If you'll get the soup out of the refrigerator and put it in a pan, I'll be in there to warm it up as soon as I'm done here. Not the one with hamburger in it. That's not done yet. It's for tomorrow night. We'll finish up the one from last night—the potato and bacon. There's cold cuts, cheese, and bread. Left over green beans, whatever you can find, okay?"

Daddy's face isn't so tight now. He nods and walks to the door. When he's out of the room, Momma sits down on the edge of the bed. She lowers her head, leaning her chin toward her chest.

"Oh God," she says. "I feel so sick." All at once I am very scared. I want

to help her, but I can't leave Teddy by himself. He's over by the pillows, and
Momma's sitting at the foot of the bed. She looks now like she's holding onto
the bed post to keep from falling to the floor. Her hair is hanging down so I
can't see her face. Teddy isn't crying, just moving his head from side to side and
pumping his legs like he's riding a tricycle upside down.

I'm still standing on the footstool so I can reach him. I rub his stomach, and
he smiles, then stops smiling, then smiles again.

"Good boy," I say.

He stares at the ceiling when he smiles. Then he makes sucking noises,
and I make them back. This keeps him from crying. He looks at me every
now and then, but I don't think he sees me, not really. He looks away fast
every now and then.

"There now," I say like Momma does, and I try to undo the safety pins.
They're stuck in the wet, folded corners of the diaper and are hard to get to
because Teddy won't stop moving his legs. I try pulling them out toward me so
I can undo the catch when Momma looks over like she's just waking up, like
she finally knows she's next to us tending to things.

"Oh, honey, no, not the pins, I'll get those. You could stick him... or yourself." She stands up and steps a little in front of me and then sits down too close
to where I've been standing.

I fall off the footstool but catch myself by holding onto the blanket that
starts moving off the bed. I get my feet down to the floor. I think Momma forgets I'm next to her sometimes.

She stands again and turns toward the bed, pulling Teddy closer to her.
Then she says to herself, but a little to me, too, "We need to get some new pins.
These're not easy to push in and out of the diaper anymore. I keep meaning
to get to MacLallan's to get some new ones, but somehow I never make it. Hi
there, little man." She jiggles Teddy's stomach. He smiles, kicking his legs, spitting at the air.

"Why don't you run get the bucket?" she tells me. "Oh, and bring a coupla
wet washrags too. I have to wash his bottom." I don't want to get the bucket,
but I go. If it's full I won't be able to carry it.

"Shike." She waits for me to look at her. "The bucket's empty now, so it's okay. I washed out the diapers in the toilet. They're soaking in bleach in the tub. If it's too much for you, get the wagon and bring the bucket in with that. Don't forget the rags, okay?"

I walk fast to get what Momma needs. Momma can always read my mind.

But once again, it's the bucket, the dirty diaper, and wet washrags. All in a day's work. And like Momma, my work is never done.

When I come back, I'm pulling the bucket, walking backwards. I put the wet washrags in my pocket, even though they're soaking through my overalls. I love my overalls. Most dresses don't have pockets. Dragging the bucket's easier than letting it hit my leg every time I take a step. I tried that, and it hurts.

Momma sees me coming and smiles. "Well, I thought getting the bucket would be easier for you than trying to carry the dirty diaper to the bucket, but then maybe not." She laughs a little.

I put the bucket down with a "whew."

"Problem with dirty diapers is that they can open up while you're carryin' them, then you've really got yourself a mess, well, as you just found out not too long ago, huh?"

She stands over Teddy with the dirty diaper wadded up beside her foot on the floor. She's washed Teddy's bottom with one of the wet washrags I give her from my pocket, and then wipes her hands with the second one. She lets both drop on top of the diaper on the floor. Finally, Momma lifts Teddy up and down, up and down, his penis bouncing a little bit with him kicking a few times before she finally lays him down for good, scooting him around the way she wants him on the diaper.

I bend down and pick up the smelly mess before Momma asks me to. My stomach jumps, so I close my nose by holding my breath until I've placed the whole poopy wad in the bucket. Then I see the dirty washrags have fallen off to the side so I pick them up, opening the lid careful and throwing them inside. I drag the bucket over to the door and start to take it to the bathroom.

"Just leave it, honey. We'll get it later." She tells me to come get the rubber sheet and hang it over the bathtub rim and wash my hands. "Use soap," she calls after me.

When I return, she says all at once, outta the blue, "You wanna try?"

I look at her, but she is nodding with a smile. I can't believe it. Teddy is boxing the air with his fists and legs.

"This is a job for somebody about twice your age." She smiles down to Teddy, but she means me. Then she looks directly at me. "But I don't see why you can't give me a hand every now and then when I especially need it, do you?"

Momma's hair is still messed up from her nap, and she's in the same house dress she wore yesterday, maybe the day before. It's all scrunched up under her arms and around her neck.

"What the heck, huh?" she sounds happy, so I'm feeling better, too. "My thinking is this," she says leaning over and whispering to me like I'm not to tell Daddy or anybody. "If you start learning now, maybe by the time you're in school, you can be Teddy's babysitter. You know what that means?" She asks me like she's got a great answer up her sleeve. Momma always tells Daddy he has all the answers up his sleeves. Now, I'm thinking she has one for me, and I've got to guess what it is.

"Answer's up your sleeve, but I don't know what."

At first Momma doesn't know what I mean. She just looks at me, but then she laughs real big, and she can't get stopped for a minute.

"No answers up sleeves," she says. "I was thinking that you just might earn a little money for that babysittin' service—watching Teddy while I'm busy around the house. Whatdaya think of that?" Then she gets very, very serious. "You just have to promise me you'll never, never do what I'm going to show you now by yourself. But you know what?" Momma doesn't tell me what. She just stands there looking down at Teddy, and she waits. I think she is crying because her eyes are red, and she's breathing in and out real fast. But she looks at me like she's made up her mind and says, "I think you can do this. Okay, pay attention, and I'll show you."

"That's his penis," Momma told me the first time I saw it. "He pees from there. A lot different from you, huh? When he's older, he won't have to sit down to pee, only when he doo-doos." We laughed together. I knew what she was telling me already because I go to the outhouse on the farm with Leon. He's too short so sometimes he misses the toilet hole when he pees and hits the boards instead. There's a stool for him to stand on but most times he doesn't bother. And sometimes he thinks he's done when he's not so when he shakes himself, he goes all over his overalls. And I've seen Daddy pee lots of times, sometimes up close when I'm in the bathroom with him.

But Momma and Daddy don't know that Tommy Don and Roy pee against the side of the barn to see which one can pee the longest and the farthest. One time Tommy Don hit the barn with his pee when he was standing a long ways away. His pee arched high in the air and then ran down the side of the barn like a little river. Leon and I watched while Roy measured by counting his steps, toe-to-heel, toe-to-heel until he stood next to Tommy Don.

"It's not much," Roy said. "Measures a bit over two steps. Two feet 'n a half's all."

"The hell you say," Tommy Don yelled back. "You got big feet little brother! It's a good three feet or better. You didn't count from where my toes were, you dumb fuck." Tommy Don always says "the hell you say" about everything or "you dumb fuck," and anyway, he didn't really care if his pee only went two feet, because he beat Roy by a country mile any way you looked at it. He told us so. Tommy Don always says "country mile." A country mile is a lot.

Momma knows now that the footstool I'm standing on is there because she says, "I'll be right here if the stool starts to move, Shike." She puts her leg behind it to make sure it doesn't go out from under me when I lean over the bed, like the chair did in the kitchen. Right now, Teddy's penis is poking up in the air like my little finger.

"You gotta watch out," Momma tells me with a smile. "If he decides to become a fountain in the middle of this bed, he could spray you quicker'n you can say 'jack rabbit,' and I don't mean maybe. I hope you know how to swim!" We both laugh. She tells me that normally we would put the rubber sheet under him but she forgot and had me put it in the bathroom, and anyway, now we're in a hurry.

I take the point of the diaper that's in front of me and lift it up between Teddy's legs, putting it down over his belly button. He is moving his arms and legs and making lots of noises. I have a hard time holding the diaper in place while I reach for the side part to bring it over to the middle. Momma holds it there for me because I have to change hands. Then I get both parts together.

"That's right. That's very good, Shike. You've watched enough to remember how. But pull this piece up tight and hold it here while you reach over and get this corner. Ooops," she says, putting her hand over mine and lifting up. "Not down so hard on his stomach, honey. He's a little tyke. There, that's it. Now, hold this corner together with the one on top, with your left hand… honey, your left hand. This hand, honey. Great." She holds out the pin to me. I take it, being very careful.

"You said I couldn't do it," I say holding the pin way out away from me. It's like it's on fire. I lay it down on the bed until I have to use it.

"Well, I know I told you that. But I don't see why you can't learn. You never know…." She doesn't finish but says instead, "I'm right here. We'll do it together." Momma shows me how to slip my finger under the diaper corner. Then she puts her fingers under mine, her thumb over the corner I'm trying to hold because it's too much for me.

"Besides, I'm putting my fingers underneath. If you stick something, it's gonna be me." Then she adds, "Or it'll be you." She smiles. "But if it's me, I'll bite your neck!" I pull back, and she laughs. "So we're both hoping it's gonna be you!" She leans toward me and says "you" like "boo." I pull away from her some more but I laugh. In a soft voice, she says, "I'm teasing you, Shike. You're doing just fine." She points with her other hand where I'm supposed to put the pin.

I take my hand away while she holds the diaper in place for me. I open the pin with both hands, the point sticking up and out like a knife.

"Put the needle part here," Momma says, moving her thumb back and forth. "That's right. Now press down slowly. Good, that's it, aw, it's stuck. Sometimes that happens. Just let me, honey—"

She starts to help me but suddenly moves her hand because the bedroom door flies open and Daddy yells at us, "What's going on with supper, Darlene? I've worked hard all day. I need to eat."

I don't know it, but I'm pushing down on the pin in a hurry just when Momma moves her hand to the side, and the pin point jabs Teddy.

He lets out a terrible scream, and Momma jumps up, pushing me out of the way, grabbing the pin out of the diaper. It falls to the floor as she lifts Teddy up.

Daddy slams the door. I hear him stomp toward the kitchen. He is talking louder than Teddy's screams. "It's always something. I can never come home to just my supper."

The announcer is back on the radio again, almost as loud as Daddy. He is telling volunteers to contact air-raid wardens. I don't know who wardens are.

"Well, that's how it is with children," Momma yells back to him, but it's not loud enough for him to hear because by now he's banging around in the kitchen again.

"I didn't mean to, Momma," I say and start to cry.

"Teddy, Teddy," she says, rubbing the place where the needle went in. "It's okay, it's fine. Let me look. Caroline, Caroline, it's fine, fine. Look it's only a little, itty bitty, tiny, tiny red dot. It barely went in at all. It just scared him. Daddy's coming in here like that scared him, that's all, just like he scared the rest of us. Stop crying now and take his diaper," she says to me. "Here, here, spread it out for me on the bed. We'll try this again."

"I don't want to do it anymore." I can barely see through the tears in my eyes. My stomach hurts.

"No, okay, you don't have to try. With the pin, I mean. That's another time. We probably shouldn'tve been doing this tonight anyway, with everything's that going on around here the way it is. Let's just finish this diaper business and get on with the man's supper."

She has a safety pin in her mouth when she finishes her sentence. She reaches over to the small table by the bed and pours some alcohol from a bottle onto a rag from a pile she keeps there. She rubs a little on Teddy's skin. He doesn't care. He just keeps kicking at the air, his face wet from crying. She hands the rag to me and I hang it over the rack on the side of the table.

Momma takes the safety pin from between her teeth and puts it into Teddy's diaper, then with the knuckle of her index finger she gives the safety pin a strong push. I hear it snap closed. She asks me to pick up the safety pin from the floor. When I find it, I'm careful when I hand it to her—the point up. Momma pins the other side of Teddy's diaper very fast and lifts him against her stomach. "See, not such a big catastrophe! Now, take the bucket into the bathroom, Shike, and then come to the table."

Momma told me we'd take care of the bucket together, but she's forgotten. I don't want to do the bucket by myself, but I push it into the bathroom corner where it belongs.

———————

WHEN I WALK INTO THE kitchen, Daddy is stirring the soup that is about to boil over onto the stove. He lowers his head and watches the flame while he turns the knob until it makes the soup slow down.

Momma puts Teddy in his crib and pulls it near the table. Teddy has his bottle. He is quiet, his eyes closed. He makes soft sucking sounds.

"The soup's made, Vernon. All I asked you to do was to heat it up. When you saw I couldn't come right away, why didn't you simply do it without turning it into a tragedy? What's the big rush over dinner?" Momma is standing in the dining room while she talks to Daddy in the kitchen. She leans against the table.

Daddy whirls around. His face is tight. His eyes are mean. He presses his lips together, then he turns his back to us again. He shakes his head from side to side, side to side.

"Big rush?" he yells. "It's nearly seven thirty."

"So where's the horse race? You got someplace important to go, is that it? When you saw I couldn't...." She stops and stares at Daddy while he stirs the soup with a ladle. I want to ask if I can help, but I know she'd be mad. "Is it asking too much for you to help yourself a little when I can't make it right away? Looks like you're managin' to do that now. Why couldn't you've done it earlier?" Momma throws her hands in the air, then drops her arms, slapping her hands against her legs. "For godssakes!"

He shrugs and stirs. "You think this's the first time I've warmed it up?"

"Vernon," Momma says, irked to no end. She sits down in a chair by the dining room table, but where she can still see him.

"What!" Then he stirs the soup very fast and says, softer, "What?"

"I planned supper. It's not like I sit around here all day. I felt sick today. If you're that hungry, why don't you just ladle yourself a bowl and eat it." Momma kinda smiles and then says, snotty-like, "You being so hungry like you are!"

"You're sick a lot, Darlene." Daddy says this like he's so tired he can't talk. He looks at her and turns the fire off under the pot. He stands looking at her a minute before he says, letting his shoulders drop, "I think we oughta eat together as a family in the evenings, so I waited."

I sit on the other side of the table and listen. I can't reach the plates and bowls on the counter to set the table. I know to be quiet.

"I am not!" Momma says, shouting the 'am' real hard. Daddy looks at her like he doesn't know what she means. "…dizzy all the time like you say I am." She waits, then says real loud, "And anyway, if I am, I am. Dizzy is dizzy."

"Well, I got a question about that." Daddy doesn't look at her. He walks over and gets a bowl out of the cabinet and brings it back to the stove while he's talking. His voice is soft, but he's still not happy. "How come you can walk to the neighbors and take Teddy over there if you're so all-fired dizzy."

"I made myself do it, Vernon, because I didn't think it was safe for him to be here with me like this. I can't leave him to Caroline when I think I'm going to pass out. I prayed each step I took on the way over there." Momma only calls me Caroline when she is very serious, when she's mad at me or Daddy or wants us to listen to her real close.

He tells her, "I don't want Teddy over there. Those people are old. They are…." he stops, then goes on, "They mean well, Darlene, but they're old and they're… strange. They just are. They don't even speak English clear. We don't know them that well. Why don't you call one of my sisters?"

"Hannah has fifty kids, Vernon, and half of our relatives don't speak English worth a damn. That's no reason for not leaving Teddy with the Kruegers. They're German, just like us." Momma so mad, she doesn't care if she's using swear words.

"Hannah has two kids, Darlene. And, we're not German, we're Dutch." He waits a minute and says, "Well, Dutch to begin with and then Dutch-German from Russia." Daddy always says *Roosha*. Momma says *Rush-ah*.

Momma laughs a little. "Do you hear yourself, Vernon? What kind of thinking is that? Our ancestors came over on a boat just like the Kruegers, and most of them couldn't speak English worth a damn either, if at all, let alone clear. Judas Priest." Momma is getting hot under the collar. She thinks cussing is a sin.

"Well, okay." Daddy gives in a little. "But the Kruegers are too old, that's the point I'm getting at."

"Hannah's got her hands full is what I'm getting at and you know it. Criminy. I'm not leaving Teddy with her, not even for a few minutes." She lowers herself into a chair. When Daddy doesn't say anything, she goes on. "And Eliza works. She's secretary at the shop with you, for godssakes. Why do I have to spell all this out? If I call Elizabeth, I might as well call you to come home from work and take care of our kids. Or would you rather I bring them to her where you work? Or maybe to you?"

Daddy ignores her. "There's Nita Jane," he says, then waves his hand back and forth. "Never mind, never mind." He waits. I think he's not going to talk more. When he does, I can hear he's getting sick of their talking. "Well, okay, she's got her own problems. I just thought… Sherman came around and said she's better again. They upped her insulin even with her being pregnant and all. He's worried silly about her, so okay, that's not such a good place to go for help. What about Josephine in a pinch? God knows we do enough for her and Clifford when they're in trouble."

Aunt Josie is Momma's sister. I stay at their farm during the summer, sometimes, to play with my boy cousins. Daddy's run out of his own sisters to help us in Clearview.

Daddy shrugs and sighs. "That's just plain out of the question I know. Shirly's over half-an-hour from here. Anyway, we do that already. And they're good to us. I'm just…." He throws his hands in the air. When he lets them fall to his sides, he slaps them against his legs, like Momma does when she's frustrated. Frustrated is when you're next to being mad.

Momma puts her head in her hands. "Vernon, I don't know what to do anymore either." She tells him she started to call him at work, but she knows he wants her to stop that. "I can have Josephine come here every now and then, but this is getting to be… it's getting regular. I don't know what's wrong with me. But it's not going away."

Momma lifts her head and looks at me like she's going to cry. "And you know how things are with Josephine. She has to drag her boys over here with her. She has to hold Tommy Don out of school or be there when he comes home. It's more trouble than if I just try to muddle through alone." I want to go stand by Momma, but I know she wants me to stay where I am.

Daddy pulls out a chair, puts a bowl of soup down on the table and sits. He folds his hands in front of him, lowers his head. I think he's gonna pray, but he looks up and stares at Momma before he picks up his spoon. Daddy asks her why she doesn't find a doctor. He's asked her lots of times.

Momma tells me he doesn't want her to really go unless it's Gramma Jantz's doctor, who sees people for practically nothing. They always argue about doctors.

"These Holdeman Mennonite doctors preach and pray over the pulpit on Sunday and preach and pray over your mangled leg on Monday," Momma says while Daddy eats. "If you're lucky they might give you a laxative."

Daddy starts to eat a spoonful of soup but brings it down quick back into his soup. He tells her she's on one of her rampages and it's not the right time for it.

Momma stops talking, but when Daddy starts eating again, she says, "You know, Vernon, your mother was probably following her doctor's orders when she gave you bluing for worms when you were a baby. It's probably why you've got blue eyes."

I try to see Daddy's eyes from where I'm sitting. They are too small. I can't tell if they're blue because he's looking down at his bowl while he eats. But I remember now they have to be blue because Momma tells Daddy his eyes are still waters and deep. He is eating his soup loud and fast. Then he stops and spreads butter on his crackers. Momma stands up this time and goes to the soup pot and dishes out two bowls. She carries one at a time to the table, putting the first one in front of me. There are no plates. We are going to eat from our bowls on the tablecloth without plates. If I get soup on the tablecloth, Momma won't like it.

"What's rampage?" I know, but I ask because nobody is saying anything, and I don't want them to be mad.

Daddy looks at me and winks. "It's going on and on when you oughta stop." He doesn't look at Momma and isn't smiling at me yet. He taps my bowl and says, "You eat now."

Momma's rampage isn't over. "You probably have the indigestion you get now from all the slaughtered and canned food they fed you as a kid, or all the lard and sugar sandwiches in your lunchbox. I'm not doing that with my kids."

Daddy slaps the table with his hands and looks over at the stove. He has his lips twisted up real tight, and he is frowning a lot. Daddy wants to know how whatever-in-the-hell-he-ate-when-he-was-a-kid has anything to do with Momma's finding a doctor, which is what she should be thinking about. Momma starts to tell him, but he stands up and says, "Just stop, Darlene. It's enough talk now at the dinner table."

He walks away to gets more soup. He's in the back of the kitchen cutting bread when Momma starts more rampage. She made homemade bread yesterday when she felt better. The house still smells like fresh baking.

"Dr. Webber in Shirly says it's only because I've had a baby. It's what Bufford told me here in Clearview. Well, I've had a baby before and never felt anything like this." Daddy comes back, sits down, and shrugs. He's heard this before, over and over. He keeps eating his soup, while Momma goes on some more.

"Finding somebody who can really look at me when I'm like I am now, isn't going to be easy. And I can't drive to Hopewell with two little kids and look for a doctor. Dear God, if I could do that, I wouldn't be taking Teddy to the Kruegers." She looks at Daddy a while before she says, "Though I've thought, lately, that finding a doctor in Hopewell might be the thing to do."

Daddy doesn't stop eating while he says, "That's right, just leave the kids with Josephine. Drive over to Shirly, leave them with her, and then go on to Hopewell. All this while you're dizzy and don't feel like you can walk across a room. Hell, go tomorrow."

He leans back some and wipes his lips with a kitchen towel that has a boy and girl kissing each other on it. Gramma Dirks gave a bunch of boy-and-girl-towels to Momma for a new house present in Clearview. She sewed them all by hand. Daddy doesn't mean anything he's saying about Momma going to the doctor because they don't have any money for it. He's just mad.

"If I can get in at some doctor's office and can drive." Momma talks like Daddy really wants her to go, but then all at once, she stops talking. It is quiet a long time. I don't know what she means about driving to a doctor's office. Momma drives, sometimes, but not ever to Hopewell anymore. She used to drive to Hopewell with me to get a hamburger and then come home. But mostly we took drives around Clearview. This was before Teddy, even when she was big with him. Momma and I would walk down the streets until we got to the parking lot at Grampa Jantz's shop where Daddy works. We'd get in our car, and Momma would drive us around.

Momma would say to me, "See that barn? That barn holds fifty cows and oooh I'd say about a dozen horses." And she'd tell me, "See that shed? That's a chicken shed, Shike. That shed's smellier than a pigpen. You know how I know? Your Grampa Dirks had sheds like that. We kept chickens in there— hundreds of chickens before the bankers took everything. I used to sit in one of those sheds and read books to the chickens when I was young, little older than you, after I'd been to school."

Momma knew lots of old barns and farmhouses and chicken sheds and pigpens and hen houses and granaries, all over the country where we went driving. And they all have stories she's told me. I liked to drive around with Momma and hear her stories.

Sometimes, we looked at houses they were building in Clearview. Momma always said ours was the best. "Prettier than that one by anybody's measure," she'd say pointing at a brand-new house and laughing. Daddy built our house for Momma, with Uncle Clifford's help.

"Built it from scratch," Uncle Clifford told me.

Momma and me drove around together for a long, long time. Then after we were done, we'd park the car in the parking lot like we never took it any- where, and we'd walk up the street to the drugstore and get candy or ice cream before we walked back home.

But since Teddy, Momma only drives when Daddy leaves the car at home and walks to work by himself. We go to the grocery store or to get gasoline. She drives back home, sometimes, before we even get to where she's driving us. Daddy keeps the keys now until she asks. But Momma made a set of her own at the hardware store in Shirly, behind Daddy's back. I promised not to tell, but she doesn't use them anymore.

Momma never told Daddy about "our little escapades," and I kept our secret. Then one day he looked at the gas gauge and caught us.

"No more escapades," he said with his eyes too little and his lips real tight, like he'd heard what Momma called them to me. We went a long time before he found out. Sometimes Momma would fill the car with gasoline at the end of our drives. I don't know where she got the money. Maybe from the jar she keeps hid high up in the back of the kitchen cabinets.

She would say to the filling station man, "Only halfway today" or "five gallons is all" or "keep it steady at three-quarters full." Daddy always says, "Fill 'er up."

Driving around was fun. When we were out of town, way out in the country where there were only pastures, I would stand next to her in the front seat and wait to see where we would go next. We drove all around in the country.

After we got caught, Daddy told Momma that she didn't know when to stop about some things. Had she gone crazy? We didn't have the money for that amount of gas. Didn't she realize he was paying for a new house they'd just built?

Now we're eating without saying anything. It's quiet except for our soup and the radio that Daddy's kept on but turned down. It's only music. The announcer is gone. Momma and Daddy have talked everything away. Daddy's saying he's sorry by playing Momma's music.

After a long time with all of us just sitting quiet, looking at the table, Daddy says, "Have Josephine take you. Have her drive. The kids can go to your mother's. She's still down the road from Josephine. She might not like it, but tell her—"

"Okay. I'll see," Momma says before he's done. She is talking down into her soup bowl.

2.

After supper, same evening

"I WANT YOU TO GO to the doctor, if you need to, Darlene. I really do." Daddy stops, clears his throat. "I just don't know how to tell you any more than I already have. How we'll pay for it, I don't have any idea, because I'm afraid that faster than any of us can say 'scat,' we might not have jobs. And I'm a-saying 'we' because it's not only about me anymore. With this declaration of war on Japan, it's hard to know what it's all gonna turn out to mean."

Daddy gets up and goes to the living room, and I think supper is over, but he comes back to the table with the newspaper. He sits back down and opens it wide, then folds it over into a square. "Here's what Roosevelt told reporters today. It's what I was trying to hear on the radio when I got home."

Daddy picks up the newspaper and reads, *"We are now in this war. We are all in it—all the way. Every single man, woman, and child is a partner in the most tremendous undertaking of our American history.'* It's what I was trying to catch on the radio. They were broadcasting Roosevelt, what he was telling us." Daddy puts the paper down and lays his hand on it. He looks like he's going to read us some more, but instead he tells Momma that he had this talk with Grampa Jantz today.

"The automobile business is out the winda, Darlene. There's gonna be this huge effort to make military equipment now. There's not gonna be any new cars or trucks, only tanks and airplanes."

"I don't understand. Just say it, Vernon."

"I'm telling you that Dad's gonna stop selling and repairing cars, and Reuben isn't gonna buy the place until cars start back in production again. The dealership's closing down. Could be next week, but if not, it's soon. What I'm saying is nobody knows nothin', for sure, yet. But everybody's talkin' about what they think's comin' next, Darlene. And the talk at Dad's shop is that everything's up for grabs."

"What's up for grabs? What are you talking about?" It's like Momma can't hear and keeps asking Daddy to say what he's telling her again and again.

"Everything we got, is what I mean. I mean my job, this house, where our next meals are coming from. You gotta have a doctor, go get a doctor, but I'm not sure I'll have a job after this next paycheck to pay for it. I just don't know what else to tell you." Daddy touches Momma's hand but brings it back quick to his knife and fork next to his plate, the plate he brought with him when he got his bread and butter. His spoon is in his empty bowl. He moves the knife and fork back and forth, hitting them against each other. I wait for what's next.

Momma keeps staring at Daddy. She sees only Daddy. "When will you know for sure?" Her voice is shaking, and she looks like she needs to go lie down.

"Who knows? But the freeze's gonna happen, no doubt about it."

"Oh God, Vernon."

"Well, some prayin' might not hurt." Daddy turns his head and looks toward the kitchen and his evening coffee in a pan on the stove. He makes coffee like the cowboys, he told me once—boils it in the pan, grounds and all. Teddy is just now waking up in his crib. His bottle is almost empty and has rolled off to the side.

3.

January, 1942

W E ARE EATING POTATO PANCAKES, bacon, and eggs. Breakfast for supper. I like the toast, from Momma's homemade bread yesterday. Daddy wipes his plate with the last corner of a slice and eats it in one bite. He holds his strip of bacon between his fingers when he says, "Dad's sayin' the shop'll close in a coupla weeks. The two sales guys got notice today. They're gone. Government's froze everything. No more new automobiles. Parts're gonna be scarce, 'cause what there is, everybody's gonna be grabbin' em up. There's not gonna be anything but what's out there right now. I'm out of a job."

Momma stops eating, puts her fork on her plate, and looks across at him. He's waited until now to tell her because he wanted supper on the table first.

"I know you've told me over and over that it was comin', but I just kept thinking something'll happen, and it won't really come true. There's too much war. Now, it's everybody fighting. Japan, Germany, Italy against the rest of us. It's crazy." Momma looks over at Teddy in his crib. He's sleeping again, sucking on his pacifier, a blanket over his legs.

Daddy eats his bacon in two bites and lifts his shoulders and lets them drop. He wipes his lips with his napkin and puts it down, laying his hand on top. When he starts talking to Momma, he scoots his fork under his napkin, holding it there with his fingers. He turns his head a little to the side, looks over at Momma direct, bringing his fork out, sliding it back and forth across the tablecloth. Finally he holds it with his fingers like it could slide off the table to the floor.

"I was offered a job in Aileen," he says, picking up his fork a little and dropping it down. It falls on the napkin with a soft thud.

"Aileen? Doing what? What about our house here? What about my doctor in Hopewell?"

Momma went to a doctor Aunt Eliza told her about. She's been happy since she saw her doctor in Hopewell. She only went one time. Teddy and me stayed with Aunt Josephine at the Shirly farm. Momma takes pills now. "Horse pills," she tells me when I watch her take one. "Real hard to swallow." She laughs when she's done, rubbing her throat. Momma takes two different kinds, one is bigger than the other.

Daddy says to Momma, "I'd be rebuilding crankshafts for one thing. And probably just trying to keep farm equipment, cars, and trucks running from parts that're in stock, from there it'll be catch as catch can's my guess, what we can get from other repair shops that've closed and the salvage yards. Who woulda thought?"

Daddy told us that the car business was booming before Pearl. No end in sight.

"Who's giving it to you? The job, I mean? You'd work on farm equipment, you're telling me?" Momma doesn't like farm equipment. Her cousin died on farm equipment.

"Well, engines still have to run, Darlene. Tractors, cars, you name it. Everybody's gonna need to continue to drive and work in the fields. Fighting Hitler and Japan isn't gonna change that, in fact it's gonna do the opposite.

"Wilbur Hilliar came around today. He used to have a dealership in Aileen. He's turning what used to be his automobile service repair into one for cars, trucks, and farm equipment. Changes like this is how these guys are gonna survive. He took me aside and said I could begin as soon as Dad closes up, if that's what's in the offing, and he thinks it pretty much will be. He knows Reuben, so Reuben's filled him in. It's how he found out about Dad and me."

Uncle Reuben gives me dimes. He says, "Here's one for the little lady."

"It's no longer a secret, Darlene. Dad's shuttin' down, and Reuben's not gonna keep it open. I mean, he doesn't want to do what Hilliar's doing. He'll wait out the war and then see if he wants to reopen. Reuben doesn't have to switch like Hilliar because Reuben's got his farm, hell, two farms. He'll be better off raising wheat."

Daddy looks at Momma and adds real quick, "Hilliar's got his hand in early, which is smart. He'll get Dad's parts for repairs, and me too, if I say yes. None of the other guys are going with him. They got other places in mind." He looks away again before glancing back at her.

Momma looks scared. Her eyes are open wide, but her mouth is all scrunched up. She doesn't take her eyes off Daddy. She lays her hand on her heart, like she can't breathe. It feels like something terrible is coming up from the table and spreading around all of us. All at once, I can't breathe, either. All the glasses and dishes and bowls look funny to me. The food on my plate doesn't look good anymore. I reach for Momma's hand, but she doesn't take it. "What about the house?" She is making short air noises. Her words are coming out in little sounds, like moans. "You're saying we're moving?"

She's not eating anymore. I think she is starting to cry. "You're gonna take it away, just as soon as we got it, aren't you? Aren't you?" Her eyes are full of tears. I get up from my chair and go stand by her. She looks at me and says, "It's okay, honey, you gotta go sit down. Go on." She moves her hand back and forth in the air and points to my chair.

I go back and sit down. I look at Teddy in his crib. He is still sleeping. I want to go to my bedroom, but I don't want to leave the table. I don't want to see and hear Momma and Daddy, but I want to know what's next.

"Well, there doesn't seem like there's much of a choice. I'm lucky to have a job offer, at all."

"What's Sherman gonna do? My God, Nita Jane's pregnant and diabetic. It's touch and go with her right now. They have doctor bills, so many doctor bills." Momma always worries about doctor bills. She still owes money to the doctor in Hopewell.

"He's gonna work at a landing field. Not in Hopewell. In Kansas. Salina. Smokey Hill Air Base, I think he said. He's got a relative up there who's got him the job. They're moving right away. He's set—not likely to be called up because of his job is the thinking. Well, he'll be called up, but he'll be exempted, reclassified, is what I mean. Mechanics are needed on airfields. But who knows?"

I can't breathe. I'm shaking all over. I hold onto the tablecloth on each side of my plate.

"Well, we can't do that," Momma says. "You won't do that, will you, Vernon? They're moving? Nita Jane's willing to move away from your parents at a time like this?"

"Seems so." Daddy waits, then goes on talking. "And we will too, Darlene. I've been trying to tell ya. This isn't play acting anymore. This country's gonna be changing and not just in the newspapers. It's gonna make a difference to all of us. You and me. Everybody. Here and now."

I think Daddy will say, *this isn't Hollywood,* like he tells Momma, sometimes. He and Momma used to go to the movies before me. She's told me about Hollywood when we do dishes together, and at bedtime—when Daddy's not around. She liked Clark Gable and Bing Crosby. And Jeanette MacDonald, best of all. She tells me her movie stories and sings her songs. Momma sings soprano.

"Aileen's not that far. You could dri—" Momma doesn't get to say everything she wants to.

"I can't drive back and forth because of the tires and gas. Japan just took over the oil fields and rubber plantations in Malaya, Darlene. America's gonna have no rubber for new tires. What there is, will be for the military. But putting that aside, even if driving as we like was allowed, we can't be spending money before I earn it."

He tells her that somebody Grampa Jantz knows came by and said that everything's gonna be changing all across America real soon, just like Roosevelt's telling us. The draft is gonna be speeding up. Rationing is gonna happen, just like in Great Britain. If the war goes on longer than a few weeks, Daddy tells her, it's gonna be more than just tires and gas that's gonna be hard to find. It's gonna be groceries, especially things we get from parts of the world where they're fighting now. No sugar. No coffee. Or pineapple.

"Who knows what all!" Daddy is worried.

"What'll we do with the house? We can't afford two payments. Can we rent this one out? We can rent it out, if we've gotta move." She told me last night during dishes that we might lose the house. She acts surprised, but she knew this was coming. She said so to me.

"No." Daddy says while he pushes his plate out of the way. He sits with his hands folded on the edge of the table, twirling his thumbs around each other.

"I think we ought to give it to Hannah."

Momma pulls her lips in and blows air out through them. "You're telling me that we built this house out of what little we could pull together and what we borrowed, and you're gonna give it to your sister? Why? Give me one good reason wh—well, I know why, don't I? When did this little scheme of yours come to mind?"

"You've known about this, Darlene. I told you some time ago that Hannah's got nowhere to go with her kids since Harry's left her again. She can't keep living out on the farm with mom and dad. They're too old. Dad's gonna be retiring now. The kids are driving him crazy and anyhow, she needs a place of her own. I feel responsible for them. We've talked about this."

Daddy's words are coming fast and loud. I can't make them all out, but I know Daddy wants Aunt Hannah off the farm. He's told Momma lots of times.

"There was no talking. What talking? You told me you were thinking about finding a place for Hannah and her kids. Our house? You were talking about our house when you were telling me this?" Momma is beside herself. "Why you, Vernon? Why just you? Where're your brothers in this? Reuben, for godssake? He's farm rich, and Willard? You're so damn close to Willard, where's he now that you need something? Your brothers own farms, businesses!" Momma hates Uncle Willard. It's written all over her, Daddy says, when they argue about his family.

"The kids were left to me. I took them on when he left her, Darlene. I've all but adopted them. I explained all this before we got married. You know how it was with them long before you and me even met. They've been mine to take care of since they were babies. I did, too, tell you."

Daddy is talking louder and louder. "It doesn't matter why. They're my responsibility and that's the end of it."

Momma's told me about Daddy's "other family." They are bigger than me. I only see them on Sundays, when they come, at Daddy's homeplace. They don't play with me, but they talk to me sometimes. Momma asks Daddy about Aunt Hannah's responsibility, how about letting Harry in and out of her life, in and out of her bed? What about that? Daddy doesn't say anything.

Momma's lips are very tight when she says, "And what about this responsibility here?" She nods her head toward me and at Teddy in his crib. Her voice is shaking, her lips twisted up.

I am shaking more. I can hardly see the table. The dishes look like they're moving. I push the fingers of my hand under my plate and pick up my spoon with the others. It is hard in my hand. I squeeze it tight. It feels good to hold it. My breath comes out fast. Momma glares at Daddy.

"That's what I'm trying to take care of, Darlene." Daddy tightens his fingers together as he presses them down on the edge of the table. "It's done, now, anyway. I had to let Wilbur know right away, seeings how he had his pick. People're panicking, Darlene. You know that? Nobody can reason out what all this means for them. We may be eating rice every night before this is over. Potatoes may be a thing of the past."

We never eat rice. I don't know what Daddy means. I cry out. I think I'll throw up. I run to Momma again. I grab hold of her arm.

"Stop it, Vern! You're scaring Shike. You're scaring all of us." But Teddy isn't crying in his crib. He doesn't even know that everything is going wrong.

Momma turns to me like she's never seen me before. I think she doesn't know me. But then she puts her arm around my waist and hugs me to her chest and tells me, "It's okay, honey. Daddy and I have to talk. Why don't you go into the bedroom and play?" She says this in a funny voice. It doesn't sound like hers. All at once, I don't know if it's her voice or not. I have a terrible feeling in my throat and stomach.

"Momma." I cry. "I want to stay here by you."

"Well, that's fine, honey. But if you do, you'll have to not interrupt us, and you can't cry because your daddy and I have important things to discuss right now. You think you can do that?"

"No." I start to tell her that I mean I don't want us to move to Aileen.

But she says to me before I can say any more, "Then you have to leave the table, Shike. I can't...."

All at once, I feel like I can't leave the room, but I don't want to hear what they are telling each other. All I can think to say is, "I'll be good. Real, real good." I cry hard.

Momma looks at the spoon I have in my hand. I am holding it up in the air, moving it around in circles. When I see that I am, it doesn't feel like I'm the one doing it. It is somebody else's. I bring it down and stare at the spoon. It got into my hand by magic. I want to put it down on the table. but I can't let go of it. Momma pats my arm, takes the spoon out of my hand, and puts it on the table careful-like and turns away from Daddy. She pulls me to her again, hugging me close. Then she holds my head against her chest with her hand, kisses the top of my head. She's holding me like this when she finally looks at Daddy.

"Where will we live?" Her voice is shaking.

"In a rental that Hilliar has in mind until we can find a decent place. It has a lotta rooms, hot running water and a toilet. It'll be rent-free. Not the place we find, a-course. I mean his rental. For now." Momma and Daddy lived in a rented house in Clearview after they got married. I was born in a rental.

Momma doesn't look at Daddy. She pushes me a little away from her when she lets out a noise like she has cut herself someplace. It is a horrible cry. She looks down at her plate, then up at me with hurting eyes, filled with tears.

I think she wants me to tell her something, but I don't know what. She wipes her cheeks and eyes with the end of the tablecloth. She doesn't remember she has a napkin at the side of her plate.

Momma and me set the table special tonight. She spent a lot of time in the kitchen making Daddy's favorite hamburger vegetable soup, but it didn't get done in time. She started too late, she told me. "So it'll be for tomorrow night after all the seasoning has set real good."

Now, she is crying so hard I can't look at her, but I can't stop watching, either. Teddy is waking up in his crib. He's not crying, but he's making sucking noises, moving his legs and scrunching up his face.

"Play with Teddy so he won't cry," Momma tells me while she cries. "I need to talk to your father." When Momma calls Daddy "my father," I know how serious she is.

I go to Teddy. My supper is cold on my plate. I'm still crying but not too loud.

"Are we moving?" I ask Momma.

"Yes, honey, surely we are, but it's okay. It will be fine. We have to go where Daddy can find work. We'll work this thing out. Just take Teddy. Here, let me help you."

Momma wipes her face with her napkin after she stands. She goes to the crib and lifts Teddy out and puts him in the wagon on his side, on his thick, yellow blanket that matches his jumper suit. She hands me his bottle from the table. "He can take his bottle. It isn't warm anymore, but it's not from the ice box, either. It'll be okay for now. You make sure it doesn't fall outta his mouth, okay?" Momma has taped some old pillows in a pile so Teddy can lean against them without falling on his back.

"This will keep him on his side." She pushes the pile of pillows up against him. "If he looks like he's gonna cry, you can pull him around the house. He likes that. Just don't pull him around where Daddy and I are talking, okay? That's a big help, Shike."

Then she says something that doesn't sound like Momma as she touches my back with a little push. She is talking in her funny voice again, "I thank you for your help."

She messes up my hair and kisses me on the forehead. Then, all of a sudden, she takes my head into her hands and leans over so her face is close to mine. "Your daddy and I will never do anything to hurt you or Teddy, Shike. We won't let anybody or anything hurt you, either. Not ever. Sometimes things happen that we can't help. Your daddy and I will find out what to do about this. That's what we have to talk about."

I nod. I will take care of Teddy like she wants me to.

Momma helps me get the wagon turned around, and I move it toward the living room. She takes the bottle out of my hand and puts it in Teddy's mouth. She takes a towel from the back of the wagon, rolls it up, and puts it under Teddy's bottle to hold it up for him, so it won't fall down.

"Turn that damned radio off when you get in the other room, will you Shike?" It's only soft music now, some singer Momma usually likes to hear. When I pull Teddy to the console, I turn the knob that shuts off the music.

When Momma gets back to the table, I hear Daddy say to her, "You know that movie star Clark Gable you used to talk about so much? The actress he was married to? Well, she was killed in an airplane crash today—or maybe it was yesterday—that they said."

"Carole Lombard?" Momma can't believe it.

"I think that's the name they said on the news. We used to see her in the movies, remember?"

I look at Momma. She is staring at Daddy like she can't believe anything he's saying anymore as I take Teddy into our bedroom and close the door.

HONEST

MONEY

1.

July, 1942

"**L**ITTLE MISS MUFFET SAT ON *a Tuffet, eating her curds and whey. Along came a spider, sat down beside her, and frightened Miss Muffet away!*" I say it along with Momma who turns around from hanging Teddy's diapers on the clothesline in the back of the warehouse and tells me, "You almost got it this time, Shike." Momma and Daddy say almost this or almost that, all the time.

"I don't know a tuffet."

"Well, I'm not sure what it is, either, but I've always thought it's something you sit on, you know, kinda like a milking stool, but, now that I'm thinkin' about it, a 'tuffet' could be Miss Muffet's behind for all I know." We both laugh big.

"Start over."

"Okay, but you say it with me. Little Miss Muffet sat on a tuffet, eating her curds and whey...."

"There's too many words."

"You mean it's too long?"

"It's too hard."

"You mean the words? The words are hard?"

"I don't want to anymore."

"Well, that's okay. Some of the words sound funny. Nursery rhymes were written a long time ago, back when people talked different than we do now. And anyway, sometimes things in nursery rhymes don't seem to make much sense exactly. You ever hear me say 'no rhyme or reason?'"

I nod, even though I don't remember, for sure.

"That means some things rhyme and some things are, well, are… reasonable, okay, let's see… hmmm, looks like I talked my way into something we'll have to pay attention to here."

Momma stops hanging Teddy's diapers, turning to look at me, holding the clothes pins she hasn't used in her hands. She bends down. "What I want to tell you is that some things rhyme and some things make sense, making sense is what reasonable means. It's like having a reason for something. I know you've heard me say that."

I nod but I'm still not sure.

Momma stands up and stretches. "Well, it's usually one or the other. Things either rhyme or they make sense, not both things together. So don't feel bad if you don't understand right away."

Momma throws the clothes pins down in her laundry basket and takes my hand and walks me to the couch. She points to a cushion next to her after she's sitting. I sit down, putting my leg alongside her leg, touching it a little.

"Here's how you'll learn what this one means." Momma stops and takes in a long breath. "Little Miss Muffet puts her behind down on a milking stool while she's eating her cottage cheese—that's what curds are, they're cottage cheese. And this cottage cheese has a lot of milk in it, that's what 'whey' is, it's lots of watery milk. So Miss Muffet's cottage cheese was pretty soupy. Then all at once this spider comes along and decides to stop right beside her, and when she looks down and sees it, it scares Miss Muffet so bad, she runs away."

"I know."

"Well, all right then. What's the confusion?"

"No. I mean, the cottage cheese. I know cottage cheese."

"Okay, I know you know cottage cheese," Momma says. "But do you know that it's also curds, is the question."

"Yes. You told me once before. I remember."

"I did? I told you all of this? Why did you let me… ah well, I've been doing that lately." Momma looks off to the back of the warehouse at Teddy who's still sleeping in his crib. "I'm sorry," she says in a whisper.

"Does Muffet take her cottage cheese along?"

Momma turns back to me. "You mean when she runs away? Well, I don't know, Shike. The verse doesn't say." She stops like she's not going on. But then she smiles and rubs my leg. "That's the point, I guess. It's just a little verse that rhymes. It only tells a itty, bitty story. This one's about a girl who was enjoying what she was eating until this spider shows up and scares her, that's it, end of story. It doesn't tell us everything about what happens to Little Miss Muffet after that."

Momma shakes her head a little, then smiles, pushing my hair out of my eyes. "The whole idea is to have a verse that's fun to learn. If it didn't rhyme, it wouldn't be as much fun or as easy to memorize." She gives my leg a couple of pats. "So let's say it together. You can say 'scared' if you want to, like you did last time. 'Frightened' is a harder word, one that grown-ups usually say instead of 'scared.' You know, I'm thinking that when people made up these verses they probably chose words that make them into a poem." Then Momma says the whole rhyme real fast. I try to keep up. She is having fun again. She says it almost like she's singing. Momma likes to sing. She sings when nobody is listening.

"I like it," I tell her.

She laughs and hugs me close.

She pushes me back from her so she can see me better. "You know, I'm not even sure you know what a rhyme is, Shike. Do you? Know what one is?"

"I don't know."

"Rhymes are words that sound almost alike so they're fun to say together... like... let's see, 'fun and sun,' or... 'say and may,' or... 'flower and shower,' or... 'now and plow,' or 'care and share.' You want to try and come up with one?"

"I don't want to." I don't tell her I feel like I won't be able to make one up fast.

"It's okay if you don't want to. I want you to like to do it when you learn it. Rhyming and saying verses that rhyme teach you new words. That's what they're about more than anything else. I have an idea! How about I give you an easy word and you try to find one that sounds like it. Let's see...."

"She," I say. I hear the "sssss" in "see," and all at once I know one.

"That's right!" Momma says. "That's the way it works, like that. What could be another one that sounds like 'see?'"

I get off the couch but stand next to her lap, looking up into her face. "I can't think of the right words."

"Don't worry, honey. Rhyming isn't easy. It comes easier when you learn to read."

"I want to read by myself." When Momma reads me stories, I point to the words as she goes. I say them with her if she lets me. Sometimes she reads fast because she wants to be done in a hurry, then I can't keep up.

"You'll get to go to school not too long from now, and you'll learn words fast then. Once you learn to read, you can rhyme faster than anything. It—"

"Shit," I say and laugh.

"What?" Momma's mouth is open. She doesn't close it. She stares at me with her mouth part of the way open. "Where in the world did you get that kinda language, young lady? I didn't know you even knew this word."

"Daddy says 'shit.'"

"Well, you're right, he does, sometimes, I guess." Momma smiles a little.

"And you say 'shit.'"

"I do? I suppose I do. But I shouldn't. It's a word that—"

"It rhymes."

Momma laughs. "Now, that's true. It does rhyme probably with… what word did I use? 'It,' I think it was. And the word you used does rhyme with 'it,' but not a rhyme you'll find in any book of verses, that's for sure." She takes my hands. "I don't want you to learn to talk like that, Shike. Your Daddy and me get mad and say things that we ought not to be saying. Getting mad isn't a good enough reason for talking like that."

"Makes sense."

Momma stops, looks at me, and then laughs a lot. "That's very smart, Shike. Having a reason means 'making sense.' Very good. You're something this afternoon, you know that? Where'd you get all those smarts, I'd like to know?" She kisses my hands and combs my hair with her fingers, pulling little clumps behind each ear. "You're growing up so fast. What a big girl you're getting to be!"

"Me."

"Yes, you." She looks close into my eyes.

"'Me' rhymes."

Momma claps her hands together. "My goodness, it does! 'Me' does rhyme with 'be.' You are so bright today. I just might have to wear my sunglasses the rest of the afternoon!" She thinks a minute. "Oh, one thing I meant to tell you about this nursery rhyme. I thought I heard you say 'curds and away.' That's not how the verse goes. It's 'curds and whey.' Whey, not 'away.' You remember what whey means? Okay then, here's another new word. You see how you learn new words when you memorize nursery rhymes?"

I nod so she tells me again, "Whey is the watery part of milk. Actually, it's a little more complicated than that. Let's see. Okay, when Gramma Dirks makes cottage cheese, she starts with whole milk that she gets right from the cows after Grampa Dirks does his milking. She sometimes puts some of it in a crock and lets it sit outside on the porch with a towel over it so flies and bugs don't get to it. When milk sits out like that, it gets sour. You've heard me tell you this, I know."

"Smells."

"That's right. And usually we don't drink that—though years ago, out on farms and back when our people lived in the old country, when my and your daddy's relatives lived in Russia, they put sour milk in lots and lots of things they made good to eat. Lettuce salad with clabbered milk is one I like or on cucumbers with salt and pepper. Clabbered milk is sour milk. When it's put in things, it doesn't smell or taste bad. But when it's by itself, it can be pretty hard to swallow unless you're used to it, okay?"

Momma doesn't wait for me to answer. "So, when milk gets sour, some of it gets to be solid, it forms into clumps. This clumpy part is the curds, and the water part that's left behind is the whey, like I told you. But here's something, too. It can take quite a while for milk to sour, so to make it curdle faster, you can put rennet in it. That's something that makes the curdling quicker, and it's got something in it that keeps the curds from becoming too soft, getting too soupy. You buy rennet in stores, and Daddy puts it in the ice cream he makes to help keep it solid, not too soupy."

Momma stops and looks at the clock on the end table by the couch. "Look at the time. I swear, Shike, nothing is ever simple with you." She kisses the top of my head. "Okay, we'll take a minute or two more. Now that we're in this, we might as well plunge on while Teddy's sleeping."

Momma sighs but smiles at me. "So, back to Miss Muffet. During her time, which I'm guessing from the illustrations in the books, was somewhere around when my grandma was making cottage cheese, the cottage cheese Muffet was eating came from whole milk with lots of cream in it. You know how good that tastes, right?"

I nod. Uncle Clifford puts whole milk or cream on lots of things because they have cows. Sometimes we get to bring some home. Daddy likes his on green beans with butter, but Momma says he drowns her good cooking in it. Momma buys milk that has the cream in a little cup at the top of the bottle. Then the other part isn't so fat, she tells me.

"Well, Miss Muffet was eating whole milk that'd gone sour and had separated into curds that still had the watery part of the milk left in it. But instead of pouring the whey down the drain and just eating the curds, she ate both."

"Poopy," I say and laugh.

"What? No, don't be silly, Shike, or we'll have to stop."

"It rhymes."

"Well, it does, soupy rhymes with the word you just used, but I don't like that kinda talk." I didn't make her laugh. She stands up, stretches, and yawns. I think she wants to go to bed. "Why don't you come over here and hand me the rest of Teddy's diapers outta the laundry basket so we can get this done?"

"I don't want to," I shout and get off the couch.

"Okay, Shike, sit back down. I want to talk to you." I fall down against the couch with my face on the cushion. I don't want to talk anymore. "I'm serious. I want you to listen to me." Momma sits back down, turns me around to look at her, and takes my hands in hers again. "You can play with this rhyming all you want. It's a fun thing to do. Nursery rhymes can really help you learn new words and learn to make up words that sound alike. And you memorize real easy, I see that already.

"But people listen to words more times than not, so it's really, really important to learn to say the right ones. I know that your boy cousins use inappropriate words at times, especially when grown-ups aren't around. They don't have a very good teacher in your Uncle Clifford, and your Aunt Josephine doesn't give them much instruction, so they feel free to say what they please. It's clear you know what some of the bad words are. So I want you to take those words out when you're talking with other people. Bad words only show how mad you are or how few good words you know to express what you want to say. They don't show people how smart you are, even when Tommy Don and his brothers think they do. They might think they're big and very grown up, like the men, by saying such things, but they aren't. They're just showing how ignorant, how dumb, they are. I don't want you to participate in their language when they talk like this, okay? And your daddy and I will try to speak better, more like we should from now on, you understand?"

I nod. Momma kisses me on my cheek and points to the laundry basket, "Now, let's get this done before your daddy comes home to talk to us about a new place to live!" She and I go over to the clothesline, and I reach down, take a diaper, and hold it up to her.

"A new place to live?" I can't believe it.

"I haven't said anything to you about it because it may not work out. Your daddy's got himself all excited, but knowing him and his notions about this, that, and the other thing, I have my doubts. I haven't the slightest idea what this place looks like or where it is, exactly. I didn't mention it to you because I didn't want you to get your hopes up if it doesn't work out. We'll just have to see, you understand?"

I nod, and I'm hoping like everything that Daddy is right.

2.

Afternoon, same day

"HOW CAN I MOVE AT such short notice?" Momma isn't happy anymore about the new place. She drops one arm to her side and pushes her hair back with her other hand. It's very hot in the warehouse. Her face is red. She wipes her face with a towel she hangs from her apron ties in front.

"Well, I'd say we're about half packed as it is." Daddy waves his hands around at all the cardboard boxes sitting along the back walls and piled up in corners. It's mostly clothes and dishes we haven't used because there's no place to put them without them getting dusty. "You're the one complaining we can't stay here. It's a warehouse attic, for godssakes."

We moved to the warehouse because the rental Mr. Hilliar said we could have wasn't ready yet. The people living there weren't able to move out when they hoped they could, so he "granted them more time," that's what Daddy told Momma after the first load of our movables was in the pickup at Clearview. "Living in the warehouse'll only be for a few weeks, till the couple can get out," he had promised. But even though Momma has changed the warehouse into a livable space—as Daddy tells her again and again—it's not really a place to live. It isn't even approved by the city for a living space, but we're doing it regardless.

"Getting away with it because of the war shortage on houses," Momma grumbled.

"Hilliar's inside connections." She tells Daddy, often, how much she dislikes Mr. Hilliar. "He doesn't have an ounce of blood in his body. It's copper and gold running through his veins."

About our move now, she asks, "There's hot running water and a toilet?" Momma doesn't trust what Daddy tells her anymore. She falls on the couch, staring across the big space that's the back part of our living room.

In his crib, Teddy's trying to reach for a block. As he does, he falls forward and begins crawling to where it is but falls down on his stomach so he snakes along the rest of the way.

"Where we're going, it'll have those things, you're sure?" Momma doesn't believe Daddy's telling her all of it. "He holds back," she tells me, "then I find out too late to resist." She keeps asking him about this and that, mostly about the toilet and hot water. Daddy starts to get up and go to Teddy, but he sits back down when Momma says, "Shike, would you go play with Teddy while I talk with your daddy?"

Momma has to heat all our water in a big pan on the wood stove when we take a bath. It takes hours and hours. It makes the warehouse hotter and hotter when she heats the water, even with the fans going all the time. While Momma is busy talking, I don't go play with Teddy, and she doesn't watch me to see. Teddy stops trying to stand up. He just plays with his blocks. He's a good baby.

Daddy tells her that she'll have running hot water. "And it's got a real bathtub!"

We take our baths like Aunt Josephine and Uncle Clifford and my boy cousins do, in a galvanized tub. Momma won't let me take a bath out on the farm unless she's there with me. "Your boy cousins," she says, "get their baths in the summer in the tank, Shike. Let me tell you, and you better be listening, you are not to bathe in the tank where the cows come to drink. It's filthy, that water, and I can't even think about what Josephine's kids are putting down their gullets when they accidentally swallow some of it."

My boy cousins can't use soap when they take their baths in the tank because the cows would get sick, so they rub Lava on and wash it off from buckets of well water outside after they've been in the tank and before they come back into the house.

"A bathtub?" Momma asks Daddy now. "What a novelty!"

"No need to get smart, Darlene," Daddy says, looking over at me, with his mouth twisted up to the side. "And there are kids on the block!" Daddy looks down at me, acting like Momma isn't there. "Wouldn't you like that, Shike? Somebody besides Teddy? Somebody your own age, how about that, huh?" He wants me to like Hilliar's rental.

"This is a house you're talking about here?" Momma asks. He's told her it's an apartment. She knows because it was what we were supposed to move into, that's after Daddy told her it wasn't a house she'd hoped for. She just wants him to say it's a real bona fide apartment, no more shenanigans. That's what she told him she would have the next time, at the very least, or it was going to be "Katie bar the door."

"No, not exactly," Daddy says about the apartment being in a house. He sits down at the other end of the couch. He doesn't want to sit next to her. The couch is the only place for him to sit, unless he gets a folding chair from the back and brings it into the living room. The warehouse is one big space. Momma's put up sheets that hang on wires to make rooms. Wood posts keep the wires from sagging down too much. Daddy made them stay in place by nailing them to the floor and the wires stay by nails bent over on top.

The day Momma finished making all the rooms with Gramma Dirks's old sheets, before we unpacked things from our house in Clearview, she asked me, "You've heard of wallpaper, haven't you, Shike?"

I nodded. Daddy's homeplace has wallpaper in the upstairs rooms, some big flowers, some little ones on yellow and blue backgrounds, in the bedrooms where my aunts stayed until they left home. It's where we sleep when we stay overnight. Gramma Jantz won't let anybody put flowers on the walls downstairs because she thinks it's a sin.

"Well," Momma said to me about the warehouse walls she'd made, "These are clothesline walls. Clark Gable and Claudette Colbert." Momma knows movies and the stars.

"Who?"

"*It Happened One Night.* You know, the movie." When she told me, she was using pliers to screw hooks into the warehouse walls to hold the lines at the end. "Claudette and Clark made two bedrooms by hanging a sheet like this across a room in the movie, *It Happened One Night,* remember?" Momma doesn't see movies anymore, but she tells me their stories when we take a break or at bedtime. Mennonites and movies aren't supposed to mix, as Momma has told me many times before.

She was happy the day she made the sheet walls. It was one of her good days but she's run out of horse pills. She keeps telling Daddy every now and then, but there's no money for doctors and pills.

"C'mon, Darlene, you know it's an apartment, not a house." Daddy is irked no end. I don't want them to talk any longer. I want to get in the car and go see.

"Oh, another apartment," Momma says, like it's the first time she's heard it. *"This* was an apartment, remember?" Momma wants a house, even if we rent. She's sick of being bullshitted around.

It's a bad word, but she says it, anyway.

"This one really is an apartment." Daddy looks straight at her.

"Where?"

Daddy waits a minute, then says, quiet-like, "At the Hilliar's."

"Oooooh. At the Hilliar's. So we'll owe Hilliar just like we do now. Now it's owing him for the favor of this rent-free apartment and in the future it's for finding us a better one that he just happens to own that we'll rent. This is one very generous man you work for, Vernon!" Momma's stares at Daddy are mean. Her hair is hanging down over her eyes. She keeps pushing it behind her ears, but it's too short and falls right back down. She's in the same housedress she wore yesterday, and she doesn't have any anklets on with her shoes. She looks puffy. She tells me over and over that she's puffy because she's holding onto her weight, after Teddy. "Keeping my baby fat." She laughs like it's a joke. She eats lots of watermelon and cottage cheese.

Now Daddy's arguing with her about rentals, houses, and apartments and whether they are bona fide or not.

"Momma?" I lean over her knees so I can look up into her face. "Can we say Miss Muffet?"

She pushes my hands off her knees. "Not now, Shike." She gets ready to say something to Daddy, but he stands and walks fast into the kitchen. I hear the faucet running.

"Momma, can we say Little Miss Muffet? *Please?*" Momma doesn't want to talk about Miss Muffet, but I say, "I want to rhyme."

She doesn't look at me but keeps her eye on Daddy as he comes back to the couch.

He doesn't sit down. He stares at Teddy as he tries again to stand up by holding onto his crib rails but falls. Teddy's face scrunches up, and he starts to cry, but, all at once, he stops crying and crawls for a block. Daddy doesn't drink his water. He just holds the glass like he's going to.

"So the Hilliars own the property. Is that so hard to take, if we actually get a decent place to live? You're not understanding how hard it is to find a place these days. People are living in shanty towns in parts of this country."

"Most of them are in the big cities working, making a dollar an hour, Vernon. I'd live in a shanty, too, if you made that kinda money. It's temporary housing anyway, not shantytown. At least, for the whites, it's not." I know shantytown. It's the colored side.

Daddy twists up his mouth. "The buck-an-hour people are working in the shipyards for the Navy. I don't know, Darlene, you talk outta both sides of your mouth. It seems to me you're never satisfied." Daddy is talking to himself. He doesn't even look at her or me. He talks to the window on the other side of the warehouse or the floor. "You don't want us to leave Oklahoma to find a better job someplace else, like Sherman did, but you don't—"

"Sherman went to work at the airfield, Vernon. He's working directly for the government in this war effort. You can't do that. We've talked about this. Does your religion stand for something to you or not?"

Daddy doesn't say this time what he's really thinking—that Momma won't leave because of Gramma Dirks. He's said it before, lots of times, and every time she stared at him when he did, not saying a word. "That's really what it's about," he usually tells her. "You two fight like cats and dogs so you aren't about to give that up!" Daddy thinks everything hard about Momma is because of Gramma Dirks. She's even sick because of Gramma Dirks, he says. But, then, he's sorry. He tells her he doesn't really mean it.

When he sits down, his glass of water spills on his lap. "Shit," he says and takes a long drink from the glass to empty it. I look at Momma, but she doesn't tell him not to say bad words. She just sits staring at him. Now Teddy is standing on shaky legs, crying and yanking hard on his crib rails.

Momma looks at me, shaking her head, but she doesn't tell me to take care of Teddy like she usually does. She surprises me by whispering, "Ignore him, and he'll stop." I don't look at Teddy, and he drops down and plays with a toy. She winks at me.

"Look, it's all there is right now, Darlene, and it's good of Hilliar to offer it to us. I know you don't like him because he's rough-talking and smokes, but he gave me a job. I'd like for you to remember that." Daddy smokes. He smokes on the way home from work, even in the backyard after dark, when Momma's in bed. I look down from my bedroom window and see him—the lifts of his hand to his mouth and a long fire light glowing from the cigarette.

I don't know if Momma ever sees him out there, but she knows he does it. I smell it on his work clothes. She doesn't say anything to him about it like she used to. She just smells his work shirts up close and shakes her head when she does the laundry, in our Maytag downstairs, that's hooked up with a long cord to a big plug against the back wall. "When his work clothes turn white from the bleach, maybe he'll stop," she says to the washing machine.

"Isn't this a little too chummy, you working for this man, then you coming home to his house? You make his money, and then give it back to him in rent? Didn't plantation owners do this kinda thing years ago, once the slaves got their freedom, to still lay claim to them?"

Daddy is fuming, just like Momma wants him to be. "You know the rent's not all the money I make."

"Pretty close these days, Vern. Pretty close."

"C'mon, Darlene! He's trying to help us out here. We've been looking for a place for months. And it's not in his house like you make it sound. Anyway, it's not connected to his house like a lot of places are nowadays, that people are forced to live in, close together, all crowded. We'll have a private entrance."

Momma can't take her eyes off of him.

"Okay, so it's on his property." He breathes loud through his nose. "There's no harm in just looking at it, is there? If you don't like it, we don't have to take it." When Momma doesn't say anything, he throws his hands in the air.

Teddy falls down and starts to scream. Momma looks over at his crib, not moving, staring at him.

"Aw, what the hell. I don't give a flying fu… *fig* anymore." Daddy wants to say real bad words. He starts to yell. "Hell, I just as soon live here outta the cardboard boxes. I mean, why not hang around in this warehouse and wait and see what else might turn up in the next who-knows-how-many years? It's no never mind to me."

He stops to take his glass to the kitchen. From there, he calls out, "But I don't know how long Hilliar is gonna be satisfied to keep us in this illegal setup—him at risk for it." He walks back to where Momma and me are sitting, waiting. "I really think the only reason he isn't in trouble for it now is because things are so hard out there that the authorities are willing to overlook almost anything to keep people off the streets."

I know Momma's thinking if Daddy'd stayed out on the farm helping Grampa Dirks like she wanted, he'd stay out of the draft, and we would have a decent place to live. She's said this plenty of times when they argue, until Daddy's stopped listening. "He doesn't hear anything but what he wants," she tells me over and over.

Momma breathes in, waits, and finally says, letting out a long breath, "Okay, then, when can we see it?"

Daddy can't believe his ears. I clap my hands. and Daddy winks at me, but Momma gives me a mean look, and I stop clapping.

"This afternoon if you want. We don't even have to wait that long. We can go right now," Daddy says.

"Don't you have to call or something, to let him know we're coming?"

I stand up. I want to go see the apartment and move. I hate the warehouse. It's noisy all day and smells bad, like too much dirt. When Momma sweeps, whole clouds of dust go up in the air, past the windows in the sunshine. Momma showed me one day. She acted crazy with her broom, going back and forth real, real fast. Pointing to the dust she'd made in the air, she said, "Watch out, Shike! A dust storm!" And it's hot in the warehouse when I try to sleep, even with the fans. I want to play with other kids, like Leon and I did with Bobby Gene before he died. Tommy Don was one year older than Bobby Gene.

"Everybody knew how close these two boys were," Momma told Daddy when she got the phone call that Bobby Gene had passed away. Tommy Don said Bobby Gene died because he drank the white juice from a milk weed, but Momma told me that was nonsense. Bobby Gene died before we moved to the warehouse. He died from fever he had that took him very fast. Everybody was quarantined on the farm for a little while. They couldn't leave until the health people said it was safe.

"He was fine one day and in the ground the next," Momma told a woman later at the Hopewell church. Momma never would say what made him die. She said they didn't know for sure—some kind of fever. She wouldn't let me go to the funeral. I stayed with Norma Janet, at Simon Nichols's house. I stayed there for a few days because of all the crying. Aunt Josephine was beside herself, and Momma had to help her with my boy cousins. But that was a long time ago, too long to remember much.

Uncle Clifford and Daddy did all the moving to the warehouse, with a few men from Mr. Hilliar's shop helping once they got each load to Aileen. "Hard times in your lives," everybody told Momma and Daddy at church.

Momma stops talking to Daddy even though she's in the middle of an argument with him. "Shike? You all right. You look sick."

"Bobby Gene—"

"What does Bobby Gene have to do with right now? Go take care of your brother like I asked you to do." She's forgotten she told me not to pay any attention to him.

"Did Bobby Gene die because of whey?" I feel scared.

Teddy is trying to stand up in his crib, screaming his head off. Daddy walks to the back of the warehouse and picks him up and walks him around. Teddy doesn't stop crying so Daddy bounces him up and down with his sing-song ah-ah, ah-ah, ah-ah. Slowly, Teddy quiets down.

"Will you stop with the whey? I'm sorry I even started this rhyming thing with you. Now you're gonna drive me crazy with it." Momma pushes me away from her. "Just stop. I mean it. I want to talk to your father."

Daddy comes back holding Teddy, who is quiet, leaning against Daddy's chest. "I can call right now if you want me to."

"I don't know," Momma says. Daddy tells her that she's out of sorts. I know to be quiet about the whey. Daddy tells her if they don't go today, the whole deal will be lost because there are people waiting in the wings.

"What's this gonna cost?"

"Ten." Daddy says.

"Ten. That's half your pay! How are we—"

"Ten a month, woman. A *month!* Not every paycheck. We get all the utilities, and there's no other costs."

"What do you mean 'get the utilities?' Do we pay or him?"

"That's what I'm trying to tell ya. We get them free. He pays."

Momma's face stops being so tight.

"So, see, it really comes out less than what we paid with our own prop...." Daddy stops. He never talks about the house we left to Aunt Hannah in Clearview, our house, the one he built Momma and me. He says real quick, "There's furniture, rugs, and even a console. By the time we get everything unpacked in there, we'll have a real place to live, Darlene."

"How do you figure that?"

"We've got things. A few things." He waits. Most of our things were left with Aunt Hannah in the house Daddy gave her. Momma will never forgive him. She said so. Still says so. He stands up and takes a few steps toward the phone. "Hey, we've got the clothes on our backs and a washing machine and a couch." He grins and even laughs a little. "More'n a lot of folks have right now when you stop to think about it."

Daddy gives a sideways look to the long extra clothesline stretching across the back of the warehouse space, now full of Teddy's diapers hanging to dry. "And we got plenty of folding chairs and a card table." Daddy starts talking to Teddy while he walks with him around in front of Momma. "Maybe your daddy should start playing some cards on the side," he says. "He could hang a bare bulb from the ceiling back over there and earn a living by hook or by crook, whatdya think of that, little man?"

Momma stands up and walks over to him. She waits, looking at him, then says, "Ah, just as I thought." Now she looks at me.

"Don't start, Darlene." He bounces Teddy up and down more. He doesn't have on his shop clothes anymore. He's changed to a clean shirt and trousers, but he still smells like his smokes.

"How much have you had?" Momma asks. Then I know it's more than just smokes. Daddy forgot to use his Sen-Sen.

"A nip is all. It was a good day. I got paid. I can have a drink now and then if I want to." He blows on Teddy's hand that Teddy's put over Daddy's mouth.

Momma shakes her head and sighs. "Well, we might as well go over there and take a look. But I'm not making any promises."

"I don't expect you to," he says. But he wants Momma to like it. He wants to move to Mr. Hilliar's apartment. I can tell.

3.

Later afternoon, same day

THE APARTMENT IS GRAY WITH white shutters and looks new. But it's a garage. Momma says her words about this even before Daddy shuts off the engine. A long row of steps go up the side with a small porch at the top. There's a row of windows on the garage doors downstairs that have lace curtains. The two windows upstairs don't have any.

"There's actually two apartments," Daddy says as he looks up and out of the windshield. "One upstairs and one down. An old man and woman live in the one downstairs. They keep to themselves, Hilliar says. He'd ask them to live upstairs so we wouldn't have to worry about steps and the baby, but they're old, and, he says, they can't walk up the steps, which makes sense."

"Reason," I say. Momma looks at me then back at Daddy like she didn't hear me. "Reason," I say louder, "makes sense." Momma gives me a mean look, so I am quiet.

Then Momma gives Daddy a mean look. Her voice is nasty-like when she says, "And you worried about the Kruegers, remember? But now it's all different, isn't it? Maybe these old folks can babysit for me, you think?"

Daddy acts like he doesn't hear her. "We're supposed to go right on up. Hilliar said he'd be inside airing the place out." Daddy opens the door and steps out of the car. He goes around the hood and opens Momma's door, reaching for Teddy and lifting him into his arms.

When we go upstairs, I run my hands along the railing and take one step at a time until I'm on the porch at the top. Momma and Daddy are behind me. Mr. Hilliar opens the screen door that almost knocks me over and stretches a big hand out for me to shake. I take it. His palm feels wet and soft.

"Hello, lil' lady," he says with a smile. Uncle Reuben calls me little lady. I like it when Uncle Reuben calls me that. Mr. Hilliar has fat cheeks and talks like his mouth is full. He pulls me up the last step into the kitchen, pushes me by my shoulders out of the way, and laughs a little. Then he holds open the screen for Momma and Daddy.

Daddy almost bumps his head on the top of the door. Momma passes me and mumbles, "And they call him Shorty!"

Mr. Hilliar breathes real loud through his mouth and nose. He looks like he's got too much hair. Daddy is small and bald next to Mr. Hilliar. Daddy's hair is flat against his head because of his hair oil while Mr. Hilliar looks like he has red cotton candy all around his face. His beard is big and fluffy, the same color as his hair. He looks like Santa Claus but not with any white, only red, even his puffy face. He's fat everywhere, especially his stomach that pooches out, making his pants look like they're way, way too big for his legs, hanging down under his belly, flapping around when he walks because his pant legs are too wide at the bottom. And they're too short. His socks show over the tops of his shoes. His shirt is very tight and all sweaty with dark circles under his arms. The leftover part of his belt hangs down from his buckle like a big tongue. When I stand close to him, he smells dirty, like BO. You have to bathe to get rid of BO, Momma's told me. Mr. Hilliar smells like smokes and whiskey, too, lots more than Daddy.

"Hey, it's a climb, I know, but it's worth it." Mr. Hilliar pulls a cigarette out of his shirt pocket and pokes it into his mouth. He offers Daddy one but doesn't wait until Daddy says no. "Sorry, Shorty. I forgot." He winks at Daddy.

"Well, here it is." Mr. Hilliar moves his hand and arm around the room like we are outside in the country, in a pasture with lots of sky everywhere, like in the picture on the big calendar in the kitchen. He yanks the cigarette out of his mouth and drops it in his pocket. Daddy smokes with Mr. Hilliar at work, I think.

"Lots of kitchen space as you can see and good linoleum." Mr. Hilliar moves his fingers back and forth fast like he's polishing the floor from high in the air. I look down at the crumbled-like white floor with yellow lines making shapes all over. Mr. Hilliar's linoleum makes me think of crushed newspaper, without the letters. Momma and Daddy are looking down, too.

Momma says, "I like the pattern on this. It won't show dirt and smudges."

Mr. Hilliar smiles. "That's the idea! I'm glad you caught that, Missus Jantz."

In the crumbled pattern, I see faces with beards exactly like the ones from the pictures in the fairy tale books Momma brings home from the Hopewell library. I move my feet around and try to find Jack in his beanstalk or the giant, but I don't see them. I lean toward the trees and bushes on the floor and say, "Fee-fie-foe-fum." I whisper real soft so Momma won't notice. I think if Jack hears me, he might come out enough for me to see him, but I probably scared him off because I sound and look like the giant from where I'm standing.

"Jack," I whisper. When I say it more, Momma turns around and stares at me. I straighten up and look at the couch in the living room. When she goes back to listening to Mr. Hilliar, I look back at the kitchen floor to see if Jack has come out, but all I see are a bunch of faces I don't know.

Mr. Hilliar is happy about this floor. "I put it in myself before they closed down on this kind of thing." He looks at us with a smile. "The government. With the war and all." He says this like Momma and Daddy might not know about the war. "In here"—he walks past us into the living room—"you got about as much stuff as you'll ever want." He's proud of his apartment. Daddy laughs a little, and Momma is smiling at Mr. Hilliar a little, too. I know she's just being nice. "Couch, end tables, coffee table, lamps and curtains, well, at least in the bedrooms. You'll have to see to the ones in the living room." Daddy is pleased with everything Mr. Hilliar is saying. "The radio works, and it gets good reception." He flips on the console and rolls the dial past the stations. There's a lot of static but music and words come on every now and then. Mr. Hilliar stops on KSRC—I know because it's louder, and I know the announcer's voice. KSRC is in the big towers downtown, Momma told me. Right now there's some soap opera on that Hilliar turns up for Momma to hear. She smiles. She really likes the radio.

In Clearview, Momma listened to *Portia Faces Life* and *Stella Dallas* and *Whispering Streets* in the afternoons while she ironed or cooked. But we left our console with Aunt Hannah. One day after we were in the warehouse, Daddy brought home a small brown radio so Momma could listen to her soap operas and music, but it had a lot of static. Momma doesn't put it on these days. Daddy tells her it's not the radio, it's the warehouse reception.

"Silvertone," he says. "It's a good name." Daddy is never home when soap operas are on the radio. He left work early today to take us to see the apartment.

"Can I get reception in the kitchen?" Momma asks Mr. Hilliar.

"Well, I don't see why not. It's perfect most of the time in the living room, so the kitchen should be fine, as well." He smiles, reaches in his pocket and takes out the cigarette and holds it between his fingers without lighting it, just shaking and flicking it around. He says, "I tell you what, Missus, if you have a problem with the reception, once you and Shorty are in the apartment, I'll look into that for ya. I'll make it right even if I have to bring a radio up and tend to it myself. How's that?" He leans in toward Momma like he's gonna kiss her. She tips her face only a little up at him, but I know she likes that maybe two radios could be in the apartment.

Mr. Hilliar is saying especially to Momma, "The bedrooms are in here, and the bathroom." He points to a small hall while he reaches over and turns off the radio.

I wait in the living room while Mr. Hilliar, Momma, and Daddy walk through the hall and see the rooms. When I step into the hallway, they have turned and are coming back again. The hallway isn't very wide, and the ceiling is low. The walls are very close together. I go over and sit on the couch.

Momma isn't smiling. She is holding her purse under her arm. I can't tell if she likes the apartment or not. I know she's not happy with Mr. Hilliar. He's smoking his cigarette now, blowing smoke from the side of his mouth. He stands by an open window and taps the ashes over like the window doesn't have a screen. Some of the ashes land on the sill. Momma cleaned the sills in our Clearview house with vinegar and water. The windows at the warehouse don't have sills.

"Well, that's about it. You have some of your own furniture, you say?"

"Yeah," Daddy speaks up quick, "Yep, we do."

But Momma says, "Not much."

"What we've got'll fit." Daddy slaps a hand against his leg. He keeps moving Teddy from one side to the other. Teddy is being good. He hasn't let out a peep, but he's pushing his legs against Daddy's stomach every now and then. He wants back in his crib at the warehouse so he can try to walk. They all stand in a kind of circle, waiting for each other to say something. For a little bit, nobody does.

Mr. Hilliar walks to the kitchen, opens a cabinet, and takes out a saucer. He smashes his cigarette in it and blows out the last of his smoke through his nose. Then he swings open another door. "There's a few dishes, too, as you can see," he calls out. A pile of plates and stacked cups, bowls, glasses are on the two bottom shelves. Momma goes to the cabinet and opens another door. It's empty. She closes both doors real slow. Everybody stands again without saying anything.

Momma asks then where she can put her washing machine. "A wringer Maytag." She waits and expects Mr. Hilliar to tell her she won't have any place to put it. Daddy looks off to the side.

Mr. Hilliar tells her that he has a large basement in his house with an outside entrance. "It's all set up for that sort of thing." He says she can wash in the basement and hang clothes and diapers on the line beside the garage. She would have to share the line "with the old man and woman, lovely people. They don't use it much." Then we all stand without talking again. I move from one leg to the other. I want to go home.

"Well," Mr. Hilliar says, his hair still standing on end. The sun is coming in from the window and makes his whole head shimmer. He looks like he's on fire. "I'll just go use the bathroom while you folks talk it over." He walks to the hall, and Daddy waits until we hear Mr. Hilliar close the bathroom door.

"What do you think?" Daddy asks Momma, very low, like he's talking behind Mr. Hilliar's back and doesn't want him to hear.

Momma doesn't whisper. She talks right out. "What's there to say, Vernon? We need a different place to live. I don't like the fact that we live upstairs over somebody very much, especially since they're old. They're not gonna like

Teddy's running around all over the place once he gets to doin' that, which is gonna be in a coupla months. He's already pullin' himself up onto the couch and tryin' to walk alongside." Daddy turns his head toward where Mr. Hilliar is, down the hall. The toilet flushes. "And I'm worried about the steps."

"You got steps now, Darlene, or have you forgotten that? You got two sets of them, as a matter of fact, and you're not gripin' about that so much." Daddy is making this up because he tells Momma she gripes about the stairs all the time. He tells her she gripes and gripes about everything. He's always telling her to "give it a rest." Seems, to me, Momma is trying to tell him that she wants to rest instead of the stairs.

"The stairs we have now are inside, Vernon, or have you forgotten that? And there are two sets of them so they don't go straight up to heaven all at once!" She glares at him. "How'm I gonna get up and down those with Teddy in the wintertime is the question. Hilliar isn't saying a word about keeping the steps clear of ice and snow. Is he gonna do that as the landlord? And there's Shike. You said there were kids around. I didn't see any, but even if there are and she meets them, how's she gonna play safe with kids in the yard with me up here tending Teddy and the housework?"

"You can't have everything, Darlene."

When Mr. Hilliar comes into the room, Momma stands, looking at Daddy without anything on her face. Daddy says, "I think we've just about decided—"

"We need some time to think about this," Momma interrupts, taking the baby from Daddy. She turns around and looks for me. "Come with me, Shike."

"Well, I have to say that there's a waiting list, Missus Jantz," Mr. Hilliar says. Momma turns around and stares at him. He stares back at her. "I offered it to Vernon because I know he's good for it, working for me. But places like this aren't a dime a dozen, like they used to be. You want it, I need to find out as soon as possible."

"When would that be?" Momma asks this so soft I almost don't hear her. She talks soft when she doesn't want people to know what she's really thinking. She's gonna be upset when we're in the car.

"By tonight, I'd say, tomorrow morning at the latest. Shorty can tell me at work tomorrow. That'd be soon enough, I guess." Mr. Hilliar looks at Daddy.

"I think that's fair, don't you, Shorty? I have others to call, if you don't take it. I want it filled by the beginning of the month, and that's in three days." Mr. Hilliar isn't happy to wait.

"Oh, I think we'll take it," Daddy says, shaking Mr. Hilliar's hand. "We just need some time to talk it over. Darlene's worried about her and the baby, about Shike and the stairs, and a few little things like that—"

"Sure. Sure. That's understandable," Mr. Hilliar says, but he doesn't even wait until we leave before he puts another cigarette in his mouth. "Well, okay, then, you call me when you've talked it over. Or at work. At work's fine, in the morning." He turns and lights his cigarette like he wants it to be a secret. He walks slow behind us down the stairs. Momma stops with Teddy and grabs the rail. Daddy tries to take him, but she only shakes her head, pulling Teddy tight against her hip. She wants to see how hard it is.

While we get into the car, Mr. Hilliar stands on his back porch and waves goodbye. He goes inside his house before Daddy starts the engine. Daddy says we can't be messing around if we want it, or we'll mess around and lose it. Momma says if there's such a long waiting list, all these people looking at it, why did Hilliar have to come early and air it out?

I stand in the back seat like I always do—one leg on each side of the bump in the middle. Daddy's told me there's a rod that runs underneath that helps make the wheels spin in the back. I hold onto the sides of the front seats. Momma tells me to sit down, but I don't. I want to hear what they're saying about the apartment.

"He's holding you to him with his business, your job. He will raise our rent as soon as we get settled in the apartment, you wait and see." And then louder, she tells him, "And he's just as likely to lower your wages at the same time because he'll have you over a barrel. You'll be working for the rent."

Daddy backs the car over the bumps in the driveway. I am trying to picture Daddy over a barrel. What Momma says, sometimes, seems crazy, like Daddy tells her.

Once we're moving down the street, he says, "What choice do you think we have? Just tell me that. Darlene? You want to leave the warehouse, I find us a place to go, but you don't wanna move. I can't win." Daddy throws his hands up, off the steering wheel, then grabs it again like he's going to wring its neck. His hands squeeze tight on it, then go back and forth, back and forth, around the wheel. Momma tells him she could wring his neck, sometimes. She'll tell him about wringing his neck before we get to the warehouse, I'm sure. She wants to wring Daddy's neck just like the chickens on the farm, like Gramma Dirks does. Momma uses an ax. Daddy presses his foot down on the gas, and we go faster.

"You didn't find us a place to live, Vernon. Hilliar offered you an apartment he wants you to rent, just like he offered you your job. He knows a good thing when he sees it."

"He's being up front and fair, Darlene. He didn't need to give me a job. Shops are closed everywhere, you know that? I'm lucky to get this job. There's plenty of mechanics on the streets looking for work. They're doing just about anything and everything to have a job. Getting to work on crankshafts for cars and trucks and fixing equipment is almost a privilege, you wanna know what I think."

I wait for Momma to say she wants to wring his neck, but she only moves Teddy around on her lap. He tries to stand up on her legs, and she says "no." He takes the fingers of one of his hands and claws at Momma's moving lips. Momma is talking low while Daddy is talking loud. She slaps Teddy's hand away, and his face scrunches up.

I say, "Hey, hey, little man," and he reaches toward my face over Momma's shoulder. It stops him crying before he starts again. Teddy likes the warehouse. He doesn't cry as much as he used to in Clearview. Momma tells me it's not because of the warehouse, it's because he's not so little anymore. Teddy gets mad though when he tries to stand up when he wants to and falls down. Now Daddy says maybe he should go work for Uncle Willard on his farm again and give up being a mechanic since it doesn't please her. He knows she wanted him to work at her homeplace, the Dirks farm, not for Uncle Willard.

"You heard him just now. He can get lots of people to live in that apartment. He doesn't need us. We need him." Daddy's yelling, and before Momma can say anything, he beats her to it. "But go ahead, talk it to death. Talk, talk, talk and I'll call and tell him no, and he'll give it to somebody else, and we'll live out of boxes for God know how much longer. And maybe not for free." He turns the corner way too fast. I grab the seat to keep from falling.

"Slow down," Momma tells him. "No need to take it out on the drivin'."

Daddy slows down but says, "Who cares anymore, Darlene. Who gives a shit?"

"It!" I say.

"Shike," Momma waves her hand at me. "Not now." But when she turns around to look at me, she is smiling a little.

Momma hugs the baby and turns him around real quick to face the windshield. All at once Momma makes him act like he's driving like Daddy. She lifts Teddy's arms, puts her hands over his, and starts to drive with him. Teddy begins to laugh. She bounces him on her lap. She makes rumbling noises with her lips, like she's driving and then putting on the brakes. *"Mmmm, eeek, mmmm, voooooom, eeeek."* She brings one of Teddy's arms down to his side and acts like he's shifting, like Daddy. She makes more noises, and Teddy begins laughing out loud. "Teddy's driving like Daddy. See that Daddy? Driving like a mad man. *Voooooooooom, mmmmmmmm, eeek."* Momma's making Teddy drive fast, shifting faster and faster.

"All right, Darlene. I get your point."

Momma doesn't stop. She goes faster and faster. Teddy leans his head back and up, trying to look at her. A smile's still on his face, but he's no longer laughing. His eyes are big. Momma pulls Teddy's arms down into her lap slow and turns to Daddy. She has tears in her eyes. She is so mad, she almost can't talk. "What's the matter, Vern. You don't like for us to drink and drive?"

"All right, Darlene, that's enough." Daddy is mad so fast, I think he might hit something. He doesn't have anything to throw in the car.

"What's the matter, Daddy? You don't like us to play? Only you get to play?"

Daddy turns the car to the curb and slams on the brakes, and I fall onto the floor. My head hits the back of Momma's car seat as I go down. My legs are hanging over the bump sideways. I don't know what's happened until I'm sitting onto the seat. I feel an ache in my wrist.

"I hurt myself. On my wrist." Crying is coming up in my throat.

Daddy yanks the gear to neutral, where the engine doesn't stop, but the car can't move. He's told me about gears. We are sitting with the engine on, idling. I don't want to stop here. I want to go home to the warehouse where there's more room. I can play away from Momma and Daddy with Teddy in his crib.

I stand back up and lean over and look for Teddy.

"What the hell do you think you're doing?" Momma says to Daddy, grabbing Teddy's head, checking it all over.

Teddy scrunches up his face and starts to cry.

"Hey, little man." I lean far enough for him to see me. He stops crying and takes my finger and put it in his mouth. I let him bite down on it, then I yank it back. His bottom teeth are getting sharp. He's left drool on my finger. I wipe it on my underpants. Momma won't like it if I wipe it on my dress. When I take my finger away, he looks like he's going to cry again. Teddy squirms until Momma lets him stand on her lap facing me, leaning over her shoulder.

Daddy says, "You gonna shut up about this, Darlene, or am I getting outta the car? I know what you're doing, hell, you've been doing it for weeks, months now. You're getting even for Clearview. It'll never get settled, will it? Not until I make it right, and I can't right now, Darlene. I can't, don't you understand? It needed to be done, and that's the truth of it. There's a war going on, and we're caught in it. You ever notice anything outside your own little world? Well, I've had it." Daddy is wearing himself out. He turns to Momma and says in a tired voice, "You gonna be drivin' home by yourself if you keep this up. I can't go on like this."

"I'm not driving anywhere. Nowhere, period," Momma tells him in a shaky voice. When she starts crying, so does Teddy. I feel sick to my stomach. Daddy said 'Clearview.' They're going to fight hard.

"You gonna drive us home like a father should or not?" Momma asks him louder. "You're just mad because you want that apartment, and I have my doubts about it. If you can't handle that, then go off like a bad little boy and have another drink and pout."

"Maybe I will." Daddy opens the door.

"Don't go, Daddy." I try to grab his shirt from behind, but he is out of the car before I can. "Please. Please be quiet. Just be quiet, okay? I wanna go home."

"Tell your mother that, little girl." Daddy slams the car door.

"We'll all be good, Daddy. Momma." I touch her shoulder. "Tell Daddy we'll all be good."

"Come back to this car, Vernon. You hear me?" Momma is yelling at the top of her voice. "I will not drive home, you hear me? You hear that?" She is yelling at him across the front seat and through the window by the steering wheel. Her face is red, and Teddy is screaming bloody murder.

"Then sit there till you rot."

I watch Daddy walk away from the car. He's not walking fast, but he doesn't look back at us.

I don't feel bad about my hand anymore. I try to open the back door, but it's stuck. I want to run after Daddy and beg him back.

"You stay right where you are, Shike. Right there. Don't you dare open that door." Momma is so furious, she almost can't breathe. "That's just what he wants. He wants us to beg and plead with him. And we're not gonna do it. Not under any conditions, you hear me?"

She opens her door, steps out onto the street, and pulls Teddy up high on her hip. She slams the door, looking in Daddy's direction.

He's walking real fast, down the sidewalk, past houses we don't know. He's walking like we're running after him. His trouser legs flap from side to side, his arms pumping up and down. He looks funny, almost like he's acting silly, like he does when he's trying to make me and Teddy laugh. But he's very serious now. He's going away, going away, so fast.

I lean out the window and watch him go down the street without him looking back at us. Daddy's never run away before. I can't stop crying.

"Is Daddy gone?" I ask Momma, but she's walked around the front of the car and can't hear me. She opens the back door and sits Teddy next to me. She reaches over and puts both of my wrists between her hands, turning them over and over.

"Which one is it?"

I wiggle the one that has the ache. "Looks like it's okay." She presses it between her fingers in one place, then more. "That hurt? What about here?"

I shake my head. "Momma, is Daddy—" I start, but she doesn't let me finish.

"Good. I think you're okay." She kisses me and then whispers, "Crazy," as she backs out of the door and closes it. "Hold onto Teddy."

Momma stands and watches Daddy for a little while, her hand on the driver's door handle.

Teddy rolls against me, his eyes open wide. He isn't crying. He stares at me, waiting.

"It's okay, Teddy." I lean over him, trying to pull him up into my lap, but he's too heavy, so I hug him best as I can.

"Momma and Daddy're having a little fight's all." He wants to stand up, so I help him lean against me on wobbly legs. I hold his body close. He touches my lips with his moving fingers. I act like I'm biting them, and he laughs big. I kiss them and the palm of his hand. They smell like sour milk and baby sweat. His eyes stay on my face. "You just sit here quiet as a mouse, and Momma will drive us home."

"Da-da," Teddy says. All at once, I love him so much I think I'll cry.

As Momma starts to sit in the driver's seat, she sees Teddy is standing between my legs while I hold him in place. She tells me he has to sit down, so I push him down onto my lap so he's looking at me with his legs spread out, one on each side of me, his huge diaper in the middle against my stomach. Teddy is fat. He is very heavy. "He's a big baby," Momma tells everybody. Sometimes she adds, "A big boy growing by the minute. Who knows when it will stop?"

Momma gets behind the wheel, slams the door hard, turns the key. The engine starts up.

"Da-da," Teddy says like he knows Daddy is gone.

Momma shifts into gear. "Now, we'll see how smart you are," she says to me, but she's really talking to Daddy.

"Da-da," Teddy says, smiling at me, playing with my lips. He doesn't look out the window when Momma drives the car up alongside Daddy.

Momma is driving the car down the wrong side of the street.

"There's Da-da," I say to Teddy, pointing out the window, but he keeps playing with my mouth as I hold him best I can on my lap. Momma needs to cut his fingernails. They are soft and sharp at the same time.

Momma puts her elbow out the window like she's on a Sunday drive watching what's happening on the sidewalk. She drives real slow, "moseying along," as Daddy would say if they weren't mad. Daddy doesn't look over at us. He keeps right on walking, his trouser legs swinging back and forth as he walks. Then in a sugary voice Momma leans out her window, saying, "You can walk home then, Vernon, that's fine with me. But if you hope to sneak a little drink into your stroll, you can sleep out under the stars. Don't try coming home like it's okay, because I won't have it." Momma puts her foot down on the gas. I hear the petal slam all the way to the floorboard.

"Hold Teddy tight, Shike," Momma yells at me.

As the car takes off with some speed, I hear Daddy yell back at us, "I make an honest living. I'll have an honest drink if I want to."

4.

Late evening, same day

"WELL, OKAY THEN." MOMMA IS talking polite-like on the phone. I hear her say this when I get up to use the bathroom. It is dark outside, and only one lamp's on in the living room that Momma's made out of the whitest sheets on wires. Two of the sheets have come apart to make a crack I can see through. The phone line runs along the floor until it gets all the way to the plug on the wall. Daddy has put black tape over it so we won't stumble and fall. In the little bit of light from the lamp, it looks like a tiny black snake sliding across the floor. Momma sits, leaning on the arm of the couch. "I appreciate you calling me. No, no, that isn't necessary. Just tell him I'll pick him up after work." Momma puts the phone down quiet.

When I come out from behind the sheet that hangs to the side of the toilet and look her way, she is saying something to me, but I can't hear her because of the toilet's noise, so she motions for me to come to where she is. Teddy is lying next to her. The bottom half of his body is naked. His legs are going up and down fast, and he is making little humming noises while he waits for Momma to put on his diaper that she's got in her hand. She pulls me up close to her and kisses the top of my head.

"Your daddy's sleeping at our new place tonight," she says. She shakes her head and sighs. "Let him sleep it off, then. I can't think about what I'd say to him if I saw him right now." She pushes my hair to the side and looks into my eyes. "He works hard, Shike, and he's worried about us. I'm not so easy to live with sometimes, am I?"

"Where's he stayin'?" I'm not sure I heard her right.

"At our new place." She sighs. "We're gonna be livin' in a real apartment. He told Mr. Hilliar yes. Would you like that?"

"Are there kids to play with? You said I couldn't play in the yard."

"I'm not sure," she says, standing up. She picks up Teddy and tries to spread a diaper on the couch while she's holding him. I spread it open for her. She lays Teddy down on it. "But Daddy can make you a sandbox, maybe, and a swing. I saw a tree with the right kind of branch. How would that be? That's if Mr. Hilliar gives us the permission, of course. But I don't see why not."

She has Teddy changed quick. She doesn't ask me to help. She wants to be done for the day. The air is full of baby powder. She hands me the wet diaper and washrag. When I come back from putting them in a bucket in the toilet room and stand next to her, she says, "When I told you that about the yard, I wasn't sure how I could manage you outside and me inside with Teddy. But I've been thinking about that a little bit. Maybe we could get some old chairs from Gramma Dirks and put them outside so I can be with you while you play with your new friends. Would you like that? We could keep them in Mr. Hilliar's basement if he wouldn't mind, that way we could get to them easy, by the washer. Daddy'll have to ask."

I hug her arm. She sits Teddy up next to her. She pats the cushion on the other side of her, and I get on the couch, pushing myself back until I'm in place.

"Book ends," she says to me like she's whispering a secret.

"Teddy and me," I say, and she laughs.

5.

Several days later

"JESSE'S AT SEMINARY, AND CLIFFORD'S trying to save the last of his wheat, you say, so what're we gonna do?" Momma asks Daddy about moving while we are eating breakfast.

"I'm thinkin' on it. I was relying on Clifford, but he told me on the phone a few minutes ago that his yield is more than he expected, which is a really good thing, since he's had such hard luck, but he's had to dump the last of his harvest in the yard because his bins in the granary are full. He got the combining finished while the crews were still able to stay, you know, before the chance for rain that could've make the fields too soggy for cutting, but now the weather men have been predicting downpours for two nights and are telling farmers it's inevitable. So his real problem's with storage. He's trying to find help to get what's on the ground to Hopewell. He's waiting on his brother, Claude, to come help from Kansas."

"How long will that take, do ya think?"

"I've no idea. You're the one talking to Josephine. What'd she say?"

"I talked to her last night, and she didn't say much, really. They're just waiting for help, she said. She didn't mention Claude, but it doesn't sound like they're gonna be available for us anytime soon. I hate to ask them anyway, since Clifford helped us the last time. Can Karl help? Never mind, never mind. I'm just thinking out loud. Hilliar won't pull this thing out from underneath

us, will he—give the apartment to somebody else? I've got us packed already."
That's what's making Momma worry. She told me in the bathroom when Daddy wasn't around. "I absolutely refuse to unpack and stay here another minute, not after all we've been through to take this new place." She means the fast packing, finding the money for the first month's rent so soon, and now trying to get help with the move.

"Of course not. I've given Hilliar my word, and he's given me his."

"But no money's changed hands, Vernon. He just strikes me as somebody who'd—"

"Darlene, if nothing else, Hilliar's not gonna do anything that jeopardizes me making the kind of money I do for him. Good God, you're the one's been thinking he's gonna tie me to him with the rent. Now you're worried all of a sudden he's gonna pull the carpet out from under us 'cause he's gotta wait a few days? I dunno, Darlene. You keep thinkin' this man is our enemy, that he's got some kind of hold over me. I'm trying to tell ya that it's the other way around. We both know he's got a buncha guys in his shop that don't know their asses from a hole in the ground."

"Vernon!" Momma says, nodding at me.

Daddy acts like he hasn't said anything wrong. "Just ease up, will ya?"

"It's the kind of money you're making's all. It's hardly enough to get by. It's like he's withholding, takin' advantage of this war situation. He hasn't kept his promises about your wages. Remember how much he told you that you'd be making with all the cars and tractors needing fixin'. So you'll just have to forgive me for not trusting him very much about this apartment deal. Besides, I can't believe he's not takin' home a whole lot more money'n we are. Something's fishy is what I'm sayin'."

"Course he takes home more than I do. For godssakes, woman, he's the boss! But I think it's the opposite with Hilliar, from what you're thinking, actually. What he's doing is giving too many of these dumb guys jobs, just so they can work, and we have to all share the take. He doesn't need the amount of people he's got in the shop, but he lives in Aileen. It's a little place, and half the mechanics he's got on the payroll are his relatives. Basically he's feedin' 'em. I work salary, not commission, or I'd do better because I'm doing most of the work."

"Like I don't know? That's exactly what I'm saying." I wait for Momma to tell him, like she always does when they talk about Daddy's job, that the money's the same for everybody regardless of how fast he works or how much work he does. They talk Mr. Hilliar forever and a day. Daddy tells Momma she talks Mr. Hilliar to death.

Daddy shrugs. "I haven't wanted to talk about this with you because I knew you'd end up piling up more resentment toward him. He's really a well-meaning guy under all the bluster."

"Okay, however that may be, what I'm sayin' now is that we need to know for sure we still have this apartment, Vern. And I won't be the one to talk to him. You do the askin' cause I'm not doin' it. Not with that man."

"I know. I will. But I don't need to ask. I'm telling you, he's holding it for us."

"When?"

"When *what?*" Daddy doesn't wait for Momma to answer. "I'll ask him on Monday."

"Oh, no, you don't. I've got boxes stacked to the ceiling, and already I'm going back through them to find every little thing here and there we need. Something's gotta happen real soon or I'm gonna lose my m—"

"Darlene there's no point to callin' Wilbur because he's—"

"Call!" Momma orders Daddy. "I need to know for sure."

Daddy looks at her like she's slapped him. Momma slapped Daddy once when we lived in Clearview, and he slapped her back. Momma almost left the house. She said she would, and she'd take Teddy and me with her, back to Grampa and Gramma Dirks's farm. Daddy went into the bathroom and threw everything outta the medicine cabinet all over the bathtub and floor. He came back in the living room without saying a word. Momma didn't stop talking. He went to bed on the couch in the living room after he cleaned up the mess in the bathroom. There was a red spot on the floor where Daddy broke the Mercurochrome bottle. Momma couldn't get the spot up from the linoleum even when she poured bleach on it later and scrubbed it on her hands and knees over and over.

When we were all packed to move to Aileen, Momma and I went through the house to see if we forgot anything, and when she came to the bathroom, she stood staring at the red spot before we left for good.

"Looks like left-over blood," she told me, gasping a sob caught in her throat. "But whatever else it is, I know beyond doubt, it's a stain on our future."

It scared me what she said. Most of all, I knew I never wanted Daddy to sleep on the couch ever again. And tonight he was sleeping on one, or something like it, away from us, on the other side of town.

Now she stands in front of Daddy pointing to the phone. He looks at her with his hands in his pockets. They stand staring at each other. I know if I move, they'll start words and then fight hard.

"Hilliar's not at home right now, Darlene. That's what I've been trying—" All at once, Daddy walks past her to the window. I don't know what he's thinking or going to do. Momma stands looking after him.

He turns around and says to her, "Clifford's here." Daddy is grinning big.

"You're kidding!" Momma rushes to the window. "Saved again, by powers way past me to see," she says when she glances at Uncle Clifford's truck and turns back around to look at Daddy who is walking fast for the stairs. "How you pull yourself outta these scrapes, Vern, I'll never know. I swear it's like some kinda magic. How did I miss hearing that beat-up truck of his? Is Josephine with him? I can't tell." Momma always calls Uncle Clifford's truck "beat-up," but Daddy tells her that old beat-up truck has saved our lives more than once.

"Nope, no Josephine, but he's got Tommy Don with him." Daddy tells her before he starts going down the stairs.

"Shit!" Momma says real soft. She rubs my hair and says she's sorry.

"Dirty mouth." I shake my finger at her.

She laughs. "You're too smart for your britches, Shike." Momma is happy that Uncle Clifford came, even if Tommy Don's along. "Well, maybe I can keep that boy cousin of yours busy somehow. You stay clear away from him while I try and find things for him to do. No nonsense today, okay?"

She goes over to the crib and reaches down for Teddy. He's been awake, rolling from side to side, with fingers in his mouth, crying every now and then, but not loud. Momma says it's a small miracle that he doesn't cry more because Teddy is cutting his teeth. "Watch out for those front ones." She showed me once by pulling Teddy's bottom lip down. A little white tooth was there, next to another red swelling to the side. I put my finger on the white edge of the swollen lump, but Momma pulled my hand away. "They look tiny, but they can really mess up your pointer if he decides to become a bear." I know about Teddy's teeth. He's already bitten me more than once.

I run out to Uncle Clifford and grab his leg. I love Uncle Clifford. He reaches down and messes up my hair. "Hiya, Shypoke! Ever' time I see you, you've grown a foot."

Uncle Clifford is storying to me. I'm short for my age. Everybody says so. Then he steps around and opens his truck door and pulls out a cherry pie from the front seat and hands it to me. "Hold it careful now, Shike, and carry it over to the little stand there by the door. We don't wanna mess up your Aunt Josephine's dessert!" He looks at Daddy and says, "Her orchard is keeping her busy, mostly with canning, but she found some time to send this along."

When I get back, I ask him why he didn't bring Leon.

"Your mother's gonna have enough to take care of without having to watch out for both you and Leon. Tommy Don's here to help with the little carries."

Tommy Don doesn't look ready to help. He's sitting on one of the wooden boxes Daddy brought home to sit on outside under the tree when he smokes late at night, after Teddy and me are in bed, and Momma is busy or asleep in their bedroom. I can barely see him sometimes in the dark, but I smell his smokes when he comes in and passes by the sheets of our bedroom walls on his way into the bathroom to take his sponge bath at night.

Tommy Don's reading a comic book that he started unrolling as he got out of the truck. When Daddy and Uncle Clifford stop talking about the harvest, Tommy Don rolls up his comic book again and puts it in the truck. Then he goes and stands behind Uncle Clifford. Daddy reaches around and pulls Tommy Don to his side with a big handshake, like he's a man. Tommy Don likes Daddy.

"We'll be needin' all the help we can get. Thanks for comin'." Daddy says right to him, like he talks to Uncle Clifford. Daddy rests his hand on Tommy Don's shoulder.

Tommy Don doesn't smile. He just stares at Daddy like he's the president, but he nods his head a little. So far, Tommy Don hasn't looked at me. He acts like I'm not around. His hair stands up this way and that, all over his head. He looked like he's stuck his finger in an electric socket. Daddy told me that's what it means when your hair stands on end. Momma doesn't want my hair to ever look like Tommy Don's. No electric sockets and no hair on ends. Tommy Don's overalls are all dirty, and his knees show through big holes in the front legs.

Momma tells me that "Josephine's boys are always filthy." When they stay with us overnight, Momma makes them scrub their skin raw. "I wanna see flesh," she tells them while she stands in the bathroom at Clearview.

Tommy Don is usually in the tub with Roy. He covers his privates with a washrag when Momma is around.

"You may not know it. But your skin is supposed to be pink. We can't hope for white, so we'll go for pink. Now, scrub. I wanna see pink skin from head to toe, no, come to think of it, I wanna see red skin so I know you've done something meaningful. When I come back in here, I wanna see the farm dirt floating on top of the water."

One evening when they stayed with us, she started to leave after she'd given them a talk about red skin but came back into the bathroom, almost knocking me down where I stood in the doorway. Tommy Don grabbed himself because he'd started getting up to sit on the edge of the tub.

"Come to think of it, the water should be red, too, given the color of dirt around here!" She laughed, staring up and down at Tommy Don, who glared at her.

We had a real bathtub then, in Clearview, and not a galvanized tub like the one out on the Shirly farm and the one in the warehouse. Momma told me, while we were doing dishes the other day, taking a break from the packing, that those galvanized tub days were soon gonna be a thing of the past. She meant for bathing because we'll still use three galvanized tubs with our old wringer Maytag—one for the wash and two for rinse. The first rinse has bluing in it when we do the whites. Maytag means lots of throwing water away in buckets and lots of filling them up again.

"A real tub," Momma said to me, dreamy-like, with a sigh. "A real tub like in Clearview, oh, won't that be grand?" She never talks about Clearview, so I knew she was putting all of her hopes on this one. But for me, it means a bath every night instead of one on Tuesdays and Saturdays. There'll be a lot to do.

WHEN EVERYTHING IS MOVED OUT of the warehouse and the boxes and furniture are all in the apartment, Daddy and Uncle Clifford put the couch in place in the living room and some folding chairs around it for us to sit and talk. Daddy, Uncle Clifford, and Tommy Don didn't stop moving everything upstairs until long after dark. Daddy tells Uncle Clifford it's far too late for them to drive all the way back to Shirly, so he and Tommy Don will stay and sleep in the bedroom on the floor on mattresses with Daddy. Momma says she will sleep with Teddy and me in the living room. We start to spread sheets and blankets down for everybody, but I don't know how to do that like she needs, so Daddy comes in and gives her a hand.

The first thing Momma does after she puts Teddy to bed is to find an end table, then a lamp. She plugs it in behind the couch and turns on the console. The music comes in loud and clear so she sits and listens with tears in her eyes. When she looks at me, it's like she's shining in the lamp light.

She's left the leftovers from the potato salad, dill pickles, baloney and homemade bread, and Aunt Josephine's cherry pie out on the kitchen counter in case anybody wants something extra before bedtime. We all go and help ourselves to seconds, but she sits and listens to music for a long time with one hand in her lap, the other over the end of the couch. After a while, she gets up to put away what's left of the food and cleans off the counter. Because I'm still awake, she asks me if I want to help her put the perishables in the ice box on the shelves I can reach. When she asks me to help, I know she wants to tell me things. But tonight she doesn't talk at all. She's settling in to the quiet.

After the men are out of the bathroom and in their bedroom, and I am back in bed on my floor mattress, just before I fall asleep, I see Momma go back to the couch to listen to the radio music some more. She's turned it down so low she has to lean over to hear it. I wake up with a jerk when she stands up and the radio is playing the star-spangled-banner. Momma looks at me and smiles. She yawns, stretches and says, "Sign off," as she turns the knob on the console.

6.

The next morning

I WAKE UP WHEN I hear Daddy's voice. He is standing over Momma, shaking her awake with a real soft "rise and shine." She's still on the couch sleeping. He's all dressed up for church. He tells her that Uncle Clifford and Tommy Don are starting on their way home if she wants to get up and say goodbye. He is holding a coffee cup. I see his broken front tooth when he grins at me. It broke off a long time ago.

Momma wipes her eyes and looks around like she doesn't know where she is. "Why did you let me sleep?" She sits up, brings her legs around to the floor, and starts to stand but can't push up enough on her hands to do it. They keep sinking down into the cushions.

"Well, Teddy wasn't awake yet so I thought you could use the rest. It was a big day for everybody yesterday, especially for you with all those stairs and the baby."

"How will I ever make church now?" She tries to stand up again, falling back down. "I've had the lesson ready since last week before we started the move, so that's not a probl—"

"I don't think you should go, Darlene," Daddy says, so soft it's a whisper. "You stay here and straighten up what you feel like you can. The church folks will understand. Your Sunday School class can go in with Alma's. There's so few right now that it's summer and late harvest. But Clifford's on his way to his truck soon. I've got them breakfast already. He didn't want me to wake you up, but I didn't want to leave for church without you knowing I'm goin'."

"How in the world did I sleep through breakfast? What did you end up feeding them, anyhow?"

"Breakfast." Daddy is grinning big.

Uncle Clifford comes into the living room from the bathroom. Tommy Don's been standing in the kitchen door with a cup in his hand. I know Daddy gave him coffee. He is looking at Daddy like he's somebody he's just met and thinks is special. Momma doesn't drink coffee. She drinks orange juice with her toast. I see the Post Toasties box on the kitchen counter. A lot of the times when I stay over at Aunt Josephine and Uncle Clifford's, we have Post Toasties, milk, boiled eggs with baloney and bread for supper and fruit from her orchard with sugar on it for dessert. Sometimes the fruit's canned. Aunt Josephine gets it from the cellar, and Uncle Clifford goes around the table pouring thick cream in everybody's dish. I like this the best.

Momma tells me that my boy cousins live on such food plus a squirt or two from the cows. She thinks her sister must buy mayonnaise by the gallon and says that Aunt Josephine and Uncle Clifford keep the Bond Bread people in business. When Aunt Josie puts bread on the table, she reaches into the bag and pulls out two handfuls.

"They eat three loaves a day most of the time, and the only way they can afford it, is to get it when it's stale, on the day-old shelf. Sometimes it's been on the shelf so long, they get it free. Josie just cuts the mold off. And that's feed for the pigs, along with the mold she cuts from the cheese!"

Tommy Don eats the most. When Aunt Josephine isn't watching, I've caught him eating mayonnaise from the jar with his spoon. Momma tells me that the only way they make it now, with everything rationed, is that they live on the farm. "They don't have a pot to pee in, but they have milk and eggs and butter for that Bond Bread, if nothing else."

"Don't get up on our account, Darlene," Uncle Clifford says to Momma, when he comes into the living room from the bathroom. "We're gonna be out the door and on our way in a few minutes."

Momma tells him that she and Daddy can't thank him enough.

"No need," he says. "We're all family here. The coffee's a treat. Beats the colored water we've been drinking all to hell." He raises his cup. Gramma and Grampa Dirks divide their coffee with us and Aunt Josephine because Gramma drinks Postum. "And there's a butcher coming up in November. I'll need some help with that."

Momma nods and tells him Josephine has already talked to her about it. She finally stands, and they all talk again about wheat in bins and praying for no rain—a change from the past, for sure—and Uncle Clifford having to drive to elevators in Hopewell because his granary is full.

"A big year for us, finally," Uncle Clifford says. "Maybe we can actually get the bankers off our back for a little while."

Momma says goodbye, tells Uncle Clifford to say thanks to Josephine for the pie, and makes her way toward the bathroom. I heard Momma call Aunt Josie last night about the pie so her saying thanks to Uncle Clifford is really letting him know she is grateful to him for bringing the dessert. Buying butter and sugar is getting harder and harder.

I stay with Daddy. Teddy is still sleeping. A miracle.

Daddy walks over and puts his hand on Tommy Don's shoulder. "You have quite the worker fellow here," he tells Uncle Clifford.

"I think you might be right," Uncle Clifford says to Daddy, not to Tommy Don. "He's started on the tractor for his mother's garden this summer, and I'm thinking he can give me a hand next summer out in the fields. He's plowing already, so that's not the problem, but I'm thinking he can drive the truck if nothing else, not to the elevators, of course, but back and forth from the field to the granary bins. But his mother carries on like there's a death in the family every time I bring it up."

Uncle Clifford stops and looks down. He's remembering Bobby Gene because Daddy goes over and touches his shoulder for a minute. When Daddy steps back, Uncle Clifford clears his throat and goes on. "She's been doing this, you know, driving back and forth, but with everything she's got going in the orchard and garden, canning and the like, she just can't do it all."

Uncle Clifford doesn't walk toward the door like I think he's going to. He sits down in a folding chair in the living room and reaches for his cigarette papers in the top pocket of his overalls bib. He puts the paper on his knee and pulls a pouch out of his side pocket, opening it up with both fingers. Then he holds it in his hand like he's weighing something, moving it up and down. He picks up the paper from his knee with his other hand and puts his finger inside to fold it over part way.

Then he shakes the tobacco from the bag into the folded paper while he says, "I've been paying Fred Haskins's kid up the road to help me get it from the field to the bins and then to spread the loads in the back of the pickup —this is after the crew's left, moving up north with their combines." He lifts his chin, showing us where the combines went, across the apartment, through the window and on down the road. "But he's just graduated from high school and wants to go to work for an uncle up in Nebraska where he can make more money. If Tommy Don takes over Melvin's chores, it'll save us money we don't really have to give away. A penny saved's a penny earned is how I'm looking at it."

When he's done talking, he uses his tongue to bring the string between his teeth and then his teeth and free hand to pull the string tight to close the pouch. He leans over a little to put the tobacco back in his pocket. Daddy is watching him real close and breathes in and out, a big sigh. Uncle Clifford runs his tongue along the edge of the paper and rolls it between his fingers, then he twists both ends. He holds it between his fingers like the tail of a mouse and stands up to go. He knows not to light his smokes in our house.

Daddy smokes with Uncle Clifford, too. I've seen him when they're out in the yard on the Shirly farm. When Momma comes out on the porch, Daddy hides his smoke down close behind his leg. Now I hear Momma splashing water in the bathroom.

"You big enough to reach those tractor pedals, Tommy Don?" Daddy asks him. Daddy sounds like he doesn't think so. He punches Tommy Don with his fist in his shoulder, not hard, only playful, and grins at him while he pulls him close. Tommy Don looks down at the floor but moves his head a little up and down.

"Rigged some blocks on there for him," Uncle Clifford says. "When there's a will, there's a way. That right, T.D.?" Uncle Clifford tries teasing Tommy Don a little. Only Uncle Clifford calls him T.D., nobody else. When Roy called

Tommy Don T.D. once, Tommy Don hit him so hard Roy fell down. This minute, he's standing without moving a muscle. His head is down. The only time
he looks up is when he looks at Daddy.

Tommy Don didn't look at me all day, unless he couldn't help it. And he
hasn't spit or said a bad word, either. He only does that when Uncle Clifford
isn't around. I think he's two Tommy Dons—one when he's with the men, and
one when he's with me and his brothers.

"Tommy Don's shoes are worn out," Momma tells me later when we're by
ourselves. "Your Uncle Clifford doesn't exactly keep his family in proper attire."
When I ask her what "a tire" means, she laughs. I think she's probably talking
about the tires that are hard for Daddy to get because of the war. "His clothes
are old and worn out is what I mean to say, Shike. When his daddy does get
some money, it doesn't go for clothes for his kids. Not that he's extravagant, Lord
knows, he's not. But his boys run around shabby. I've seen Tommy Don without
a coat in winter. His brothers wear each other's hand-me-downs—short, long,
big, small, or threadbare. It's not right. I know they don't have much when the
harvest is low, but there're ways to get coats and shoes for your kids. Clifford's too
stiff-necked. He won't take anything from anybody. I don't dare give Josephine
anything from our church relief fund or even our clothes drives. It's not a bad
thing to accept help when you need it. Churches have these drives for exactly this
kinda thing." She sighs. "Josie would do it, but Cliff'd kill her, if she took anything
from charity. Doesn't stop him from bringing his family to eat our fried chicken
or baloney sandwiches over here on Sundays when they run out, does it?"

Now, Momma stands in the hall and motions for me to come with her to
the bedroom. Teddy is in his crib, changed and laying on his side drinking milk
from his bottle. "I don't know if I can find some clean underwear for you and
me, but we've gotta try, Shike. Let's look in the boxes. I'll do some hand laundry tonight." She looks around at me. "Good, you already put on your overalls. Let's try for a clean something for the top. I gotta tell ya, I'm about one
step from getting you some of those shirts like boys wear, without the flouncy
sleeves. When we have a clothing drive at church, I'll sneak you a couple, how's
that? I only had that one leftover dress of yours that I could alter, and you've
outgrown it. You're a weed these days."

Walking behind her, I go toward her and Daddy's bedroom. I don't know for sure where Teddy and my bedroom will be in the new apartment. I'm happy about wearing the boys' shirts from church drives. But Momma changes her mind about lots of things she says she's going to do.

All at once, I hear a loud crash and a crying out. Momma starts running down the hall. "Oh God," she is saying in a shaky voice. "I knew those stairs would be the death of somebody."

———————————

I STAND WITH THE KITCHEN screen door open and watch Momma start down the stairs. She runs her hands along the outside wall as she goes, looking at the wide gap left where the railing has been broken and Tommy Don must've fallen through. I lean over the porch and see pieces of wood scattered in the yard around where Daddy and Uncle Clifford are bent over Tommy Don. They're trying to hold him steady as he rolls from side to side, screaming and crying, like he's hurt real bad. His legs are going up and down, and he's rolling from side to side, like Teddy does when he's crying with all his might.

Daddy looks around at Momma as she starts coming down the steps. He calls out to her, "Watch the railing, watch the railing. Be careful where it's broken out there." He points toward the railing that's gone. "He's fell, Darlene, he's fell hard."

All at once, Tommy Don turns on his side and throws up in the yard. Uncle Clifford jumps back while Daddy holds Tommy Don's head up. Momma runs down the rest of the stairs and rushes to where they all are. She drops to her knees, but she can't get to Tommy Don because Daddy's still holding his head in his arms. I hear her let out a cry. Daddy looks over at Uncle Clifford who's bending over Tommy Don on the other side now.

Daddy says, "We gotta get him to the hospital, Clifford, soon as we can. My God, you can see bone." Momma stands up fast and runs for the stairs.

"Don't call nobody, Darlene," Uncle Clifford yells at Momma. "Not even Josephine, and no ambulance, you hear?"

Momma turns on the steps and calls back, "Clifford—"

"I mean it, Darlene. I wanna get him to Shirly and Doc Webber. He'll be fine."

But Tommy Don doesn't look fine to me or to anybody but Uncle Clifford. Tommy Don is holding his arm close to his stomach and crying so hard I can hardly look at him. All at once, Uncle Clifford reaches in front of Daddy for Tommy Don's overall straps. He starts pulling T.D. up to his feet. He can't stand up, his legs give out, so Uncle Clifford grabs under him fast, lifts him up and swings him in his arms, carrying him toward the pickup. Tommy Don is screaming so hard, I start crying. Daddy is running after Uncle Clifford, begging him to stop, but he keeps on going like Daddy isn't talking to him. When Uncle Clifford turns Tommy Don a little to the side so he can open the pickup door with his hand from underneath, I see throw up all over the front of Tommy Don's clothes. Daddy beats Uncle Clifford to the door and opens it so Uncle Clifford can sit Tommy Don down on the passenger's seat.

"You can help out best if you get us some wet towels," Daddy yells toward Momma, but she's already in the house. I hear her running hot water at the kitchen sink as I open the kitchen screen door and step inside. She is saying down to the water, "C'mon, c'mon." After the towels are soaked, she barely wrings them out. They are dripping all over the floor while she runs out the door, past me, and down the stairs again. She tells me not to follow her. She doesn't want me to slip on the water or be on the steps with the broken rail.

"You'll just be in the way," she yells at me. "Look after your brother."

I don't stay in the kitchen, though. I stand on the little porch at the top of the stairs and watch. The railing is solid all around the porch. Teddy is trying to stand in his crib. He is crying but not real hard. I don't say anything to him because he cries harder if I talk to him and don't pick him up.

When Momma's halfway down the stairs with the wet towels, Daddy looks at her and shakes his head side to side, over and over. I can't hear what he's telling her. She stands with dripping towels in her hands. Daddy is about as upset as I've ever seen him. Uncle Clifford is wiping blood from his hands on a rag he's pulled out of his back pocket. He is standing in front of the truck. Momma tries to hand him the towels, but he shakes his head and sucks in air through his lips. Tommy Don's crying very loud through his teeth and is shaking like he's cold. Then I hear him moan through the side window, "Oh, ooooh, oh, Daddy."

Momma walks over to his window and leans in and after wringing out the extra water, helps wrap his arm in the hot towels. She turns to Uncle Clifford and says, "Clifford, you can't just...."

But Uncle Clifford walks around the hood of his pickup to the driver's side, smoking his cigarette fast, while he lets it hang from his lips. He opens the door, as he says, "He'll be fine, Darlene. I'll tend to it."

Daddy steps up to Uncle Clifford's window and talks with him for a minute. Uncle Clifford shakes his head over and over, puts his hand on Daddy's arm, and then he starts the pickup and begins backing up to turn around. Momma's walked to the middle of the yard so Uncle Clifford can finish his turn and steer his pickup down the driveway. She is crying so hard it sounds like slow, soft screaming.

I am crying, too. I want to go down the steps, but I know I'll get a spanking if I do. My legs start to shake. I try to walk inside but can't make the step into the kitchen, so I hang onto the screen door handle to keep from falling down on the porch.

After Uncle Clifford's pickup is on the street toward their Shirly farm, I stand up, again, and walk over and wait by the porch railing. Daddy's talking to Momma.

She presses her hand over her mouth. Then she takes her hands and put them in her hair. All at once, she starts yanking her hair very hard this way and that, and then just as fast, she drops her arms and grabs the sides of her housedress. Her knees bend, and I think she's going to fall, but Daddy puts his arm around her, holding her up, and turns her to face him. He holds her tight in his arms. He lets her cry, while he rubs her back and holds her head against his chest.

She cries awhile in his neck, then she steps away from him and starts throwing her arms up and down and screaming, "Crazy, crazy, crazy... the sonabitch." I sit down on the top step and wait. I don't hear everything they are saying, but when Momma turns my way I hear her say, "What is the matter with him? This is insane—it's plain crazy. I don't know what to do."

Daddy keeps saying, "I know, I know, Darlene. I know… but he can't be talked to, you know how he is."

Momma runs toward the stairs and up. She is at the kitchen screen door, fast. She runs past me saying, "This child is in shock. I cannot believe this crazy man my sister is married to."

I go up the step as fast as I can, Daddy behind me, watching that I don't fall, putting his hands under my arms picking me up and helping me step into the kitchen. Momma grabs the phone, and I know she is calling Aunt Josephine.

After a little bit, she bangs the receiver down. "Where the hell is she, anyway? It's Sunday morning, but services haven't started, have they? Out there? I don't even know if she went today. She doesn't go every Sunday." She looks at me and says, "She's probably in her garden. I don't know what to do."

Aunt Josephine and Uncle Clifford don't go to church together. Aunt Josephine goes by herself. She usually takes my boy cousins. Leon tells me.

"Let her become a Baptist if she wants to," Momma told Daddy, once. "At least she's going someplace, and, God knows, her boys need it, even if Clifford doesn't believe and won't attend."

Daddy comes into the kitchen looking down at his best shirt and tie. They have blood and vomit all over them.

Momma looks at him and says, "I can't get Josephine. What do you think he'll do, Vernon?" She doesn't even see Daddy's shirt and tie. Teddy is starting to cry louder.

I go talk to him, and he stops for a little while. I throw him blocks that he throws back.

"He's promised he'll get ahold of Doc Webber." Daddy tells her. "But since it's Sunday, knowing Clifford, he may not want to bother him on his day off. He absolutely will not take him to the hospital. The man's so stubborn he could stop a freight train head-on, single-handed. He's always been like this, Darlene. It's enough to make you wanna take his kids away from him. I mean it. It's not right, but what're ya gonna do? Josephine's the only one who can make him listen to anything. Let's just hope she's there when they get home. Otherwise, it could be hours, tomorrow, before Doc Webber."

Daddy starts undoing his tie. He gives it a yank to take it off. He stands staring at it in his hand before he looks up at Momma. "There's no going to church, now." He shrugs and waits.

"Just tell me that child isn't going to suffer all day."

"Josephine will do something, honey." Daddy doesn't call Momma, "honey" very often. He's helping her calm down. "Clifford's a lot of things, but he's not totally without feeling, well, at least, he gives a damn about what other people think of him." Daddy waits and then says, "Most of the time."

"Well, yes, that's if they know. Josephine doesn't exactly talk to other people about this, does she? I'm stumped today. I don't know quite what to do." She waits a minute. "He does listen to her, if only she's home soon. She'll lay down the law."

"What about calling your mother? That's providing they're home, of course, but, at least, she'd know about it, and she's not gonna let that slide. Let's just hope and pray this is one of those Sundays your dad got stubborn and refused to drive your mother to church."

"Actually, Josephine could be there right now, come to think of it. This is exactly when she'd visit, if Mother isn't in church. Thank Almighty God, Hilliar got our phones working for us before we moved in. By the way, where is he? That rail's gotta be fixed and right away."

"Went to visit his wife's mother in Garber, that's what I've been trying to tell ya. Don't ask me, Darlene, about where he gets his gasoline, because I don't know. Maybe he saved all three gallons this week for the trip, though I didn't see him walking to work!" Daddy is being nasty about Mr. Hilliar. He never talks bad about Mr. Hilliar, so I know he's upset. "Then again, he's got an engine repair shop now, doesn't he? Government claims everybody's treated the same, uh-huh, my ass... behind!" He looks at me and winks. Daddy talks about gasoline and tires all the time. He gets gas from Uncle Clifford when he goes to the farm. When we need some to drive someplace, they get it out of the tractor or the gasoline barrel by the car shed that the government gives Uncle Clifford for farming. When they get it out of the tractor, they suck on a hose to get it in our car. Daddy almost swallowed some one time. Momma said that would do him right, because when he lit a cigarette, he'd be blown to kingdom come. Momma patted my leg and told me she was only kidding.

Momma goes to the phone and talks to the operator. After a minute, she starts talking to Gramma Dirks. She waves to Daddy, and, with her lips moving, her head nodding up and down, up and down, and her finger pointing to the phone, she lets him know that Aunt Josephine is there. After she hangs up she tells Daddy that Aunt Josephine and her kids were just getting ready to leave and are now on their way back to their farm. Josie knows Webber's number, Momma tells him, and will call before she leaves.

"It's probably what Clifford had in mind, anyway. He can't take a piss… relieve himself without Josephine holding his hose for him." I know what she means by Uncle Clifford's hose, but she doesn't know I do.

Daddy nods, his lips twisting into a small grin. He says, "That's no lie."

Momma lifts the phone again and tells the operator she wants to talk to Reverend Ervin Classen of the Hope Mennonite Church in Hopewell. It isn't long before she has Reverend Classen's wife on the line. Momma starts by telling her that she and Daddy can't make church today.

I ask Daddy as we walk from the living room and down the hall to the bedroom, "Why won't Uncle Clifford take Tommy Don to the hospital?"

"He's goddamned stubborn is what it is!" Daddy says this to himself, not to me. He hardly knows I'm there, even when he's answering my question. He throws the tie on the dresser top and unbuttons his shirt, takes it off with a couple of jerks and throws it with the tie. Next, he unbuckles his pants and steps out of his trousers, looking them over, carefully. He nods his head and stands in front of the bed in his underwear. He looks at me with a smile. He is in his best white undershirt and his shorts with blue lines on them. Then he frowns very serious-like, looking down at his undershirt which has a light red stain from Tommy Don's blood that's seeped through his dress shirt. He sits on the bed with his trousers on his arm. The belt's still in the loops. He holds his pants up and folds them once and lays them out over his lap and legs. He sighs.

"No, Shike, saying your Uncle Clifford's stubborn, that's not exactly right. He's stubborn, but there's more to it. You should know this about him." He waves his fingers several times, toward me and away, showing me he wants me to come where he is. When I walk over to him, he lifts me up on the bed, beside him. He takes my hand and holds it for a little bit. His hands are hard and soft at the same time. All at once, I feel that Daddy loves me. I grab him around his stomach and squeeze. He laughs a little and squeezes back, rubbing my back. Then he pushes me away and brushes my hair from my face the way Momma does. After he looks at me a minute, he cups his knees with his hands, even with his suit pants on top of his legs. He doesn't care about the wrinkles he's making, like Momma does.

"I want to put your mind at ease about what's happened this morning, okay?"

I feel like crying again, so I ask real quick, "Will Aunt Josephine and Dr. Webber drive Tommy Don to the hospital? Will he get pain killers?"

"Pain killers?" he asks me, surprised. "Where'd you hear about pain killers?"

"Momma says pain killers, sometimes."

"Okay, but, Shike, I don't want you to worry about this. Your mother was upset this morning, mainly, because she couldn't get ahold of your Aunt Josephine right away. Aunt Josie will definitely see to it that Tommy Don gets pain medicine for his broken arm." Daddy rubs his forehead. "But I don't want to fool you about any of this, either, because when you go out to the farm, you're gonna see and hear some things for yourself."

Daddy thinks a minute before he speaks. "First off, it's not likely Tommy Don will go to the hospital, unless Dr. Webber insists on that, because neither your aunt or uncle want to spend money that they don't have on things like the hospital. And to be perfectly honest, I don't know that they need to. The doctor will set Tommy Don's arm himself is my guess and then put it in a cast. That's what doctors do. You don't necessarily need a hospital for that, okay?"

I nod.

Daddy squints his eyes a little. "I hardly know where to start, Shike." He holds the edges of his trousers while he looks off toward the wardrobe and closet, puckers his lips, then says, "Your Uncle Clifford is like he is for a reason, though sometimes, it seems like what started out as a good reason for how he acts has hardened into something really difficult to explain." He takes my hand for a minute, then puts it down on the bed with a little pat. "Right now, I'm not very happy with your uncle, myself. I know you love him a lot, and you should. He thinks the world of you, so it's not easy for me to tell you what I'm going to say, but you should know why your mother is so angry with him. You've seen her mad at him before, right?"

"She thinks he's mean. She says so."

"I know she does, honey, and she's right about that, but there's more to it than she takes into account, most of the time, seems to me, at least, in the moments she gets as mad as she was at him today.

"Your Uncle Clifford came from a very, very poor family. There were five kids, and his father was sickly, and his mother just couldn't handle everything the way your Gramma Dirks and Gramma Jantz did when their children were growing up. Leona, Clifford's mother—Leon's named after her, did you know that?"

I shake my head.

"Well, she made a garden and did her best, but your Uncle Clifford and his sisters and brothers were hungry a lot—all the time, really. She worked him and her other kids past what kids should do, to make ends meet, and Clifford's dad was mean, I mean, really, really mean. Even before his sickness, while he was still up and around, he hit his children every chance he got, over anything and everything. He probably was in a lot of pain before he allowed himself to show it, which can make a person act mean. He had cancer, Shike, and he died when Clifford was just a teenager, in high school, about the time he met your Aunt Josephine. In fact, that's where he met her, they were in school together."

Daddy clears his throat. "Your mother went to school with him, too, because they all were in the same high school in Shirly, okay? So she remembers how Clifford acted with some of the bully boys at school." He doesn't look at me to see if I'm listening because he knows I am. Daddy is thinking careful about what he wants to say to me about Uncle Clifford.

"The Ratzlaffs, Clifford's family, were very proud people, maybe because they never had anything and didn't want people to see them as shameful. People can get... well, I almost said mean again, but what they can feel is very mad at other people when they themselves don't have much. Being poor, especially when other people know it, can make you feel bad about yourself, and you can feel very, very angry toward people who have things that you'd like to have, too, but you can't, and you can't figure out how to get them.

"But I have another idea about this as well, and your Uncle Clifford is the perfect example of it, in my opinion. He doesn't want anybody to know he's poor to the point that he'll go without what he, Josephine, and his kids need rather than take anything from anybody, even if it's free. If he did that—took what people gave him—he thinks everybody'd know he didn't have the money to buy for his family himself and, to him, that's about as low as a man can get. But, to my way of thinking, and your mother's, too, that's being too proud."

Daddy waits a minute like he's thinking what to say next to me. "There was a time when your Uncle Clifford could have had a farm, a whole farm, for almost nothing from the government, and he wouldn't take it because he thought doing that would make him obligated, he'd owe the government. Clifford didn't want to be grateful, not even to the government. When you're grateful to somebody, it's for something they give you, and he didn't want to accept anything from anybody—he wanted to do it on his own, not with any help, not even for free, especially not for free." Daddy stops and pats my leg. "That's about the best way I know to tell you. You think you understand about the hospital a little better now?"

"Yes."

Daddy starts talking again, like I've just told him no. He looks out toward the wall. It's like Daddy's talking to somebody far away, past the dresser.

"It's this attitude that just drives your mother crazy. If your Uncle Clifford has trouble earning a living because of the weather or illness, or this, that and the other thing, and then when somebody tries to help him, he feels ashamed, like he did when the government wanted to help him get started proper in life with his family."

Daddy pulls his Sunday trousers up higher on his lap and lays his hands on them so they won't slip down again. He sees the wrinkles he's made so he runs his hands over his pants. I'm guessing he'd rather talk than hang up his pants. It's hot in the bedroom, even with the window open. Maybe, it's like he wants to wear shorts, like Leon and my boy cousins wear cut-offs in the summertime. Some men do that but not Daddy. Shorts aren't right for Mennonites to wear, not even the men, regardless how hot it gets.

Now he's saying, "And here's the thing too, when you're down and out, there are some people who will take advantage of you, make you work hard for a little of nothing, because they have you over a barrel."

I can't believe Daddy is saying "over a barrel," especially like Momma does about Mr. Hilliar. "Do you know what 'being over a barrel' means?"

"No. Momma says 'over a barrel.'"

"Uh-huh. Well, I know why your mother says it, most the time lately, but God knows I don't want to get into that with you. But 'being over a barrel' means somebody has you in a position, in a place... ah, Shike, how can I tell you so you'll get this?" Daddy stops and says "ah" again before he starts. "Okay, let's see. It means you can't help yourself because of circumstances, that you have to take whatever happens because you don't have a choice, like... well, let's say, if you don't have a job and you've looked everywhere for one, okay? And somebody gives you the job you're asking for all right, but they pay you less money than what your work is worth because they know you need the job so bad you'll take almost anything to have the work. They have you 'over a barrel' because you gotta take what they dish out 'cause you don't wanna lose the job they've given you." Daddy shakes his head from side to side. "I have no idea where the expression came from, but, well, that's the best I can do with what it means, you understand?"

I nod. "'Over a barrel' means you gotta work at a job even when your boss is mean."

Daddy smiles. "You got that perfectly right, Shike. That's how it is." He pats my arm again. "I think 'over a barrel' is a saying from back when people used to try to ride over water falls in a barrel. Once you start going over a huge waterfall in a barrel, it's a pretty scary proposition because you can't stop going over even if you wanted to. Once you've started, you gotta see it through." Daddy nudges me a little. "I don't know if that's where it came from or not. Could be about the barrel of a gun for all I know. But the point I want to make about your Uncle Clifford is that he will move heaven and earth so he doesn't get himself in a place where bosses can treat him unfair and make him look bad to others. You see?"

I nod again.

"So when he's down and out—and that's pretty much been as long as I've known him—your uncle doesn't trust anybody. He expects they'll cheat him. So he doesn't put himself in a position so he has to be in debt to the other guy. He wants to work on his own, not for anybody else. He thinks working while you owe the other guy something is like working for nothing."

"Momma says you work like crazy for nothing."

Daddy makes a little "ahhh" sound and laughs nervous-like. "Well, your mother and me don't see eye to eye on this always, but that's the idea, yes, you're catching on to what I'm telling you. She looks out for me because she thinks I should get paid proper for my hard work. But there's this about that too—your mother always wants more, Shike. She thinks I should get more money for what I do because she wants to buy more things, for you and Teddy, too. She wants you to grow up with things like other people have. She doesn't want us to live by the skin of our teeth like Uncle Clifford and Aunt Josephine do, especially with their boys."

Daddy doesn't stop to tell me about skin on teeth. He goes on talking to me like I understand everything he's saying. "She wants things like everybody else because she believes we're just as good as the next guy down the street. Okay? She doesn't want me to work for nothing. That's what that means. Working for nothing is living too close to what you make, never having anything left over for extras.

"But in this business of being poor and wanting things, your mother isn't that far behind your Uncle Clifford. They just have two different ways of dealing with it. Your mother thinks we should push and push for more money until we get extra things, and your Uncle Clifford thinks he should save and save until he's got enough to get the things they need. That's why he doesn't want bills at the hospital he'll have to pay on for a very long time, you see?"

"Like horse pills," I say.

"Ah… yes, like your mother's medicine and doctors. Well, you have me there. It's a problem that's not going away easy, is it? It's always about money and getting what you need, well, and what you want. Big arguments about all of that, Lillun." Lillun is my other nickname. It's close to being called "Lil Lady," but it means "Little One," which I don't like as much.

I nod again so Daddy goes on telling me more. He smells nice, like his shaving cream and his coffee and hair oil. It feels good with him next to me, talking by ourselves. And he's not trying to get up and leave, like he needs to go to church or work. I don't want him to stop talking. I want him and me to sit like this, together, in our new apartment, in the bedroom, all by ourselves for a long time. He's getting ready to get up and leave for the kitchen. I can feel it.

"Daddy, I want you to tell me more about Uncle Clifford and poor."

"Okay." He reaches into the back pocket of his Sunday pants and pulls out his wallet. He snaps open the coin pouch and, putting it in front of me, tells me to take out a half-dollar.

I look down at the money but don't take anything.

"No, go on, I told you to. Take it." I reach in for the half-dollar but just when I have my fingers pinched on it and start to pull it out, Daddy closes the pouch around my fingers with his hand and says, "Okay, Shike, you get this half-dollar, but if you take it, and I'm telling you that you can spend it like you want to, but—and here's a really important thing to learn—once you take it and spend it, I'm going to come back around real soon, on Saturday, let's say, and I'm going to tell you that you have to give me a dime for letting you have the half-dollar. And"—Daddy says "and" like it's the most important part— "I'm going to ask you for a dime every Saturday until the half-dollar is paid up and then ask for a couple of weeks extra. Now here's the thing, Shike, you have to pay me each and every week or I'll come take some of your toys, your paper dolls, or a couple of your pictures books for the dimes you don't give me."

I take my fingers out of Daddy's coin pouch.

"So how do you feel about that?"

"Pretty low," I say, and he laughs big.

"Uh-huh. Something to think over real good, huh?"

Daddy reaches over and pats my hand. "That's what it's like to borrow money—owing people for what they give you. That's how the banks make their money. They give you money, but then they ask for it back plus a little more than what they gave you to begin with. That's called a loan." Daddy closes the coin pouch with a snap and puts it by his side on the bed. "And the extra money you pay to them for loaning you the money you've asked for is called interest."

He asks me if I understand. I tell him I do.

"With loans, you always pay interest—more money than you got in the first place. Your Uncle Clifford knows this the hard way, you see?"

I nod, but I want the half-dollar really, really bad. I start to ask him for it, but he pats me on the leg like he's not done yet.

"Now, pay attention, Shike. If you have a job and you work each week and you earn money for your work, that's called your wages or your salary. You've heard your mother and me talk about my wages, my salary, right? Okay. Well, let's just say that I make pretty good money—I make real good wages, okay? And I get paid every two weeks. My wages come in a paycheck, right?"

I nod, and Daddy picks up his wallet again and takes two half-dollars out of the coin pocket and puts them on his trousers. He puts his wallet down on the bed on the other side of his leg. "Now let's say these two half-dollars are what I earned for my work this week. So I take this money and go to the grocery store and buy food for two weeks and then I go and buy gasoline for those weeks as well."

"Stamps, not just money, Daddy." I know about stamps and rations.

"Okay," he says. "Right now we have to have stamps from the government for a lot of what we buy, but stamps are the same as money, because if we don't have them, we can't get the things we need. Gotta watch how we use them." Daddy picks up one of the half-dollars and throws it over his shoulder. It hits the other side of the bed and slides down to the floor, and we laugh. "All gone, Shike, because we bought gas and groceries with it." I look at the other half-dollar. "Okay, I still have half of my wages left. But then Teddy gets an earache, we have to pay the doctor and pay for the drops, and—"

"Momma needs her horse pills." I laugh.

Daddy laughs too. "You're really stuck on those pills, aren't you? So okay, Momma needs her horse pills, though she hasn't been getting those lately. And there's the rent, oh, and we also have to pay for the electricity and the water."

"We do?"

"Sure, Mr. Hilliar's paying for that because of the special deal I have with him about the warehouse and now with the apartment, but when you own a house like we did in Clearview, or even rent one, you make a payment to the bank or the owner of the house or land plus all the electricity and water. Those are called utilities."

Daddy waits a minute before saying, "Well, your aunt and uncle get their water from a cistern, but in town we pay for it, and if you have an inside toilet, you pay for the sewage and for trash being carried away and on and on it goes. So see, things add up and guess what?"

He picks up the other half-dollar and throws it up and over his shoulder where it hits the wall. I laugh, but I look to see if the half-dollar left a mark on Mr. Hilliar's wall. I don't see any, but I saw where the money fell. Daddy doesn't even look around.

He says, "All gone. All the wages are gone. And we haven't made the car payment. We bought a car from the bank, remember? They put up the money for the car—gave us a loan—so when I get my wages I have to pay back some of the money for it when I get paid, like I told you about paying for the half dollar, a dime every Saturday, see? Every month, I have to make a car payment plus a little interest. But there's no money. So now what happens?"

"I don't know," I say, looking down at his trousers. "Will they come get my toys and paper dolls?"

Daddy laughs. "You got the right idea, but if it's for our car, what do you think they'll take if we don't pay for it proper?"

"Teddy and me?"

"Oh God, no." Daddy shakes his head. "Oh, Shike—"

"Our car!" I pipe up, knowing, all at once, how loan and interest work.

"That's right. We're only playing around with money, right now, today, but if it's for real, yes, they can take our car if we don't pay them some of the money each month that we took to buy it. You see how this works, now?"

"I don't want them to take our car."

"Well, if there's no more money, what can we do?"

"Get money from the bank."

"But if you can't pay back the money you owe the bank for your car already, why will they give you even more money that you can't pay back?"

"You said Uncle Clifford got more," I say, a little worried.

"You were listening really, really good." Daddy smiles and pats my leg again. "The bank did give him more, and they might let me have some more for the car but remember how hard it will be to pay it back, especially when I may not make very good money the next pay check and the next and the next. That's how it works. That's what it's like when you hear me and your mother talking about what to do sometimes. And that's what your Uncle Clifford and Aunt Josie worry about when they don't make the harvest."

He waits, then asks me, "Well, what would you do when the bank wants more payment for the car, let's just say, for learning purposes, okay? What if they won't give me any more money as a loan?"

"I'd go to Grampa Dirks!" I say.

Daddy laughs so loud all at once, I jump. He starts to talk to me but keeps laughing and has to start over again and again. After he stops laughing, he says, "Okay, Shike, good thinking, but let's say your Grampa Dirks doesn't have enough. He can't help you because he doesn't have enough himself." Daddy reaches over and hugs me again and then he says, "But I gotta tell you, Shike, that's how the rich people do it. There's always somebody in the family who has money they'll give you to keep you afloat. But I'm seeing that you're getting this idea real quick."

"Simon Nichols!" I remember church people help each other.

"Hmmm. That's supposed to be how it works in Mennonite communities and still does in some, but times have changed. We help each other in other ways, but with money, well, we're pretty much on our own. But I gotta say, Simon has been watchful about my needs for finding work and a place to live, and he supports my views at church when a lot of others don't, so helping you doesn't always add up to money."

Daddy is serious now. He stands up and walks to the closet and lifts a hanger off the rod. The hanger has an old towel folded on the bottom. This is so his pants won't get a crease on them from the hanger. Momma told me when she was ironing. She showed me pants that had creases on them from hanging too long on wire hangers without towels.

Daddy puts the hook under his chin while he hangs his Sunday trousers over the towel. Then he puts the hanger on the rod in the closet and hunts for other clothes to wear while he talks to me, then turns around and stands in front of me in his underwear and socks before walking back to the bed and sitting down next to me again.

"Now, when your Uncle Clifford ran out of money and couldn't pay off the money he owed the bank, it's true, the bank did give him some more money to tide him over—for another planting and harvest. But then he had another bad year and couldn't pay them back again. And when he went to ask, they gave him money once more, but they told him if he had another bad year, they wouldn't give him any more money. He knew that meant he'd have to sell the farm in order to pay them back all that money or he'd have to let them come get the farm so he wouldn't owe them anymore.

"Worrying about whether the harvest is going to be good is over his head all the time as a farmer. He never knows until he's finished the wheat whether he'll have any money or not. This is why he hates owing people anything because it can pile up and up and up until you're way, way over your head and you feel like you can never get out from under it, you see?"

Daddy stands again and walks back to the closet and takes a pair of work pants off a hanger too fast sending the towel over the wire that falls to the floor. "Uh-oh!" he says when he picks it up and throws it on top of the dresser that's got boxes on it plus his dirty shirt and tie. He comes back to the bed and sits down like he did before, only this time with his work trousers on his lap.

"But I also want you to see that your mother and me think your Uncle Clifford is too stubborn about easing his worries. If he'd let your Aunt Josie take some clothes from the church for their kids and some government's relief money every now and then to tide them over, they'd have a little for things like taking Tommy Don to the hospital, if that's what's needed." He must not be ready to stop his story yet because he sits quiet for a minute without putting his trousers on.

"Your mother just sees red over all of this. But here's the thing, Shike," he touches my arms as he talks, "a really, really important thing to know. You don't mess in other people's business. I don't believe it's any of our business to go nosing around in your Uncle Clifford and Aunt Josie's business. You understand? They do things their way, and we do things ours.

"I don't want you saying anything to Tommy Don or your aunt and uncle about what I've told you because they will be upset that we've even talked about their troubles. Your mother, sometimes, gets more into their business than I feel like she should, but I can't always do anything about all that. Josephine's her sister, and she feels like she needs to interfere. But you need to stay out of it, Shike. You let your mother settle this with your Aunt Josie, if that's the way she wants to do it, okay?"

"Okay."

Daddy stands up, and I'm glad we're going to stop talking for a while, but suddenly he sits down again. I can't believe he's going to tell me more. I'm getting hungry. I want to go see when we're going to eat dinner. I start to slide off the bed, but Daddy puts his hand on my leg.

"Just wait up one more minute, Shike. You got me started on this so I want to finish it up right. Your Aunt Josephine makes a huge garden, tends the orchard for canning and such and helps with the butchers on their farm so they can keep from owing anybody anything. And it's a good thing, too. They help us by sharing their eggs, milk, and butter, and your Aunt Josephine is very generous with her baking, like the pie we got from her yesterday. Do you know how hard it is to get sugar and flour to make this? She had to save and save her stamps to do it."

"Gasoline," I say.

"Yes, they give us that, as well, from time to time. You're right about that. They are both very good to us, like your uncle coming to help us move, as he's done before. But we help them, too. I fix Uncle Clifford's truck and equipment and help with any number of things around on the farm when we go visit, plus the butcher coming up this November. We do that almost every fall, remember? And when they get tired of eating the same old thing and want something else, they come over and eat with us." He laughs a little. "More baloney sandwiches! But you know what I'm getting at, right?"

He pats my hand. "You see any of what I'm trying to tell you? We got started on this because of Tommy Don. I'm hoping you understand a little better how this works now with them and with us, also."

"Tommy Don won't go to the hospital because Doc Webber will fix it so they won't owe the hospital money. Momma says he needs shoes. They all need coats because Uncle Clifford won't take money from banks and pay loans. He's scared because he might not have enough money from harvest."

Daddy is so surprised at my answer, he laughs and hugs me tight. "That's the best part of it, Shike. Yes. Your uncle Clifford isn't exactly being selfish, though he gets himself his tobacco and whisky when he feels like he wants it bad enough. But his biggest hope is to live all to himself without help from anybody, if he can, because he hates the pay back."

"You buy tobacco and whiskey."

Daddy looks like I threw something at him. He looks up quick. His mouth opens, then closes, his lips smile, then pucker up, and, finally, he pushes one side of his mouth into his cheek. After he sighs, he says, "Okay, Shike, you have me there. But that's another story for another time. This morning we're talking about your Uncle Clifford, where his ideas and circumstances are different from ours."

"Okay."

"Okay." He stands up and looks down at himself.

I start to laugh. I think he looks funny in only his striped underwear, socks, and shoes with his work pants on his arm that he's taken out of the closet. I try to get off the bed, but it's too far, so Daddy reaches out and lifts me down.

When I am standing in front of him, I point to the suspenders for his socks. I've never seen these before. "What are these, Daddy? Suspenders for your socks?"

He smiles and winks. "Those? They're kinda like suspenders, I guess you could say, yes. But they're called 'garters,' and they hold up my good socks so they won't fall down around my ankles or look wrinkled." I reach down and pull one garter out and let go. It snaps his leg.

"Ow, watch it now. You could start a war you can't win!" We laugh big.

I step back and look at him for a minute. His knees are wrinkled all around and look like lids on jars. Daddy's legs are skinny, very skinny, and they have hair all over them.

"You reminded me, Shike. I almost forgot to take these off. Can't wear these with my everyday clothes."

He sits on the bed now and pushes each garter down his leg and over his feet.

He pinches the garters clips and takes each sock off. Then he walks to the dresser, lays the garters on a box, and reaches over to throw the socks in the hamper near the closet door. He takes off his stained undershirt and pulls his work shirt off its hanger very slow and looks at it before he unbuttons the top button and puts his arms through the sleeves. He's going to wear it without an undershirt.

"Don't have much else outta the boxes yet," he says to himself. "At least these are clean. Sometimes, your mother is some kind of miracle worker."

He buttons all the buttons down the front of his shirt. "She thought to get my clothes ready for tomorrow." He reaches for his work pants on the bed and opens them wide again and this time steps into the legs and pulls them up, buttons and zips and then while I watch, after he's totally dressed, he sort of shakes all over like a dog and laughs.

I laugh too. I stand and wait while he pulls his belt through all the loops and buckles up.

He wads up his tie, shirt, and undershirt to carry to the kitchen for Mother to bleach and wash them, though I know she'll take the tie to the cleaners. He waves his fingers again to show me he wants me to walk down the hall in front of him. When I stop, Daddy runs into me. He makes a little noise.

"What's got into you? You okay?"

"The half-dollars're still on the floor," I say.

Daddy turns me around, and we walk back to the bedroom. When we get to the door, he says, "Well, finder's keepers, I always say!"

I can't believe it! I race to the back of the bed and find the money real fast. I am so happy, I think I'll cry. I hold up the half-dollars in the air.

"I found them!" I yell.

"Well, that you did, Shike. That's what you get for being such a good listener. And you know what? I won't even come around and ask for a payment next Saturday."

I run down the hall yelling at Momma. I've never had so much money ever, in my whole life.

When we come in the living room, Daddy looks over at Teddy's crib. "Oh boy, we may be in for a good talking to, Shike. We stayed in the bedroom longer than I intended."

But Momma is on the phone with Teddy sitting up against her on the couch, pressed against her legs while she listens in the receiver with one hand and rubs his back with the other. I smell cooking on the stove, frying chicken and gravy and mashed potatoes, and I don't know what all. Green beans, too, probably. Momma tells Daddy with her lips, the phone still pressed to her ear, receiver a little under her chin, "I'm talking with Josephine." In a little bit, she says her goodbyes, puts the phone in its cradle, and leaving Teddy to Daddy, she walks toward the kitchen.

Daddy picks up Teddy and goes to pour himself a cup of coffee with one hand while he holds Teddy against him with the other.

Momma looks down at me and opens the refrigerator door. "You haven't eaten a bite yet, aren't you starved by now?"

I nod, but she isn't looking.

She pours me a glass of juice in my favorite Shirly Temple glass. Momma tells Daddy, while she's moving the chicken around in the skillet with a long fork, "Josie says that she just talked to Webber at his home, and he's sending her to the hospital because the bone is showing, and he can't take care of that at his office. So Clifford be hanged. They're on their way to Hopewell General whether he likes it or not. That makes me feel a whole lot better. At least my sister has some sense."

"Will Uncle Clifford be able to pay the bankers now?"

Momma stops taking down bowls and putting them on the kitchen counter, turning around to me, saying with real surprise, "When, in heaven's name, did you learn about the likes of money and bankers? You never cease to amaze me, Shike!"

Daddy's back is to Momma when he lifts his finger to his lips to show me, "Sshhh." He winks, then leans over to ask Momma if she wants him to put Teddy down in his crib while he makes some corn bread in a hurry.

NIGHT
VISITORS

July, 1942

I WAKE UP WITH A jerk. I don't know where I am. I think I am dreaming. I roll over on my back and try to sit up but my feet are held down by somebody. I start kicking and funny sounds come up out of my throat. I finally push myself up by my hands and see my feet are twisted up in a sheet Momma's covered me with when I went to bed. The window in my new apartment bedroom is open, and a cool breeze is coming in. It's still night. I get up to go to the bathroom. On the way across our bedroom, I see Teddy sleeping in his crib that Daddy's pushed to the corner, against the walls. Teddy moves around a lot while he sleeps.

Momma says Teddy likes to have accidents and doesn't even take his time to decide where. He's learning to walk along the front of the sofa couch and chair, and sometimes he does that well enough, but lots of other times he doesn't get very far before he wobbles and falls on his butt. He usually sits down hard. When he cries, Momma doesn't pick him up and tells me not to help him, because, she says, if we leave him alone, he'll get up and try again. If we start helping him every time he cries, he'll learn to wait for us to help him stand, and, then, it'll take longer for him to walk without us. For a while, Momma worried that he was falling down too much, but the doctor says there's nothing wrong with Teddy's bones. He's just thinking faster than his legs can carry him.

"Teddy's got a real temper," Momma says. When he thinks things don't go his way, he wails. The last couple of weeks he's been crying more, like he did when we lived in Clearview. But he was littler then. Momma says little babies cry all the time. I think Teddy's mad because he didn't want to move from the warehouse, where we lived before the apartment. It was one big room with sheets for walls. Teddy liked to watch me run like my tail was on fire. I could run even through walls!

Sometimes, when he cries real long, Momma tells me not to pay so much attention to him because he wants to eat all the time, and, then, after he's been fed, he wants to sleep and be left alone. He cries hard when Momma tries to clean his face and hands with a washrag. Sometimes, he holds his breath. He stops when Momma blows on his face and takes him into another room. I think Teddy doesn't care if his mouth is dirty.

Momma tells Daddy that more and more Teddy is turning out to be a hard baby. "A real bear." She tells me that he's growing to be a big boy, but I think he's fat. He weighs twenty-two pounds, and he won't stop eating. The doctor told Momma to slow down on the treats and the bottle, even if giving him those makes him stop crying. Teddy takes the bottle all the time, but Momma doesn't tell the doctor this. He likes to eat like she does, she says.

Now, he's sound asleep with his face pressed against the rails of his bed like bars in a cage. I go over and squat down and put my lips on his cheek through the rails, but he doesn't know I'm there. Teddy can sleep standing up, I swear—although I'm not supposed to swear. I've found him draped over the sofa, sleeping with his face on the cushions, while sucking his thumb. He sucks his thumb forever and a day.

In the bathroom, while I'm sitting on the toilet, I see faces in the crumbled-up pattern of the linoleum floor. Momma likes this flooring because it doesn't show dirt. But I'll help her mop it every day, anyway. Momma hates dirt whether it shows or not.

In the night light that she's plugged in for me, a jungle full of people, most of them men with beards and tiny eyes and very fluffy eyebrows, are scattered across the floor in front of me. They are crowded behind lots of bushes and each other. They look like the people in the picture books with fairy tales that Momma gets from the library to read to me at night.

"Fee-fie-foe-fum, I smell an Englishman," I whisper. Gramma Dirks talks about the English this and the English that. She tells me when I grow up I shouldn't marry an English boy. Momma says that Gramma Dirks is old-fashioned and thinks everybody is English that isn't one of our people, the Mennonites who came from Russia. The giant in Jack and the Beanstalk thinks like Gramma. He thinks everybody he smells, who isn't a giant, is English. I look for Jack and the giant in the crumbled-up shapes on the floor. The giant is there, but I can't find Jack anywhere. Lots of faces are smashed together. I see a queen and king and maybe Miss Muffet but no spider. And then I see Rumpelstiltskin. His pointed hat is almost covered up by the beard of an old man with a big nose. Momma read me the story of Rumpelstiltskin but stopped before the story was over. Moving her lips in a whisper, she read ahead by herself. When she finished, she patted my arm and told me there was too much in this story about the love of money and about the devil helping with the making of it.

"All about greed, pure and simple," she said. "They just make up these stories to the point that some of them are lies too big for grown-ups, let alone children." I wanted to hear the end of the story even when I was a little scared of Rumpelstiltskin, but she mumbled to herself, "How a little man could tear himself asunder is beyond anybody's caring one way or the other. It's absolute nonsense!" Rumpelstiltskin must have torn himself up at the end of the story.

Momma helped me find another story instead. She read to me about Rapunzel. I look for Rapunzel in the bathroom floor and find her off to the side of where my feet hang down. But there's not a castle anywhere, and I know she's locked up inside, so I'm not sure it's Rapunzel at all. After I finish the toilet, I flush and splash my hands in the water Momma leaves for me on the sink at night because I can't reach the faucets. After I run my hands through the towel, I get down on my knees and try to find Rapunzel, but she's gone once I'm down on the floor close by.

"Rapunzel," I whisper, "let down your hair." But she doesn't come out from where she's hiding. I think if the person I saw is her, she might be afraid of me. Maybe she's hiding because she thinks I'm the witch that cut off her hair and threw her into the wilderness. She may not be in the castle anymore. She could be living happily ever after with the prince and their two children.

Momma sometimes sings, "Tea for two, a boy for you and a girl for me." I put the toilet lid down real quiet and sit down again so I can try to find her from where I saw her before, but she's run off. While I'm looking for her, a little dwarf comes out but he's without the others. Nobody any place on the floor looks pretty like Snow White. I look for Lassie and Peter Rabbit and Mary and her lamb and the three pigs and the three bears and the three blind mice and the three little kittens. But I can't find any animals, at least not any I know. So far, there are only people. Then out of nowhere I see Mr. McGregor, but he doesn't have his glasses on. I wonder if it's really Mr. McGregor.

When I turn my head, I see the face I didn't want to find—the troll. He isn't under the bridge like he is in the story but behind an old man's beard, partly hiding, looking up at me with a grin. The Billy Goats Gruff aren't around either, and there's no bridge for them to cross over, like they're supposed to. The troll is all by himself, waiting. He's probably been waiting for me to come live in this apartment. He wanted us to move here so he could watch me when I come into the bathroom. He probably wants me to pay a toll. I wonder why he didn't ask me for one right away when I came through the door a few minutes ago. Maybe the door is his bridge in this new place. Maybe he was so far behind the old man with a beard that he didn't see me at first.

"Who's that tramping over my bridge?" he asks me now. I sit without moving, looking around to see if somebody else could be talking to me from the floor. But I know it's him.

"Oh, it is I," I say from the fairy tale. "I am not a very big Billy Goat Gruff. You don't want to eat me. You want to wait until somebody fattier comes along." The fairy tale doesn't say it just like that, but I don't have a bigger brother goat for him to wait for, and I don't want to tell him about Teddy. Way deep down, though, I think he probably already knows Teddy is in his crib, sleeping. But in case the troll doesn't know, I am dead silent. I'll let him eat me before I'll ever let him take Teddy. Teddy is fat, and even though he looks fattier for his size than me, I weigh more. I'd be the best meal because I weigh forty pounds. It says so on my ration stamp book.

"Fee-fie-foe-fum," I say because I want him to know I have a giant on my side, at least I know one.

"An Englishman? No Englishman for my toll. My toll is you. You will never leave this bathroom unless you give me a toll that's fattier than you are."

I want to run, but I am not moving. I say real fast, "I know you usually eat goats. I'm not a goat, and I'm not even very fat. In fact, everybody says I'm skinny—"

"Your brother is fattier than you are, even though he's half your size. His baby fat will be much more delicious than yours. And baby fat sticks!"

I can't talk I'm so scared, but I'm more scared not to. "You don't want him," I say real, real fast. I think I'm going to cry. "He has very sharp front teeth, and he cries and kicks all the time. He will be awfully hard to stuff down your gullet." I'm very proud I thought of this to save Teddy.

"Then I will eat you instead. That's okay with me. I haven't had anything but Post Toasties lately, and I need to have something that will really fill me up."

While he is talking to me, I see him move. I know he is starting to come out from behind the old man with the beard in front of him. I am so scared I think I will yell for Momma, but I know when she comes in the room, he will hide, and she'll just think I'm making things up, and she'll stop reading the fairy tales to me.

"Don't you even think about calling your mother or your father, Little Lady, or you will be in more trouble than you want to be, you understand me?"

"He can read my mind, he can read my mind." I'm too scared to get off the toilet, where I've gone back to sit, and run. But I think to say, "Will you take money?" I have the two half-dollars Daddy let me keep and feel good I thought of them.

"Money? What good will money do me if I can't leave this floor to go to the store and buy anything? Can't you see I'm glued to this spot?"

Daddy says he is always glued to his spot, but he moves around. I'm not sure if I trust what the troll is telling me.

"I can get things for you, anything you want, just tell me, and I'll go to the grocery store and get it for you. I go to the grocery for Momma all the time," I lie.

"Do they sell Billy Goat Gruffs?"

"No," I say. Then I have another idea. "I can bring you curds and whey, that's soupy cottage cheese, if you want. We have that in the ice box, and Miss Muffet likes—"

"You are a silly, silly little girl. Are you trying to tell me that because I'm short, just a little man, I do not want a whole meal like other men twice my size?"

"No, no, I think you are a very big man. For your size." I don't know what to say to keep him from being mad at me. "I can bring you a real supper, some food off my plate next time. My daddy eats a whole meal, and he's short. His friends even call him 'Shorty.'" Then I think of something that might save me. "Momma's gonna make meat loaf for supper. There'll be leftovers. Daddy loves her—"

The troll doesn't let me finish. "If your father doesn't mind being called 'Shorty,' that's his business, but don't you ever call me that! And as for my supper, I can't wait that long. I haven't eaten anything for ages. Maybe I'll just take one of Teddy's toes, just one. I'd leave him with all the others so that he can still walk, or maybe I'll take a finger, he won't miss his little finger. A little snack, something to tide me over until you bring me a real meal!"

"No, no, oh no." I am sobbing now. I can't help it. Maybe if I cry, he'll give in. Momma does, sometimes, when I'm real upset. "Nothing of Teddy's. You can take something of mine if you want but not Teddy. Pleeeease."

"All right, all right," he says falling back some behind the old man again. "Stop your sniveling right this minute or I'll pluck out one of his eyes, I will, I will."

"Okay, okay. I'll be good. I'll get you anything out of the refrigerator that you want. I can be awful quiet. A mouse."

"If I let you go, you'll only go back to bed."

"No, no," I say, about to cry again. "No, I'll go right now. You want baloney and cheese? We always have those."

The troll doesn't say anything for a long time, but I think I see him nod a little. I get down from the toilet and start to run to the kitchen, but when I'm at the door, he says real loud, "I've changed my mind, Lillun, I don't think baloney and cheese will do."

I start to ask him what he wants then, but when I stop and turn around and try to find him on the floor, I can't see him. I might be able to tiptoe through the door, but I look down and find him right there by my bare feet. I jump back and yell, then grab my mouth and look around to see if Momma or Daddy heard me. I wait with my hand over my mouth until I think the coast is clear.

When nobody comes, I whisper, "What do you want?" He can move fast as I can, I see that now, but there's no way I can keep track of him if he moves out of the bathroom. I want to ask him if he can go through the door, but I'm afraid to. I almost yell at him because I am getting as mad as I am scared. He's being too picky about his food. Momma and Daddy have told me over and over that they don't like picky eaters. Momma thinks we should eat all of what's put before us, no questions asked. Before I stop myself, I ask again, "What do you want? You tell me right now or I'll...." I think quick, as quick as I can. "I'll cover you with Mercurochrome!" I run to the toilet seat. I run like the wind, like Leon and I do through the Mexican sandburs without getting stickers caught on the bottoms of our feet. I crawl and then stand on top of the toilet lid, open the medicine case, and grab the Mercurochrome bottle. I whirl around and show him his poison.

But everything is absolutely still inside the bathroom. I look down and around on the floor, and he isn't there anymore. I look over by the door, and he isn't there, either. I get off the toilet lid and stand without a hair moving. I run my eyes all over the bathroom floor, but I don't see him anywhere. I walk to where he was hiding behind the old man with the beard and wait, but he is gone. I look under the bathtub, sink, toilet, and gas heater. Nothing moves.

But then I hear a small noise, like a tap, tap, tapping—I almost can't breathe—it's the tap, tap, tapping of hooves across a bridge. I know it is. I just know it is! I look this way and that way. I look everywhere. I turn around in circles, around and around. I see nothing but crumbled-up gray lines on the white linoleum floor.

Tap, tap, tap.

I look at the sink and my water dish, at the towels hanging down, the washrag drying on the side of the bathtub. Then I look up at the wallpaper with its long vines going all the way to the ceiling. They look like Jack's beanstalk, only small, a lot smaller than in the storybook. Could the giant come down these stalks into the bathroom and hide in the floor? If he tried, he could beat up the troll, because the troll is little and the giant is so big. I would tell him the troll is English. That would do it, for sure. But the vines are way too small to hold a fat giant. The vines would break, and he would fall hard, probably not able to get up because he weighs so much.

Tap, tap, the tapping of hooves again across… and then I see the open window with the shade half down. The string with the pull moves in the breeze and the wooden circle pull is what's hitting the windowpane. I didn't know it until now, but my fingers are pressed against my lips so tight I still feel my teeth on them when I take my fingers away. I've been holding my breath without knowing it. I let out a big sigh.

And then I tiptoe around as many fairy tale people on the floor as I can before I am walking, then running, back to my bedroom.

Teddy is sleeping now on his back. The moonlight is coming in through our open window and is falling across his legs and feet. I crawl into my bed and turn on my side so I can watch Teddy sleep. I pull the sheet up to my chin, feeling sleepy too, but I'm not sure I can close my eyes. I need to watch.

I look out the window and see the tree move slowly back and forth, back and forth. I think I hear a tap, tap, tap of hooves over a bridge, but then I see the shade-pull to our window moving in the breeze, and I smile.

The troll can't leave the bathroom. He's glued to his spot. He told me so himself, so he believes he can't move from the floor, even if I know he can. And anyway, I think slowly, very slowly now, that he knows that I know he is afraid of Mercurochrome. I touch the bottle under my pillow before I let go and fall asleep.

ARGUMENT, ARRANGEMENT, AND AGREEMENT

August, 1942

I AM SLEEPING WITH MOMMA and Teddy tonight. Teddy is already asleep in Momma and Daddy's bedroom in his crib. She told me after dishes in the kitchen. Daddy is sleeping on the sofa couch.

An agreement, Momma says.

I don't know for sure what she's telling me, but they aren't yelling anymore. When I go stand next to Daddy, he says that him being on the couch is a new sleeping arrangement.

Arrangements make everything quiet, so I'm happy they are having one.

They were fighting when Momma kept saying Daddy needed to look for work in Hopewell if he wasn't going be a farmer, because Mr. Hilliar wasn't "doing him justice." And Momma couldn't let it rest, so after supper it started up again. Daddy says Momma never lets anything rest. She starts everything up, again and again, he tells me, especially about how he gave the Clearview house to Aunt Hannah when, Momma says, it wasn't his to give away. They say Clearview now all the time. When Momma shouts at Daddy, he spreads his arms out wide and brings them down against his sides with a slap. Their arguments over the Clearview house are always the same, only some of the words are different.

"Of course, of course," Daddy shouts. "I'll never live this down, will I? No matter how much explaining I give you, it only fans the flames. When we have an argument over anything—and lately it's about everything—but it doesn't matter what we're talking about, does it? Because when that comes to a halt, here you go toting out the Clearview house to taint everything with that sin. What do I have to do to atone for this one, Darlene? You want me to wear sackcloth and ashes? Or would you rather I stand in front of a train? That's more like it, isn't it? Why don't you just stone me to death. That make you happy? Because what you're doin' is about the same thing. It's killing any peace and quiet I can find over much of anything. But you know that, don't you? It's your plan."

"It belonged to our family, Vernon. Teddy and Shike included."

"So it's our kids against Hannah's kids, is that it?"

"Yes," Momma screams. "Yes, yes, and yes. And we see by what you did where your heart is."

Daddy is so suddenly mad his face and neck are puffy and red. It looks like he will come on fire. "So here we are again. I'll never make recompense now that it's done. Want me to go to Clearview, reclaim the house and throw Hannah and her kids out on the street?"

"Yes," Momma says again, her face very big and shiny. When she yells at him, spit flies out of her mouth. "Yes, yes, *yes.*"

Daddy walks to the dining room table, sits down, and puts his head in his hands. When he looks at her again, he has tears in his eyes.

"You don't mean that. You're just mad."

"No, I'm just right."

They both walk away from each other. Daddy goes into the kitchen. I hear the water running and see him drinking over the sink. He is still gulping at the water in his glass when he comes back into the living room. He puts his glass down, half-full, on the end table and bends over to start making his bed. He opens up the davenport and grabs bedding from underneath. He sighs as he snaps the sheet open and folds it around the corners of the mattress the way Momma does when she puts clean bedding on for me. Daddy's sheet smells like outdoors. He opens and spreads the blanket like the sheet. When he's done, he sits down and pulls me to him for a hug. He's in his underwear—boxer shorts and undershirt. He still has his socks on.

When Momma leaves from the kitchen to go to the bathroom, I ask Daddy why he's sleeping on the sofa, but I know. He says he needs to get some rest for work tomorrow. When I tell him that Momma didn't say anything about him sleeping on the couch, he says, "Your Mother is not likely to let me sleep very much in bed with her tonight. She'll talk her head off, whether she gets anywhere with it or not. She's still worked up over this whole house deal. Good God, how long's it been now? I've only seen Hannah and the kids once, maybe twice, since we moved. And if we still lived in Clearview, where would I work? It makes no sense but it's not about making sense anyhow. It's about me being the bad guy. Oh, well."

He waits a minute, then pushes me away from him a little. "Look, I don't want you to worry your head about any of this, especially our sleeping arrangements, Shike. Things will be back to normal by tomorrow, I'm sure."

He always says no worrying my head. Sometimes he says my pretty head.

Now he winks and says, "Have you ever tried to sleep with a wet hen?"

I shake my head, and we both laugh. He reaches out and pulls me to him again.

"Well, that's about what tonight with your mother would be like. You better go join her now to get ready for bed, or I'll be in trouble for that as well."

Daddy has his mechanic's uniform laid out on the dining room table with his clean underwear and socks. His shoes are under the clothes tree on the shoe tray. He always leaves them there after work and puts them back on when he leaves in the morning. He walks around the house in his work socks, the ones he takes out of his bedroom dresser drawer after his bath. They look dirty, but they're not. He won't wear slippers. Momma buys him a pair every Christmas. He wears them around on Christmas day, then he pushes them into a corner in the closet. He tells me, "This way I can't find them to wear the rest of the year." Momma sighs and shakes her head when she pulls them out and gives them to the church's clothes drive. She keeps trying to find "the right kind," so he'll wear them all the time.

Momma sticks her head out of the bedroom door and starts to call me again, but I am already walking toward her.

"Well, come along then." She doesn't look at Daddy, but she looks at his half-empty glass on the end table before she turns back into the bedroom, walking down the hall to the bathroom. I stand in the doorway and look back at Daddy.

"Shike," Momma calls.

"Go mind your mother now," Daddy says. "I'm fine."

"Bite the bedbugs," I tell him, and he laughs, a little.

When I turn to go to the bathroom, he's standing with his back to the bedroom door. I watch him bend over, hiding from Momma and me what he's doing, but I know he's getting his bottle out from its secret place under the davenport, and he is going to pour his whiskey into the water glass later when we can't see, when Momma is done in the bathroom and closes the bedroom door.

Teddy is sleeping so deep, he doesn't hear us talking. He is on his back, not even his lips are moving. He's a good baby now, doesn't wake up anymore during the night. Momma is grateful for small mercies these days.

———————

"COME OVER HERE, HONEY, AND curl up with me." Momma is holding open the sheet to let me in next to her when I come out of the bathroom, after washing my face and brushing my teeth, and Momma's brushing my hair for one hundred strokes. I have my pajamas on. She still has on her house dress. She tells me she's too tired to take it off and put on her night gown.

I don't go to where she is so she closes the sheet and rolls on her stomach and pushes her face into the pillow.

"Oh Shike," she says to the pillow, holding herself up on her elbows, her chin in her hands.

Then she rolls over onto her back and puts an arm across her forehead. She talks to the ceiling. "It's all so complicated." Then she adds real quick, "Don't ask what complicated is. You know what it means, even if not exactly." But she decides to tell me anyway. "It means everything is hard to explain to you. I don't know how to tell you why Daddy and I aren't getting along, especially why we're fighting so much lately."

She looks at me and waits. I stand still, biting my lip so I won't talk. "C'mon, you're a smart girl. You listen. Your father and I disagree on so many things, and that's got to be confusing to you, but I don't know what to do about it, because I have to be honest with myself. Neither one of us is easy to live with. He's easier than I am, I admit. But that's because he doesn't ask questions. He's a simpler person."

"He is not," I yell at her, but I don't know what she means. She's going to say more, but I am crying and don't want to listen about Daddy. I want to get into bed with her but don't want her to touch me. I stand beside the bed and wait.

"Okay, honey, that's fine but come to bed, and we'll talk about it. I can't promise for how long, because I'm so tired, but I'll try."

"You're always tired. You go to bed all the time, even when it's day." I'm just saying what Daddy says to me and even her, sometimes. I look right at her, telling her like Daddy, right to her face.

Momma looks back at me a long time. Then she lets out a little sob.

"I know I'm in bed too much, but I don't know what to tell you about that, Shike. Do you want me to lie to you?" She waits, and I don't want to, but I shake my head. "Okay then. The truth is, I'm tired, and I don't know why. The sickness seems to be coming back, and I don't know how to keep it at bay. It comes and overtakes me at times, and, lately, I have to just grab a hold of what I can to keep my balance. It's like being on a sinking ship, that's what it feels like. And your Daddy doesn't always help me out. He asks me to do what I can't, and he is so... so *ooltmoodsch!*" She laughs real big, all of a sudden, forgetting to cry. "I don't know where that came from," she says, still laughing but slowing down. She reaches out and touches my arm, and I let her. *"Ooltmoodsch* means old-fashioned. Sometimes, I think your father is just like a... a nineteenth-century male, like his father. He doesn't know how to—"

"He is *not*," I yell at her, crying, pushing her hand away.

"Okay, honey, I understand. He's your father and you want to.... Okay, Shike." She motions for me to come into the bed with her, but I stay standing where I am. "What's happened here is that he's charged off doing this thing without having me a part of it just when I thought we had a home, when we were being a family. We had something together. This has... it's been so... upsetting to me. I don't feel like I have my legs, my balance anymore. And we've moved three times in only a few months, and now we may have to move, again, which I admit I'm trying to get him to do, but taking off and moving, again, feels so up in the air. What I'm trying to tell you is that I don't want to go, but I feel we have to because… because of bad circumstances."

I don't move but ask her, "What's circumstances?" But I know the argument by heart, even if I don't know all the words.

"Circumstances are, well, it means a situation, something that's happening, and if it's a bad situation, you have to do something about it." She tells me again what I've heard them talk over and over. Momma thinks we should move to Shirly with Gramma and Grampa Dirks, and Daddy should work on the farm with Grampa, or, at least, we should live there until Daddy finds a better job in Hopewell. She's scared he's going to take the wrong work, and then the army will get him. The one thing she does know, she argues, is that Daddy can't keep working at Hilliar Repairs because they're hardly making ends meet.

Daddy's work is their big, big argument, almost always. When Momma asks him about moving to her homeplace, he tells her that she just wants somebody to take care of her when she's not feeling herself. Well, what about the kids, she wants to know? If we move to Hopewell, even if we find a place to rent and Daddy finds a decent job—two big ifs, Momma thinks—when he's drafted and has to leave, she'll be left all alone without anybody she knows, except church people, and they live all over town, most even live in the country. She doesn't know them well enough, she tells Daddy, to ask for help like she'd need.

Daddy doesn't want to leave Aileen. He wants to give Hilliar Repairs more of a chance, believing things will get better in time. But Momma's idea about being on the farm, well, Daddy tells her that's bullshit. If we have to move, we would all do better in Hopewell.

"Shike knows the Toews and the Nichols families. We've gone over for dinners several times. And Shike's stayed with Norma Janet and the Nicholses when Bobby Gene died. It was fine. They would be glad to help if need be." Daddy's idea is that I'd be able to start school better in Hopewell, and I'd have friends that would last. We wouldn't have to keep moving over and over. "You worry ahead about every little thing that hasn't happened yet."

But Momma's worries are about life without Daddy. She doesn't know if she can make it alone with Teddy and me. She's told me. I know.

After Momma tells me about not making ends meet, she says, "Why don't you come on to bed, and we'll try to settle it, at least for tonight. What do you say to that?" She holds open the sheet again that she's using like a blanket. "Come quick before I fall asleep!"

I get up onto the bed and slide in beside her.

"Curl up against my stomach. There. That's the ticket!" She hugs me up tight against her. It's hot, but the fan is on, blowing the sheet in little ruffles. The windows are closed because it's raining. "The rain is making everything a little cooler already," Momma tells me in a sleepy voice.

I twist halfway around and try to look at her. "What's 'the ticket' mean?"

"Old saying," she says, her chin on the top of my head. "I've never seen anybody in my life as curious about words as you are. Half the time I don't even know what I'm saying till you make me aware of it. I haven't the slightest idea where 'that's the ticket' comes from, but it means that's exactly perfect, just exactly what I needed, that you're helping me feel close again. You're my little toaster, warmin' my heart. So that's what it means right now, anyway." She kisses my hair by my ear, then the top of my head, as she settles in to sleep.

"Daddy's feet are hot all the time." She doesn't get upset when I talk about Daddy, so I say, "He lets me pull his socks off, sometimes."

Momma just sort of hums and kisses my head again. She says, "Pickled pig's feet! Yuck, and I don't mean the kind you eat." We both start giggling, and before we know it we are shaking all over each other.

"Oh," Momma says. "I knew you were going to make me feel better. What would I do without you, Shike?"

I curl deeper against her stomach and lay there with her for a long time. "Are you better now?"

She says, "Un-hum" real soft, and I hear her starting to breathe deep, sleep-like. She doesn't want to talk about Daddy and regrets anymore. She wants to sleep. I want to talk, but I am falling into her breathing against me. Soon I am not just me. I am her and me, together, at the same time. The clock is ticking on the side table, and, after a while, I hear her say, very far away, "Spoons. You and me are spoons."

Then I think I might dream about us running away with the dish.

———————

I DON'T KNOW IF I'M awake for sure, but then I see the clock's hands shining 12 and 1. I am sleeping against Momma's stomach. I am sleeping inside the circle of her body. She is soft, like a pillow. I fall into the smells of her. I smell her skin, her mouth, her hair, her clothes. It is her time of the month, she told me. She is bleeding now, I know. But when she was pregnant with Teddy, no blood came from between her legs.

She told me about having babies one night not very long ago, after dark, in her bedroom, with only the night light on, shining against her face while she talked. When I asked about Teddy coming out of her stomach, she said she could tell me only as much as the little space with her fingers. Later, when I'm older, she will tell me more. But she didn't want me to worry when I saw blood on her private napkins. She told me not to worry, nothing was wrong, that bleeding was natural—something all women do. It's about having babies and women's monthlies. Now I think about monthlies sometimes. I ask her every now and then if she's having a monthly, and she smiles and says yes or no. I can't keep track. She told me that monthly talk was private, it's not talk for me to have with other people. It's not conversation with just any or everybody. Women have their monthlies, but they are personal—until they are pregnant.

I curl my fists under my chin and push my head into the soft pillow of her chest. I sleep against Momma's chest and stomach. I feel her breathing on my back. She breathes toward me and away, toward me and away, in and out, the warm touch of her belly, and then the being away of it and then the touch of it and the away of it, in and out, toward me and away, our breathing around my body and her body and our bed. She breathes in and out, toward and away—our bed and our breath, inside and out, falling, falling. I am falling with our breathing. I'm falling against Momma's body, falling against her belly and her chest, her breathing is toward me and away while I sleep and wake, sleep and wake.

She whispers while she sleeps, but I am away. I am away. I am floating away, away from my bed and from Momma. I am away from her now, at the window, watching the rain falling, the rain falling like her breathing in our bed.

My breath comes in a jerk and a sound. I am no longer falling. I am awake. I sit up and push away from Momma's breathing. I walk to the window and watch the rain falling. I stand and wait and watch the rain. It is cooler outside. The fan makes whomping, shooshing noises, in circles, around and around, louder, then soft, louder, then soft, whomp, shoosh, whomp, shoosh, whomp, shoosh. My breath comes in and out with the fan. Everything in the house is quiet, except the fan and my breathing, and Momma's far, far away breathing, breathing so far away from me.

I listen to the sounds of the rain hitting the windowpane. They ping against the glass hard, like little stones moving toward me, hitting the window and then sliding to the ground. The sounds are hard and loud and far away from where Momma is warm in her bed.

I touch the window and see my hand-mark and watch it stay and then watch it melt away. I push my hand against the glass and step back watching my hand-mark disappear from the glass. I put my hand in the mark I've left on the pane before it melts away, but then before I put it back inside, it is gone. I smell the rain on the glass-mark and my hand.

The house is quiet. There is only the rain that melts on my hand, on the outside of the glass, running down. Everybody sleeps and doesn't see where I am, what I'm doing. I am awake, and they are sleeping far, far away from me. I want to be by the window and watch the rain never stop. I want the quiet to go on and on.

When I look back at the window, the hand-mark is gone again. I put my hand on the glass, where it's been, but it doesn't leave a mark. It is wet and cold, and the wet and cold stay on my hand, but when I take my hand away, the wet and cold run, slow, very slowly down the windowpane.

A shudder goes through my hand and arm and through my stomach and my legs and feet. I can't move. There is something in me that makes the hand-mark happen on the glass, but there is something out there, too, something not me, that makes the hand-mark happen. It is the warm in me and the cold outside that makes it appear and disappear.

I push air out of my mouth onto the glass and a spot of fog suddenly appears. I watch it go away, so very slowly, two small rivers in the middle of the fog run down the glass. I touch one with my finger and make it stop. I can make my own wind and rain against the windowpane.

I push air out against the glass in one place and then another, pushing "ah, ah, ah," watching little fog spots come to life on the glass. At once, little pools of water begin all over the glass and the rivers began falling from the pools down the windowpane. I write my name in the foggy places, but before I can finish the letters are gone.

I stand and watch them fall, run all the way to the sill where they disappear. I touch the glass and my hand comes away wet from the fog. My hand leaves no hand-mark on the windowpane. I smear the foggy glass with my hand and then put my wet hand under my pajamas and touch my stomach. My hand is cold and wet but doesn't get warm fast. Then I take it away.

Where I've touched my stomach feels like me but doesn't feel like me. My hand feels like mine but doesn't feel like mine.

All at once, I am terribly afraid. There is something in what is happening that I should know. There is something I should know inside, deep inside, and I don't know what it is. It is moving through my mouth, my eyes, my neck, my shoulders, my arms, and into the palm of my hand, this one hand that holds the wet and cold that doesn't turn warm right away. I think I am more than my mouth and eyes and neck and shoulders and arms and hands.

Suddenly, I am alive in my hand, all of me is a breathing hand. Something has grabbed my breath, and I am rushing into my hand. I want to wake up. I want to wake up and not be in my hand anymore.

I call out to Momma, but she is too far away. I hold my teeth tight and stretch my lips wide against my cheeks. I can't open my mouth. My breath is coming out fast and quick, and I can't stop it. I squirm in my hand to get free. I want to run from my hand, back to Momma, but I don't know where she is. I am the breath of my stomach and my legs and ankles and feet. I am breath everywhere. I am my hand that is my body, and I am the air that is breathing outside of me and inside of me and the breath in Momma who is sleeping in our bed, far, far away.

I am alive with the breath of everything. I am floating, I am floating up and away, flying up and up, toward heaven when I come to life with Momma shaking me awake.

"Shike, Shike, you're dreaming, honey, wake up, wake up."

I fall back against her stomach and my pillow. Little whimpering sounds come out of my mouth. I can't stop them. Then I am crying against Momma who holds me against her and tells me over and over that everything is all right, everything is all right.

Slowly, I come back to being with Momma in our bed.

"Oh, honey," she says, sitting up a little. "Your hand is wet and cold, how did you get so... wet, so cold? Honey, are you all right?" She stares at my hand a little while, then wipes it dry with her house dress. She looks across the room as she says, "Did you walk to the window to see the rain?"

She lowers herself back into the bed, pulling me to her.

I shake my head a little. "I've been sleeping all the time."

I don't think she hears me, but she asks, "Until your nightmare?"

I nod the back of my head against her chest.

After Momma has talked me awake, dried my hand and pulled me to her, I wait until I hear her sleeping again.

I hold out my hand and look at it. I look at the window and try to find smears and river marks on the pane but see only the rain splashing on the clear glass from the outside.

Suddenly, I want to look over the side of the bed, and when I do, I see my pajama bottoms in a pile on the floor. Momma didn't notice I was in bed without them, and I am asleep again before I can pick them up and put them back on.

HOME AT CHURCH

1.

April, 1943

"**H**ERE'S NOT WHERE WE'RE GONNA live forever so you can put up with it until—" Daddy doesn't finish what he's saying to me because Momma finishes for him.

"Until we say so." Her lips are tight.

We're at the table except for Teddy who's in his high chair next to Momma. I'm sitting next to Daddy. We've moved into the church basement because of Simon Nichols, and I'm mad at him and Daddy for it. It's not living in a church basement, our church's basement, that's so upsetting. It's that it's only "temporary," a good word for Daddy, a bad word for Momma. Temporary means it's not going to last, which means moving again, and maybe again and again. Temporary housing is "the way of the world these days," Daddy says. I hate the world and its "progress living." Progress living is "living one day at a time," Momma says. "Progress means 'moving forward,'" she's told me. "Big laugh on everybody." I know about moving, by now. I know we aren't going to stay here. They don't need to tell me this over and over.

We've moved from Clearview to Aileen, and in Aileen, from the warehouse to Hilliar's upstairs garage apartment, then downstairs into the old people's garage apartment, when they moved out, and now that we're in Hopewell, it's the church basement until we can get something else, when and where that can be. I look around, and all I see are boxes piled high along the cement walls, and even an idiot knows this is how we will live for a long time, just like we did in the Aileen warehouse. We thought we'd live there only a little while, and it turned into forever and a day.

The cement blocks make the rooms cooler, and I'll be grateful for that come summertime, Daddy tells me, so he knows we aren't getting out of here soon. But in the same breath, he says that living here is only temporary, and when, not if, we move—in a few weeks, a month or two, at the most—I'll get to start school, permanently, and that's a promise.

I don't know why we didn't stay where we were until they found a house in Hopewell, but when Daddy wasn't around, Momma told me she felt like we had to do something soon, because she couldn't stay in Aileen with Daddy's friggin' boss a minute longer than necessary.

"That man simply wasn't proper. But that's nothing you need mention to your father. He's perfectly convinced that the man was well-intending. Ha. I happen to personally know otherwise. It was far too uncomfortable at night there, when your daddy wasn't home, when he had to work after dark."

Now Daddy reaches over and takes my hand. "Your supper's not getting eaten, Shike, but okay, here's what you need to know. I'm going to make this clear just one more time, okay? We've told you this already—"

"Over and over," Momma interrupts. "It's enough, Vern. She knows."

Daddy acts like Momma hasn't said anything. "—but I think you don't understand that we're not in this basement for good. It's to get us outta of a sitchawation—"

"Sit*u*ation," Momma corrects him.

He looks up at her with mean, dark eyes. Daddy's eyes are blue, but now they shine almost black. "Indigo," Momma says, when he's mad, and then she laughs.

"I know 'temporary,'" I shout at him. "But no house is ever gonna happen."

"Watch your mouth," Momma says.

"It will happen." Daddy glances at Momma and away. "It's just that we don't know when."

"Where is it?" I ask. Momma wants to reach over and slap me. I see it in her eyes.

"We don't know yet, like I've been telling you. But we'll find one, and whichever one it is, it'll be permanent, where we stay and not move again. I'll see to that."

Daddy reaches over and shakes me back and forth a little with his hand on my shoulder. "Now, do you understand?"

He's told me all this so many times before I have it memorized. He doesn't want me to answer. He wants me to nod and eat. He taps the plate of hamburgers he made in a hurry after he got home, while Momma was tending to Teddy in his highchair.

"Stop the pestering, Shike. I mean it," Momma says. "Believe me, you're going to school as soon as the doors open because I'm gonna push you out the door myself. God knows, I'd do it tonight, but it's only April, and school doesn't start for you until... well, I don't know, for sure, what day, but I'll take you on that day, which is... oh Lord, Vernon, help me out, here, when's the first day after Labor Day?"

Daddy looks around as though there's a calendar hanging somewhere on the empty cement block walls. He grins. "It's the first school day after Labor Day is when it is."

"You're a big help!" She pushes her hair out of her face. "It's on a Tuesday, is that right? Oh, it's too many days for me to count, Shike, and I shouldn't have to." Momma whirls around, looking at nothing and, then, back at me. "I wrote it down, so stop worrying about it. It'll be in the paper when the time comes. We'll go then."

Momma changes real fast from being mad to being almost sad. "Look, I'm just tired," she says to me. "I don't know what my name is, let alone what day it is."

Daddy stops eating his hamburger, lays it down on his plate, and looks around for something to wipe his hands on. He walks to the counter on the back wall by the sink and wipes his mouth and hands on a towel and comes back, pulling something out of his back pocket. "Just a minute."

"It doesn't matter," Momma says to Daddy, like I'm not there, but then glares at me. "Shike, this is crazy, your incessant asking about school and hoping I'll fix it so you can know for certain about when and where."

Daddy clears his throat. He's holding a small calendar in his hand. He runs his finger down, stops and says, "Ah. Shike, you'll be home all day for your Mother's birthday because school won't be started yet. See, it's a good thing, this waiting you have to do. School will start on Tuesday, September seventh." He holds the calendar out for me to see, then turns some pages, flips it over to show Momma her birthday circled in red.

Momma looks up and stops feeding Teddy, for a little bit, to see. "Well, I'll be, circled and all!"

Daddy asks, "And what number might this one be?"

Momma says, "You have to ask?"

"No," Daddy says, putting his wallet calendar back in its sleeve and his wallet back into his pocket. "I know. I'm just wondering if you do."

"Very funny." When Daddy sits back down and picks up his hamburger to take a bite, she says, "Well?"

"Well, what?" His hamburger is filling his mouth, so he keeps it from falling out with his fingers. "What?" But then, after he's swallowed, he grins. "Twenty-five. You see, I do know."

"How do you remember this, I'm wondering?"

"I keep track of you and your numbers," Daddy says.

Momma stops messing with Teddy's food dish, her fingers up in the air, greasy with hamburger meat. Teddy opens his mouth and tries to grab Momma's hand with one of his. "No, Teddy, here, use your spoon." She puts his spoon in his fist. "You subtracted, didn't you, the fast thinker you are!" She grins at Daddy.

Daddy grins back at her and swallows big.

"Didn't you? You subtracted. I'm on to your ways, Vernon Leland Jantz."

"How did he do it?" I ask.

"Something you're gonna learn in school, just not with numbers that high at first." Daddy tells me.

"Oh thanks a lot," Momma says grinning, busy again with Teddy.

Daddy picks up a pickle slice that's fallen out of his hamburger. Daddy's made Mennonite hamburgers for supper from a recipe Momma wrote down from Gramma Dirks's cookbook the last time we visited their Shirly farm.

"Okay, Momma," she said to Gramma Dirks, "now all I have to do is figure out how to divide a bucket of lard and a tub of ground beef to feed four instead of fifty!" They both laughed big. Mennonite hamburgers drip down your arm with grease and have onions already mixed up in them. You're never supposed to put pickles with them or pick them up to eat them but Daddy does both. The rest of us use forks and cut them up to eat a piece at a time. We eat our pickles on the side. Daddy calls Mennonite hamburgers, Mennonite Sloppy Joes.

"I want to read," I tell them both.

Daddy says. "Yeah, we know. So you can keep your mother and me busy explaining the meanings of even more words."

"Words like 'disgruntled' and 'dissatisfied,'" Momma says, feeding Teddy again.

"I will *not!*" I say. I know what those words mean, but I don't know what she's telling Daddy about me and them.

Daddy holds up his hands, sees that they are greasy again, and goes to the counter, this time bringing back the towel with him that he knows Momma doesn't want him to use for his napkin. He puts it over his leg carefully and pushes his plate back when he's done. I think Momma will tell him she doesn't like him using the towel this way, but she doesn't.

"What your mother is trying to get me to do, Shike," he says, leaning over and wiping my fingers with his towel, "is explain why I can remember her birthday number this year. And she thinks it's a matter of subtraction—me taking my age and subtracting nine from it because your mother is nine years younger than I am." Daddy holds up his hand. "Subtraction is a matter of taking a number and counting backwards until you get the sum you're looking for."

"What?" Momma's voice sounds a little like music. "Don't listen to him, Shike. He'll only make matters worse for you at school. Subtracting is...." Momma waits, trying to figure out how to explain it to me.

Daddy says, "Ha, hum, not so easy is it?"

"Well, maybe not for you, just let me gather my thoughts a minute."

"Go on," Daddy says. "We're all ears. I'm only here to learn!"

"Oh shut up, Vern," Momma says, but she isn't really mad. "Okay, Shike, you begin with a number in mind—choose a number."

"Four," I say.

"Okay four," she says. "Now let's say you want to take two away from that, from four." I nod. "Okay, you're gonna take two from four, you got that?"

I look at Daddy, and he is grinning. He winks at me and taps my arm and says, "Two from four, we got that, right?"

Momma stares at him. I'd like to tear your head off, Momma's eyes are saying. But she says real nice and sweet, looking only at me, "Okay, what the difference is between adding and subtracting is the difference between whether you make more of something or less of something."

Daddy leans back in his folding chair and folds his hands over his stomach and sighs.

"Vernon, I'm not going on with this unless you stop being holier-than-thou over it. You had your turn, now, let me try."

Daddy just says "ah" again and squeaks a little on his chair as he moves, folding his hands in front of him on the table like he's about to pray.

"Try away!"

"So," she begins, "say, you have four and you want to take two away—"

"It's two."

"Ah, I see. And subtracting two from four?"

"It's two."

"Are you just saying the same answer over and over?"

Daddy taps my plate. "I think what your mother wants to know is if you know what subtraction means. Do you know?"

"Yes," I pick up the last of my hamburger like Daddy did, but it falls apart. Now I'm going to have to eat it in wads with my fingers. My hands are so greasy I just leave them there, fingers over my plate. Momma tells me to wipe my hands on Daddy's towel, then use my fork. I stare at her.

"It's okay," Daddy says, handing me the towel. "So did your mother teach you what subtraction is or did you get your answer from your Grampa Dirks?" he asks.

I look at him without answering. I want to tell him Grampa and me memorized together, but I wait to see what Momma wants to say.

"She wants to eat her hamburger before it gets cold, right, Shike?"

I nod.

"Oh, no, you don't," Daddy says, only looking at me. "You know what a test is, Shike? You know you'll have to take tests in school to see if you know what you've learned, otherwise, your teacher wouldn't know if you really got it right. So what is—"

"Four minus two is what, Shike?" Momma asks.

"Two." I've already said twice, but I say it again.

Momma looks at Daddy and says, "See, she knows."

Daddy starts to say something, but Momma asks me, "And what is the sum of four and two?" She adds real quick, "The sum is what the final answer is, is all."

"Six," I say.

"You see, she knows how to add and subtract." Momma stares at Daddy and says, "Six. Six is the right answer. So much for your test."

"Shike," Daddy leans over toward me and my plate. "What's subtraction?"

Momma says. "That's too hard for her, the idea of subtraction. She has to learn her tables before she can—"

"Tables?" I don't know tables. "What's tables?" I look down.

"Not like table, table, not like this table," Momma puts her pointer finger on the folding table we're using for our supper and taps it a little. Our dining room table sits against the side wall with boxes on it. "In school, you'll have charts with all your addition and subtraction numbers on them."

I nod.

"So you know then." She nods at Daddy. "They call those charts "tables," sometimes. Anyhow, you memorize what's on them so you can always know things like four plus two equals six and that four minus two is two, just like you're remembering them now. Only in second and third grade, you're gonna have to do really big numbers, and, in order to do that, you have to understand what addition and subtraction mean. How to use them as a general principle, you see?"

I nod and finish eating my hamburger in pieces, slowly with my fork.

Momma starts to tell me more, but Daddy says, real fast, "Shike, pick any number you want again, only make it bigger, like twelve or twenty, something like that."

Momma looks up, quick. "What're you doing, Vern? What're you *really* doing?"

"Just pick one," Daddy says, looking at me close. "Just do this one more."

"Twelve," I say fast, I can't think of anything else.

"This isn't right, Vern," Momma says, standing up. "And you know it." She starts to pick up Teddy's plate, but she stands, waits and watches Daddy.

Daddy acts like she isn't there. "Okay, now think of another number, one that's like twelve, big like that, with two numbers in it."

I don't want Momma to say anything so I say, "Twenty."

"Okay, now, what's twenty minus twelve?" Daddy looks at me with a little smile on his face as he moves his cup, back and forth, slowly across the table. I listen to it scrape, back and forth and back and forth. "Well?" he asks after a minute.

I know the answer, but if I say they'll fight because they're mad at each other. They each want to win about me and numbers.

I start to say, "eight," but I wait too long. All at once, Teddy's plate flies past my ear and toward Daddy's face. He ducks, and it hits the cement wall with a loud crash, three pieces hitting the floor, one of them rolling next to my foot. We all stare at the wall like the plate is there still in one piece.

Then Momma says, "All right, Vernon. You've had your fun at Shike and my expense, so, now, just stop. I know what you're doing, and you know what you're doing, but she doesn't, and it's not fair."

"What?" Daddy acts like he doesn't know what she's talking about, but I can tell he does. Now he's really mad. He gets up and starts to leave the table.

"Oh, no, you don't," Momma says. "Don't you dare go. We're having this out right here and now."

"Eight," I shout. "Grampa and me are already at one hundred."

Both Momma and Daddy stop and stare at me. "He's told me that once you know twenty, you can go to a hundred easy. It's just a bunch of tens with one to nine in between."

But I don't want to add and subtract anymore. I want to go back to the Momma birthday number and start again so we won't fight. For one minute everything is very still, nobody moves.

"So why didn't you say so?" Momma asks. The whole room feels like it's going to explode.

I look at Teddy. His face is scrunching up like he's getting ready to cry, but he doesn't. He looks at me, and then Momma, and then me, and then at Daddy. He just looks with his scrunched-up face and waits, and then like a shot out of a cannon, he throws his spoon hard. It hits the table and bounces all the way across until it falls to the floor next to Daddy. Teddy still doesn't cry, even though he has tears in his eyes. He looks at me and kinda laughs. I'm the one that starts to cry. I stand up and walk past Daddy, pick up Teddy's spoon, and walk it back to his highchair. I try to cry without making any sound. I start to say to Teddy, "Hello, Little Man," like Daddy does, but I hear somebody else say, "Hello, hello," like I've said it out loud, and it's ringing in my ears.

"Anybody home?" Simon Nichols asks, opening the basement screen door and walking in.

2.

Same time, same place

SIMON NICHOLS LOOKS AROUND THE room and knows something bad has happened, but he says with a smile, "The door was open, I'm sorry, should I have knocked?"

Daddy stands up so quick, he almost knocks over his chair.

"No, no." Momma's voice is shaking and very loud. When Simon Nichols looks down at the broken pieces of Teddy's plate lying against the wall and behind my folding chair, Momma says, "We just had a little dispute over... school."

Simon Nichols looks at me. "Are you worried about school? Yes, I bet you are. I can see how you would be." He walks over to where I'm standing and bends over to look me in my face. I'm not crying anymore, but my cheeks are wet, so I wipe them with my skirt. "Here," he says, handing me his clean handkerchief. It's very white with letters in the corner in blue thread. "Not a nose's been on it, yet."

He pulls me up out of my chair and hugs me against his legs like Daddy does. "I've been doing a little of that myself lately, so I carry a few extras with me, just in case. It's amazing how a clean hanky can wipe away the tears, at least for a little while. Give it a try."

I put my eyes in his hanky that smells like Clorox and Ivory Snow, like our clean bath towels. Simon Nichols walks to Daddy and shakes his hand. I want to be mad at him, but I can't with his hanky in my hand.

"I really didn't mean to barge in like this. I just dropped by to see if everything was all right. I couldn't make it today, until now."

"How's Edna?" Momma asks.

"She's as good as she can be, under the circumstances. Thanks, Darlene. Sylvia's leaving from Chicago tomorrow, if she can get off that soon from her job. The drive's at least two days, so she'll not make Sunday services. Well, all that's beside the point, isn't it? She wouldn't, anyway. It's not an important point, probably, but nonetheless…." Simon Nichols looks around, like he'd like to sit down but doesn't know where. He looks very old, like he might, all at once, fall over. He's got white hair, is skinny but much taller than Daddy.

Momma starts to say more, but Simon Nichols speaks first. "I only have a minute, really. I wanted to drop by to see if there's anything I can do or anything you need but also to invite you to dinner one night at the beginning of the week, say Monday or Tuesday?"

"Oh, Simon, that's so generous, but I don't know. Seems to me you have about all you can handle in your house right now. We don't want you to feel that since we've moved to the church, you need to—"

"Glynda Faye absolutely insisted on sending this invitation along. She says to tell you that Edna would welcome your company, and she does. I asked her myself. She was very excited about your coming over. It would cheer her up from her hard-to-hear news, and it'll give you a chance to meet Sylvia—that's if she arrives in time—and learn to know a bit more about Hopewell. I mean, the town. I promise we won't talk church." The hard-to-hear news is that Edna Nichols has cancer. Reverend Classen announced it in church, so we could all pray for her. Momma and Daddy have said, "colon cancer," and mentioned her in our prayers at big meals.

Simon Nichols turns to Daddy and smiles, even laughs a little. Looking at Momma he says, "Here's how Glynda Faye put it to me, 'Don't you dare come home without an acceptance to supper.' Glynda Faye can have a stubborn streak, so, let me put it another way, if it's more of a help than a hindrance, then we'd like for you to come one night this next week for dinner. There. Leaves a little wiggle room if you feel you can't get away right now." Simon Nichols looks at me and smiles. "You know about wiggle room?" I shake my head. "It's where your toes go to squirm around in your shoes. See if your mother agrees with that!"

"We'd like to come very much. You tell us the evening, the time, and what I can bring, and we'll be there."

"Wonderful," Simon Nichols says, happy that Momma says yes. "That's wonderful. I'll settle the day and time with Glynda Faye, and one of us will get back to you very soon." He looks around again, especially at the boxes.

All at once, Momma is very flustered. "Oh, where are our manners. Sit down, Simon, please, please sit down." She reaches for her folding chair, but Daddy says, "No, I'll get it, Darlene," and carries a folding chair leaning against the wall over to where Simon Nichols is standing.

"Vernon, if you place the chair by the table, we'll offer a cup of coffee to Simon." While Daddy puts the chair next to the table near Simon Nichols, Momma hurries to the stove to make more coffee.

Simon Nichols raises his voice more than he usually does. "No, no, Darlene." He reaches out his arm like Moses on the picture cards I look at in Sunday School class, the one where Moses is parting the Great Sea. Simon Nichols lowers his voice and arm and sort of laughs. "I'm sure your coffee is the best ever made in the church basement, but, believe me when I tell you, I'm sloshing now when I walk! Glynda Faye has this idea that coffee is going to solve any sad feelings I'm having about Edna. And I have this idea that I can't refuse when she keeps filling my cup without hurting her feelings. Now, I'm wondering if I'm ever going to sleep again, less from the sadness in our house, than from the amount of caffeine pumping through my veins."

Momma walks back to the table and takes Teddy, who's wanting out of his highchair. She rocks him, back and forth. Simon Nichols still hasn't sat down. "Again, Simon, we are so sorry—"

Simon Nichols raises his hand. "Thank you, Darlene."

Everybody just sort of stands there, Momma rocking Teddy, Daddy's hands over the back of his chair, Teddy sniveling like he's missed supper, and me waiting and wanting to push Simon Nichols down in his chair so we can go on.

All at once he says, "How're things going?" as though he just came through the door. But he doesn't wait for an answer. He looks at me. "We have to get this school business out of the way before anything else. You're probably thinking that since you don't live in a proper house or apartment like the other kids, there's not going to be a school bus route that comes past the church. Well, I looked into this and found out that if you are still living in the basement—which I must say is highly unlikely as we have church members looking for you another place to live—you will be registered in Thomas Jefferson Elementary School only three blocks from here."

He hands Momma a card he's pulled out of his wallet. "Registration is from seven forty-five in the morning to two thirty in the afternoon on the days on the card, at which time you will automatically be signed up for ration stamps through that school. They'll be transferred here from Aileen for the whole family." Simon Nichols looks up at Daddy, then back at me. "They'll be giving those out to you, at school, every month through your teacher. And then the first day after Labor Day, you'll report to the room assigned to you for that school. They'll show you which room it is when you register. The only other thing you need to know is where the school is. Have you seen it yet?"

I shake my head. Momma nudges me with her hand and says, "Give Mr. Nichols his handkerchief back, and say 'thank you,' Shike." I hold out the hanky.

"I tell you what, I'll make an exchange. You give me my hanky, and I'll give you this map of how to find your school. Since it's only three blocks from here, once your Mother knows the way, you can easily walk there, I'm sure. The only problem is crossing Van Buren Street which in the morning and afternoon can be kind of busy. So you'll have to decide on that with your parents."

"Say 'thank you,' Shike." Momma says, but Daddy beats me to it.

"We surely do thank you for this, Simon."

"It was no bother at all. I enjoyed talking with the folks at Thomas Jefferson. Saves you the trouble, as I see it. Well, I must be going back. Glynda Faye doesn't trust me when I'm around you two, too long. She'll think I've decided to live in the basement myself. She tends to think I live at the church as it is. Her last instruction when I left the house was, to quote, 'Stay only as long as you need to. They're busy. Don't move in for a week.'"

We all walk Simon Nichols to the back door, and Momma says goodbye.

Simon Nichols gives her a hug, even with Teddy in her arms, and she laughs a little bit, embarrassed-like. Simon Nichols says, "Well, then... until... soon."

Momma turns on the parking lot light, and Daddy walks Simon Nichols to his car. Daddy doesn't come back for a long time. When he does, he looks at Momma while he stands by the door.

"The man never ceases to amaze me. I don't know what to make of all this. Seems he may have an arrangement for us to have a house. He knows a man who has one that might be available if the people living there leave when they say they will." He looks at Momma's face and then at me. "But we can't get too hopeful, he says, because everybody's hanging on to their rentals, because they're scared they won't find another place until they do, and the landlords push for the most they can get every time they change renters. It could be out of our reach." Daddy says this like Momma doesn't know about houses that are out of our reach.

"What house?" Momma doesn't believe in the house Simon Nichols found for us.

"Well, that's the thing, but we may not have a choice."

"Where?" Momma isn't mad. She's just tired and short-tempered. Grampa Dirks explained short-tempered and ill-tempered to me. When I asked him about "tempered," he told me it's like temperature, how hot or cold you are with feelings, how mad or glad you are. Ill-tempered is mad and bad and short-tempered is quick mad and bad.

Daddy looks at Momma fast and then shrugs. "It's not going to come up anyway, Darlene. Well, I'm pretty sure not any time soon. So don't worry about it until we have to worry about it."

Now Momma is short and ill-tempered. "What house, Vernon?"

"It's south off Randolph." Daddy's not looking at her.

"But that's... that's colored town, Vernon." She waits a minute, then looks at me like it's my fault. But she says, "Oh no, not a move from here, and then, a move from there. We can't live there permanently, for godssakes. And what about Shike's school? No buses will come for white kids from there."

"He didn't say we had to move right away. We've got until the end of July. But beyond this, it could be a problem."

"What kind of problem? What aren't you telling me about all this?" Momma throws her free arm out and around and then jerks Teddy to her other arm so fast his head bounces back and then forward. He looks up into her face so she rocks him up and down. "I see a problem in this from start to finish, but there's something else, isn't there? What about July? We have to be out of here by July?"

"Ervin's...." Daddy sits down so hard I think the folding chair will break. "He's retiring, Darlene."

Momma stands, keeps rocking Teddy, bouncing him up and down, up and down. He's getting heavy for her, and he wants out of her arms. He starts sliding down, so she pushes him against her stomach, but he keeps sliding, so she sits in a folding chair by Daddy and stands Teddy on the floor by her legs, holding him with her hands against his back.

"Retiring?" Teddy tries to crawl-walk away, but Momma grabs him by the straps of his jumper suit. "When?"

"Nobody knows yet. Simon says by the end of the year. It's real sudden because there's some health problems with him. He didn't say what, because he doesn't feel free to yet, but Ervin's got to take it easy. I'm guessing it's his heart. Anyway, they'll need the basement for retirement festivities—dinners and the like."

"But that's the end of the year. Why July, then?"

"The incoming pastor—which hasn't been decided yet, of course—but whoever it is may need to stay in the basement while the Classens get out of the parsonage."

Momma doesn't know what to say. She sits and looks around at all the boxes on tables and the floor, and when she looks back at Daddy she has tears in her eyes. "It never stops, does it?" she says, real soft. "How many times can we move, Vernon, and still feel like we can go on? Why are we just hearing about this? Now? It's what Simon came about, wasn't it? What he really was here for."

Daddy waits and throws his hands in the air. "I don't know, Darlene but doesn't seem like we have a choice one way or the other. He claims he just heard and that Ervin has only decided and told him a day or two ago."

"What was all that about Shike's school, then? Acting like she could go from here to Thomas Jefferson in September when he knew all along that we might have to be out by July? He was lying is what he was."

"I think he wanted to put Shike's mind at ease, knowing that regardless, there is always a way to get to school. I dunno, Darlene. He said there were lots of variables is what he said about the circumstances. We very well might be here in September, if Ervin changes his mind, if the new minister finds a house, if—"

"If, if, if. Always the ifs. I'd call this an 'iffy' situation all around, wouldn't you?" Momma glances around at all the boxes. "So much for unpacking."

Momma and Daddy sit very still. Momma doesn't try to get Teddy when he crawls under the table and grabs his rubber ball, throws it and crawls after it. I sit down in a chair and wait. I don't move a muscle. I want to kick my legs back and forth to tease Teddy, but I know not to move a muscle.

"Where off Randolph?"

Daddy sighs. "Let's not talk about this now, Darlene. It probably won't even be necessary. Somebody else in the congregation could find something—"

"Where off Randolph, Vernon?"

Daddy sighs and squints his eyes. When he opens them, he says, "It's on the edge, not deep into... other streets. It's off Randolph two blocks, is all. Other whites will be living around us. In fact..." Daddy hesitates and stops.

Momma's eyes are so big I think they will pop out of her head. "It's a duplex. Okay, let me get this straight. Simon Nichols, the great white father of us all, is willing to get us a duplex in colored town? "

"It's all there is right now, Darlene, and, by what he says, we'd be lucky to have it."

Momma's eyes are now so small I think she will close them and they will disappear. "Tell me I'm dreaming, that this is all a nightmare that will go away when I open my eyes." She holds her eyes shut real tight and listens to what Daddy says next.

"Actually, now that your eyes are closed, Darlene, I'll tell you the good part. It is a duplex, but the other side is a nice, white newlywed couple."

When Momma opens her eyes, she is killing Daddy with her looks, but she speaks so fast I think she is joking. "Tell him we'll take it, first chance he has to get it for us."

MOMMA,
GOD,
AND
GRAMPA
DIRKS

June, 1943

GRAMPA DIRKS IS DRIVING HIS gray Ford through the streets of Hopewell, his hand on the side window frame, his fingers drumming a tune. He's singing in his head. He moves his lips a little, looks at me and smiles, then drums his fingers some more on the window frame, looking out the windshield. When he moves his lips again he sings soft, to himself.

Momma sings "I've Got You Under My Skin" with the radio. She sings with the woman singer and the band. She tells me every single time it's Frances Langford with Jimmy Dorsey. The first time she was singing it, I told her I liked the band. "No, no, the Jimmy Dorsey Orchestra." she said. "This very song hit the radios right after me and your daddy got married in Kansas in August of '36." Momma always sings too many "deep, deep, deep's" so she gets behind and has to sing words together fast to catch up.

I don't know what Grampa Dirks is singing because I can't hear all the words. He sings, "duck and geese better scurry" and "fringe on top." He doesn't remember I'm on the front seat with him. He's looking out over the hood like he's all by himself, but I know he's happy he's taking me for a drive in his new used car. When Daddy first saw what Grampa Dirks had bought—them standing in the driveway of Grampa and Gramma Dirks's farm in Shirly—he shook his head and said, "Fords are the most cold-blooded animals on the face of the earth. What did you go off and do that for? I probably coulda got you a deal on a Dodge or Plymouth through people Dad knows in Clearview. Now you're gonna be pleadin' for your old crank-and-run engine when temperature drops below freezing."

Grampa bought a used car because there aren't any new ones to be had. Daddy says "to be had this" and "to be had that." So does Momma. She says, "nothing to be done, nothing to be had." When I asked Daddy about "to be hads," he said it meant "things are gettin' scarcer and scarcer."

I don't think Grampa Dirks knows where we're going. It's Saturday, and Gramma is helping Momma with Teddy. I asked Daddy why Momma couldn't get up. "She seems to be sicker and sicker these days. I don't know what the problem is and neither do people who know these things a helluva lot better than I do. Get yourself up and about, because I gotta work today, and we've gotta take you out to the farm or get your grandpa and grandma over here. At the very least, Darlene's mother."

I want to ask Grampa Dirks about Momma, but I'm not sure when I can because he's "lost to himself." That's what Daddy tells me. "Whalen's the kinda fellah who can get totally lost to himself. He'll be thinking along in his head and what he doesn't realize is that you aren't in his head with him. All at once he'll start in on something like you've been listening to what he's been thinking all along. Always sets me back."

"You probably should sit down," Grampa tells me after a while. "If I have to make a sudden stop you could be a catastrophe."

"That's when something terrible happens."

"That's right, Shike. It means a disaster, a horrible accident. We don't want that on our day out and about."

"Do we have gas?"

"Course we have gas or we couldn't go. Oh, you mean do we have enough gas. Well, that's a good question." Grampa Dirks squints, looks at the gauge. "Yup, I told the man to fill 'er up, and he did. But then I shot my rations for the week—two weeks, to be truthful—so we better decide here pretty soon where we're gonna land. How's about the park? I have baloney sandwiches from your grandmother and some potato salad. I even remembered to bring plates and forks. We'll eat our lunch and then watch 'em swim, how about that?"

"Okay."

"I think she threw in a pickled peach for you and some cottage cheese for me. I know we have peanut butter cookies. Your grandmother's one resourceful woman. She can bake when there's a teaspoon of not-much and another teaspoon of less-than-that, and whatever comes out of her oven smells like high-priced everything at the store and tastes like she's chief baker for the White House!"

I laugh and can't keep my legs still on the seat. Momma wouldn't let me wear my overalls today, but Grampa doesn't care if I climb all over things in my dress.

It takes Grampa a long time to set up our picnic even with my help. He won't let me run back to the car to get the basket he left on the back seat. He wants to do it while I sit where he can see me and not have me running around to the swings or slides. Once we have our lunch spread out, everything on one of Momma's old tablecloths and the food on our plates, Grampa Dirks picks up his fork and starts right in. He doesn't pray, and I'm glad because I don't want to take the time. He's sitting across from me.

He says, like he's talking newspapers with Daddy, "The rich always profit during hard times. Guess who made the thirties world-wide economic depression? Now guess who's gettin' us outta it with this war?"

Daddy tells Momma that Grampa thinks out loud most of the time. "The man spends so much time reading and listening, that he forgets there are real people around him. But I can't complain too much. I learn a lot just keeping my ears open."

Grampa has told me before about capitalists and how the rich are richer and how they made war to make everything better for themselves. He's probably telling me this morning's headlines from The Hopewell Herald. I can read but not the newspaper yet, so I wait and listen. Daddy reads the headlines to me sometimes before he starts the evening news in his sofa chair. And then all at once I know who Grampa's talking about—who got us in and who got us out—who made the war. I know the answer to this morning's rich is richer, so I say, "Roosevelt." I say Rose-a-velt like Grampa does, not like Daddy's Roose-a-velt.

"You know your politics, Little Lady." He laughs. "It's your silver-tongued, shifty-eyed, money-grabbing Captains of Industry and the politicians who're riding in their hip pockets, that's who, well, anyway the ones who're left after all the suicides. But they aren't the ones getting us out, I can tell you that. Our boys with their blood, sweat, and tears are doing the job and all around the globe."

Suicides are when you kill yourself, but I'm not sure about rash. I heard Daddy talking to Grampa Dirks when he didn't know I was listening. He told him he worries about Momma and suicide. I've heard him say to Momma, "Promise you aren't gonna do anything rash, Darlene. Because I can't be worried all day at work when I'm away from here. Think of the kids."

"What's rash?"

"Wwhaaat? A rash? Where in the world did that come from?" But he doesn't let me tell. He says, "A rash is when you get—" and a car driving into the parking lot honks real loud. Grampa turns and looks for a minute. He watches a colored boy almost get hit when he runs in front of a car. When the car comes to a stop in the spot with a jerk, the driver gets out and yells, "You little nigger bastard."

The colored boy is running as hard as he can down the street. Grampa Dirks says soft, still watching the driver, "What's that kid doin' on this side of the park? He's gonna end up gettin' himself in trouble. Just what we need, another incident at Highland Park!"

Grampa Dirks looks over at me and asks real careful, breathing kind of hard through of his nose. He's still upset. I'm not sure if it's about the colored kid or me. "Do you have a rash? Is that it? Where, honey?"

"No. I don't know. What's a rash?"

"It's when you have little red bumps all over your skin, but you know what a rash is by now, right? And hives and chigger—"

"Hives are bees, their houses."

"Well, hives are bees houses all right but...." He smiles at me. "Well, here we are, you and me, with language tricks, again. Remember I told you that words can have more than one meaning. Hives are also red bumps you get when you're allergic to some foods, like some people get hives when they eat strawberries. But what's this business about rash? You think you have a—"

"No, not me. Momma."

"Your Mother has a rash?"

I nod. "Daddy asked Momma to not have any. He made her promise."

Grampa Dirks is quiet, staring out at the bridge and creek running through Highland Park. Some colored boys are playing with a dog on their side of the park, throwing it a stick that it chases and brings back to them.

"Honey, I don't know what you mean. What did your daddy say exactly? Can you remember?"

"He said, 'Darlene, don't do any rash, promise me,'" I say.

When I look at Grampa Dirks, he has a little smile on his face. But then he gets very serious. He says, "Shike, honey, I think you heard your daddy telling your mother not to... oh God... let's see. Okay, how about this, sometimes rash means not giving any thought to our actions. It means not thinking carefully before doing something that can hurt yourself or others. Did you overhear your daddy talking with me about your mother the other day?"

I nod. "He's worried about her doing rash."

"Well, let's see what we can do to make this easier in your mind."

Grampa starts to eat his sandwich, then puts it down, wipes his mouth and rubs his hands together. "Okay, here's what I want to tell you, Shike. Your mother is a head-strong girl. She's always been willful, wanting her own way, and when she was growing up, we had our difficulties. I'm talking about her and me. I wasn't known for my patience when my kids were little like you are now, when they were growing up. I didn't take the time to explain things. I didn't talk to them much, well, not at all really, unless I was telling them what to do or not to do. I didn't... well, I lost my temper. I lost my temper a lot."

"Daddy does."

"I'm sure he does. He's got quite a load to carry these days. Your daddy and I talk, and I think I pretty much know what he's thinking when he told your mother what he did, about not doing anything rash. What he meant by that, I'm sure, is that he didn't want her to say or do something she would be sorry for later."

"Is Momma sick?" I ask. "She says she's sick. Daddy says she's getting sicker and sicker."

"I don't know how to answer that, Shike. It would appear something's the matter with her, but she's been to her doctor and several others as well. And so far they haven't been able to find anything wrong with her. But she says she's tired most of the time, and she stays in bed when your grandmother and I think she should be up and around. I can't say she's doing that on purpose, but it doesn't help for her not to do her housework. After a while when you sit and lie around all the time, you lose your get-up-and-go." Grampa waits a little bit while he chews his sandwich and moves his potato salad around with his fork. "And the other side of this is that she does get up sometimes and go. She's up, has lots of energy, wants to go everywhere, do everything. But she always seems to eventually end up right back in bed. We don't know what to make of it."

"Daddy tells her to get up and start doing something right now."

"Uh-huh. And does she listen to what he says?"

"Sometimes she does, I guess but, most of the time, she only lays in her bed and cries."

"Well, I have my own thoughts about this, but I don't know how to cure her, and when your daddy comes to me, I just listen to him while he tries to figure out what to do next. He doesn't know what's the matter with her, either. What do you think?"

"I think she's mad… mostly."

Grampa laughs, pats my arm, and coughs off to the side of his bench. He drinks some water he brought in a jar that he poured into two glasses for us.

"I'm sorry, Shike. Your mother's predicament isn't funny. It's just that you've come up with something similar to what I've been thinking myself. Sometimes, I think she's just mad, just mad at the world, only I wouldn't've thought to say it so directly. But the question then becomes why does she feel this way? Have you ever asked her?"

"She says, 'find someplace else to be.' Daddy tells me, too. When they're really mad, they say, 'Get lost, over with Teddy.'"

Grampa nods at me, but before he does, he grits his teeth together. He picks up his sandwich and takes a bite and chews. "You know your Daddy loves your mother, loves you all, don't you, Shike? He's just overcome by what's happening with your mother, with his world. You'll have to be patient with him, but, if something happens that isn't… that seems bad to you, I want you to tell me. Will you do that?"

I nod but feel a little scared.

"Why don't you ask your mother when this happens again, when she's down in bed and doesn't want you around, when she tells you to go someplace else, ask her, 'Why are you mad?' Would that work, if you asked her like that?"

I shake my head.

"No?"

"She'd get madder."

"Well, how about saying, 'Don't be mad, Momma.' What do you think she'd do then?"

"She'd tell me not to tell her what to do. She says I don't know how she feels and that I don't have clues. I tell her not to be sick, and she says she tries, but she is anyway. Sometimes she says for me to just stop pesterin' her and find another place to be."

"Yeah, well, that's a hard one. Maybe the best thing to do is to let your daddy take care of this. He's trying to figure out what to do. Your mother isn't sick like people who go to the hospital, okay? It's a different kind of sickness."

Grampa Dirks and I eat. He finishes his plate, and I eat most of my sandwich, leaving the crust behind. He wipes his hands on his paper napkin, so I do, too. We drink our lemonade together.

"Sometimes when women have babies, they have problems after. They get down and find it hard to have energy. They're anemic." Grampa Dirks leans over and grins at me when he says, "…and that meanz-z-z-z that they're tired all the time. They have what the doctors call 'tired blood,' so they have to take a tonic to get their blood built up so they can get up and go. Having a baby can take a lot out of the mother, though why that's true for some women and not others, I can't tell you. But seems like your mother is particularly fragile when it comes to having children. It takes her a long time to recover. It did when she had you, too." He pats my arm and squeezes my hand. "But your mother's gonna be all right in the end. She's a tough cookie. I've known that from the day she was born. You'll have to trust me on this one."

Grampa Dirks looks off toward the swimming pool while he finishes his sandwich. "When your mother was born, she came out of the womb, all red-faced and crying. I was told they didn't even have to smack her bottom, though I don't know if that's true or they were just telling me she was a—"

"Tough cookie?"

"You got it! Being defiant is pretty much your mother's nature. Your momma's about as stubborn as they come. She's like her mother in this."

"Is she gonna get better?"

"Oh, I'm sure she will. If it's what women have after having babies, she should start kicking out of it pretty soon. She'll take her medicine—"

"Her horse pills?"

"Whaaat? Oh, you mean vitamins and iron tablets the doctor has given her? She takes 'horse pills,' you say?"

"She used to before there wasn't any money."

"I see. Well, with this new batch, I think it won't be long before your mother is good as new."

"How long before she's better, Grampa?"

"Oh, honey, I don't know what to tell you. That's what we're all wondering and keep hoping for. We'll just have to see what the new medicine does for her."

"Okay." I want to cry.

Grampa Dirks comes round to my side of the picnic table and pulls me next to him, hugging me hard. "It's not easy, is it? Your daddy's having a hard time, too. Oh, no, honey, don't cry. Can't have any of this today."

He pushes me back a little, and at the same time he reaches for his handkerchief in his back pocket. I can't stop. I cry holding his handkerchief against my eyes. He holds me while I cry. He smells like Daddy only old, like more sweat and more musty smells in his clothes.

"Goddammit!" he says out loud to himself. "I could just shake her, and I would, too, if I thought it'd do any good." He lets me cry against him until I'm done.

Grampa wraps our plates and forks in the tablecloth and closes the jars with leftovers, putting them all in the basket. We finish our lemonade with quick slugs and slurps, Grampa racing me to the finish. He tosses the empty glasses on top of the tablecloth. When I hear a clunk, I look to see if he broke something, but he smiles and closes the back door to the car.

At the swimming pool, we sit on the benches where people go to watch through the fence. I ask Grampa Dirks if I can call him Grampa Whalen. I think if I add Grampa, he might let me call him this all the time. He hands me another peanut butter cookie he had wrapped in a napkin.

"Just for today," he says, looking at his pocket watch. "For another hour or so."

"Guess that'll just have to do for now."

He laughs and pulls me so close I have to wait until he lets go before I can eat my cookie.

"DO YOU BELIEVE IN GOD, Grampa Whalen?" The swimmers are splashing around in the shallow side of the pool near us. Two boys water fight while their mother watches in a lounge chair, catching the sun.

"You always come up with a fistful of surprise, you know that, Shike? I just get settled with my cuppa coffee, and I get hit with God." Grampa has poured some coffee from a thermos into the top that he calls a cup.

"Joe," I say.

Grampa Dirks looks puzzled at first. "Ah, cuppa joe! Daddy talk." He laughs a little. "I thought there for a minute you were calling God, 'Joe.'"

Now I laugh. "Nooo. God's name is Almighty."

"Well, He's called other things, too. Some of His names aren't so well-intending, but we won't get into that. Calling God 'Joe' wouldn't be too far off for some of the soldiers out there on the battlefields right now, Shike."

Grampa's bottom lip moves a little as he drinks his coffee, and a dribble runs down the side of his cup. He puts the cup down fast and wipes his mouth with the back of his wrist. The wrist is where most people wear their watches, but Grampa carries his in a special pocket with a gold chain. When he takes his watch out, every now and then, he lets me press the long button that flips open the lid so we can see the time. I know seconds, minutes, hours, and half and quarter-hours, but it takes me a minute before I can say out loud what time it is by where the long and short hands are. If they're not right on a number, I have to count, and counting doesn't always add up to what the time is. Grampa tells me to keep working on it, that it will come in time, and, then, he laughs at his joke. I don't know what the joke is, but I'm happy when he is.

"Do I believe in God?" he asks himself, looking off over the swimmers in the pool, then back at me. He drums his chin with his fingers. "Well, I'm praying to somebody up there." Grampa nods his chin toward the sky and watches the clouds for a while. Then he says to me, "So there better be somebody listening or I'm a dang idiot!" He winks at me like Daddy. "Okay, hmmmm, so, yes, I do believe there's a God, but to me He looks a little different than you've been taught He does, probably. Do you know what 'belief' means, when people say they 'believe' something?"

"Momma says 'to believe' is to think something real strong. I asked her because she talks about 'believing this and that' a lot, 'specially about Scriptures."

"That's a good answer. But when most people talk about their beliefs in God or their country, they mean they feel very, very strongly about them. When you believe something strongly, you think it's true, so you act on it. You're willing to do things that show yourself and other people that you believe it. For example, your mom and dad believe in God, so they go to church. Now, you don't have to go to church to believe in God, but if you believe strongly in God—especially in a certain way—you probably will go to services, you see what I mean? The same is true if you believe in your country. That's why some people think Mennonites don't love their country, because, they say, they aren't willing to go fight for it. But even though we—well, our people, let me say—don't believe in fighting and killing other people on the battlefield, they're willing to do other things to show they believe strongly in our country."

"Stamps, bonds, and bandages. That's what Momma says." Grampa smiles and pats my leg. "So do you believe in God strong?"

"Oh, boy! You aren't going to make this easy, are you? Okay, just remember you asked for this, Shike. Here's what I believe, at least for today. I believe that God is the Supreme Being, and that He manifests Himself in all things—in plain Shike-talk that means we can see Him in everything around us, especially in the breath of life. I mean by that, that we can see Him in the breath of all living beings."

"We sing 'breathe on me,' in church. It's a hymn. Is God breathing on me when I sing it?"

"I think that's exactly what the song means. The song's saying that God's breath is giving us life, eternal life, life forever, beyond this life on earth."

"Forever and ever, amen."

Grampa thinks this is funny. "That's pretty much how they say it. At the end of prayers, you mean?"

I nod.

"That's because most of the folks we know believe if they believe in God, well, and in His son, Jesus, they will live forever and ever. They also say that because they believe the Bible is the Holy Word of God, and what it says is true forever and ever."

"Amen!" I think Grampa will laugh again, but he doesn't. He asks if I know what "Amen" means.

I shake my head, but then I say, "It means 'the end.'"

Now Grampa does laugh big. I don't always know when he will. "It means 'so be it.' And that means 'not my will but Thine be done.' And that means that in the end we surrender to what God wants, not what we may want."

"Daddy prays about wills before meals. Momma talks about wills all the time."

"So do you understand what God's will is—means?"

"Is it He says, and you do?"

Grampa laughs again. "It means that if something happens and we try our best to understand it and attempt to do something about it, and it doesn't change because of our actions or it changes in a way we don't like, we say it's God's will and accept it. So in a way, what you are saying is right on target. God tells us what He wants us to do, that it's His will, not ours."

"God's like Daddy. He says no ifs, ands, or buts."

"Hmmm. In a way, then, yes." Grampa waits so long to go on, I think he will look at his watch and stand to leave. But he asks, "Can you tell me about 'forever and ever.' You understand that expression, what that means?"

"Always. Going on and on and on without ever stopping. Aunt Josie told me that one."

Grampa nods, and when he doesn't say more, I ask him something that's been my question a long time. "If God is forever and ever, why did he die?"

"He didn't. Oh, you mean Jesus?"

"On the cross."

"Yeah. That's kinda hard to explain. Jesus is God's son and God made him both a spirit like He is Himself and a person like us, like you and me and everybody on earth."

"Only Jesus died, not God?"

"To most people God is the Big Guy in the Sky, Shike. I'm calling the sky 'heaven,' because Christians always look up when they think about heaven, okay? God's bigger than anything else, so we look to the sky because it is without limit. The earth has limits. It stops, even the vast sea stops... it is measurable. It ends—has a bottom and shores. But the sky, Heaven, goes on and on and up and up, without end. But most people express the limitlessness of God by saying that He exists unto Himself.

"That's really, really big stuff. It means God doesn't need anybody or anything to exist, to be—He just is, has always been, will always be. He was alive before anything was made, before the world and even before the heavens, and so everything that is—the earth, all the stars and planets in the sky, the oceans and rivers, all the animals, including all of us human beings—He created.

"But when we talk about creation we usually mean things. After this, there is a parting of the way, for most people. They disagree and even argue, and, frequently, fight, have real wars with one another, about how God lives in us and how we should live if we want to be with God."

"God's in heaven with Jesus. Norma Janet says."

"Uh-huh. You mean, Simon Nichols's daughter. Your mother's told me she's your Sunday School teacher, is that right?"

"She shows us pictures of creation. We punch them out and stand them up. She makes us stand them up in order, one before the other ones and then the next and next, on down the line."

"Uh-huh. Well, when people talk like Norma Janet is telling you about God and creation, they talk about God like He's a Presence, like he's a Spirit, like He can't be seen, is invisible, unless He wants to make himself known—that's what 'manifesting Himself' means. I'm sure you've heard that in church, how God manifests Himself. Well, that means He becomes something so we can see Him—like in the way trees grow and the sun shines, flowers blossom, even people, how all of us look and act."

"Momma is finding pictures and cutting them out about creation."

"Naw, really? Your mother?" Grampa Dirks can hardly believe it. "Why's she doing that? Helping with Norma Janet's lessons?"

"She says she has an idea. It's about me, but she won't tell me yet. She's cutting pictures out of magazines, lots of animals and flowers and trees, and she's laying them out on old flannel shirts. I'm learning lines."

"Lines? Like in a play? Ah, you're going to do some part in a church play, is that it?"

"She won't tell me how or when yet."

"Well, that's a puzzle."

"Like jig-saw. I have one of Jesus with the animals."

"Ah, well, like that, but when I said 'puzzle' now, I meant, it's a mystery." Grampa rubs his forehead. "To be 'puzzled' means I'm trying to figure out something I don't know the answer to, like your jigsaw puzzle, yes, like that, only not shapes, but about something I'm trying to figure out in my head."

"Clues."

"Exactly. Like clues you use to figure out a puzzle in your head." Grampa slaps the table. "Thank God, we have that settled." He laughs a little. "You certainly keep me on my toes—which means, you make me think hard and keep thinking hard to find the answers."

"Believe!"

"Uh-huh." Grampa pats my leg. "But here's what I want to tell you so you don't misunderstand what I'm trying to say to you. When I say that I believe God is the Breath of Life, I mean that most people believe He gives us life or takes it away. When you're alive, you breathe. When you die, you no longer breathe, right? To them, God exists outside of them, and He lives in our hearts, only if we let Him in."

"We believe!"

"Yes, that's right. Now your mother and dad believe this, and it's what they teach you at the Hopewell Mennonite Church. It's like God or his son, Jesus, knocks at the door of your heart, and you have to open it and let Him in to belong to Him, so that you can live like the Bible teaches you to live and not just go off in your willful ways, on your own, without any consideration to what He wants you to do."

"His will."

"Yes, you're getting the hang of this. When you let God into your life, or when anybody does that—lets Him in—well, then they say He lives in you, and in everybody else who lets Him into their lives."

"Have you opened the door and let God in?"

"That's really a good question, Shike. First, you need to know that that's just an expression, a way of talking. It's not a real door in your heart. When I say this or some preacher does, it means you're willing to believe in God so strong you'll do the right things, live the right way. For Christians that means like the Bible teaches."

"Momma worries about living right all the time."

"Uh-huh, I know. And for that reason I'm probably not the one who should be talking to you about this. Your mother, in particular, has very strong ideas about who God is, how you can have Him in your heart and life, and what she believes He does and doesn't do for us—for them and you, and everybody else who believes. God is undoubtedly the biggest thing you can ever talk about, Shike. You know what religion is?"

"It's going to church."

"That's not too far off, actually. You're full of good answers today. But churches are called different names in different religions, and people do differ- ent things when they go to their… well, let's call them houses of worship, okay? The Jews go to synagogues. The Muslims go to mosques. The Buddhists go to temples, and Christians go to churches."

"Lois has a temple."

"Who's Lois?"

"Norma Janet's friend from high school."

"Yes, well, all this church business can be kind of confusing because some places of worship can have more than one name, such as synagogues can also be called temples, and the Mormons have a big temple, and they're Christians, not Jews."

"Her temple is Saints."

"Saints? Does Lois say she belongs to the Latter Day Saints?"

I nod.

"Ah ha! That's another name for Mormons, and the whole name for them is The Church of Jesus Christ of Latter Day Saints, and their biggest temple, the major one, is in Salt Lake City, Utah."

"She said 'Salt Lake.' She doesn't say 'Mormon.'"

"Probably not. It's just another name for the religion she belongs to. You know the Holdemans, the people we come from, right? They have a long name too. It's The Church of God in Christ, Mennonite. All religions have different names and different ways of believing about God and different ways of holding services when their believers go to their different places of worship. Not everybody goes to worship on Sunday."

"You've got to be kidding?" I slap my forehead, and Grampa laughs. I almost say "Mein Jäajna." Momma's taught me Mein Jäajna from Plattdeutsch because she says it sometimes. I think it means "oh my ever lovin' God," but I'm not sure. Grampa is talking again.

"Not everybody does what Mennonites do in church either. Some people have little pieces of bread they hold over a cup. Their priest does that, and they all eat it, and the priest drinks from the cup, like the Last Supper at your church, only you don't have a priest, you have a preacher."

"I don't drink grape juice at church because I have to belong, and I'm not old enough yet."

"That's right. You do that when you're twelve, I think."

"It's Christ's body."

"So they say."

"Daddy says 'so they say.'"

"I know. I probably got it from him or the other way around. Your dad and I talk about religion a lot."

"And the newspapers."

"And the newspapers." Grampa laughs again. He laughs a lot with me.

"Do other people sing in their churches? Or temples and whatever the Jews call houses of worship?"

"Synagogues," Grampa repeats for me. "Some beat drums. I know that seems strange since there are Mennonites who argue over whether or not there should even be piano music to accompany singing in church. But there are all kinds of different sacred rituals people have during church services. Rituals are ceremonies or services people do over and over. Some hold sacred scrolls and walk through the congregation with them. That's the Jews with what they call the Torah, it's the history of their people and their laws that God gave them directly from Mount Sinai. Others hold open Bibles in their hands while they preach. Some pray on carpets on the floor and others pray sitting in pews or standing up or kneeling down. In some churches they sit, stand, and kneel, up and down, the whole service. Mennonites do some of that. You ever been to a Holdeman church service?"

I shake my head. "After Wesley Schmidt, Momma says she doesn't care if she enters a Holdeman church door ever again."

"Yeah, I've heard about this Schmidt character. Your daddy's pretty much on your mother's side with that one. Well, the Holdemans stand and sing and recite scripture with the preacher and then sit and listen and then kneel to pray, but the men sit on one side of the church, and the women on the other. Catholics have special prayer stools in front of the pews that they pull down and kneel on. The Holdemans turn around and kneel in front of their pews. But—"

"Momma says who wants to put your nose down where you've been sitting, huh?"

"My sentiments exactly!" Grampa laughs until he coughs. "But regardless of how people do it, they pray in all religions. They also sing or chant—that's saying lots of words together without singing. If they do sing, they sometimes use pianos or other musical instruments."

"'No pianos for the Holdemans,' Momma says. She couldn't go to church without pianos."

"Sounds like your mother has it in for the Holdemans plenty! But I think I understand where this is coming from. Your mother has an exceptionally beautiful soprano voice."

Grampa Dirks sighs and sits watching the swimmers for a long time. Finally, he says, "There are more ideas about God and how to worship Him than just about anything else on earth. There are even ideas about ideas about God. People have different places of worship because they argue about whether He wants you to do one thing or the other, or if this is so, or that is so, or if this is wrong, or that is right. Sometimes, they get so mad or upset with each other over what they believe, they leave one church and join another one or start a completely new church with brand new ideas. Believing in God is a big, big deal."

"Is yours a brand new, big deal?"

Grampa Dirks thinks that's funny.

"Are you a Mennonite? Momma says, yes, you are, but you just don't go to church anymore. Daddy says, no, you're not, because you have your own ideas about God. He's not even sure you're a Christian. When he said that, Momma got real mad."

"Well, I'm not going to touch that with a ten-foot pole, Shike. But I can tell you one thing. Right now I don't belong to a Mennonite church, but I was raised in a Mennonite home, actually, in a Holdeman home. My mother was a big believer, but my father wasn't."

"Like Grampa and Gramma Jantz. Gramma goes to church, but Grampa Jantz wouldn't go if his life depended on it."

Grampa nods. "Maybe I should be asking you what you think about God."

"He made ever'thing in one day and rested for seven."

Grampa Dirks laughs so hard and leans over so far, I think he will fall off the park bench. "I think maybe you need to study your addition tables a little more, Shike, or read your Bible during daylight, because Genesis says He created everything one day at a time for six days, and then rested on the seventh day."

"That's it!"

"Anything else you believe about God?"

"He made Jesus."

"He did. What do you believe about Jesus?"

"He makes us all get born again and live forever and ever. He's magic."

"Magic?"

"He made water into wine at a wedding, once. Norma Janet says that's like magic. A miracle."

"So they say," Grampa Dirks smiles and winks at me.

"The Bible says."

"It does." Grampa nods his head up and down a while.

"Do you think about God?"

"I do. All the time. I believe God is spirit, that he lives in us—"

"The Holy Ghost."

"Well, you could call it that, maybe, but the Holy Ghost or Holy Spirit they teach you about at Hopewell Mennonite comes into you when you accept Jesus as your personal savior. I believe that this God-spirit lives within us from the time we are born, that it's in you all the time, from the very beginning, not just when you are born again through Jesus. I believe that we forget it's there. We get busy and forget. So to remember it's there, we have to sit down and get real quiet and wait and pray, and then, we remember. That's a lot different than being a Mennonite."

"Do you read the Bible? Daddy does. Momma does, too, when she isn't too sick to read. At night, she has Daddy read it to her."

"I do read the Bible, every day. I also read other Scriptures from other religions, as well."

"They have Bibles, too?"

"Yes, you can say that, I suppose, but they don't call them Bibles. They have writings from prophets and holy men that their followers teach are sacred, holy, just as the Christian Scriptures are. You ever hear of Buddha?"

"What is Buddha?"

"He was a man who lived a long time ago too. He lived five hundred years before Jesus and Buddha's disciples wrote down many things he said, like Jesus' followers did, which became what we call the Bible. One of Buddhists' sacred writings is the Tripitaka. And then there is Muhammed. You know this name, Muhammed?"

I shake my head.

"He was a prophet born five hundred years after Christ, give or take a few years. His disciples wrote down what he said and things he did, and those sacred writings are called the Koran. Muslims—that's what his believers are called—all over the world believe in the Koran like we do our Bible. Some Muslims memorize the entire Koran."

"Like my lines? Like Momma is teaching me from the Bible?"

"If your lines are from the Bible, yes, exactly like that. But the Muslims memorize not just some of the lines, some verses, but the whole thing. I'm talking about their holy scriptures, not ours. Can you imagine if you had to memorize our whole Bible? I don't know what the difference is between their holy scriptures and ours, in length, but I know memorizing either one would be a whole lot of memorizing. People spend a lot of time writing down and reciting—that's reading out loud, sometimes from memory—their holy texts." Grampa stares out over the swimming pool water, the sun shining in our eyes off the surface, but he doesn't seem to mind. I look down or at him to keep the glare out of my eyes.

"Benedictine monks for centuries have read through the entire Bible during their mealtimes. Jewish scholars spend an entire year following very strict rules when they write out the Torah to make their sacred scrolls. I read the Bible myself once from Genesis to Revelation, some each day, and, in order, not skipping around. It took me a whole year to do it. And that's just reading it. So you can imagine how long it would take to memorize it." Grampa has been talking to himself again. Now he nudges me and asks, "Pretty amazing, don't you think?"

I nod but don't say anything, just watch the swimmers get out of the pool and jump back in from the diving board, with my hand over my eyebrows. I don't want any more religion. "There's too many Bibles. I can't remember them all."

"You're right. It's enough for today. Long, long lesson in religion, but remember you asked."

Grampa looks at his watch and starts to tell me we have to go home, but I have one more question I want to know. "Do the coloreds have their own swimming pool?"

"No, they don't, and that's what the incident was about I mentioned before. There was a town meeting to see if they could get one, and the Negroes were not allowed into the meeting, and a crazy group of men—probably belonging to the KKK—came and tried to outshout—"

"What's KKK?"

"Ku Klux Klan. It's a group of people who believe coloreds should not have the same rights as white people. A long time ago Negroes were slaves on big plantations in the United States. After President Abraham Lincoln and the civil war, the Negroes were freed and didn't have to be slaves any longer. But they still don't have much. It's a long way from the civil war until now, and they still don't have the rights they were supposed to get at the end of that war.

"Anyway, during the town meeting over the swimming pool in Hopewell, the KKKs shouted and got other people all fired up. A fight broke out—the Negroes had gathered outside the meeting place, and one ended up getting very badly hurt. Since it was a colored man, it wasn't as bad as it coulda been. Last I read about this, the man who was hurt was going to be all right, but his jaw was smashed up pretty bad. It's set the whole project of getting the Negro kids their swimming pool way back. The mayor of Hopewell and the town council are still saying they're gonna try and get something done about it. So the colored kids may end up with a pool just so there's no more trouble. The Negroes are very upset, as well they should be."

"Tommy Don says 'chocolate drops,' and when I do, Momma doesn't like it.'"

"Other children and many adults call the colored kids a lot of names. It's best to just say 'Negroes.'"

"Momma says God loves them just like us."

Grandpa says, "Uh-huh. About this, your mother is right." He taps my hand, and I open his watch, while he holds it. "Time to get you home before I get skinned."

1.

G RAMPA DIRKS SITS ACROSS FROM me at the picnic table in the backyard of the duplex in colored town. Momma is in bed. Teddy is sleeping in his crib next to her with fans that whir between them. We have just moved from the church basement, and boxes are piled sky high and unopened all over the house. Daddy tells me every morning that he's going out "on the job," which he told me means "he labors from dawn until dusk to earn a living." When I ask him about living, he tells me he drives from one job to the next fixing cars and equipment to earn enough to keep us with a roof over our heads and a bowl of cereal on the table. More often than not, he heats up his own supper or makes it himself, sometimes for Teddy and me.

"We're eating enough alphabet soup for you to forget about your first year of school," he says, but then he promises no such thing will happen.

Grampa has pulled the table under the shade tree. He is sitting next to me with a cup of coffee just like Daddy does only he doesn't keep his spoon in his cup. He twirls it around and then puts it down on the picnic table where it leaves a wet spot. He sits next to me because the table is so big. If I sit across from him, he says he'd need his glasses to see where the heck I am. He looks at his watch and slides it back into the little pocket just below his belt and just above the big pocket of his trousers. I don't see the time, but I know it's about when Daddy comes home from work—that's if he comes home when it's still light.

"Your mother asked if I could have this little talk with you, Shike, because there's a couple of important things you need to be told, and I wanted to be the one who talked about them with you." Gramma Dirks is in the house with Momma. I can hear them talking while they make supper.

"Since we're going to have a little talk by ourselves, can I call you Whalen?" I ask. "I have once, you remember? By the swimming pool? You let me, and Daddy does."

"He does, but your mother calls me Daddy. You ever notice that?"

I nod.

"You ever think about why?"

"You're her Daddy."

Grampa Dirks laughs to himself and rocks over to the side and then back again. "Well, yes, that's true, but let me explain a little more about that. Your mother is related to me by blood, by birth. She's my daughter, and your father is related to me only because your mother married him. To your dad, I'm not his dad, so he calls me by my first name. To your mother, I am her dad, so she calls me that. You don't call your mother, 'Darlene,' or your dad, 'Vernon,' do you?"

"They say no."

"Well, you see how that works now and why."

"But they call me 'Shike' and not 'daughter.'"

"Oh, Lord, and I suspect you're going to claim that I don't call you 'Grand-daughter.' That going to be your argument? Well, I've got a comeback for that."

"Daddy taught me 'comeback.'"

"Okay, then. My comeback is that the custom is there to show respect to those older than you are, a reminder of the place these people hold in your life, the people we should look up to for who they are to us. They know more about the world by living longer and having more experiences than we do."

"Teddy doesn't call me, 'Sister.' Teddy doesn't talk, but if he did, he would say, 'Shike.'"

"Actually, the Amish and Holdemans do call each other 'Brother' and 'Sister,' or they used to. Even the older people call each other that with their last names."

"Gramma calls her church people 'Brother' and 'Sister.'"

"Yes, she does. The point is to honor the life these people have lived that you haven't yet—that's when you're young—and when you're older, it's to show respect for their place in your family, even if it's your church family. It's usually about family. Outside that, you won't be calling your teacher by her first name, will you?"

"No." I almost laugh.

"'Course not. See? And Reverend Classen at church. You use his title to show respect. He's a reverend which means he's revered."

"Like Paul Revere? I know that story."

"Oh boy, oh boy. How did I know this was going to end up with me in deep water?" When Grampa stops laughing, he says, "Revered means respected, that means you have deep admiration for somebody. On the other side of the argument, when we use familiar names, like our first names, it means a kind of specialness as well, especially nicknames. It means we are close to them, know them well enough to use a name their family would use. Calling you 'Shike' is very special, see? So I don't mind if you call me Whalen when we're out here by ourselves, because it's my first name, the name my friends use with me. But once you're back inside, or when your mom and dad are around, I think it's the best idea to call me 'Grampa.' Then there's no problem. That an agreement?"

I know agreement, so I nod. I'm lucky he's letting me call him by his first name and not his last. I know about first and last names, even before school. But then I have an idea.

"I call you Grampa Dirks."

"Ah, yes, well, that's a little like Reverend Classen, I think. You'd never say, 'Mr. Dirks,' would you?"

I laugh. "No."

"It all has to do with how well you know a person. Now, do you think we can go on with what I'm out here to talk about with you?"

"Okay, Whalen," I say.

Grampa hesitates but begins without any more talk about revere and family. "The first thing I want to talk to you about is reading and writing. You're getting ready to go to school, and I've got a proposition to make today about that. But first, I want to talk about language. Your parents, your mom and dad, were raised in homes where the German language was spoken rather than English, at least, most of the time. Do you understand what 'language' is?"

"Sometimes."

"What do you mean 'sometimes?'"

"Momma says sometimes."

"I guess I don't understand."

"Babble."

Grampa Dirks looks at me a minute. "Oh, you mean like baby-talk, babbling that sounds like words but aren't. Like Teddy. But he's talking better all along, isn't he? He really doesn't babble so much anymore, even though you can't make out some of his words all the time. But he has words in mind when he says them."

"Teddy doesn't talk much. Momma worries. She thinks something's wrong with him. He's been to the doctor. But she doesn't believe everything is all right."

"I know about Teddy's problem. I'm not inclined to take your mother's view because she fixates on things. Right now it's Teddy's language—"

"What's 'fixate?'"

"It means obsessively focusing on something. Oh dear, that didn't help, did it? 'Fixate' means to become preoccupied. Well, that didn't help, either. Let's see. It means to think about one thing over everything else. Your mother can't stop thinking about Teddy's talking. And when that gets solved or better, she'll probably find something else she can't stop thinking about. How's that?"

I nod.

"So we got side-tracked here a bit. What do you mean by babble?"

"Not like baby-talk. Like babble in the Bible. Momma reads me the story in the book from the library."

"Ah, like the tower of Babel. Well, yes, in the Bible the story goes that the building of the tower is how we got all the different languages in the world, that's true. I'm not sure I'm remembering this correctly, but I think it's that the people thought so well of themselves that they decided to build a tower to heaven and God stopped that by making the builders not speak in the same language. You've got a good memory for your Scriptures, I see that." He stops, says, *"Ve willa noo staut forta.* Do you know what I've just said?"

I shake my head. "Is that Momma's language?"

Grampa Dirks looks at me, surprised. "Your mother's taught you about *Plattdeutsch?*"

"She says words and tells me what they mean when I ask... sometimes."

"Well, you know enough then to see that different languages can't be understood if you don't know what the words are, how they sound, how you say them. You ask about words all the time, so you understand, right?"

"I know *mein jäajna.*"

Grampa Dirks laughs so much I think he'll fall off the picnic table bench. He slaps the table with his hand until the spoon rattles.

"Oh, God, kid, you're a scream!" Grampa Dirks's looking off to the side.

"Momma screams, but she doesn't like for me to."

Grampa Dirks nods and gives me a hug. "'You're a scream' is an expression people say when they mean you're funny and nice to be with, because you say outrageous, funny things. I know, it doesn't make very much sense, but that's the way language can be." Grampa waits a minute and then asks me, "Do you know what *'mein jäajna'* means?"

"Momma says it's like 'Oh my God!'"

Grampa starts laughing again, so I say, "Momma says it's bad to use God's name in vain, even when she does it. When I say 'Oh my God' Momma makes me stop. When I say *'mein jäajna,'* she just laughs like you did."

I've licked the butter off a cracker, so I start eating it, drinking some milk from a plastic glass. Momma doesn't like me to lick the butter off, but Grampa Dirks doesn't care.

"Well, that's because *'mein jäajna'* translates—literally means 'my adversary' or something like 'my enemy' in English. It's hard to take words from one language and have them mean exactly the same in another language. 'Mein jäajna' is like slapping your forehead and saying, 'Oh God, that's really, really awful!'" Grampa slaps his forehead a little bit and then says, "It's like somebody you don't like very much has shown up, and you want him to go away, so you're praying to God that He will get rid of him for you. So what your mother told you isn't so far off. It's like saying, 'Oh my God, help me out here!' Kind of like that."

"I don't like Barbara," I tell him.

"At church, a girl at church?'"

I slap my forehead. "I want God to make her go away."

"Good Lord. You can't go around mein jäajna-ing Barbara, Shike. Your mother finds out about this, I'll be buried alive." He stops and looks at the sky. "Oh, God, help me out here. I'm sinking in deep doo-doo, not by inches, by fathoms!"

"You praying now?"

"Plenty."

"What for?"

"Knowledge!" he says and then adds fast, "Don't ask. I just want to know how to get out of the hole I've dug myself into. I'm on the Shirly schoolboard, for godssakes. I should know how to talk to a kid about language!" Grampa Dirks is talking to himself again. Finally, he says to me, "You think it's possible for us to start this conversation over again?"

"Okie-dokie, Whalen," I say.

He laughs real loud and slaps his forehead again. He moves his head back and forth in his hands, elbows on the picnic table.

I'm happy I make him laugh. I swing my legs back and forth, lick and eat another cracker.

Finally, he stops laughing. "So here's what I came out here to talk to you about. Let's get back to it, or I'll never finish in time for supper! Having a conversation with you is like walking through a snake pit, Shike." He holds up his hands. "I'll explain another time. For now I want to tell you some things I promised your mother I'd discuss with you.

"The first is to help you understand why your mom and dad are upset about this move to where they are—here in colored town—and their finding out that the Birch Street house is not going to be available until March, well after you've started to school. You've guessed at some of this, no doubt. And I'm sure they're talking about it where you can hear. They arguing and throwing lots of statements around about your schooling?"

"Yelling even."

"Uh-huh. I thought so. Well, I want you to know that this isn't because you're doing anything wrong. It has to do with their own hard times at school when they were kids, anyway, that's my opinion. You think you're up to my explaining that to you a little bit?"

I nod.

Grampa Dirks drinks his coffee soft, his bottom lip sort of shakes around the edge of the cup when he slurps. It looks real different from the way Daddy drinks from his cup. Daddy gulps big, then sometimes wipes the rim with his tongue or finger. When Grampa sets his cup down he says, "Language is a very important part of your mother and dad's life as Mennonites. English is the language you and I are speaking together right now and is the language most of the people you know speak, at church—at least, most of the time—and at school, in stores and the like. All around you, everywhere in this country, people speak English. But when your mother was growing up in our house she and your Aunt Josephine, and Uncle Jesse, too, they all spoke *Plautdietsch*—that's Low German, a completely different sounding language." Grampa Dirks says "plowt-dēētch" which sounds funny.

"They say 'plot doych.' Not what you say."

"Ah, yes, well, that's a dialect pronunciation. The name I'm using is the one that actually means 'Low German.' It's the one most Mennonites use, but the way your parents call it is correct, as well. The way they speak it is spelled differently, too, but you don't know that yet. Do you know what 'dialect' means?"

I shake my head.

"It means a particular way a group of people, usually from a certain area of a country, speak a language. Some of the words can sound different. Your mother spoke *Plautdietsch* from the time she was a little girl. The words I used when I asked you if you knew '*Ve willa noo staut forta*' are *Plautdietsch*. In English that means 'We will go to town.' When your mother started to school only a few of the kids in her class spoke the language we spoke at home. Most of the kids spoke English."

"Gramma says 'English.'"

"Oh, you mean, when she says *the English* this and *the English* that?"

I nod.

"That's right, but your grandmother calls anybody not a Mennonite, 'English.'"

"Momma thinks it's 'old *moldsh.*'"

Grampa Dirks laughs again. When he stops, he says, "Ah, you mean *'ooltmootsch,*' which means 'old-fashioned.' Well, that's because when our parents came to this country from Russia, everybody around where they lived spoke English, so they thought everybody different from themselves were people from England even though some of them came from other places. And because our parents called them English, we grew up calling them that, too."

I eat my cracker and listen.

"What I want you to know is that Low German, or *Plautdietsch* or *Plattdeutsch*, was the language that your Grandmother Dirks and I grew up speaking first, and so did your mom and dad. We only learned English after we'd gone to school."

"I don't know *plot—doych.*"

"I know. In some ways, I wish you did, but it can make it hard to learn English. And this is what I want to tell you. When your Daddy talks to you about him not being able to read and write English very well, he's telling you that he had a hard time in school because he didn't hear much English at home. When his mother and father talked to him, and his brothers and sisters, they always said everything in Low German, in *Plautdietsch*. So your Daddy didn't learn lots of English words, but as he grew up, in order to talk to everybody around him, he had to know more and more English words. He learned to speak and listen to English, but because it was hard for him to read English, he grew up not liking school very much.

"Everything you learn in school depends on reading. So your dad grew up pretty much only reading the newspaper and his Bible. It bothers him, a lot, that he doesn't know very many English words. Now, your mother, on the other hand, couldn't stop reading. She wanted to read everything she could in English, but there's been a problem with your Grandmother Dirks about this. She doesn't think English should be used as much as *Plautdietsch*, and so she tried to keep her girls from reading or speaking English any more than they had to. Your grandmother is from the old Mennonite religion, the Holdemans, so she reads even her Bible in *Plautdietsch* and tries to use that language as much as she can.

"I don't agree with her about this, so I told your Aunt Josephine, your Uncle Jesse, and your mother that in our house, English would be spoken and read. Your Aunt Josephine was really, really good at school and learned English quickly. Your mother did, too, but she had more trouble with your Grandmother Dirks, and so she didn't do as well at school.

"Now, I'm telling you all this because I want you to know that your mother and father want you to do well at school. They want reading and writing to come easier for you than it did for them. Your mother doesn't care if you don't learn *Plautdietsch*, because she wants you to get along easier with people who aren't Mennonites. Your daddy feels the same way, but he still loves the old language and wishes there was a way to teach you both. But...." Grampa sighs and pats my arm, "I don't think it would sit well in your house if he tried to teach you *Plautdietsch* because your mother would raise Cain over it. That means she wouldn't like it and would make him stop in no uncertain terms. She's worried that *Plautdietsch* could mess you up in school the way it did her and Vernon… your dad."

Grampa Dirks drinks more of his coffee and asks if I got any of that.

I nod.

"I just want you to know that your parents are very worried about moving you from school to school right at the time you are going to start to learn to read and write. Your mother doesn't want you to go to this new school close to colored town, for two reasons. One is that the bus service is not out here for whites—to their school—and she'd have to drive you every day. Secondly, in a short while, when you move to another house from this one, you'll be going to a different school. She's afraid you'll give up and won't like school anymore."

"I want to go to school bad."

"That's what I've been telling her, and I'm very glad you do, Shike, because I do, too. Even though I don't go to school to learn any longer, reading is one of my favorite things to do. But you know this already because you look at my magazines when you come to the farm, don't you? I see that you want to read, and I think that's mighty fine." Grampa Dirks puts his hands around his coffee cup and winks at me like Daddy.

"Soooo that brings me to the next important thing I want to tell you."

Grampa Dirks pats my arm again. He keeps patting my arm. Maybe he thinks I'm going to fall asleep or daydream. Momma's told me daydreaming is when you're dreaming about things with your eyes open, not minding your business. Grampa Dirks must wonder if I'm sleeping with my eyes open because he says, "How are we doing? Are you still up for this, or do you want a break?"

"I'm up for it."

"You want more crackers? Well, we better not ask for more of those before supper, I guess, but you better drink, at least, a little more of your milk, or your mother'll have my head."

I drink a little milk. It's not all that cold, and I don't want it, but I drink it for Grampa.

"It looks like I'm going to be around some to help you with your reading and writing—your homework."

"Homework? I don't know homework."

"Oh, I don't know what I'm thinking. Of course, you won't have homework right away. Homework's when the teacher has you bring extra schoolwork home to work on in the evening. But being in the first grade, you probably won't have any of that, at least not for a while." Grampa Dirks leans over and says, "But we could practice at home a little, don't you think, like we've been doing with numbers. It'd make your parents feel better about your change of schools with all this moving around. What d'ya say?"

"Oh goodie!" I can't believe Grampa is going to help me with my reading and writing.

"That's what I'm thinking, oh goodie! You know, your Grandmother and I live twenty-five miles from here. And so I can't come to help you with your schoolwork unless we live closer to each other. So your parents—now this is strictly upon your approval, you are going to be the one to decide—but they are considering you coming to live out on the farm with your grandmother and me until you all move to Birch Street."

He waits a minute, looking at me like he wants me to say something.

So I ask—because I'm not sure I heard him right—"I get to live out on the farm with you and Gramma? Yippee! I want to—no ifs, ands, or buts about it."

Grampa laughs, but he puts his hand over mine. "Whoa, now. This would mean you would stay with us, which means living with us, Shike. Give this some thought, because it might be for a long time."

"Can Teddy come, too?"

"No, that's what I'm telling you. You wouldn't see your momma and daddy or Teddy except on visits and weekends."

I want Grampa's reading and writing on the farm but with Momma, Daddy and Teddy. "I want Teddy."

"That's part of what you'll have to decide about. Your grandmother and I have too much to do on the farm to take both you and Teddy. Teddy is very young. He needs to be near your momma and daddy now. He's not even potty-trained, yet. I know your mother is starting this but he needs to be with his mother for it. And we would take you home on weekends most of the time— Saturday and Sunday. You'd still see your church friends."

"How would I get to school?"

"School is in town these days. I would drive you to Shirly Elementary every weekday morning, or you'd ride the bus. We have bus service out in the country now for school, which is in town, less than four miles away. It's a big change, Shike. But your mother, especially, has convinced me that it's a pretty good idea." Grampa Dirks waits before he says, "You don't have to decide now but sometime soon, okay?"

I nod.

"Thing is, your grandmother has agreed to not teach you *Plautdietsch,* though she'll be speaking some of that with me, beyond doubt. Your mother is concerned about that but is more worried about the beginning of your schooling in town. She thinks you and I could work out any difficulties you might have, since we've done so well with numbers together.

"I want to read with you, Grampa Whalen."

"Okay, we'll be talking some more about this in the weeks ahead then. It's a good start, don't you think? I'll answer any questions you might have—"

"Hey!" Daddy calls from the side gate of the yard, and after he's come through, he latches it from the inside. "How in the world did you two get the yard to yourselves at this time of day? Isn't Darlene up? And where's Teddy?"

Grampa helps me get my legs over the picnic bench, so I can run to Daddy.

I grab his legs, and he almost bangs my head with his lunch pail when he brings his arm around to hug me. After I let loose, he walks toward Grampa Dirks and sets it down on his newspaper, so it won't blow away from the picnic table.

"How are things going?" he asks. He's looking at Grampa, not at me.

"Shike and I just had a heart-to-heart talk, and as for me, I enjoyed it very much." Grampa Dirks looks at me and waits.

When I don't say anything, Daddy asks, "Well, how about you?" Tonight Daddy only smells a little like tobacco. The whiskey smell is gone.

"I feel mighty fine," I say. They smile and nod and laugh and talk about supper, so we start for the back door. I do feel mighty fine about Grampa Dirks helping me with school, but there's a little sad feeling, too. I wonder how often Teddy will miss me.

2.

Late August, 1943

MOMMA'S FRUSTRATED. SHE FLIPS A towel in the air hard, folds it and then rolls it against her apron. Teddy is playing with blocks in his crib over toward the wall and is being a good baby, for once. He thinks it's a game to throw a block, crawl or try to walk to where it is, and throw it back where it came from. Dumb game, but he's a baby. I watch him play while Momma talks to me. She isn't happy.

"I'm not going over this time and time again, Shike. I've made up my mind and that's that. And..." she holds up the rolled-up towel like it's a stick, circling over her head with it, saying, "your daddy agrees with me. You're going to Roosevelt School just off Randolph. I'm going to register you tomorrow, period, and you'll be coming along because they weigh you and measure your height for your ration book. And the teacher will want to meet you. You give me anymore trouble about this, and you won't like it."

I am crying, but not making any noise, because she'll just get madder.

"Your Grandpa was going to come and talk to you again about this, but he has a cow that the vet is tending to and some new chicken houses he's got to move his laying hens into, so he can't leave the farm."

"But Grampa said. He said."

"I know, Shike. And that is my fault. I admit it. I was only trying to figure out the best way to do your schooling. How many times do I have to tell you?"

"But why not?"

"The answer's the same, regardless of how many times you ask. It's too hard on them. They can't do everything that's required, and I don't know—"

"It's Gramma. And *Plattdeutsch*. And—"

"I'll take you to your new school myself, each morning, without fail."

"You'll fail. You'll be tired."

"Watch it, Shike. You're dangerously close to a problem you won't be able to get out of. Now, drop it and come hold the end of this sheet. C'mon."

"No," I scream and run toward my bedroom. When I get to the door, she calls out, "If I hear the door close, Shike, you will be dealing with your daddy when he comes home."

I stand by my door with my hand on the knob. There is silence except for Teddy's moving around in his crib.

"Oh, for godssakes," Momma says. Her voice is soft and almost pleading. I think she wants me to come back to talk. Maybe she's changed her mind again, but in the dining room I find her lifting Teddy out of his crib. He smells like poo.

Momma turns and looks at me. "Give me a hand here, will you? Get the bucket from the bathroom. Hurry."

3.

Same day, later

"YOU'RE DRIVING YOUR MOTHER CRAZY with this, are you, now?" Daddy's hair is sticking out over his ears, and a few strands are high up in the air on top of his head. He takes his hand and smooths his hair when I look at it. He wants to read his newspaper before supper, but he has to deal with me.

"I want to live on the farm."

"You think you do, Shike, but you don't—not really. It will be a full eight months with only your grandma and grandpa every night. Your grandpa tells me that every time you talk with him about the move, you mention Teddy. And don't bring up the weekends again. It won't be enough. Your grandparents go to bed with the chickens."

"They sleep with the chickens?"

Daddy laughs. "No that means they go to bed when the sun goes down, because that's when the chickens get on their perches for the night. And they get up at the stroke of dawn. For Whalen, it's actually way before sunrise. He gets up around five in the morning. Do you know how early that is? You're still dreaming with the angels."

"He'll teach me reading and writing."

"I know he promised that, and he's told me that he will come some week-ends, though not all the time. Here's the thing, Shike, we decided to try this idea before your mother and I had thought it all the way through. She's worried now that, first, you'll get lonely, especially for Teddy, and you'll want to come home when you can't. No, hear me out, now. It's not just your grandpa who won't let you come back home in the middle of the week, it's the gasoline. He can't drive just anytime he wants because the rationing of gasoline is restricted. He has a barrel but not one as big as Uncle Clifford's, you understand, because your grandpa doesn't do wheat anymore, only pastureland. You don't want to be in bed upset because you're lonely." Daddy sighs. "And second, your grandmother is not an easy woman to live with. She will be more patient with you, but she won't like you listening to the radio with your grandfather or reading the newspaper with him, like you do with me, and on and on. She's got her old school ways, I mean, old, old school.

"This idea your mother had, it was a very dumb idea, and I shouldn't've gone along with it. But I did, and your grandma and grandpa wanted to help, so now, we're in this mess. I want you to un-mess it. Just agree to this, and I'll make it up to you."

"How?"

"Well, if you aren't the little negotiator, though!"

"Bigger than candy!" I say this sometimes when Daddy and I are bargaining for something. He taught me how to bargain.

Daddy laughs. "Okay, how about a used bike?"

"Yippee!"

"That do it?"

"Cowboy boots, too."

"Oh, no. One bargain chip is all there is in this negotiation."

"Okie dokie, Daddy. An agreement."

Daddy laughs. "Okay, but here's the deal. We have to look solemn, and you can't tell your mother yet, or she's see it as a bribe, and I'll be in lots of doo-doo."

I nod and laugh. "Grampa says 'doo-doo.' What's 'solemn?'"

"Serious as the devil. Oh, and another thing."

"Only one bargain chip, Daddy."

"I forgot to add this in the contract—that's a solid agreement, remember?

You have to go to Roosevelt with your mother on your best behavior and in your best dress, no overalls, not even a little argument. Got that?"

I'm silent, hesitating.

"No ifs, ands, or buts, Shike." Daddy holds out his hand. It has grease in all the cracks, but he smells of lava soap, so I know his hands are clean.

"Shake," I say.

"Shake." Daddy lifts his newspaper while he grins at me. We shake hands. Daddy's hands are hard—like leather—Momma says.

"When?"

"Oh God. No hounding. I should have put that in the contract, as well. First opportunity. Actually, to put your mind at ease, next Saturday, how's that? I know exactly how, when, and where to make that deal."

"Thank God Almighty," I say.

Daddy smiles. He doesn't scold me.

Momma comes to the dining room door to ask me for help in the kitchen. As I walk to where she's standing, I think I'll miss Gramma and Grampa Dirks and Shirly schooling, but farm life may not have agreed with me very much with all the sunrises and sunsets so early and late. And anyhow, I got a bicycle out of the deal.

A HEART
TO HEART
WITH
GRAMPA
DIRKS

THE
NOTICE

1.

Fall, 1943

"YOU'RE ALMOST THIRTY-FOUR YEARS old with two children!" Momma tries to hand Daddy his draft letter from the army. He's barely in the door. He has a folded newspaper and his lunch pail in one hand, his hat in the other, that he's holding tight against his chest like he does when he says the Pledge of Allegiance. Before he kicks the front door closed with his foot, I can see the wind's picked up so much the bottom branches of the trees are almost hitting the ground before they spring up and whirl around with the rest. Daddy looks like he's been hit in the face by one. What little hair he's got has swirled into jagged spikes, and his face is red, his eyes squinted closed. He looks like a clown from the picture books I used to look at when I was a baby.

Once he's inside, the closed door, he stands, shaking all over like a wet dog, and when he opens his eyes, he looks down at what Momma's trying to hand him. "What's this?" he asks, not looking at her. He knows what it is. "Darlene, let me get my bearings for the love of God. I damn near got blown away coming from the driveway."

Before the mail came, she was watching the skies outside the kitchen window, walking back and forth across the living room to listen to the weather reports on the radio and then back to the kitchen window, leaning over the sink, trying to see what she could. She was praying out loud that Daddy would get home before the storm hit. Now that he's here, she acts like she never prayed for him at all.

Daddy looks from me to Momma and back to me again. He wants me to tell him what Momma's shaking her head about, regardless of what he knows. I start to say it's about his notice, when Momma waves the letter in front of him like a fan. He'd better take it now, right now, because she wants this whole thing out of her hands and into his.

I almost reach for the notice so he can get a hold of himself and put his things down. Daddy takes off his shoes quick, puts his lunch pail by the clothes tree along with his newspaper. Only then does he take the letter from her, twisting his lips up to one side. He's playing along to keep her from going to pieces. Momma goes to pieces easy since they started talking about Daddy being called up for real, not just maybe. His number was called on the lottery a few days ago. When she began her why, why, whys, he told her, "Darlene, I'm called along with all the other men in the country who held number five hundred eighty-three. It's not like the government's out to get me alone, you know!"

But it was waiting for the letter that told Daddy to report immediately to the draft board that made Momma upset. "Until it was in my hand, anything could've happened," she said to me when it came. "By the grace of Almighty God, it could've gotten lost—the Lord's hand being in it, you see."

The radio Momma's left on is telling us that the storm that's tearing things apart outside our front door has winds that are sure to snap power lines and is bringing rain and hail that will make floods and beat down roofs. Just when the announcer says some gusts will be up to fifty, maybe sixty, miles an hour before the storm blows out of Hopewell, the lights flicker and go out a few times before they come back and stay on.

"The storm in all likelihood will follow a path to Okeene, Drummond, and on toward Hopewell," the radio says. "It has been gaining strength as it moves across the state in a northeasterly direction. All those in the path of this dangerous storm should take necessary precautions and stay inside but away from windows."

Daddy asks if the radio has said a tornado is likely. Momma tells him she's not giving a damn about the storm right now. She's only concerned about when he's going to the draft board and how he's going to act when he gets there.

About the storm, Momma's not telling the truth because she's terrified of storms. She wants to go driving across town every time there's "a nasty cloud in the sky"—that's how Daddy puts it. Sometimes—when she has the car because Daddy's tied up in a more-then-one-day job out of town, with the farmer getting him and bringing him home—she grabs Teddy and tells me to get in the car, that we're not gonna stay in this rickety house on the outskirts of colored town and get lambasted. Once we're in the car, I ask her where we're going. She just keeps looking out the windshield, past the wipers, saying, "We'll just have to outrun it, won't we?" I ask her again where we're going to outrun it to, but it's always her homeplace.

When I told Daddy, once, that's where we'd gone, to Gramma and Grandpa Dirks's in Shirly, he yelled at her. First of all, he told her, it's the gasoline we can't afford—that driving to Shirly and back's a whole week's allowance—and second, he says, Shirly is on the path of most of the storms around here. If it's on its way to Hopewell, it's probably hitting Shirly as she's driving there.

"You're not outrunning it, Darlene," he says. "You're running into it!"

But about Daddy going to the draft board, Momma's not lying. She's been more scared of the mail than any storm that might show up. After lunch today, like every day after lunch, she watched for the mail, walking back and forth from the kitchen to the front door and peering outside toward our mailbox at the side of the road. I don't see her do this every day, because I'm in school except for Saturdays. But when she carried the mail into the house today, she had her eyes closed. For a minute, I thought she might run into the table, but she opened them just in time. She looked down at the envelopes like they'd shown up in her hand out of nowhere. She tells me over and over that it's just been hell for her to go and get the mail every day, to look at what might be waiting in the box.

"I have to grit my teeth to bear it!" If that's so, I want to know why, then, she's running to get the mail as fast as she can, almost falling over before she can pull it out of the box? But I don't ask.

This afternoon, she stood out there holding all the envelopes with one hand and laying them against her stomach, flipping through them, one by one.

When she pulled out one toward the last, she made a terrible sound that anybody could have heard up and down the block. After that, she walked fast into the house and laid all the other mail on the dining room table, standing and staring at this one envelope in her hand. She couldn't take her eyes off it. She kept turning it over and over, running her fingers across it, like she was wiping it clean or trying to erase what was inside. Then she laid it down on the table without opening it and ran into the bedroom, crying.

I tried to figure out whether to go open the envelope and see for myself or go to the bedroom to help her stop crying. I decided instead to be with Teddy on the couch. Anything else, she'd be mad.

After a while, she came flying out of the bedroom and stood in front of Teddy and me, her eyes and cheeks all wet and red from crying. She stood looking at us, just looking at us without moving. It felt funny to have her staring and staring at us.

"What?" I asked more than once, but she kept raising her hands and letting them drop by her sides, bending over a little so they slapped her legs. Then she held her stomach like she had cramps.

"Is Daddy called up, for sure?"

"I think so, yes. Yes, it's finally here, for sure." She walked to the table then and tore the envelope open so fast and hard, it came apart in two pieces, one part falling to the floor. Her lips were twisted when she unfolded the paper, reading it to herself. When I went over next to her and asked if I could see, she pushed me away and told me to just sit and be quiet.

"You knew this was coming," she said down low, holding the letter out away from her, like it was gonna grab her face. She fell into Daddy's sofa chair. She never sits there. She let the letter fall to her lap, while she continued staring at it. She couldn't look anywhere else. What did she mean, "You knew this was coming?" Did she mean me? But down deep I knew it was both of us she was talking to, because before Daddy's registration number was announced, some of the boys, who weren't married at the Hopewell church, had been called up, and I heard Daddy talking to her about how the older guys—whether they were married with families or not—were going be called, too, right away, because the army doesn't care if you have kids.

Daddy said, "Darlene, the draft ages are eighteen to forty-five, period. Why would the United States government think I should be exempt?" I asked once when we were on the way to Hopewell for church what "exempt" meant, but neither Momma or Daddy answered me. Momma always says it's not for little kids to know, not to worry. But later, Daddy told me it meant not having to go to the army because of some reason the government thought was all right. When I asked him if he was doing one of those reasons, he shook his head.

"Not really, not the kind that would let me off the way your mother wants. To her way a-thinkin', I should manufacture a reason. But even if I could come up with something in time, I won't do that. She doesn't seem to realize you don't mess with the United States government without consequences." He poked my belly, jiggled it. "And don't ask about consequences. It means 'getting caught up with what you've done.'"

"When's the storm coming, Momma? Are we gonna get a tornado?" I asked her while she sat in Daddy's chair this afternoon, the letter in her lap, her staring at it, but not reading it yet. She waved her hand in the air. Then she sat very still with her elbow resting on the sofa chair and her head leaning against her hand. She sits this way a lot. It's like her head is too heavy to stay up on her neck without help. I think she can't hear anything but what's in her head, and everything she hears weighs her down. She says that this war weighs her down and wears her out all the time.

"It just goes on and on and on, doesn't it? It's never going to end, is it? At least, not in time to help us." She asks me like I know something she doesn't, and I won't tell her, like I can hear what's on the radio, and she can't, because there's something wrong with her hearing, or her brain's too full to take in the news. But she's gotta be able to hear it. Well, she does, I know she does, because she says things that tell me she does.

One afternoon a news flash came during her soap operas, while she was ironing. "They're beefing things up, they're not slowing them down. What happened to the Neutrality Act, I wanna know?" she asked me, whirling Daddy's shirt around on the board, ironing fast. "They said we wouldn't get involved, we'd support the British and the French, but we'd stay outta it. Well, now we're in it halfway around the world. Where the hell are half these places they're telling us our boys are fighting in? I can't even pronounce half of them." And she tells me over and over, "The politicians say one thing one day, and, then, the next, they're doing the opposite, so why do we believe them like we do? We follow our leaders who lie to us, just like our enemies are doing to their people. I'm done with it."

Sometimes, she acts like she never talks to Daddy about the war. She asks him questions, then acts like she hasn't heard a thing he's said.

So the afternoon, when she said "Neutrality Act," I said, "Pearl Harbor."

She stared at me.

"Pearl Harbor makes it different," I told her.

She stood the iron up and put her hand over her mouth while she looked at me, horrified. "You've been listening to your father. Has he been talking to you direct about this war again? I thought we'd put a stop to that, Shike. These aren't things to talk about with children. Well, you can believe this's gonna end for good. I mean it. I don't know, sometimes, what gets into your father that he thinks—"

"No, Grampa Dirks. I sit on his lap when he talks with Daddy. Grandpa Dirks says, 'Pearl Harbor makes everything different. No more signing away the war, leaving friends standin' alone.'" I don't understand what she's talking about. She sees me help Daddy with his maps and newspaper clippings at night, knows I sit and listen to the news with him after dinner, before bed.

"Well, there'll be no more sitting on Grandpa Dirks's lap when war is discussed, from now on." Momma turned up her soap opera on the radio. I don't know if I'll get to sit on Grampa's lap anymore or not. Sometimes she remembers to do what she says, other times she forgets.

She doesn't like it when Daddy has the radio on for the news while we eat. A long time ago, when she asked him why we can't have supper in peace, he told her that if he had to choose between her supper or the news, he'd just have to miss her supper. She doesn't say anything these days, only raises her hand and waves it over her head while she keeps eating. I think Momma wants to listen but wants to get mad at Daddy for it.

After the news is over, and he turns the radio off, Daddy talks about "our guys" and "our boys." He especially talks about our guys coming in from all over the country and from England who're training as pilots at the Hopewell Landing Field.

Momma told him one night, "You make it sound like all these men going to war are part of our family, Vernon, and they're not. For one thing, there're more Mennonite boys going to the wheat fields than the battlefields. And some are going to camps or even prison for unwillingness to serve, as you well know. It's not you making your decisions for yourself anymore. There's Jesse, too, you know. What's gonna happen to him, in the end, after this war? You ever give that a thought to that?"

"Your brother needed to enlist, if you want my opinion. The army woulda straightened him out like he needed to be straightened out. God only knows what he was really doing at seminary, probably drinking and screwing his way through, while he left your parents behind to do all the work on the farm. Well, he got his due, didn't he? We'll see what being in—" Daddy put his hand up before Momma stopped him. "Okay, regardless of what I think of Jesse, and what he's done, tell me how he's going to get out of this one, Darlene? Oh, right, he's a half-preacher now, isn't that what he's writing home about, to your mother, instead of stating it like it really is?"

Momma was furious. She looked at me and told me to go play someplace else and take Teddy with me. But she didn't wait to see if I went, so I stayed and listened. "He was on his way to ordination when he got himself in trouble."

Momma glared at Daddy. Now it was her turn to hold up her hand to stop his rampage. "First of all, we all get ourselves in trouble, now and again, wouldn't you say? But Jesse is neither here nor there in this argument we're having tonight, Vernon, and you know it. So don't cloud the issue. When we were running around all over Oklahoma and Kansas with Josephine and Clifford, Sherman and Nita Jane, and Jesse and his girlfriends, I didn't hear you complaining. You were right in there with the drinking and horsing around. And as for my father, he's not keen on the war. He's got some anti-German opinions, is all.

"He doesn't like all this talk of brutality coming on the news about Hitler and Mussolini, how they go after anybody they hate, especially the Jews, and try to annihilate them. That's the word Hitler's used, you know. Annihilate.

Jesus was a Jew, remember. If Jesus was alive, he'd be saying these men would be out to annihilate Him. That's pretty extreme, I'd say."

"Well, actually that's what happened to Jesus during His time, if you really look at it."

Momma almost couldn't breathe. She sputtered when she talked. "Maybe so, but you're trying to get me off my message here, Vernon."

"All I'm trying to say is that you and me are in agreement more than you want to admit, Darlene."

"Oh, I don't think so. My dad takes what Hitler's doing personal, seeing's how we're all German. We were raised pacifists, speaking the German language, calling it our own. He reads High German, and he and Mother still speak *Plattdeutsch* in the house. The present political situation in Germany troubles him. He feels we need to do something to make things over there right, but that doesn't mean he's for the war."

"What Whalen is for is called Just War."

"What're you talking about?"

"It's a theory that allows people, who don't believe in war, a way of justifying the use of force and violence under certain conditions."

"And what might those be, for the love of God?"

"You've heard Reverend Classen talk about Just War versus the pacifist position. I know you have, because our church is conflicted at the moment over it."

"I don't remember him using that term."

"Well, he has, but term or not, he's talked about what it means in a couple of his sermons lately."

Daddy waited for Momma to ask.

Finally she asked, with a grudge, "Which conditions?"

"First off, people who believe in Just War think it's the last resort, that all other means of resolution should be tried first. And in our case now, that's been done with Chamberlain and others signing an agreement with Hitler in Munich that gave him Czech borderland, which was supposed to appease him but didn't. Then, Hitler and Stalin signed the German-Soviet Pact, which Hitler used to take over Poland, so Stalin wouldn't attack him. So it was pretty easy to see that no amount of appeasement was going to stop this man's aggression.

His speeches and *Mein Kampf* told us what he was going to do from the beginning, but we gave appeasement a try."

Momma stared at Daddy, like she was hypnotized. Her mouth hung open like she couldn't believe what she was hearing.

"So your dad believes that our going to war with Hitler and his allies is justified because we tried all the other options."

After a minute, Momma found her voice. "Dad'll have to tell me himself he believes in this Just War theory of yours. I don't believe it. He's never said—"

"Darlene, for the love of God, it's not my theory—"

"Okay, the theory."

Then Daddy was furious. "Your dad's not going to say outright to you he believes this. He doesn't want to get your mother riled, for one thing. But Just War people's major belief is that you have a right to defend yourself and help out your friends when they're attacked. You aren't punishing the enemy. You're protecting your rights and that of your allies."

"But that's what Hitler thinks he's doing, that he's got a right to do what he's doing, just like we say about ourselves. It's all over the news. So it goes back and forth until it has to be settled by fighting it out until somebody wins. So many lives lost for nothing."

"Well, that's pretty much the pacifist position, actually. If you do fight, it may solve something in the short term but not the long one. So war is futile. Not all pacifists argue this way. Some think killing is one of God's commandments, so you simply don't ever do it, which is what our ancestors have—"

"I'm with the ancestors."

"Well, maybe, but if somebody came in here and started killing our kids—"

"Vernon!"

"Okay, okay, but I listen to you talk, Darlene, and so help me God, I cannot figure out which side of the fence you're on most of the time. You protect your father's pro-war views, even while you try to say that's not what he means, but then when I talk like he does, you say I'm pro-war, me thinking Mennonite pacifist views should be hanged. All at once, you're so far to the anti-war side you're practically a Holdeman. I don't get this."

I know about the Holdemans, that they wear beards and head scarves.

They aren't the Amish but close. Gramma Dirks wants to be Holdeman, but Grampa Dirks won't join the church with her. She goes to a Mennonite church without beards and scarves now, but she always hopes one day she can be with the Holdemans. Gramma Jantz is a Holdeman, but Grampa Jantz won't go to church with her, either. Momma's explained this to me.

"I can understand the other side without agreeing with it, Vernon," Momma said real quiet. "Isn't that what you tell me, all the time, that I should be doing like you think you're doing—trying to see the other side? I know that the boys being shipped over there believe they're fighting for what's right, and maybe they are, but—"

"So in a way, they are 'our boys,' then, aren't they, Darlene, whether you want to say so or not, because they're dying for our country, the one we live in and belong to and where we enjoy freedom of religion. You remember, our ancestors came over here by choice. They didn't do very well anywhere else, did they? But then again, maybe you want to be shipped back to Russia and live with the few distant relatives we left behind, after being run outta Holland and then Polish Prussia. Boy Howdy, I'd like to see how that'd pan out—you living the old life in Russia! Something worth watching, I'd say, you making plümemooss while wearing a black kerchief, wool socks, and Old Colony-style shoes, with Stalin breathing down your Mennonite neck!"

Daddy was on a rampage, with no end in sight. He stood up, leaning over the dining room table toward Momma. "And he is, you know! Can you imagine what it's like to be a German-speaking Mennonite refusing to serve in his army, right now? Exactly one year ago, Darlene, Germans in the Volga area were rounded up and sent to labor camps in Siberia and other places. A lot of these Germans were Mennonites, thrown in with the Lutherans, Catholics, and, God only knows, who all. We're talking about over a half-million people!"

Daddy is breathing hard. "I keep up with this, Darlene, because the world—in places once dear to us—is falling apart. I talk to your dad and pay attention. Those newspapers you seem to think I read just so I can argue my side against you, well, they tell me how things really are." Daddy left the table and started to walk to the kitchen. As he got ready to leave the room, he turned around and added, "Everybody's in trouble over there right now unless they are in the Red army." He looked away and sighed. "And Stalin's soldiers have their own grief from what I can make out on the news."

Momma waved her hand over her head again and mumbled something about Stalin being the United States' friend. Did Daddy want to really fight alongside friends like that, she wondered? She put her fork on her plate and stared at him until Daddy left the room.

Momma believes like she does because of Gramma Dirks. Daddy's told me so when we were by ourselves, him getting ready to read his paper in his chair. "She listens to her Mother and gets all convicted about how this war is leading us down the road to sin and ruin. But she's just scared. She admits it when she's got her right mind."

Now, with Daddy reading his draft letter, I turn my head to try and make out the sign on the top of the page, a circle with words on the outside and an eagle inside holding something in both feet. In school we learned the bald eagle stands for The United States because it is free. It lives high up on mountain tops and needs to be strong and have lots of courage to fight the weather and other birds to keep its families safe. Daddy pulls me over so I can see its picture better on his notice.

I look toward the door. I can't believe nobody in our house is watching the weather. They're both acting like it's sunny outside, and everybody is just going about their business. I hear the wind tearing around the house and ripping through the trees, with hail against the windows, but Daddy stands next to me pointing to what he wants me to see.

"This makes it official," he says. "That's the seal of...." Daddy looks at the circle close without his glasses and tells me that it's from the Selective Service System. He hums and tells me, "And that's an eagle, which is our country's national bird. And it has..." he pulls the paper up almost to his nose, "olive branches in its talons on one side and arrows on the other side. That stands for peace on the one hand and... well, standing up for yourself on the other." He looks at it a while longer before putting it down for me to see again.

"You mean to fight against our enemies domestic and foreign?"

Daddy laughs a little. "You learn that in school? They teaching you this?"

"Oath for the Constitution."

"Well, it's an oath of office for the President and Congress in support of the Constitution. Could be that service men have to say it, as well." He winks as me. "I guess I'll find that out."

He hums a little, looks down at the letter again. "There's the stars and stripes as a shield in front of the eagle that's got its wings spread open. I've seen this seal on lots of things having to do with the President. It means the Selective Service Office is sending this in the name of the President. See here? It says, 'The President of the United States,' and then it says, 'to,' and here's my name on this line. So it's addressed to me."

Momma slaps her hand down on the dining room table, and I jump. Daddy watches her as she wipes her eyes on a tea towel that she's been wearing around her dress like an apron, walks toward the bathroom door, and throws the towel in a hamper nearby that she keeps for Teddy. The lid comes down with a bang. She stops for a minute at the bedroom door but doesn't turn around when he calls out to her.

"Darlene, what do you want me to do? Throw it in the trash and go to prison? It's here now." He waits a minute, says, "You knew this was coming. They called my number on the lottery. It was just a matter of time before I got the actual notice. C'mon! This isn't a surprise." He waves the notice in the air like it somehow got wet, and he's trying to dry it off. "We have to face it now." She said the same thing to me when she finally picked it up off of her lap and read it this afternoon while sitting in Daddy's easy chair.

Momma lets out a low moan but doesn't slam their bedroom door when she goes in to be by herself. Daddy gives his draft notice to me and says, "You can look at it, Shike, as much as you want, but when you're done, you leave it on the table, okay?"

"I can't read the words," I tell him.

He takes the notice again and points, "This line says Order To Report For Induction. It means I've been notified to report to my local draft board so they can classify me—which means they'll be telling me what I'll be doing for the government during this war."

"Will you serve?" I ask him. Momma and Daddy both say "serve" when they talk about Daddy being in the army.

"In some capacity, yes. I have to take a physical and have an interview. We'll see what happens after I go to the draft board." He points to a line with a number on it. He's grinning when I look up at him. "I am one thousand four hundred and forty-two. That's only for Cleveland County, here in Oklahoma. Says that right here." He points to a place on the paper. "But you best not call me one-four-four-two in front of your mother. She's not anywhere near liking any of this."

Then he kneels down beside me and runs his hands down my arms before he puts his hands around mine. He does this sometimes when he's mad. But when he's like he is now, his hands feel soft. "Everything's gonna be fine, lil lady." Momma says he calls me "lil lady" from a song he's listened to on the radio, some song she says is a "Cowboy Number." Momma doesn't like cowboy music.

Daddy pulls me to him and gives me a hug. He smells like axle grease. I know axles are what hold the tires on. He uses grease to make them run easy.

"Men are being called up all over the country. They have numbers too. It's not just me. You understand?" Daddy stands up with the notice in his hand.

"I know." I heard him tell Momma, but Mrs. Tate told us during questions-and- answers time about the war at school.

Daddy is very serious. "Regardless of what happens from now on, I want you to remember that I've told you this. Your mother over-expresses herself when she gets worried. She's likely to come up with all kinds of ideas about what's gonna happen before any of it does. And chances are most of it isn't gonna happen, okay? She's trying to cover all the bases is how you can think about it. Like in baseball."

I nod. He knows I play throw with Leon on the farm when we visit. During summer, I listen to games on the radio with my boy cousins when Uncle Clifford does.

"Well, your mother wants to have her glove on when the ball gets thrown at her. She doesn't wanna get socked by any bad news. She wants to be at the ready when we have to do whatever we have to do next—after I've been to the draft board, okay? So you keep your eyes open and your chin up over what's gonna start happening around here." He nods his head at me, and I think I see tears in his eyes, but his voice isn't shaky when he says, "I'm gonna go talk to her now for a little bit and try to calm things down."

"When do you go away?" I ask.

"It'll be Saturday, is what it says. Early, at eight o'clock. But I'll be back." He hands the notice to me. I take it easy-like, because I could drop it and spoil everything. "But I only report to the draft board. They're just on the other side of town, and then they'll tell me about my physical, when that is. It's not all going to happen in one big swipe like the newscasters make it sound, you know." He looks toward the bedroom door and raises his voice so Momma can hear. "They're not gonna grab me, throw a helmet on my head, hand me some combat boots, and put me on a plane to New Guinea before I can say boo, baa, or kiss my butt, like your mother thinks." I laugh.

Then he lowers his voice to almost a whisper. "Just remember to put the notice back on the table, because I have to take it with me when I go." Before he reaches the bedroom door, he turns and says, "Don't show it to Teddy, okay, because if he grabs it, it'll be gone for good."

I know not to do that anyway, because Teddy can't read anything, and he puts everything in his mouth. He's likely to eat Daddy's notice as anything.

I stare at it. I try to make out the words, but I want to wad it up and throw it away. I'd make Momma happy, but it won't keep Daddy from going into the army or some camp when he tells the government he's a Mennonite and won't fight in a war. Some of the boys at church have said yes to the government and have been sent overseas already. They've been fighting for a while. The radio says where, but the names are hard to understand and say. Daddy listens real careful when he lets me sit on his lap in his sofa chair, and we listen to the news. The first time I heard Solomon Islands, I asked Daddy if it was named after King Solomon in the Bible. He said he didn't know, but it was a darn good question.

At church, the fathers of the boys who've been shipped overseas tell Daddy when they get letters from them and what they say. I listen by Daddy's side when the men stand in the parking lot and tell him they don't get mail very often from their sons, and when they do, they can't tell them where they are or anything about how bad it is. All they say is that they miss being home. Harold Mueller said he hadn't heard from Sammy for so long he figured he'd get a letter any day telling him his son was missing or dead, but, then, lo an' behold, two days ago, he got three of Sammy's letters on the same day. "We live letter to letter," he says, "with prayers in between."

Once in a while, somebody shows Daddy an envelope with a sticker along the side that says their son's letter has been read by a censor. Daddy looked at a letter for a long time that Winslow Becker handed him one Sunday that had cut-outs on the pages. I could see the envelope had the censor's number on it.

"Government secrets," Daddy told me on the way home, when I asked why some of the letter was chopped up.

"Loose lips sink ships," Momma explained. "Censors read the boys' mail so what they accidentally say won't fall into the hands of the enemies of our country who could use it against us."

"Spies," I said.

Momma grabbed my hand and shook it a little. "Where in the world did you hear about spies?" She looked over at Daddy.

"Don't look at me," he said, grinning.

"No, not Daddy. Tommy Don. He says they're standing on every street corner just waiting to hear something they can give to the enemy. He says if the Japs and Gerries know where our soldiers and sailors are, they can bomb them before they can shoot back."

"Dear Lord. It's not funny, Vernon. Josie's kids just spout off anything they hear. That's why—"

"C'mon, Darlene. Kids're bound to hear things—at school especially—and they have their own imaginations about what they do get here and there. You can't shelter them from all a-this."

Momma asked me, "Do you even know what a spy is, what it really means?"

"Sure," I told her. "It's bad guys who listen to what you say and tell other bad guys who buy it for money."

"I think that's called a gossip column, Shike." Daddy laughed out loud.

"Oh, murder," Momma mumbled from behind the fancy hanky Gramma had given her for her last birthday, the one with lace and the yellow flower embroidered on it. I knew Momma was laughing even though she wasn't making any sound because her shoulders were shaking up and down.

———————

MOMMA IS CRYING IN THEIR bedroom, and Daddy is talking to her low. I can't hear, not even very much when she talks to him loud because her words are coming out in little jerks. I'm putting the letter on the table when Daddy opens the door all at once and tells me to put the radio on and stay with Teddy. I put the radio on quiet but still can't hear what Momma and Daddy are saying. He's told me to put on music, but the news has started up again. The newscaster talks in an excited but hushed voice for a long time about the war in Italy and the Solomons. He says General Douglas MacArthur and New Guinea over and over. He says New Guinea more than any other place where our boys are.

When the bedroom door opens again, Momma flings it wide and walks fast to the couch and picks up Teddy, kissing him on his cheek, even though he tries to squirm away. He wants to stay on the couch and bounce his head against the back cushion, but Momma doesn't put him back down. She just holds him tighter. All at once, Teddy brings his head back and then forward, fast, and knocks Momma hard right in the mouth.

She pushes him back, yells, then swats his behind. "Bad boy. Bad, bad." She wipes her mouth and looks at her fingers. Teddy starts crying real loud, trying to squirm out of her arms. Momma looks at me like I'm the one who's made him knock her in the mouth. Her eyes are swollen something awful. They're so red they look like they're bleeding. She's about the worst unhappy I've ever seen her. But then, even with Teddy screaming in her ear, squirming so bad she almost can't hold him, she reaches down and touches my face, holding my chin in her hands a little bit, before she lets go.

She looks me hard in the eyes. "We'll be all right, you'll see. We'll make it, regardless of where we are, with or without your daddy." Her fingers feel warm, but she is far, far away from Teddy and me. I'm seeing something about her, something she's feeling, that I should know a lot better than I do. What's it gonna be like when Momma, Teddy, and me go live someplace without Daddy? Momma asks Daddy, sometimes, if he thinks she can't make it without him. She asks this when they're fighting. She tells him, "Well, I can, you know," and puts her chin out like she can take it even if he hits her.

But she means something different now. I think she means we can make it without Daddy by living someplace else while he's away from us, but it's gotta be the right place. And her homeplace in Shirly—living with Gramma and Grampa Dirks—is the only place she wants to live when Daddy is gone. She keeps telling him that this is the best answer for everybody.

"Where is Daddy going? When he leaves, when will he come back?"

"That's the thing not clear in all of this," she says to me. "I can't explain it to you now, Shike, but I will as soon as things are settled."

I am so scared my whole body shakes. I run to her and Teddy as she walks to the kitchen. I grab her dress. "Momma… Momma," I begin, but I can't ask her again what I want to know, because she doesn't know. I want her to give me an answer that would make me feel better, but she could tell me one that would change our family so much it wouldn't be my family anymore. Then I think something I've never thought before, and once I do, I can't stop thinking about it. What if Daddy never comes back? It feels like he's dying, that he's been shot already or a bomb is just outside the door that will fall on him when he goes outside.

Momma and Daddy have said that whatever happens about the service, it's not going to be the same. They've argued when they talked about what's next. I don't want there to be any more fights, but I want Daddy to be home even if they never stop fighting. I keep thinking that their arguments will stop if we just moved from colored town or Daddy somehow made more money or the war would end before he's sent overseas. I get up every morning, looking at them to see if anything has happened different since I went to bed, thinking that they might tell me The United States has won the war—it came over the news, while I was sleeping—and now we get our old life back.

Momma sits down with Teddy and finally puts him beside her. He starts bouncing his head against the couch right away, fast, with his thumb in his mouth. She's almost broke him of the thumb-sucking habit with oil of cloves that burns his lips when he sucks and later a thumb cage that he keeps trying to pull off until his skin bleeds.

"If you're big enough to try and pull it off, you're big enough to stop sticking your thumb in your mouth every two seconds," she tells him. He keeps trying to take it off, anyway. But today she leaves him alone.

Finally, she tells me to come next to her, as well. I stand by her side. She messes with my hair. "Your daddy's going to the draft board to get his assignment, what the government wants him to do, and where they want him to go. A lot depends on what your daddy decides to tell them, do you understand?"

"Yes." It's like she thinks I haven't heard a thing they've said all the time they've been fighting. It's all they fight about now—whether he'll say "conscientious objector," that will sends him to a camp or "non-combatant," that will send him to the war to help the soldiers but not carry a gun.

Daddy comes out of the bedroom, and without looking at me, stops at the table, re-reads his notice, picks it up, and carries it away. He is gone quite a while before he comes to the cup of coffee Momma's set for him on the dining room table. He's washed his face, and his hair is wet and combed against his head.

I sit on the couch with Teddy, holding him against me until he pushes me away. Then Daddy walks to his easy chair, watching his cup real careful, looking at it every now and then so it won't spill, holding it out in front of him. He winks at me, leans over and puts his cup on the floor next to his chair before walking to the front door and opening it. The storm is gone. The trees are dripping big rain drops on our sidewalk and porch. He steps back when a burst of wind splashes water on his socks. The air is cool and smells like rain and grass and wet dirt. He closes the door, walking back to his sofa chair, bringing the newspaper with him that he left folded under the coat tree when he first came in.

"That's one way to get rid of a storm," he says when he passes me and Teddy. "Just don't pay it no never mind! Woo-wee." He laughs a little, taking off and shaking one sock and then the other on the rug in front of his chair. He bends down, lifts his cup, and takes a noisy sip of his coffee before he sits down and puts the cup back on the floor.

"Cold." He shakes his head at his cup, then opens the newspaper, but he stops, crumbles it up a little in his lap when he leans over and drinks more coffee. I watch his face. He has the same look he had when he took the letter out of Momma's hand. He's not feeling the same way Momma is about the army. He feels good inside, and it's coming out all over his face. He snaps the paper open with a little pop like it's got something very important about the war in it he wants to see.

2.

The days before Saturday

EVERY DAY BEFORE SATURDAY, MOMMA calls Daddy's draft notice, "his letter," like it's all his fault he's had it mailed to him from the President. When he tries to talk about it, she says she doesn't want anything more to do with it. But it's not true because she talks to him about it when she wants to.

I asked Daddy one evening what the army is going to do to him because he's a Mennonite. He folded the newspaper and pulled me up to his lap and brushed my hair back before he told me that he wasn't sure exactly, but the main thing he was going to tell them was that he wasn't going to carry a gun, wasn't going to kill anybody.

"What will they say then?"

"I don't know what to tell you, because I've never done this before. I only know some things they might say, but I don't see that talking to you about them now will help because none of what I'm thinking may come up, at all, and what I do know is hearsay." He grinned at me. "Okay, hearsay means only things I've heard from other people at church and at work who went to the draft board. Everybody's different. The hard thing is waiting. That's especially hard for your mother."

Momma was in the kitchen, so she couldn't hear him. He was talking low, just to me. "She wants to know what's going to happen next, too, so she can stop worrying, but then that's not exactly true, either. She's gonna worry one way or the other. You have to be brave and wait. We'll know day after tomorrow." They both want me to be brave.

The night before Daddy goes to the draft board, they start up at supper about moving to Shirly. For Momma, it's Shirly and the Dirks's Farm over and over. Daddy says for the fortieth time he doesn't want us to do anything until we find out exactly what's going to happen next. Momma's comeback is what she's said the fortieth time.

"So do you have anything else in mind?" She means other than going to the draft board and telling them he's a conscientious objector. "You know what, Vernon, until you settle this thing inside, maybe I should pull Shike outta school, altogether. Maybe she should stay at home to learn like the Holdeman kids. I'll teach her. Could be that's what we need to do so she doesn't get all taken up with her classmates and teachers and wanna stay here, when we know damn good and well we're probably gonna have to move, anyway, because I'm not stayin' here in colored town all alone. That's for damn sure. Why we can't move now, I just don't know."

After this rampage, with no comeback from Daddy, the room goes quiet and stays that way for the rest of the evening. The only sounds are dishes clattering, cupboard doors opening and closing, me talking to Teddy, him saying a few words back, and Daddy reading his newspaper. Even the radio is silent.

Momma's told me all about how Holdeman kids go to their own schools that the Holdemans build themselves, or they have school at home with their relatives. The Holdeman kids' parents take turns teaching them, or they hire one of their church members as the teacher. When Momma was little, she had cousins that went to Holdeman schools or learned at home, and when she begged Gramma Dirks to go with them or learn at home, her mother told her she'd like that, but Grampa Dirks wouldn't allow it. And when Momma went to Grampa and begged, he told her, "I'd sooner send you to Africa and let you sit on bleachers under a thatched roof with the missionaries."

So Momma went to a one-room schoolhouse that was hard to get to when it rained and snowed, but "as hard as it was and as much as I had to miss, he wasn't about to give in," she said. "Your grampa is a strong believer in public education, let me tell you." Later when Momma went into town for high school, he drove her there when she couldn't find a ride with the neighbors.

So I don't know what she's trying to tell Daddy about me staying at home for school like the Holdemans. Grampa Dirks is sure to hit the ceiling if she tries. But when we're alone before bedtime, she tells me that she's changed her mind about homeschooling, that she doesn't exactly agree with Grampa about public education, but she certainly can't and won't teach me herself, and Grampa sure as heck won't.

"Hopewell Mennonite doesn't believe in their own schools because they aren't as closed-off from the world as the Holdemans. And I have to admit that I don't want to be as cut off from society as they are either—at least not to the degree they are, anyway."

She does worry, though, about some of the things that I'm taught at public school these days, she tells me, like about how the earth was created, how some history is taught, and now, especially about the war effort and other social activities. Mennonites don't want their people participating in dancing and lots of social ideas such as how Santa Claus is taking the place of Jesus at Christmastime. But she explains each Mennonite church has its own rules about what is allowed, about what is acceptable for their children to hear, and to what degree they allow them to participate in teachings and activities at school as they are decided by the congregation and church board.

I ask her if the church board is like the draft board.

"It is in a way, Shike, because, like the draft board, a group of men decide on how the church will be run and what they will allow and not allow, a lot like the draft board does about the army. But it's always the people on the boards who decide, just like they will with Daddy. And when people don't know or can't decide, they usually take it to 'a higher authority.' At church that's a larger committee that's over all the churches. In the army, it probably is a person higher in rank."

Momma then tells me she wants me in public school with the other kids, and Daddy has more than agreed with this. "I'm just aggravated that he's being so damned secretive about what he's going to do with his classification."

I don't ask about classification, because I know about 1-A and 1-A-O and the difference between non-combatant and conscientious objector. Non-combat people do army without guns, while C.O.s go to camps where they do no army work but work the government tells them to do—cleaning and repairs parks, fighting fires, making roads. So I tell Momma instead that I don't want to leave Hopewell because I like Mrs. Tate and the kids at my school. She rubs my back and says we'll know soon enough what we'll do, but I can stop worrying about being homeschooled.

"After all, how would it look," she says, "to have my father on the schoolboard in Shirly and his grandkid staying home for school?"

3.

Draft board day

ON SATURDAY, WE ALL SIT at the breakfast table for a long time without saying a word. Teddy is sitting on Daddy's lap, making rumbling noises while eating eggs and bacon from Daddy's plate. Momma usually doesn't like Teddy to eat from Daddy's plate, but this morning she acts like it's not happening. From the time Momma came into my bedroom to wake me up and show me what to put on, there's been only quiet in the house. We're doing everything the same but without words, and underneath, it couldn't be more different. This is the day Momma doesn't want to have happen. And they've been talking about it for so long that now that it's here, they don't know what to say.

Momma stands at the stove stirring oatmeal, and Daddy's drinking his coffee in huge gulps. She's already given us eggs and toast. It's a special breakfast with everything Daddy likes. Momma hands Daddy his bowl of oatmeal without looking at him, but she does it slow and easy. He splashes his oatmeal with cream and sprinkles it with brown sugar that Momma told me she got from Gramma Dirks. Finally, Daddy starts talking a little to Teddy about breakfast, and then, he nods to me.

"Shike, hand me the butter there." He points to the dish in front of me. It's oleo, but he calls it butter. Momma makes it look yellow by stirring in a little red dot that comes in the package.

She's handing me my bowl of oatmeal when she says, "Don't leave the eggs behind." Then, all at once, they're both talking, not to each other, but to Teddy and me. "Use your spoon," they say. And "That's enough now," and "No more complaining, just eat," even when I haven't said anything. "Stop stirring your food around," Momma says. "What's the matter with you? You look like you've just been killed."

I look up at her, but she doesn't look back at me. She doesn't want me to answer her. She wants Daddy out of the house. She wants him at the draft board, so she can take me into the bathroom and wash my hair. That's what we'll do next because that's what we always do on Saturdays, and we're going to do everything we always do today. I start thinking there must be a way to make all the Saturday things stop, not let them happen, at least not like this, not so quiet and scary. We're all going along, because we have to, even though we don't want to. It's like when I dress for church, when I don't want to go, and Momma keeps putting on my dress and shoes, regardless. It doesn't matter how I feel or whether I say anything or not. What's going to happen is going to happen.

I'm afraid to ask anything now, and, anyway, I've asked everything before, every day. They just keep telling me they don't know this or don't know that. But they could tell me the things they won't say.

Then, all at once, I want Daddy to go like Momma wants him gone. I want her to wash my hair, put it in rollers, and let me play with my paper dolls while Teddy bounces his head against the back of the couch.

When Daddy stands up and finishes the last of his coffee, I start to get up and go with him to the door, but Momma tells me to stay where I am. She tells me that Daddy's coming back, that he'll tell us what's happening once he's home, later. She wipes Teddy's mouth and combs his hair with her fingers. She doesn't walk Daddy into the living room like she usually does when he goes to work. At the door, after he's opened it, she says, "My God, Vernon, I just noticed, you have your work uniform on. Why are you—"

"It was this or my suit. A suit doesn't seem right for the draft board, do you think?" Momma only nods. She gets up from the table, finally, and walks to him as he stands at the door and puts her hand on his, the one that he's got around the doorknob. He leans over and kisses her on the mouth. She hugs him for a minute.

"How long do you think?"

"I have no idea, but I'm guessing a couple of hours." He smiles quick, then looks down at the floor, swings around, and walks out the door.

She doesn't move. She calls after him in a whisper, "Well, okay then," as he closes the door, leaving us behind.

Momma comes back to the table and starts to pick up the dishes. I think she might cry, but she looks at me instead and says what I know she will. "Shike, get down to your underwear. Let's get ready to wash your hair."

———————

IN THE BATHROOM—ME STANDING in front of the sink, while Momma washes my hair, pushing me this way and that, telling me to stand up straight, stand to the side, bend over more—she doesn't say anything about what is happening to Daddy, to us as a family. But when she dries my hair with the towel, she says, "I know what your father's likely to do. He'd just as soon leave and go overseas. I'm praying to God that he won't do anything foolish." She's never told me that she thinks he might actually sign up to leave because he wants to, but I know what she means. I see it in Daddy's eyes when he talks about the war and listens to the radio.

She gives a sudden twist to the towel as she pulls it off my head. I stare at her in the mirror. Her eyes look somewhere beyond both us standing there.

"He's going to war like everybody else?"

"Not exactly." She slips the towel back over my head and wiggles it around, covering my face so that I can't see her anymore. "If he does what I think he's gonna do, he's likely to go as a non-combatant."

Right now, as we stand before the sink as Momma dries my hair, Daddy could be saying what he shouldn't say and be sent away from us forever. All at once, I know he wants to go so bad that he will go.

"It's the god-damned radio," Momma says fiercely, throwing the towel in the tub, taking a few steps away from me. "Momma's right." She stands with her chin in her hand, her elbow against her waist like a statue, her other hand grasping the rim of the bathtub as though it's holding her up. "We've brought evil in the house with it!"

I want to ask her about her soap operas, but she'd just tell me she'd be willing to give them up if Daddy wouldn't listen to war news ever again. "He's not gonna listen to me. He's married to his news and newspapers!" I heard her tell him the other night while she was folding laundry at the dining room table, "If you sat any closer to the radio, Vernon, you'd fall into the newscaster's lap."

"Where's he going? To the Solomons?"

Momma stares at me, her eyes wide, her mouth open. Finally she says, "Well, yes, that could happen if he becomes a non-combatant. You've heard us talk about this. You know by now, Shike." She mumbles "Solomons" while she shakes her head and moves my hair around, fluffing it in the air, looking at me sideways, for a minute. "Your daddy could go anywhere the troops go. He could be on the front driving a truck with supplies or be an assistant to a medic on the battlefield or be in a hospital tent helping the wounded right there in the middle of the fighting." Looking right at me, in the mirror, she whispers, "He could be called to go to another country, be shipped overseas like all the other men. He'd be in the thick of battle, like the soldiers totin' the guns. It's actually more dangerous, to my way of thinkin', because he wouldn't have any way to protect himself. But carrying a gun, even your daddy knows how wrong that would be." She makes this sound like being a soldier with a gun is something so awful that you could get in trouble with God over it. He punishes people in the Bible all the time who don't do what He says. When you're a Mennonite, God is a lot like the army. You do what He says or else.

"When would he go?" A huge bubble of air forms in my chest.

"Right away. In weeks, maybe even days, I'm not sure, but it will be too soon." When I start to cry, she kneels down in front of me, hugging me to her. When she finally holds me out away from her, her hands still on my arms, she says, very soft, "But that's just one way to look at this, Shike. I've talked to people at church whose sons are working in hospitals overseas. They aren't on the battlefields. The hospitals they're at are in countries where the allies are stationed, and they are safe—as safe as they can be during war. We have to believe that God is hearing our prayers and will take care of your daddy and bring him safely back to us, even if he doesn't do exactly what he's supposed to do."

———————

MY FATHER COMES HOME AFTER dark. Momma was pacing the floor, too worried to make anything to eat for supper. She called Aunt Josie at least six times, which was going to make Daddy awful mad, as our telephone bill could "skyrocket way past our ability to pay."

Instead of being mad though—after Momma gets done telling him how worried she's been and how she's called Aunt Josie umpteen times—he just shrugs and tells her that she shouldn't've worried. After all, she knew he was in safer hands at the draft board than probably walking down Hopewell's streets! Tonight Daddy's in too good a mood to let himself get caught in Momma's worries. He goes into the kitchen, pours himself a cup of coffee Momma's had waiting for him, and tells us to sit down and listen to the amazing story he has to tell. Momma stands up to say she needs to go make supper—that he'll have to talk up a little, but she'll be listening.

Daddy nods and begins.

At the draft board office, the woman who signed him up happened to live, at one time, next door to his sister, Caroline, my Aunt Carrie, who's named after Gramma Jantz just like I am. She said that she knew how our family felt about the war, how we are good Americans but just don't believe in fighting on the front with guns. She believed there was a way he could be loyal to both his country and his religious beliefs and not have to be shipped away from Momma, Teddy, and me.

She was acquainted with the head of air repair on the other side of the Field, she said, and since Daddy was a mechanic, he might be able to stay in Hopewell at the Landing Field, working in a capacity that he could accept, not as a non-combatant, like he was going to sign up for, but as an exempted civilian. While Daddy waited, this woman called and arranged for him to meet the head of airplane repair, who sent him on to the Colonel, at the base, who interviewed him.

"And, lo' and behold, Colonel Myers hired me on the spot. Amazing, don't you think?" Daddy grins, shoving his coffee mug back and forth from hand to hand over the wrinkling tablecloth, the mug's brown liquid almost jumping over the rim. "Here's the interesting part that I didn't know, Darlene." Daddy's talking to where Momma was sitting at the dining room table—at her chair like she's still there. "You have to be a civilian to work on trainer planes because they don't hire men from inside the military to do that work. I guess they figure it would be a waste of manpower they could better use more directly in the fighting or, maybe, in other ways. Darned if I know. Probably has something to do with war contracts and money, it's usually about money. But for whatever reasons, they kicked me outta the army before I even had a chance to join up!" He says this after a great slurp of coffee and then a gentle tapping of his thumbnail on the mug which he does during the rest of the telling of his story.

Every now and then he makes smiling faces at Teddy and winks at me, but I notice he only glances at Mother when she comes to the dining room door to hear better. When she looks at him a long time, he looks away. When she walks back to the stove, he starts up again.

"I'm supposed to report in twenty-one days at the base as an airplane repairman." He scoots his chair, leaning his weight back until I think he might fall over backward. Momma keeps stirring whatever she's making silently at the stove, not looking our way. I can't tell if she's crying because she's so happy he isn't going overseas, or she's upset because Daddy didn't get sent to a C.O. camp so that he can be a better Christian.

Daddy swishes the last of his coffee in his mouth and swallows with gusto, the smacking of his lips followed by a great "ah" as he sets his coffee cup back down on the table. Teddy and I sit watching Momma's back. Even Teddy's quiet for once. He's stopped playing and is looking around at each of us. He knows something important is happening, even if he doesn't know that the airplanes on the base are used to get pilots ready to drop bombs on the enemy.

Daddy talked with Uncle Clifford about these pilots who trained at Hopewell Landing Field, how they fly overseas straight into battle. Daddy says some of the RAF guys were probably trained within throwing distance of our

houses for the Battle of Britain! He says this like it's some great honor for everybody living in Hopewell.

Finally, Momma turns around, and we see she has been crying. Daddy and
I are quiet while Teddy starts his rumbling noises again, running his car back
and forth over the tabletop, crashing into his plate. He sits on high pillows next
to Daddy's chair. He's strapped in with some of Daddy's old belts. Daddy gets
up and goes to Momma, putting his arms around her.

"It isn't exactly what we hoped for, Darlene, but I'm gonna be here instead
of out there or in a camp." Momma nods and sobs into his shoulder. I start to
get up, but Daddy shakes his head. "It's okay, Shike," he says gently. "Everything is going to be fine, now."

I begin to cry without noise, like Momma.

AFTER MOMMA SERVES UP SUPPER, and Daddy says the prayer, he
tells us that he's supposed to report to a Captain William Hornsby. He says
this like Hornsby's more important than anybody else we know or are ever
going to know.

"Small world, don't you think?" Daddy picks up his soup spoon. When
Momma doesn't look up from her bowl, he adds, "I mean, it's something that
the woman I talked to at the draft board knew Carrie and put herself out
enough to find me an opening like that, right here in town. Carrie and Harry
live way out in Farmington, for godssakes. I mean, that this draft board lady
lived right next door to her and knows this about me, even remembered—how
likely is that?"

Momma wipes her mouth and nods, smiling a little at Daddy.

"Amazing," he says. "Just amazing." I'm amazed. This happy turnaround
of everything that Momma was worried about means my father isn't going to
be shipped away to some hospital tent or someplace far away where bombs
could kill him dead.

Finally, she twists her napkin into a ball and places it at the side of her plate.
"I gotta tell you, Vern. This may not be perfect, but it's better than anything

I had going around in my head for too long to say. I'm not sure what they'll make of this at church, but it's something I'll accept whether they do or not." She wipes her eyes again, untwisting the napkin and using it to hide her face for a little while.

Daddy makes an "ah" sound, nodding his head, and reaches for something in his front pocket. It's a folded piece of paper I saw tucked there since he came into the house. "There's something else," he says real careful. Momma looks up and sees the paper laying on the table under his hand.

"What's this?"

"I heard from Reverend Classen today."

Momma's surprised. "Reverend Classen? About what, for heaven's sakes?" Then she looks disgusted. "It isn't a dun, is it? They wouldn't dun us for…. Good God, that would be the absolute end." She means the tithe. We don't pay the tithe like we're supposed to because we don't have the money. The church is having money troubles. Wesley Schmidt thinks the church should send people bills every month, just like the bank does for loans. Momma is beside herself over this idea.

"They've asked me to join the board."

Momma is so surprised, her mouth falls open, and she drops her spoon next to her bowl. "The board? How in the world do you rate the board? Why you?"

Daddy stares at her for a minute. "Why not? I mean, why not me, as well as the next guy?"

"Of course, Vernon, I didn't mean it like that. I just… well, first off, there're men who've been members at Hopewell Mennonite for years and years! It's so early in our membership, is what I meant. I wasn't sure that you'd be asked, ever, to be truthful. I thought—"

"Apparently the tithe doesn't matter." Daddy opens the letter and glances down the page. He puts his finger on the line he wants to read. "This invitation to the board does not necessitate your payment of the tithe as these are difficult times, and the board is taking the view that members keep this obligation according to the dictates of their hearts and their ability to pay." Daddy puts the letter down, slides his finger along the fold, and puts both hands over it like it might jump out from underneath his fingers and run across the table. His eyes are shiny, and he's moving his lips around real funny before he presses them up against his teeth. It looks like he's holding his lips together tight to keep them from trembling. I want to ask about "obligation," but I know not to interrupt.

"Wonders never cease. That takes care of Wesley Schmidt and his money-grabbin' ideas!" Momma is overjoyed. "Who woulda thought! I knew Karl and Verna were our supporters and that Ervin Classen and Simon Nichols liked us... well, you, but... talk about amazing. This is amazing! It's too many amazings for me to get ahold of, to tell you the truth!" She leans against her hands, her elbows on the table. "I guess this means we have a place in this church after all, you think?"

"It's not all that surprising, is it?" Daddy's voice is strong. He gets up to get himself more coffee. From the counter in the kitchen he calls out, "They need honest people right now, is how I'm seeing this."

"They do, and now they'll have that—with you and Karl in it, together. Classen's no dummy is he? He's maneuvered this one, I do believe. Oh, this is gonna be rich, you and Simon Nichols on the same board together with Wesley Schmidt sitting there sucking his thumb." Momma and Daddy both laugh.

They've talked about Wesley Schmidt being too young to be on the board. He owns a farm, even though he's only twenty-six. Daddy's idea about Wesley Schmidt's farm is, "Hell, I'd own a farm, too, if I'd had it given to me. If I didn't have any brothers, I'd have three or four!" I know from Daddy's rampages on the way home after church that Wesley Schmidt is an only son. He has sisters but no brothers. "Wesley's a handful all right. A bit more than a handful, I'd say, but maybe that's why they asked me, Darlene. Ervin called me yesterday at work. He thought I'd gotten the letter already—"

"And you didn't tell me?"

"It seemed like we had enough to think about with this other board... situation." Daddy hesitates to let Momma know he doesn't need to be corrected about this word. He clears his throat. "I didn't want to throw too many irons in the fire. Besides, I wasn't sure how the draft thing would turn out. No use getting all worked up over the church when I may not even have been here."

When Momma nods, Daddy says, "I asked him if it was unanimous—the vote for me to join—and he said a-course, has to be. I told him I knew that, but were there any questions that came up about me becoming a member, and he hesitated, so I figured it was Wesley and the tithe, you know. But he said there was an abstention."

"I didn't know that was allowed. I thought it had to be consensus." Now there are two words I have to not pay attention to. I try to remember them so I can ask later, but the words get lost in Daddy's talk.

"Evidently not. He did say that the tithe was mentioned, but now with the war and all—folks losing their jobs right and left—I wasn't the only one not able to meet the tithe, it seems. Of course, Ervin wasn't going to tell me who was or wasn't paying. And he was talking about the board members, not members of the church. We know a lot of members aren't meeting the tithe. But on the board, well, I think we can be pretty sure who at least one of them is who isn't meeting the obligation other than me."

"Obligation," I whisper, but nobody hears me, or everybody's ignoring me.

"Karl and Verna have all those boys. They couldn't possibly do it."

Daddy nods.

Then Momma asks, "After today there's another concern, you know. What do you think the board's gonna say when they find out you're working at the Landing Field?"

"First of all, I haven't said yes."

Momma says, "I didn't think you had a choice."

"Heavens sakes, woman! I mean the church, not the army. I mean I didn't tell Ervin I would join the board. I told him I wanted to discuss it with you. But how they're gonna feel about me working at the Field, I haven't any idea, but we can pretty well guess how Schmidt will take to it."

"I'm surprised you didn't mention to Ervin that you were called up."

"I thought about that, but then I wasn't sure, as I told you, what would happen today. No use getting everybody at church riled up if something happened like it could have. Let's see, I got the draft notice on Wednesday, so if you haven't talked to anybody—and I sure as the dickens haven't—then nobody from the church's had a chance to know. I decided to leave it at that, for the time being."

"Who was the abstention? Did Reverend Classen say?"

There it is, the second word. I whisper "abstention" but not loud enough to cause a ruckus. They want to talk without interruption. I know "interruption" plenty and "ruckus," too.

"No, Ervin wasn't about to tell me, but we know who it was."

Momma nods. "Wesley, of course. It wouldn't be Simon, would it?"

"Noooo," Daddy says. "We respect each other too much, even though we don't agree half the time. No, it's Wes. That Ervin let me know there was an abstention tells me that."

"Why did he?"

"I asked him if there were any questions raised about me by anybody. I wanted to know if Wesley raised a stink, and I got that answered."

"We've been over this a billion times, I know, but this kid shouldn't know who pays or not. Reverend Classen should be the only one who does."

"In all fairness if you did the church's books, like Schmidt does—okay, his wife does—with all the taxation exemption forms and such, you'd know. You'd have to."

"My question is why Belvanna even does the books, since they are so thick with the Holdemans who don't believe in civil services—"

"They pay taxes, Darlene and keep their own budgets."

"Okay, but you wouldn't go using this kind of information against anybody, Vernon. That's the problem."

"In all honesty, Wes never said names, and he only makes the suggestions he makes toward the whole group, nobody in particular. His abstention is a show of fairness, and here's the thing, Darlene, he doesn't have to say why. He can just abstain because he feels his conscience tells him to."

"When do you have to let them know? Maybe if you called Classen...." Momma knows the only time Daddy uses the phone is when somebody calls him. "Don't you think it bears knowing, finding out what they're gonna think about working out at the Field before you go through—"

"Let's just wait and see what's gonna happen with this Air Force thing, okay?"

"What's to know? You're gonna be working for the Air Force. They aren't asking, they're telling you, right?"

Daddy nods and moves Reverend Classen's letter around, picks it up, folds it, and puts it back in his pocket. "I don't know what the Colonel woulda said if I'd told him that I couldn't work on trainer planes, but the whole thing's moot, because I signed the papers and report in three weeks. It's done."

He glances at Momma. "It all happened really fast, and I felt it was a chance to stay, instead of go. You can pretty much guess what the other options woulda been. I thought you'd be glad."

"I am glad. I told you I am." Momma waits. She has something else on her mind. "What's the pay?"

"I don't know, Darlene. But it's gotta be better than what we've been trying to survive on." Daddy's been running all over the county working on equipment, cars, and trucks as best as he can from his toolbox and gasoline allowance. He calls himself an itinerant mechanic when anybody asks. "Itinerant" means he's on the go, working from place to place. It's wearing him out.

"And it's gonna be steady. Oh, God, Vernon. It's got its downside, but if the church doesn't throw a wrench into this, it might just work, at least for now."

"There's something else." Daddy hesitates as he finishes his second cup of coffee, putting the cup down with a thud.

"More? Oh God, what, Vernon? What? Why are you coming out with all this in spurts. It's enough to give me a heart attack!"

Daddy puts down his spoon slowly on the tablecloth. "Hornsby told me that he has a house he can rent to us down the road, but, right now, he feels he can't pull the house from underneath the folks who are renting it. But they've notified him that they're moving to Stillwater, within the year. He said he would rent it to us for a fair price." Daddy holds up his hand. "I know, it seems like another inside deal, but this would be a little different from Hilliar, since Hornsby doesn't pay me, the army does."

"You aren't in the army, but the army pays you? Sounds crazy to me."

"Well, I don't know exactly how it's done. Probably by government contract to some business outfit, who knows? But I'll get my paycheck at the Landing Field, I was told. Once a month, so it'll be a little different than we're used to, but we can plan because we'll know what's coming in."

"A house? A real honest to goodness, whole house?"

"He says it isn't the biggest thing in town, but it's across the street from

Monroe Elementary, so Shike will have to change schools, but it's permanent—
as permanent as a rental can be."

"How much? And there's quite a wait?"

"He didn't say the rent, but he's a reasonable man, I'm telling you. Just trust
a little bit and have a little patience, okay?"

"And you're gonna be the best man he's got, don't forget that. You always
are, everywhere you go."

Daddy smiles. He's pleased with what Momma just said to him.

4.

Two weeks later

"OKAY, FESS UP!" DADDY SAYS to Momma, sounding tired, when he comes in the door and puts down his lunchbox while he takes off his jacket and shoes. "Let's get it over with." He's been working at the Landing Field for two weeks, and since he started his new job, we've had to watch our "Ps and Qs" about the money, because Daddy has to wait a whole month before he gets paid. He worked night and day running all over Hopewell and even back to Aileen on extra jobs to put enough money in the jar for us to make it to that first paycheck by the army. He told Momma he's never rested up from working for himself, and now he's got to be on his toes for learning everything new at the Field.

"After all, I've never worked on airplanes before. I'm told I'm learning fast, but I'm under a lot of strain helping the other mechanics keep the boys in the air."

Daddy sees Momma's face and is guessing that she has something hard for him to hear on her mind. So Momma tells him straight out about my dress. I guess she's keeping the one she bought for herself a secret until she "can spring it on him, when he's primed with supper and nearer to beddy-bye time." These were her words to Aunt Josie, me, and Leon in the car, after what she called her "buying spree." But she doesn't seem to be able to hold her secret now after Daddy's "Fess up!" So she tells him not just about my dress but hers, and that she used grocery money to do it. While she hung our dresses up in the closet, she'd said to me, sliding her hands over the fabric of each like they were the most precious things in the world, "Finally, just finally your daddy has steady work."

Now she stares at him staring at her, him standing in the living room, not moving.

"Don't you say a word against this, Vern," she says, taking my hand, as though I'm going to give her more ammunition to fight him with. "I mean it. Why are you still as stone? Why should this surprise you? It's time we look the part, you being on the board and with a special job at the Field. Your new suit is at Newman's on layaway."

Daddy walks stiff as a board across the room past her, his shoulders pulled up around his neck, him falling into his sofa chair with a crunch on his folded newspaper. She speaks to the quiet in the room, telling him that this wasn't anything she'd planned, that she'd picked up Aunt Josephine who took all her boys except Leon over to Gramma Dirks's for the day, so we could look for houses in Hopewell.

Daddy looks up at her with total shock on his face. His voice, on the edge of shaking, his face getting redder and redder, he asks, "Why... why would you do this, Darlene, when in just a week or two I'm going to know about Hornsby's house, if we get it and when?" His words come out slurred, like he's been drinking, but he doesn't smell like whiskey, and when I look closer, I can see his rage laying low, ready to come out full-blown any minute. When it does, this isn't good for her or me.

"You should know why by now," she tells him in a calm voice, like Mrs. Tate does while teaching at school. It's the voice I hear when Momma changes for everybody at church. She's that other person, the one who acts like she isn't around Daddy and me. "There's been an awful lot of the unexpected going on around here lately, and I want to be ready for any eventuality likely to arise. I'm looking, simply looking, in case something falls through with this Hornsby house. Is that so awful?"

Daddy pushes his shoulders down, and then suddenly his whole body slumps back, as though he's gathering himself to spring out of his chair and slap some sense into her. He's never done it, but he's threatened to enough times. He stares straight ahead at the wall on the other side of the room as she talks to him—she says he doesn't need to worry because there isn't much out there in our price range that we could rent anyway.

When Daddy doesn't look at her or say anything, she whispers like she's praying. "Please, God in Heaven, let the Hornsby house come through or we just might live and die the rest of our lives in colored town." But wasn't it helpful to know that our choices are limited ahead of time? She goes ahead with her story like he's sitting there hanging on her every word.

"When we stopped to eat the packed lunch we'd all brought along, in case we ran into noontime, well, that's when I saw Shike's dress in a shop window right across from where we were parked. It was like we were supposed to see it! So we went in, nothing like simply looking. Shike tried it on, and it suited her so perfectly, I bought it because I thought about taking our picture for Gramma and Grampa Dirks for Christmas. Don't you remember, Vern, how we'd talked about this?"

She waits, but Daddy continues staring at the wall, his lips set tight, his hands rubbing up and down on the arms of his sofa chair. The dress was a little expensive but affordable, she tells him, pulling out a dining room chair to the side of him, sitting and waiting for him to answer.

"Have you gone stark raving mad?" Daddy shouts, his hands waving around over his head and around in front of him while he talks. "We are up in the air about everything, including the pay on my job, and not knowing how this house deal with Hornsby will go." So he wants to know if he's got this right, "that she's been driving around Hopewell like a crazy woman, looking for houses we don't need, on gasoline we don't have!" Daddy grabs the ends of the arms of his chair and starts to jump up but sinks lower, shouting more, almost knocking over his coffee cup that Momma has brought him and put on the floor by his foot. "Where'd you get the gas, Darlene, siphon it off of Clifford and Josephine, again? How long do you think we can keep doing that before the inspectors figure out his gasoline drum is getting low too quick? It's not harvest time anymore, you know. And then you bought… you bought Shike something to wear for Christmas? Christmas? Christmas is what? Six weeks away, is what it is." Daddy pauses and sees Momma's smile.

"Light coming on, Vernon?"

All at once, Daddy's balloon poofs. "Well, okay, but what will she and Teddy have to open on that day, now that you've spent it on her dress? I'm a working man, Darlene. This new job isn't a free ride just because it's steady work!" And, then, the other light comes on about her dress and then another one about his suit. "Tell me there's fucking more, in hiding, just waiting to jump out and take the rest of my first paycheck?"

I stand quiet, waiting, watching, as he grabs the newspaper out from under him and slaps it down on top of the arm of his easy chair before laying his arm over it so it won't fall to the floor.

He's right. We did siphon gas out of Uncle Clifford's drum by the car shed in order to go. "The government giveth," Aunt Josephine had said, laughing, when she put the hose in the gas tank of our car. "And we taketh," she'd finished off when she put the hose back up on its hook. Momma and Aunt Josephine had laughed, crazy-like again, clapping their hands and walking fast to the car, where Leon waited with me and Teddy in the back seat. Roy had been dropped off at Gramma and Grampa Dirks's for the day, because it was Saturday, and there wasn't any school. Tommy Don was working with Uncle Clifford in the barn. So much for all my boy cousins, except Leon, at Grampa and Gramma Dirks's.

Daddy was also right about our driving all over Hopewell like mad trying to see "For Rent" signs, even after Aunt Josephine couldn't find any more "Houses for Rent" ads in the newspaper. There were only three of those, and two of them were in colored town. Momma was curious as to where these were since she hadn't seen any signs in the block around our duplex, so she drove us further into what she called "shantytown," where we found only one sign standing next to a house that she claimed was no bigger than a hen house and looked like it would fall down in the slightest wind storm. There were no whites anywhere, only colored people who stopped and watched our car drive past, Momma hitting the slush puddles so fast and hard, I could see water spraying onto the shanty-houses' front lawns.

Momma whispered that there was no way she'd move deeper into colored town than we already were, that this side of town made her feel destitute as it was, so why would she want more of the same or worse? When I asked about "destitute," she told Aunt Josephine to tell me what it meant while she "high-tailed it back to civilization."

"'Destitute' is when you're down and out," Aunt Josie told me. When I asked her if we were "destitutes," she laughed a little before saying, "No. First, 'destitutes' isn't a real word for describing people, but, if there were such a word, it would be a name for those who are so poor and hard up that they'll do just anything for food and a roof over their heads."

"Are coloreds destitutes?" I asked.

Aunt Josephine and Momma looked at each other very serious. Momma said, softly, "Yes, Shike. Yes, surely, many of them are." Aunt Josie and Momma didn't say anything more about destitutes while we drove out of colored town to a nearby filling station on Randolph Street for some Cokes.

Momma started to pull to a side street so we could eat the baloney and cheese sandwiches she'd packed for us and drink the Cokes she'd bought from the filling station's pop machine. Momma calls all pop, "Cokes," but mine and Leon's were really Orange Crush. Before she turned off the engine, Aunt Josephine told her to drive downtown so we could people-watch. That was then Momma saw the dress she wanted me to try on.

When Aunt Josephine got out of the car, she told Momma she wished she had a little girl to moon over and dress up like a doll, but then, seeing's how low they were with money all the time, it was probably destiny that she didn't have one. That was when she looked at me and said, "Don't ask about destiny, Shike. It may sound a little like destitute, but it's only with some people that being destitute is their destiny."

Momma looked at her for a minute but kept walking toward the shop. Momma's told me once that Aunt Josephine is very smart—just not very smart about men. And that was a shame to her because her sister was the smartest person in her class at Shirly High School. She gave a speech when she graduated. Momma thinks Aunt Josie is Grampa Dirks's favorite because of her brains.

Leon begged to go in with us even though it was a ladies shop, but Aunt Josie made him stay in the car, because he had on his overalls. Later, he didn't get to go into Newman's Department Store with us, either.

While she pulled the dress down over my head in the shop's changing room, Momma told Aunt Josie that if she decided to buy, she knew what she was doing. And she said this again when she was trying on her own dress at Newman's, adding that she may not know much about a lot of things, but looking nice, this she knew.

"That's a mighty pretty purse you're carryin' there, Darlene. I don't dare ask where the cash came from," Aunt Josie exclaimed when Momma walked out of the department store with her dress in a box she had swinging from her arm. Aunt Josie was carrying Teddy like he belonged to her. She never stops kissing him, and Teddy lets her, at least for as long as she holds him. Teddy likes Aunt Josie.

"So we eat less for a week." Then Momma laughed. "Or better yet, I just won't go home, at all. Me and the kids'll stay with you, Clifford, and the boys. I'll help kill all the chickens we can eat, pull up all the potatoes we can mash, and all the green beans we can boil, while Vernon stays in Hopewell packing in the Landing Field dough."

They both laughed silly-like, throwing themselves against each other in the front seat. Aunt Josie always slaps her legs when she laughs, but she had Teddy with her so she clapped hands with him, her hands over his. I smiled with them, but I didn't think it was as funny as they made it out to be. I knew Momma was only kidding around, but I wanted to go home to Daddy, even though I was worried about what would happen when she told him about our dresses.

And tonight the last thing Daddy wants to do is eat less for a week so that we all can have new clothes to wear to church and our Christmas picture.

"I give up," Daddy says in a tired voice. "I just give up!" He sits drinking his coffee, without saying another thing. I know he's upset, because he doesn't read his newspaper. He sits slurping his coffee and staring past the living room, on through the outside window.

Momma walks into the kitchen and starts banging pots and pans, not loud, but enough for Daddy and I to know she had argued about as much as she was going to. Nobody has anything to say while we eat our supper. Teddy makes rumbling noises while rolling his cars over the tablecloth.

5.

At the church

ON SUNDAY, WHEN WE OPEN the church doors and walk in, all talking in the vestibule stops. Daddy shakes hands with the men and gives his brown fedora to Ronnie Toews who is putting hats on shelves and coats on hangers in the cloak room. He doesn't look at me, even though he knows I'm here. Daddy has two fedoras, one brown and one black. The brown one has a shiny wide ribbon with a little red feather in it, off to the side. He doesn't have an overcoat. He runs his hands over his head, like he's got lots of hair to smooth down.

The women smile at us, especially at me, because I have on my new dress. Momma's dress, that she bought at Newman's, is blue gabardine with a white collar and puffy sleeves. She hands Daddy Teddy while she takes off her overcoat so people can see it, even though the church is a little chilly since the heat hasn't been turned up much yet. I look at Momma and see how careful she's put her hat on so her hair shows around it. She spent extra time in the bathroom this morning fussing with her hair and hat. She looks like a movie star, even though she doesn't like her clunky black heels. She would like to wear wedges, but she says she knows she'd just get nasty stares from the people at Hopewell Mennonite. Daddy didn't say one word about her dress when she put it on. She told him that they would pay on his suit every check until he got it out which wouldn't take long at all. He'd be looking stylish as can be in less time than he might think. No need, she added with a little teasing smile, to believe that's a bad thing when you feel the part and aren't simply window dressing.

At church, I know something's not right but don't know what it is. Momma and Daddy know, I can tell. At first I think it might be Momma and my new dresses, but from what Momma and Daddy have been discussing the last two days, it's more likely it's about his job at the Air Field.

Daddy hands Teddy back to Momma and nods this way and that with a little smile, as he starts walking with me in front of him, his legs nudging me slowly along toward the sanctuary, his hands on my shoulders. Momma looks like her smile is stuck on her face. Teddy is being good for once, letting people shake his hand, telling him how manly he looks in his shirt, trousers, and suspenders. Daddy stops when Karl Toews puts one hand on Daddy's shoulder, gripping tight on his jacket, and shaking his hand with the other.

Verna Toews bends over and tells me my dress is very pretty. Her hair is shaped into two huge rolls on each side of her head coming together in the middle of her forehead in the shape of a sharp "V." The rolls move when she nods her head as she talks. I stare at the rolls of hair thinking they might suddenly open up like flowers and show me her brains. But she's wearing a little hat between these rolls which is pinned down, so it won't slide off the back of her head. Her face has freckles all over it, like Ronnie's. They both have red hair.

Verna holds out a piece of peppermint which I take and say "thank you" when Momma nudges my back. Verna tells me not to eat it until after Sunday dinner. Ronnie Toews stares at me from where he's leaning against the wall, waiting on his mom and dad. His twin brother, Donnie, stands with his other two brothers, watching over them. Glynda Faye Nichols starts playing the piano, and everybody walks to the pews so Ronnie must be done with hanging up all the hats and coats. His three brothers walk off to the side, looking at me without smiling. I think of Tommy Don, Roy, and Leon. Maybe all the Toews kids will get to be my other cousins when my real ones aren't around. The two littler kids play with me—or more like I play with them—when Momma visits with Verna in the kitchen, when we go to their house in the afternoons and evenings. Ronnie and Donnie are too much older, like Tommy Don, to care about me. I rhyme in my head over and over, Ronnie, Donnie, and Tommy. I think of the three bears. Or better still, the three little pigs, though these boys aren't very little. But seeing them as pigs makes me laugh inside.

Momma takes out my crayons and a piece of drawing paper with a cardboard from Teddy's diaper bag and hands them to me.

During the service, I draw our new house we haven't moved into yet. I put a "For Rent" sign in the yard and a swing on a tree branch like I had at the apartment in Aileen. Daddy is waiting to push me to the sky. Momma explained to me that she was bringing my drawing materials to church this morning, but that it was about time I started sitting and listening to the messages before and after Sunday School. She said that by the time I was eight, I would be doing what the adults do during church, which is sitting in the pews, listening. Teddy gets to be in the nursery downstairs where we don't hear the little kids make noises when they play and cry.

At the end of the service, after the benediction, Reverend Classen announces that there will be a special board meeting while the ladies prepare lunch in the basement. Everybody is invited to lunch, not just board members and their families. As we all get up to leave, some of the men go into the pastor's office. Momma leads me down the stairs where long tables have been set up with white tablecloths on them. Some of the women have come down to the basement during the service because the tables are already filled with plates and bowls of fried chicken, mashed potatoes—with gravy in small pitchers— green beans, carrots, corn on the cob, and sandwiches with some kind of pink filling that Daddy's told me before is salmon salad.

In the middle of the tables are plates of canned pickles, spiced peaches and beets, and homemade bread with hand-churned butter. Cake slices and cookies are on platters at both end of the longest table, along with pink peppermint candies in special dishes. Donnie Toews, who has the darkest red hair of his family, is a little shorter than his twin, has dimples on both cheeks, and does everything Ronnie tells him to do. I watch him walk up to the table taking some candies in his fist and quickly walk back to his place, passing the pieces out to his brothers. Ronnie grins at me when he throws one in his mouth. I know that look. I've seen it a thousand times on Tommy Don's face. When Momma's gone into the kitchen to get more napkins and utensils for the table, I take out the candy that Ronnie's mother had given me earlier, unwrap it slowly, while I stare at him, and pop it in my mouth. He turns his head like he doesn't see me do it, but I know he does.

———————

IT DOESN'T TAKE LONG BEFORE the men on the church board come down the stairs. Whatever wasn't right has been fixed behind the pastor's of-fice door. Everybody is easy with each other, and they're all talking at the same time, some even laughing. Everybody is happy that the men have come down-stairs so we can all have lunch. But Wesley Schmidt and Simon Nichols aren't with them. The little kids have already eaten at a small round table off to the side and are waiting to get cake and homemade ice cream. Miss Stutzman is watching so they don't get out of their chairs and run around all over the place while they wait for their dessert.

I went to a Holdeman church in Shirly with Gramma when I was visit-ing her and Grampa Dirks for a few days last summer. The women all looked like Miss Stutzman, wearing what Momma calls "sensible shoes," black head scarves and long-sleeved dresses she calls "feed-sacks," even though it was hot, without fans in the church. Miss Stutzman is an old maid because she's high up on years and has never married.

Now I can hear women talking as they crank ice cream makers in the sink in the kitchen. They laugh every time the crank catches on the ice, and they have to make a big racket to get it turning again. The board members who've joined the line are pointing to bowls of food on the tables, talking to those nearby, moving their feet like they're about to go someplace else soon. Momma's helping with the macaroni salad and coleslaw, so when Daddy waves me over to where he is in line, I run to him and ask for cocoa. He says, "Pretty soon." Teddy's sitting in a highchair behind Momma. He doesn't sit in a highchair at home, but, here in church, it's a way to watch him while Momma helps with serving the food. He's too little to sit yet with the other kids at the round table. I'm surprised Momma doesn't have me taking care of him like she usually does, but with so many people in the room, he wouldn't do what I wanted him to.

Teddy looks over at us, and I wave. Daddy winks at him, and Teddy closes both eyes to wink back. All the men in line laugh. This makes Teddy slap his hands down all over the tray and make rumbling noises with his car during Reverend Classen's blessing. Teddy is the only baby anywhere today, so everybody is fussing over him. There are babies in our church, but the families with them must not have stayed for lunch, or the babies were taken upstairs in the cloakroom where two girls—one is usually Norma Janet Nichols—are watching over them like they do in the basement during the sermon. I look around for Wesley Schmidt and his wife, Belvanna, but they didn't stay. They have two little girls, one only a tiny baby. There aren't a lot of kids my age in this church, but there are some girls a little older than I am. I know them from Sunday School. We only have six in my class, and three of them are eight and nine years old. They aren't coming over to play, because we have to eat first.

Marijune Mueller waves at me. She will come over to where I am as soon as she gets done eating with her parents. She wears French braids. They have short ribbons tied at the ends but not bows. Our church allows bows, but Mari's mother is very religious. Momma says she will learn French braiding and make me some. Mari Mueller always wants to play games I don't know. I think she makes her stories up, but she says they're what everybody plays at her school. She has jacks in a bag, but her mother doesn't like for her to play games at church. I went home with her one Sunday dinner and came back with the Muellers for evening service. Mari and I played jacks and pickup sticks. We got to draw with crayons on paper in tablets.

Most of the time we spent making up stories, lying on her bed and laughing ourselves silly. Mari had some of her stories written down, but her writing was all over the page, and the stories were best when we made them up as we went along. We laughed so hard her mother came once to see if we were all right. Mari can't play with paper dolls because dressing up, her mother says, isn't what God put us on earth to do. Mari doesn't have a View Master either because it's too much like fancy photographs. There are photographs in frames on the fireplace mantel and in the living room on a small table in Mari's house, but they're family pictures taken in studios. Mari tells me her parents argue a lot about what's sin and what's not. Mrs. Mueller was raised in a strict Holdeman home, and Mari says that her mother thought her father would join the Holdeman church when they got married, but he backed out. Hopewell Mennonite was the only church he'd go to. Her father is on the board with Daddy and good friends with Karl Toews and Simon Nichols, too.

"So that was that," Mari told me about her father's not joining the Holdeman church. She knows a lot. She's a year and a half older than I am. But she's scared of her mother, I can tell. She has lots of things hidden in her closet and under her dresser in little envelops she hopes her mother won't find, like soap that smells good and special colored strings and ribbons. She doesn't want to wear braids anymore, but her mother won't let her wear her hair down until she's twelve. Mrs. Mueller isn't going to make her wear a head scarf because her father says she doesn't have to when she stops wearing braids and joins our church. Her mother doesn't wear a scarf, but her mother always wears a hat except inside her own house. Her father listens to the radio, but her mother tries not to be in the room when it's on, like Gramma Dirks.

In the lunch line now, Mari motions for me to come be with her and her family, but I don't want to eat lunch with her because of her mother. I shake my head, and she turns back in line, disappointed. When Daddy and I get to Momma with our plates, she puts a spoonful of macaroni and cheese on mine but looks at Daddy and says, "The men seem friendly enough. Things must not've gone too bad."

Daddy smiles down at his plate and says to her, very low, "Far better'n expected!" He looks up and smiles at the man next to us who's turned back around from talking with the man behind him. Daddy moves on down the table and gets his fried chicken from the woman next to Momma. He says "thank you" to this woman. He didn't say "thank you" to Momma, because he knows her too much.

While Daddy and I are eating, three men walk up to him and shake his hand. They come up, one at a time, and say, "Glad to have you on the board" and "It's a pleasure to learn to know you." Reverend Classen made an announcement before his prayer at lunch that Daddy would be serving on the church board. Daddy stands and smiles. He sits and stands, sits and stands, sometimes only half standing before sitting back down as more men come up to him and thank him for "serving." Daddy now serves his country at the air landing field and his church on the board, but I think these men are only glad about Daddy's church service. None of them sit down next to us but go with their families to sit somewhere else. The women don't talk to Daddy. They only smile, nod, and push their kids to tables.

When Simon Nichols comes down the stairs, a few men stop talking and nod his way. He nods back, then looks at the food on the long tables. I have to twist around to watch. I wonder why he's coming down the stairs late, not when Daddy and the other men did. Daddy swallows a piece of chicken hard, coughs, and then waves at Simon Nichols when he looks our way. Simon Nichols points his finger at Daddy and shakes it a little. I think he's a grandpa, because his hair is gray and white, but if he has grandkids they aren't in our church. His youngest daughter, Norma Janet, babysits with me at her house. She's still in high school. She talks about her older sister, Sylvia, who lives in Chicago. Norma Janet's never said if Sylvia has kids. I don't think she's even married.

All at once, Glynda Faye Nichols, the pianist who is also Norma Janet's sister, comes running down the stairs, walks up to Simon Nichols while he's getting food from Momma. He puts down his plate on the serving table and talks real quiet to Glynda for a little while, touching her shoulder, nodding every now and then, and looking over at Daddy. She stretches her arm out toward the stairs, waving her hands around and then toward the back door, and finally she nods at Simon Nichols and hurries back up the stairs. She looks worried. Daddy makes me turn around and mind my food. But after he looks down at his plate, I twist around in my seat again, so I can watch more.

Simon Nichols is picking up his plate when Reverend Classen comes out of the kitchen, calls to him and walks to where he is. Simon Nichols puts his plate back down again. Reverend Classen has his hat in one hand and a big brown bag in the other. I'm sure it's his lunch, and he's going somewhere. Simon Nichols shakes his hand. Reverend Classen turns and says good-bye and waves to everybody. Some people say, "Drive carefully," and one calls, "God Bless."

When Simon Nichols comes to the end of the of the food line, he talks and shakes his head a little bit to the last woman handing out cake who brings back to the platter the piece she was going to give him. He turns around, finds

Daddy, nods his head and starts walking with his food toward our table. He walks up to us and says a big hello to me.

"I'd like to sit with you and your father if it's okay." Nobody calls Daddy "father" unless Momma is mad at him and she's talking to me. Then, it's "your father" this and "your father" that. When Simon Nichols says "your father," it sounds like he's praying.

Daddy is already standing, wiping his hands on his napkin. He holds out his hand, but Simon Nichols's hands are full with plates, one is a salad. Daddy laughs a little and waves his hand back and forth and says, "Of course, of course. Shike, can you move over to let—" I start to get up and move to the empty chair next to the one I've been sitting in, across from Daddy.

"No, no." Simon Nichols smiles at me, then says to Daddy, while walking around the table to sit in a chair next to him. "There's plenty of room right here." And there is because Simon Nichols is very skinny, skinnier than Daddy. Momma says that if Daddy didn't spread his toes when he lets out his bath water, he'd slide down the drain. And Aunt Josephine told me once that Daddy was so skinny that when he turned sideways, it was a wonder he didn't disappear. Simon Nichols makes Daddy look "positively fat," Momma said once on the way home from church.

When Simon Nichols walks past me, he smells spicy and sweet, a lot like Daddy's shaving cream and hair oil. I don't see how he can smell like hair oil, because hair oil makes your hair stay against your head like Daddy's, and Simon Nichols's hair is sticking out all over his head like Mr. Hilliar's, except it isn't red, and his face doesn't look like Santa Claus. First off, Simon Nichols doesn't have a beard. And second, his face is long and skinny, like the rest of him, even his nose. When he smiles, he has lots of teeth for such a little mouth.

Once he's in his place with his plate in front of him, he says, quietly to Daddy, "I want to talk to you by my side. I might have some things to say that I don't want overheard." He darts a look around the room, not at me.

Simon Nichols doesn't eat right away. He puts his napkin down and places his knife, fork, and spoon on top, one at a time, very, very careful-like. Then he looks straight ahead and clears his throat.

"I would imagine you have some questions about all that's been going on around your appointment to the board, Vernon. I know I would, and Ervin asked me if I'd try and catch up with you as soon as I could." Simon Nichols looks at Daddy for a bit, then takes a bite from food on his plate. After he's wiped his mouth with his napkin, he says, "He's been called out of town on peace church business, as he announced this morning. But I'm not exactly sure what he's said to you and what he hasn't, I mean, about your appointment and board business. At any rate, I've been sent to fill in the gaps, if there are any."

"Gaps?" Daddy asks. "More things I should know?"

"Not necessarily, just questions you might have. Ervin's usually pretty thorough with these things, but lately there's been a stir over a case in Okmulgee that's he's very involved in, and he hasn't been as attentive to some of the finer points of church matters here. He wants to make sure you're filled in and are comfortable with where you are on the board. No loose ends, is how it he put it to me."

"I'm fine, I think. What's the Okmulgee case, that's if you can talk about it."

Simon Nichols takes a small bite of a fried drumstick, chews and swallows. "Well, yes. Seems a Creek Indian who's a converted Mennonite tried to register as a conscientious objector, and the local draft board threw him in jail on the grounds he's a slacker and not really a full-fledged member of the area's Mennonite church. The Creek is waiting on some kind of judgment by a higher court as a lawyer was brought into the fray. It's a complicated case that could set a precedent, and since Ervin is the peace church rep from our area, he's been called in to negotiate with the Mennonite Peace Committee over this one. He's their spokesman to be exact." Simon Nichols nods his head a little toward the food tables. "He's just picked up his lunch and is on his way to Tulsa where the MPC is convening this afternoon and then tomorrow with other members of the Peace Churches." Daddy says he hadn't heard of this Indian case.

"That's not unusual, Vernon, as it's not likely anybody would, and probably won't, unless some reporter hears and wants to make a federal case out of it. I mean that quite literally. Indians on the whole have responded to the draft without question. Ervin tells me that Indian volunteers have exceeded any other group in America. How he keeps up with all this, I don't know, but he can just about tell you the population of every town in his district and the membership in every Mennonite church within each of those towns, and, probably beyond, truth be known—and how each member stands on the war issue. Anyway, the problem that Ervin foresees with this Mennonite Creek is that he hasn't been a member of the church very long, and there could be a sensational headline out of 'a warrior turned coward' sort of thing." He says in an exaggerated but quiet voice, "You know, heap big war chief trying to hide behind heap big no-no church." Simon Nichols sighs, shakes his head, leaning back a little before going on. "Looks like the authorities see an opportunity to take on two wayward situations—an un-American Indian and an un-American church.

"There's an increasing number of cases making their way to the appeals court of Selective Services, Ervin tells me. The MPC and Quakers especially, well, and The Brethren churches, too, are working together to get information out to ministers on how to counsel their young men about the options they have when they're called up for military service. But in some of these smaller churches, in deeply rural areas, there isn't always follow-through, and making a decision can be hard on young men especially when some of their families don't see eye-to-eye with them. There's so much pride for one's country all tangled up in this draft business which is what this case is about, actually. The Mennonite Creek is getting as much pressure from his tribesmen as he is from the local draft board. There's a lot of intimidation used to try and get Mennonite boys to join up, especially when local boards make them feel like they're traitors if they take the A-1-O status."

Simon Nichols takes tiny bites from his plate and swallows. He keeps his fingers on his fork but doesn't lift it again. "The government hits them with all kinds of arguments, including what their decision will do to their record for future employment, especially if they end up in prison." Simon Nichols nods his head up and down and wipes his hands on his napkin.

"You've felt this yourself with your recent draft situation. So you know."

Daddy nods but is quiet. He knows Simon Nichols wants to go on with his Indian story.

"In the Creek case, the tribal pressure comes from the tribesmen's desire to be viewed as Americans like anybody else and not viewed as natives sequestered away on reservations wanting to have their own nation and not be part of the American one." Daddy is busy eating and only nods as Simon Nichols talks. "You pretty much already know where I stand on all of this 1-A, 1-A-O service, non-combatant, and C.O. business from our board meeting today, but I'm not as fierce as I sounded in there this morning, maybe. And I can tell you this for certain, as I'm sure you know by now, Ervin Classen is about as receptive to individual decisions about this war as I've seen anywhere among the Mennonite clergy. He's very open to any of the choices any man wants to make based on his own conscience. And to tell you the truth, I'm getting there myself, slowly but surely. It's a far cry from where I started out, I know. But live and learn, I guess. Something about old dogs and new tricks, perhaps."

Daddy wipes his mouth with his napkin, listening closely as Simon Nichols continues. "I do have to say, I'm also very conflicted about what the Scriptures teach us about all this and the positions that churches are considering now. It would appear most are forming battle lines from within, and I'm talking about within each church, not just where conferences are standing on these issues. But, as always, my primary concern is first and foremost about Hopewell Mennonite and what we decide." Simon Nichols hasn't eaten any food in a while. He sits with his hands folded over his plate, his elbows resting on the white tablecloth like Uncle Clifford does when he's listening to Daddy at Sunday dinners out at the Shirly Farm.

When Daddy only nods, Simon Nichols unfolds his hands, picks up his fork, and scoots it under some potato salad. Then he leaves his fingers on his fork, his other hand to the side of his plate as he says, very polite, but stiff, as well, "Do you have any questions about your appointment to the board or our vote today to allow draft decisions and war effort choices based on personal conscience? I'll try to answer what I can, but to be truthful, it seemed pretty clear the way Ervin expressed it before and after the vote."

Daddy now puts his fork down with a clatter. His plate is empty. He wipes his mouth with his napkin, then holds onto it like it might scoot away from him across the table. "If we're being completely truthful, I'd have to say I'm flabbergasted over my appointment. I was totally caught off guard with this, mainly because... well, first off—don't misunderstand me, I'm very pleased to serve—but Darlene and I haven't attended very long. The congregation knows us, of course, but with Darlene's absences and my coming as I can, I'm just surprised is all. I know that Darlene's dad and the Dirks family is known by every Mennonite from here to the old country but—"

"Whalen Dirks or his family—I take it you're referring to his mother and her influence—didn't figure in this at all. You earned the appointment on your own merit, Vernon."

"I'm pleased to hear that. But I'm still left wondering why I was picked when there're men in the church who've been going here so much longer than me, who coulda served knowing so much more than I do about this church in particular—"

"Harold Mueller and Karl Toews spoke out very forcefully on your behalf, Vernon. And I was right behind them, if you must know. I think you're too shy about yourself to see you have an ability to look at things from a more… a broader point of view. I like that in a man, and we need as much of that as we can get right now.

"Okay, let me put it to you like this. You've said enough about this war, about points of view on the Anabaptist tradition, to let it be known that you stand firmly behind your convictions, and some of those aren't exactly square with others who are stubborn as sin in their interpretations of what should and shouldn't be accepted in our churches, especially at this time. Whole congregations are being ripped apart over this war. Some of us on the board felt that we needed some, I'll say, gentler ways of looking at non-resistance, in particular. What's almost funny about all this, to me, is that when we decided to approach you about board membership, we had no idea you had taken your job at the Landing Field. It was an added nudge the board needed to confront this situation head-on. What we don't want here is divisiveness to the point where we have a splinter group—and there is one forming—trust me on this, well, you have to have seen it yourself. We just don't want them running out the door—anyway not yet. As you know, Mennonites are far too comfortable, in my books, splintering off and forming small autonomous fellowships that turn into more churches. To me, it's a bit like being too quick settling for divorce in a contentious marriage when a little reconciliation and compromise is called for.

"And I have to admit, I've been old guard about a lot of church policy surrounding the pacifist position. I've thought that reigning in some of this modernity taking place is best, even healthiest, especially, in this church under Ervin's more liberal leadership. But upon second look, I see we're all—and I'm talking about Mennonite churches in general but especially those within our General Conference—we're just too vulnerable now, and, okay, yes, I'll say it, some of that vulnerability is financial as well as in other ways. Such as the young people leaving in droves."

Simon Nichols waits. When Daddy stays quiet, only nodding, Simon Nichols goes on.

"You can see for yourself how strong the conservative element is and who they are on the board. The first word out of Wesley Schmidt's mouth is 'de-fellowship' where non-combatance is concerned. Forget the boys who are 1-A! They're to be automatically shunned, if not excommunicated. This young man and his minions—who, by the way, are growing in numbers here at Hopewell—are for 1-A-O status among Mennonites, period. There are to be no options to their minds. And they interpret that to mean basically farming or CPS. camps, with work outside of any military framework.

"Vernon, you may not know this—not being very long in our group—but our membership has dropped fourteen percent over the last five years, and take a look around." Simon Nichols stretches his long arms out around the room, turning in his seat to do this. "Our congregation isn't exactly in the thousands to begin with. And as our young people more and more mix with the world out there, being a Mennonite isn't very attractive, especially when your church makes 'worldliness' out to be every sin you can think of."

Daddy and Simon Nichols smile at each other. Simon Nichols takes a bite of food from his plate, chews, and swallows quickly. "I'm very torn myself, as I told you. But I've been a businessman all my life, and I can tell you that a no-compromise stance doesn't move much forward. But," Simon Nichols sighs, "I suppose that's the whole idea behind this conservative group. I think that's why Wesley is here, you want to know my opinion. Why he's on the board, I mean. He's speaking for more than just our congregation. He's attempting to back, if not cause, a rebellion or, no, a reformation might be more accurate.

"I can tell you more about what's going on with this in a broader sphere another time, but he's got the backing of his father's influence which stretches far, let me tell you, about as deep and far as the isolationist position goes which is now resonating with a lot of members in our churches." Simon Nichols eats more quickly, like Daddy is about to interrupt him. He holds up his hand a minute, then lets it drop to the side of his plate. "Speaking frankly, but when your son is being called up, and a line has to be drawn for or against—it gets dirty really fast, when it's personal. The point is, Ervin and I are against this internal movement and are doing a little conspiring of our own to hold this congregation together—if necessary—by hook or by crook!" Daddy and Simon Nichols laugh a little together again.

"And *I'm* the crook." Daddy is still laughing but not as much.

"You're the crook." Simon Nichols nods, eating some more. "And, by God, I'm the hook!"

"Okay, I've taken the bait, looks like!" Daddy is grinning big. "I just hope I can—"

"It's not quite like that, Vernon—that's if you were going to say you don't want to let us down—especially, it's not with Ervin and me. You've been selected because we believe you will stand up for yourself and tell us why. We need you, need your arguments but, also, some moderation during that argumentation. We need weight on the other side. It's starting to get heavy on Schmidt's side of the seesaw.

"But...." Simon Nichols pauses, and I think he's going to say "hell," like Daddy would if he was talking to Momma. Instead Simon Nichols says, "Well, who knows how any of this will turn out in the end? It could be that this war will tear the heart right out of our whole Mennonite tradition. But we need to look at what's going on with an open mind, or we may just blow ourselves apart to the point that there won't be much left to put back together. This hard-hat conservative element has me concerned."

I think of Humpty Dumpty but know not to interrupt. Daddy and Simon Nichols are very serious.

Simon Nichols waves his hand in the air. "Okay, that's enough of that. But before I bring down my gavel, let me tell you that Ervin, Karl, Harold, and me are there to give you any support you need. Harold, by the way, is the most liberal man on our board, believe it or not, despite his wife and her family. He's a good man to bounce any idea off of that's coming from left field." He slaps the table lightly and says, "There, I really am done," and he looks at me and adds, "You have been very patient, young lady. Thank you."

Nobody ever thanks me for listening. I don't know what to say, but Daddy grins and laughs a little at me, so I tell Simon Nichols, "You're welcome." He thinks that's very funny, so he laughs with Daddy.

Then he asks Daddy about his job at Hopewell Landing Field, the kind of work he will be doing. Daddy doesn't seem upset, and neither does Simon Nichols. When they talk about the pilots, especially the Brits and what planes they use for training, Daddy tells him that they train pilots with BT-15s. Then he tells him the Brits don't see the war quite as we Americans do.

"From what I saw during my tour of the Field, before I started this job, our boys think this is some kinda big game. But, you know, they're young and are looking forward to sowing some wild oats in the skies over Germany. But the Brits are dead serious. When Captain Hornsby went to take a call at the back of the hangar, one of the English flyboys told me that his home in London had been bombed during the Battle of Britain, and although he hadn't lost anybody from his family, he knows personally what it means to have Hitler invade your country.

"His idea is that Americans need to be vigilant, not just overseas, but on the home front, because we're wrong if any of us think it couldn't happen here—though I can't imagine there're too many Americans left around who think invasion is impossible. But I gotta tell ya, my brother-in-law told me just the other day that he and a farmer up the road were talking about this very thing, and Clifford said this guy'd told him he didn't see why the heck we didn't just leave the Europeans, Japan, and China to fight out their own troubles. Seemed to him that since we'd entered the war, it had escalated outta control. I wonder what this man thinks we shoulda done when the Japs bombed our ships at Pearl? Try to negotiate? Really? This was a totally aggressive act, one meant to surprise. It wasn't retaliation for anything.

"There are those, Vernon, who believe that regardless of the intention of such acts, the Christian thing to do is to never stop trying to negotiate."

"Isn't that what Chamberlain tried to do? What happens if you can't negotiate? You let them take what's yours?"

"It's a position. One that I've come to see as too extreme, but you know as well as I do that it's what Wesley Schmidt is advocating. The Quakers believe that ultimately the pendulum will swing the other way. It's just that most of us are reluctant to die, see hundreds of thousands die, before that happens. But that's what's happening in any case, is it not?"

"Darlene and I've talked about this, and that's her position, as well."

I want to say, it's Momma way of thinking sometimes, but Daddy wouldn't like it. She's saying yes to him working at the Landing Field.

Simon Nichols looks over at Daddy and smiles a little, then starts eating again. I watch him while Daddy watches him, too, staying quiet. Simon Nichols moves back in his seat and touches his tie when he brings anything up to his mouth. Sometimes, he turns to the side and looks at me and smiles. When Daddy eats fried chicken he holds it with both hands, but Simon Nichols only uses one hand for everything. The other hand holds his napkin that he brings up to his mouth after he's finished with each bite and after he puts his chicken down. He looks at the hand he uses to eat with to make sure no chicken grease is left behind. His fingers are long and skinny and very white. I don't think he works, not like Daddy. If he ever worked with his hands, he's stopped a long time ago, like old people do. Grandpa Jantz doesn't work anymore, either. Daddy told me he's retired. I know that means Grandpa Jantz doesn't work like he used to, but when I first asked Daddy what being retired meant, he said, "It means you get tired over and over." He was kidding me. Momma shook her head at him, saying, "Oh, Vern."

As Daddy and Simon Nichols talk, I watch Daddy. At first he only listened or answered Simon Nichols's questions with real short and quick answers. But now, he's talking a lot. He's looking at Simon Nichols long and hard, saying he thinks Mennonites should start looking at pacifism a little different than they're used to doing. They should ask if their ideas about nonresistance would remain as they are if the war came here, in this country, like the Brit pilot was suggesting.

Simon Nichols eats and nods as he listens, stops and says a few words, and then starts listening and eating again. Daddy never talks this much, except with Momma, but I wonder if maybe he talks more when he's at work, at board meetings, with Captain Hornsby, and other people Momma and me don't know. Daddy talks with Grandpa Dirks, all the time, and with his brothers, especially Uncle Willard, when we go to his homeplace in Clearview on Sunday visits. But they usually talk together outside, so I don't hear what they say. Aunt Josephine says it's because men don't want to talk when women are around.

"It's men-talk," she says. She calls it boy-talk when it's my boy cousins. "No place for the likes of us," she explains.

Momma argues with her about boy-and-men-talk. She tells me when Aunt Josie isn't around, "If your Aunt Josephine ever talks anything substantial in this world with her husband or our dad, I'd like to hear it. It's ridiculous for a woman of her intelligence. She doesn't speak enough of her own mind, far as I'm concerned. She lives First Timothy two, eleven to the letter." Momma says, in a snotty voice, "'Let the woman learn in silence with all subjection.' Sometimes I wish the Apostle Paul had been struck by bandits very hard up the side of his head on the road to Damascus before his donkey had a chance to speak to him! We women would be a lot better off."

"Amen," I said at the time, and she laughed big. Momma says, "Amen to that," to Daddy. Momma added, though, "Don't think you get off so easy, Shike. Little further down in the same passage—believe me, I have these passages all memorized—Paul tells men they oughta rule their own houses properly, which means that fathers should have their children under their subjection, too. And before you ask, 'subjection' means 'under their thumbs.' So there you see, we're both hung out to dry, kiddo." She smiled at me, taking her eyes off the road for a minute because she was driving us somewhere.

After she drove a while without saying anything, she said to herself, "You never heard any such advice from the Lord, Himself. He was very close to Mary Magdalene. So that's what I go by." She puckered her lips and looked at me. "Always go to the main source for advice, Sweetie-Pie." She laughed a little, but I didn't know why.

Now Daddy's sitting at the table talking to Simon Nichols like his life depends on it. When Momma watches Daddy talk to Grandpa Dirks, she nods and tells me that they're talking like their lives depend on what they're saying. I've watched, too, and found out that when their lives depend on it, their hands are always moving around while they're talking, and they point with their fingers this way and that, usually at each other. But mostly, Grampa Dirks and Daddy sit in chairs on the porch or in the barn. I sometimes walk to the barn while Daddy is helping Grandpa Dirks milk the cows and listen to them talk. But Daddy can go on and on, too, with Uncle Willard at the Jantz homeplace. But usually they don't talk war as much as about people they both know and what these people are doing that's stupid.

Daddy leans over the table where we are sitting to say something I think he doesn't want people to hear because he's practically whispering. He taps his pointer finger on the table many times while he asks, "How does a man survive? What will he do or not do in order for him to believe he doesn't have a hand in any of the wrong things that are happening around him? Which is better? To raise wheat that'll show up in the mess kit of a soldier on the battlefield or to patch that soldier up in a medical tent so he can be sent back to the battlefield and aim his gun at the enemy again? Or, better yet, to sit it out in a CPS camp while his family has to live off a relative who's a farmer that's raising wheat and selling it to the government that's using it for the soldier toting the gun or feeding the families of the men who are fighting for the cause? That's what Harold Mueller and Karl Toews were arguing, in their own ways, in there today with Wesley, and I'm right by their side, Simon. It's not possible, in this country, today, to get around the war effort. It's everywhere. Wesley Schmidt is kidding himself."

"I don't know the answer either, Vernon. Everything is connected to it. There's no neutral position on any of it. I understand that's why the vote went the way it did. But as I told every man in the room, I feel like I'm going against the grain when I vote for rather than against the fighting." He raises his hand for Daddy to wait before talking more. "This all-pervasive war effort argument is why I voted on your side—really 'our side,' if you like, rather than 'their side.' I don't know how to keep our pacifist position anymore, and I understand why some try to. It's easy to say, 'go to the camps and lose your jobs' or 'let your relatives work your farms while you're in prison,' because none of us righteous ones is going to sell to the government who's waging the war. I don't see any of them leaving their wheat in the fields to rot, do you? And you're right. What good would that do?

"We left the old countries, time and time again, for this. And now here we are confronting it once more. Did our ancestors have it any easier back in the old countries when they were threatened with the confiscation of their property and their livelihoods if they didn't serve in the military? Remember, they were asked to pay a fine or to choose somebody to go fight in their place. When they said no, they were given the same options that our men are given now—there's never been a war in which these same options haven't been presented. It's why our ancestors said no to it all." Simon Nichols decides to eat a little more, finally finishing his plate.

So Daddy says, "It's different now in some ways, though, don't you think? Our ancestors were considered foreign people in a foreign land in Germany, Switzerland, and Russia, even after we'd lived there for hundreds of years—because of our beliefs, our traditions. We wanted to remain separate, to keep our own language as much as anything else. When we immigrated to Russia, Catherine the Great promised us exemption from military service and their schools if we would come and transform unusable lands into productive ones. Our people wanted to keep, not just the Mennonite faith, but the Mennonite way of life alive."

Daddy sighs, letting air through his mouth slowly. "Language. We talk about resistance to military service so much in our history, but language is such an important part of our being a self-proclaimed people. Nothing kills a people quicker than the loss of its language. And everywhere we immigrated, it's one of the first things the host nation wanted us to do—send our kids to their schools where they'd learn to speak the national language.

"The thing that hooked us on the Russia immigration was Catherine's promise that we'd have our exemptions forever. Well, forever didn't last very long, did it? The length of her reign is the length of that 'forever.' So when she died, here came the agents with their edicts for the Mennonites—and the Jews, too, don't forget, who were badgered pretty much for the same reason. They wanted us both to be assimilated into Russian society by giving up our languages, our schools, and our isolated ways of life. They were met with direct resistance from the entire Mennonite and Jewish communities. Well, you know the story."

Daddy looks away and then back at Simon Nichols. He's excited because Simon Nichols is listening close. "Well, look at us now. Most of us are sending our children to public schools and speaking English more than Low German, and we consider ourselves Americans as much as the next guy. We're not isolated, Simon. Not anymore. Used to be that farming separated us, kept us to ourselves, but even that's changing as more and more of the young Mennonites are finding city jobs."

"Yes, all that is very true. And the techniques of farming have changed. Whole crews come up from south to north to help with harvest. And the selling is being sold to the hubs—where the elevators are. It's getting co-opted, just as you're saying."

Daddy is nodding, real fast. He pushes his plate aside and wipes the table in front of him with his hand, letting crumbs fall to the floor or on his lap. "Wesley Schmidt is the exception these days—the farming family. You can stay isolated that way, at least for now. But more and more young people—and I count myself one of them—see ourselves as American first and Mennonites second, just like the Presbyterians and Lutherans and, okay, the Catholics and Jews. Our boys want to join up like other Americans. They want to become part of the larger society."

Daddy doesn't let Simon Nichols get a word in edgewise. He's on a rampage about the war. "It's a whole different world. Only the Old Colony, Amish, Holdemans, Hutterites, and a few other branches are keeping to the old ways. And I have to tell you, I deliberately chose not to be in those communities because I want to be a part of American society, not apart from it. I still want to be a Mennonite, but I want to be...."

"A more liberal one?" Simon Nichols asks, quietly. His fork is on his empty plate, and he's sitting straight as a board in his chair. I think he might get up and leave.

Daddy says, "There wasn't a man in the room that didn't agree with you, realize what you were telling us, especially about our heritage, the lives that our ancestors sacrificed in order to be who we are. Consarnit, Simon. What I'm trying to say is that I'm conflicted about this, too. I get it, but I want a different outcome than Schmidt, because I don't think his outlook is facing future reality."

Daddy wipes his mouth with his napkin, which he doesn't use at home very much. When Momma wants to fancy-up the table, she complains because Daddy never unfolds his napkin. Now he uses it real careful, the same way Simon Nichols uses his. He takes a quiet drink from his coffee cup. Then he pushes his cup toward me and asks for me to go and get him more, but I want to listen.

"Go on, now."

But I ask if I can finish my potato salad first. I only have two bites left.

"Okay, but don't take until you're seven, okay?"

Simon Nichols acts like he's surprised that I'm that big. He holds up his hand, his bony fingers together like he's stopping traffic. He looks at Daddy and says real soft, "Just a minute, Vernon." Then he says to me, "I don't think you should take a chance on ruining your pretty dress. Why don't you ask your mother to bring your father his pie and coffee? I want to say hello to your mother, anyway. You tell her that for me, will you do that?"

Daddy nods for me to go. I stay to listen a little more, moving the last bite around on my plate.

"Here's the thing," Daddy says to Simon Nichols, who sits up straight again. "In those days, back in the old country, even though the agents of the government came around, constantly changing the laws to try and get us to assimilate, a man owned his land. But even if he rented it, he could live off of it. He was independent financially for his survival. He sold his harvest and other goods in order to make enough, but he could survive off his land, from his orchards, his gardens, his chickens, cattle, and hogs. Families canned, butchered, preserved. They had smoke and ice houses. They were self-sufficient and self-propagating. In a lot of cases, they even managed their own seeding, passing their seeds down and around. They started their own red wheat in Russia that they brought with them to America." Daddy is talking hard and fast. I don't want my plate to get done, so I just keep licking my spoon. Daddy keeps right on talking, forgetting about his empty coffee cup. "At least that's what our history tells us as you know so well. Your family's not Ostroger is it? Isn't Nichols a Swiss Mennonite name?"

Simon Nichols shakes his head. "No, we came from Russia, Volhynia area, so we Nicholses are Ostroger just like your family. You may be thinking of Edna's folks. She was a Yost which is a Swiss-Southern German name. Actually, Yost is Amish, too. But her family—her siblings, I should say—have become Presbyterian. So the conservative Mennonite part of her family has changed quite a lot. Her parents are gone, and they must have been what were holding the Anabaptist part of her family together. Her father especially was pretty fiercely old country Mennonite. But no, I'm Ostroger."

"Well, forgive me, then. I'm spouting off here about things you already know too well for me to be saying anything more, especially about this way-back-in-Russia business. But my point is that with everything now linked to the government or the bank—to money owed for machinery and for mortgages on the property in order to stay ahead, especially with the depression just over—it's different. There's no way most of us can live off of what we have. Darlene's and my parents are still working the land. In my family's case, my brother is working Dad's land for him since he's retired. But farmers everywhere are finding it harder and harder to be as self-sufficient as they used to be. They gotta have help."

"New Deal," Simon Nichols says.

"Yeah, that's saved a lotta people, but it didn't help Whalen. He didn't just owe for his equipment—which he lost—he owed for the seed he planted and for the feed for his animals. Our people in the past had an agricultural community. Everybody now keeps hollering, our ancestry, our tradition, our way-a-life. If we're thinking that, we're way off the mark because only half of the people in the pews are still farming—if even that many any loand not so longer. It was our tradition. We wanna go back to what we were back then, we'll have to do what the Amish and Holdemans are doing, and that's a different game altogether, isn't it? And anyway, you and I both know that's not gonna happen. Look at the young people sitting in our pews, just like you say. How many are there? And they're not going back to the old ways. It's a pipe dream, even for those who still want that life."

"Not to belabor the point but like Wesley Schmidt."

"*Especially* like Wesley Schmidt. I think he's trying to save what doesn't exist much anymore."

"So what do you think we should do, then, Vernon? To remain Mennonite and not something else, like everybody else, every other 'Protestant else?'"

"It's something I keep asking myself. You know, if I didn't work at the Field, part of any salary I make anywhere will go to the government for the war effort whether I want it to or not. If we put in gardens in the backyard like Darlene and Josephine are doing, then we're helping the food situation connected to the war by allowing more food for our boys over there. It's something isn't it, when you make a garden that helps the government's rationing program and keeps you alive so you can work for the government which takes part of your earnings for the war."

Daddy stops and brings his hands down like he's dropped them on the table, but when they land flat, the sound is soft. "I know, we said a lotta of this during our meeting, but we only skimmed the top, because I think it hurts for all of us to say it, hear it outright, like it is—which is that our way a-life is being eroded and not so slowly, but beyond doubt, surely it is."

Simon nods, but he is thinking deep. His face is sad.

"And here's the thing, in my view—and that's what you've asked for—there's no saving it, Simon. It's not just going—a good part is already gone. It's true that our way of life has always been threatened this way, but now, this time, it's not just that it's more out in the open, more direct, it's everywhere. I'm not sure we understand this, especially the farmers. Think about how different our world is from our ancestors in Russia. Everything is a part of everything else in a way it wasn't back then. For one thing, we have information in a way they didn't then. We know what's happening closer to when it's actually happened. We can see the larger picture in ways they couldn't. We hear and see the world as it's happening, and so we're a part of it."

Daddy is talking about as fast and hard as I've ever seen him talk to anybody except Grampa Whalen. "I know it's always been felt directly in the lives of our relatives back in the old countries when they had to pick up and move and do that again and again, leaving their gains behind—whole farms, livestock, all their investments of time, money, and worry. That's how they got to

America in the first place. I do get that! But now, the threat to our way of life seems like there's no picking up, going somewhere else, and getting away from it. Where the heck can we go, immigrate to? This isn't just one country threatening another country anymore. This is whole parts of the world threatening the other parts of the world.

"What I'm wanting to say, I guess, is that we all agreed about this with each other in that meeting today, well, with the exception of Wesley and his followers. But underneath our agreement that we'll let every man decide for himself is the reality that we need to rethink what pacifism really is to us. I mean, is it even possible the way it used to be—unless we isolate ourselves and become one of the plain, peculiar people, and how long will that even be possible? I'm not sure I understand what a man is doing when he doesn't go to war."

Simon Nichols is listening to Daddy's every word. He looks at Daddy, nodding. He's done with his plate and is eating the cake he had Miss Stutzman get for him. He takes little itty-bitty bites and chews forever and a day. Daddy was done with his dinner a long time ago.

He tells me to go get his coffee, now, not tomorrow morning, and what am I still sitting here for? And see if there's any pie left. He will just be a pig and have another piece, he says. He and Simon Nichols laugh. They both know how skinny they are! Momma always says to Daddy when he tells her to have another helping of this or that, "Go ahead and laugh, Vernon, you don't have to worry about such things. But we're all hoping to be around to get a good look at you when you turn sixty!" I don't have any reason to stay at the table and listen. My potato salad is gone.

"To be truthful, I don't know if there's a big difference between shooting a man in the head yourself or patching one up in a hospital tent so he can go out there and do it. Is there a difference between my flying the planes that drop the bombs or my working on the planes that other people fly to drop them? Wesley Schmidt sat in our meeting telling us that the only way around such dilemmas is to do neither. But the question then becomes what can we do that doesn't in some way support the doing of that? He claims that he raises the wheat, and what happens to it after he sells it isn't his moral responsibility. He puts it in the Hopewell granaries and is then absolved of any wrongdoing with it? Is what he's saying true? If I'm hearing him right, he believes that there's a way to be free of this altogether—"

"I think what Wesley is saying, Vernon, is that wheat is neutral. It's food, and food is something every living thing has to have to live—even plants take nutrients from the soil. He's saying that he grows a product that generates life, not death. Trainer airplanes and bombers aren't neutral. They are specifically made for killing. It's not my argument necessarily, you understand. I'm just clarifying the issue he's raising."

"Okay." Daddy looks like he will pop. "But what if a person is allergic to wheat, if they eat it, and it kills them. Does Wesley feel responsible for that? Wait," he says when he sees Simon Nichols is smiling and is going to say something. "I know this is stretching the issue to ridiculous lengths, but what if you take the argument of airplanes and reversed it on itself. What if they're being used, as I think they are, to kill in order to save lives, they allow people to be free and not live under the terror of death? What about that?"

Simon Nichols clears his throat and smiles again. "Actually, the argument many young Mennonites are using about this very point is called Just War Theory. You accept a lesser evil to stop a greater one." Simon Nichols doesn't know that Daddy has argued Just War with Momma.

"I think your argument about all of us not being able to stay on the farm and raise wheat is the better one, Vernon—the one that speaks to why pacifism needs a new definition. This one about allergic to wheat and killer airplanes is taking on a hue that looks a bit shady to me." He laughs, laying a hand on Daddy's shoulder. "You know, the Amish and Holdemans would tell you that whether the world changes or not doesn't figure in any of this as the Scriptures are the divinely-inspired Word of God, and they say what is allowed and forbidden, forever and ever, amen." Daddy shakes his head and snorts a little. Simon Nichols takes his hand from Daddy's shoulder. "Still, as a man who has farmed earlier in his life and then later had a hardware store, I'll offer a moral analogy in the shape of a hammer."

"What's that?" Daddy asks very serious now.

"Hammers, like most everything else, when put to it, are tools. They can destroy or they can build, have a destructive or constructive purpose, allowing for a pun here and there. So, I don't think your first argument is a total loss. I'd argue that about anything—wheat, airplanes, and hammers, too—when extended to the farthest ends of what it can do, can bode well or ill for mankind. It's what's done with them and how they affect us.

"Your argument about the trainer and bomber airplanes speaks to that, seems to me. It's an argument of the end justifying the means, and it's been used over and over in order to get people to kill one another from the beginning of time. And it's why, despite all that, I voted as I did today. Because I truly believe it's up to each man to decide how he's going to use the tools at his disposal. And, as for me, I have to decide if how I'm using my tools is ultimately for good or ill. I guess, I'd have to say I believe unequivocally in free will, the right to choose."

Daddy keeps nodding his head as he pushes me out of my seat, telling me to beat a path toward Momma and what he asked me ages ago to do.

As I get up to tell Momma to bring Daddy's pie and coffee, Simon Nichols starts talking about the depression and Roosevelt's New Deal, how the President did care about the farmers but wasn't able to bring a lot of his programs to more farmers in the South, and that Daddy was right, this exit from farms to towns has to do with farmers not making it without help. And the weather of the thirties figured in all of this, too, don't forget, he says.

As I walk away, Daddy's telling Simon Nichols that Americans seem to be okay about this war, this time, because it's making jobs for people the way that the New Deal did when Roosevelt first became President. Daddy turns while he talks and points me in the direction of where Momma is and holds up his cup.

When I get to her, she leans over the food table to ask me what in the world is happening at our table, that she can see the men have been talking for over an hour, so what in heaven's name have they been talking about? I tell her Simon Nichols and Daddy are talking war, ancestors, tools, and depression.

She looks surprised, glancing toward their table. Daddy starts waving his cup in the air again for her to see. "Doesn't seem they're upset or anything. Oh, he wants more coffee." I turn around and look at them, and she tells me not to do that. "Heavens sakes, Shike, Simon Nichols will know we're talking about him!" I want to tell her that he's listening to Daddy's men-talk and doesn't care about us women, but I tell her instead that Daddy wants pie with his coffee and that Simon Nichols wants to talk to her. She smiles, then, and moves fast to gets what Daddy asked for. She tells me she'll never stop believing in miracles.

"Amazing, don't you think?" I ask.

She laughs out loud, saying, "It surely is!" I don't know what this all means, but Momma is happy about Simon Nichols and Daddy's talking, so I'm happy, too. Daddy stands up and starts to come around the table's end to take his pie and coffee from Momma as we walk up to him.

"Stay where you are, Vernon, I'll get it to you all in one piece, I think." She says this like she's carrying too much and is about to drop it. Her voice is polite, but she's breathing kinda shaky-like. She's carrying a coffee pitcher along with everything else. She wouldn't let me help. She hands Daddy his cup and plate and then asks Simon Nichols if he would like more coffee. She puts the coffee pitcher over his cup. I think Momma looks beautiful in her dark blue dress with puffed sleeves and white lining around the collar. And her new heels. She wears what she calls "light make-up," even though Mennonite women aren't supposed to. "I put on as little as I can and still see that I have some on," she explained to me when she was at her dresser getting ready for church. "I'll just have to deal with the stares until somebody makes too bigga fuss." She took her white apron off before she came to our table.

Simon Nichols tells her no more coffee, thanks, and puts his hand over his cup. Momma asks him about his wife, tells him we all missed Edna in church today. He tells her that she stayed home as she isn't very well and that Glynda has gone to take care of her while he stayed for lunch and talked with "the newest board member." They all laugh a little because he means Daddy. "Right now, Edna's dealing with a lot of conflict over acceptance and denial. She tells me she isn't feeling bad physically as much as finding it emotionally difficult."

"I'll give her a call, if that's all right," Momma tells him.

"Oh, she'd love that, I'm sure."

Then he tells Momma that he's really stayed far too long already, that he needs to attend to Edna at home, but he's enjoyed his discussion with her husband about the board vote and the state of the union in this war we all find ourselves in. Momma asks him if it's true that the church might lose Glynda

Faye as the pianist because she's leaving for college. He tells her that at first they thought Glynda might go to the university in Norman but that now it looks like she'll be staying out her first semester in the spring, going the winter term to the Westminster Presbyterian College here in Hopewell at least for the first year so she can stay near Edna.

"She'd be willing to go to a Presbyterian college?" Momma asks.

"It's the only college in town, and it has accepted her application, even though it was past registration time. They made an exception because of her circumstances."

"So she gave up on going to The University of Oklahoma?"

"She did, insisting on Westminster in town, so I let her have her way. Sylvia wasn't so happy as she thinks Glynda needs to fly away from the nest. But we've compromised as Sylvia can't come back here to live and help care for Edna. Chicago is her life now, she says. Down the road Glynda can transfer somewhere else if she decides to." Then Simon Nichols says, very low, "I'd rather you two didn't say anything as yet since we're trying to keep the seriousness of Edna's illness to ourselves as long as possible. All of Edna's family doesn't even know yet—she has family in Chicago she needs to contact. But her prognosis is promising. The last doctor's report, day before yesterday, showed clearly that the cancer hasn't spread greatly and that treatment might be helpful." He glances around and then turns back to our table to say, "It's been difficult keeping the ladies of the church away from visiting, using the excuse that first we weren't sure of what she had and thought that infection could be an issue—both for Edna and for others. But we know now what's happening and can't very well hold off much longer. I thought I'd have it announced next week when Ervin is back."

"She's having surgery then?" Momma asks.

"Actually she undecided about that, and the decision will be her own doing. Edna's... well, she's old school about all this. She's taking some new antibiotics, and we'll have to wait to see how much influence that will have. She's simply asked that we, the doctors and her family, not interfere with God's will. What that is, she says, is according to what's revealed to her, personally. I'm finding this a very hard decision to honor, but I've promised her I will respect what she decides."

"I'm so very, very sorry," Momma says. She puts a tea towel down on the table and places the pitcher of coffee on it, standing with one hand on its handle.

"So are we all. She hasn't felt well for a while. She didn't even have a doctor, I'm ashamed to say. I don't know when the last time was that she'd had a decent check-up. We only learned the diagnosis a few weeks ago. Glynda Faye is beside herself. She and her mother are very close. But then everybody likes Edna. She's a shining beacon in the community where we live, at church here, and to her family and friends. I'm hoping that if recent treatments fail, she will reconsider surgery for the sake of her family and friends. But for now, Edna's putting her foot down about any invasive treatment, but that could change. She's a staunch Calvanist Presbyterian at heart, you know, God's will and predestination at the center of her upbringing. Her doctor has boosted her energy with iron, but it won't last, he tells us. I have to let her family know this week. It will mean some visits, I fear, and I'm not sure she's up to that at the moment."

Simon Nichols stops and looks straight ahead, his mouth open a little, as though he's going to say more, but he remains silent. Everybody is quiet. Simon Nichols looks like he's going to cry, but he looks at his hands, rubs them together a little and continues, his voice quiet but strong. "Her spirit is still lively. It's hard for us to believe this is really happening."

"I... we... I should have called." Momma starts to say more, but Simon Nichols interrupts her, closing his eyes and touching her arm.

"She's quite a well-endowed woman, as you see for yourself," Simon Nichols says, looking right at Momma's face and smiling. Momma looks down. "I like that in a woman," he says softly. "She enjoys her own cooking but now... well, we'll simply have to...." He falters, looking toward Daddy and after folding his napkin real careful, puts it on the table like it might break. "I've been away from her far too long this morning. But I wanted to make sure we were set with this board business. And Vernon, I've enjoyed talking with you about the world's affairs." He stands, smiles, and shakes Daddy's hand. "And it's been a double pleasure," he adds, offering his open hand to Momma, holding hers a little while, putting his other hand over their handshake.

She smiles but acts like she doesn't know what else to say. Finally she adds,

"Our prayers go home with you, today," She slips her hand from Simon Nichols's. "Tell her that for us, please."

Momma steps away from the table and then suddenly reaches out and touches Simon Nichols's white shirt sleeve, whispering, "Thank you." I don't know for what, and when I looked over at Daddy I don't think he knows either. I want to ask, "What're you thanking him for. You say he's rich and hard to go through the eye of a needle." But then, Simon Nichols brings his hand up to take hers and turning around to look right at her, he says, "You are welcome. I am very glad you both are part of our church community."

He reaches in his pocket for a handkerchief which he brings up to his eyes. He doesn't move.

Daddy stands with a funny smile on his face. He has tears in his eyes, too. He moves from one foot to the other with his mouth a little open. Suddenly, he says in a shaky voice, "If there is anything we can do… we want to help, if we can." I've never heard Daddy talk like this. He's crying a little. It's very quiet all at once.

Momma looks around the room, so I do, too. Everybody has stopped talking and nobody is moving. They are all looking at us. Simon Nichols lets air out of his mouth and says "ah…." to Daddy, putting the handkerchief back into his pocket. "It's out now, I fear! No, no." He shakes his head at Momma who says, again, that she's so sorry. "This is a good thing. I leave it to you and Vernon to break the news as you see fit. I really must go home, Vernon." He bends down a little like he's going to sit back down, but he doesn't. He says in a whisper to Daddy, "Would you mind walking me to the parking lot? Your coffee might have to be warmed up when you get back, but I need a friend to see me out the door."

Daddy rushes around the table, but Simon Nichols stands up straight and says, "I'm fine. I don't need help walking. I'm not that fragile. I just need someone steady by my side." And Daddy walks out the back door a little behind him. Nobody moves in the room until they close the door. We can see Daddy and Simon Nichols's legs from the basement windows walking along the sidewalk, then across the parking lot toward Simon Nichols's car.

In the basement, everybody begins to talk and move at once. Some people pick up their plates and carry them to the kitchen. When Momma is behind the food table, tending to Teddy, thanking the women for watching him for her, they gather around her, and she tells them about Edna's diagnosis as they ask her questions. One by one, they crumbled their aprons in their hands or lay their fingers on their chests and make gasping sounds like soft cries in their throats.

6.

On the way home

WHILE TEDDY IS SLEEPING ON the back seat, I am standing against the back of the front seats to hear what Momma and Daddy are saying. As he drives, Daddy is talking to Momma about the church board meeting.

"Far as about half the men were concerned," Daddy begins, "the question of whether men should serve had already been decided a long time ago, by tradition. Wesley Schmidt, as you can imagine, wanted very strict rules for non-combatant and conscientious objector status. Actually, he wanted only one rule—out the door for anybody accepting 1-A status. His view is that those who choose to carry a gun or enter the service in any capacity are to be immediately dismissed from membership. To his mind, Mennonites aren't allowed to be involved in military service, that non-combatance is an illegitimate category. He compared it to the Catholic notion of purgatory. 'An idea totally made up,' he said. 'It has no Scriptural validity at all.'

"His idea is that our Mennonite tradition is based on a number of foundational tenets—we have a language of our own, believe in Christian education, adult baptism, pacifism, free will, humility, and community discipleship. To his mind, there are only two ways out of the pacifist position. You either are exempt by the government from service or you are sent to a Civilian Public Service camp. He says conscientious objectors can only work in jobs that'll serve the

general population such as medical services and jobs with the Civilian Conserva-
tion Corps. And exemptions should only be for agricultural reasons or because
of enrollment in seminaries and colleges for teaching." He even hesitates, Daddy
tells her, on this last point as Schmidt doesn't believe ordination is necessary for
preaching—only God's call is needed for a man to preach. This, of course, is the
Holdeman view. But since the General Conference advocates divinity degrees,
and he belongs to a General Conference Church, he'll go along with this."

Momma turns around and tells me to sit down when Daddy suddenly slows
down as a car enters his lane from an intersection. I nod but keep standing as she
becomes involved again in listening to Daddy.

"What Schmidt really believes, of course, is that there's no work acceptable
on the battlefields or on overseas bases, not even teaching school to the kids of
military personnel. He believes any non-combatants serving in capacities other
than those he's named should be shown the door, period, end of discussion."

"Don't the Holdemans believe in preacher selection by lottery?"

"Well, yeah, if you mean when there's more than one candidate. Anyway, I
think they do, or, at least, they used to. They had the candidates go into a room
while the elders took the number of Bibles as there were candidates and put a
marker in one of them, shuffling them around, at random. Then the candidates
were led in front of the congregation, lined up at random before they came in.
Then, the present preacher handed out the Bibles, one by one, and the man who
got the Bible with the marker was the one they thought was chosen by God. I
never saw this myself, a-course, and my mother never discussed her church business with me. Could be I have it mixed up with the Amish, but I think your dad
told me this."

Momma nods and waits a while. "Well, in spirit, I'm on Wesley's side about
conscientious objector status for members of our church, I'm afraid, but, how's
that position gonna happen with only so many jobs not directly connected to the
war available here at home?"

"That was my question, but I phrased it a little different to the group, and
later, to Simon. I said there aren't any jobs period that aren't connected—"

"I know what you think, Vernon. You've hammered it home enough."

Daddy hesitates before he goes on. I think he might tell Momma about Simon Nichols's hammer for good or ill, but he doesn't. "Well, at the meeting, I didn't have a chance to say there weren't any non-war jobs because Harold Mueller beat me to it. He started right away about how everything was being touched by the war, and once he said that, the full discussion was on about what conscientious objection really meant to us—was it about each individual man deciding how to serve, according to his conscience, or, was it about Mennonite tradition, which was scripturally-based? And, a-course, scriptures were thrown back and forth, most of them from Matthew and Luke—especially the one about not resisting evil with evil and the golden rule".

"'Do not use force against an evil man,' is pretty clear." Momma says, and adds, "Matthew five, thirty-nine."

"Okay, Darlene, I'll tell you, just like you got through telling me a minute ago—I know where you stand by now." Daddy goes on without waiting for Momma to add more. "I gotta tell ya, though, it was pretty surprising because the whole thing didn't last very long, not as long as it could have. First of all, everybody in the room knows that Wesley is on the board because his dad's so well-known in Mennonite circles around the area—all over Oklahoma and Kansas, you really wanna know. So my question is this. Why is Wesley a member of our church, at all, since he's thinking like a Holdeman? Forget about the board, which is another issue, isn't it? Why the he… heck doesn't he belong to his dad's church, huh?" Daddy looks at Momma like he's deciding what to say next. He curls his lips up and then says, "Simon thinks Wesley's at Hopewell to keep us in line, or at the very least, to report back about what we decide to his dad. But my question, then, is why should Schmidt Senior care?

"You think they're losing members to our church?"

Daddy doesn't hear her, or he doesn't want to stop and answer her. "Why I didn't suspect this—that he was on a mission from his dad's church—I don't know. The kid looks exactly like one of these young Holdeman guys I've known all my life, including his careful-cut beard. I wonder if that's why they didn't want him in their pews? His dad's Holdeman community probably objected to Wesley's having a modern appearance and attitude, especially being the pastor's son, so Schmidt Senior thought up this great mission he's sent him on. What did Simon tell me? He's twenty-six. How many twenty-six-year-olds do you know on church boards anywhere? To say nothing of owning his own farm! But the real question, for me, is, how the heck did he get elected to our board? All these men had to come to some kind of agreement to put him there. I had my suspicions, but—"

"Was the same group of men on the board when he was voted in?"

"Good question, Darlene. But you know…." Daddy suddenly stops and studies Momma so hard she tells him to watch what he's doing and nods toward the windshield. Finally, he sighs and says, almost to himself, "It looks like there's something hard to figure out here until you take a look at the family trees of their church and ours."

"Family trees? You mean there's a family connection between Wesley and somebody else on the board? Who?"

"Not just the board. The pulpit."

"You gotta be kidding me? Ervin Classen is related to Wesley Schmidt?"

"Simon told me today that Wesley's his nephew. Ervin's sister is Wesley's mother."

"Oh, boy, we have a lot to learn, don't we?"

"I'd say so. But that's not all." Daddy swallows and waits, like he's telling something he's promised not to. "Harold Mueller is married to Classen's only other sister, Mary. So you tell me if that doesn't present some problems. Harold is downright liberal. Thing is, I don't like the man very much. But maybe that's only first impressions. He's… let's just say, he's stuck on himself. It's his opinions and nobody else's, is how he thinks. He can't listen. But there's Karl, thank God, and oddly, Simon, looks like. Gotta say, though, I can see now how each and every one of them is lining up and why."

"Well, the plot thickens, doesn't it? The influence because of relatives makes sense when you think about it.

"Yes, that, but Mom's church is like this, why wouldn't ours be? Churches have bylaws, policies like any other organization, when you think about it. Policies mean trouble because people are always going to disagree on something about them. And far as this pacifist thing is concerned, it's never been in contention, anyway not for us, until now—now that we're in a war up to our necks. Nothing ever changes. You'd think churches would be different than ordinary politics, but they aren't." Momma is having a good day. She isn't messed up like she is sometimes about the war.

"Maybe they are, actually." Daddy looks at Momma, then back through the windshield as he drives. "I mean, about changing. I gotta say my opinion of Simon Nichols is shifting and quick. I've liked the man from the start simply because he's so fair-minded, welcoming us the way he did, especially. But I didn't realize until we sat and talked, just now at lunch, that he listens to every point of view, all sides with the kind of attention I haven't seen in anybody except your dad. And, at this meeting, he was willing to bend his ideas when he thought it was best for the group."

It's quiet a long time. I almost decide to sit on the back seat with Teddy. Momma looks back to check on Teddy and sees me still standing against the front seats.

"I thought I told you to sit down, Shike. Daddy could suddenly stop, and you could get hurt. Now do what I told you and sit down with Teddy."

I sit down on the back seat, but when she turns around, I stand up again, real slow, so she won't notice I'm listening.

"Why do you think Simon didn't tell you about this family tree business before, Vern? I take it he's the one who told you about the connections."

Daddy nods. "I don't know, Darlene. Probably didn't want to influence my opinions, with me so soon on the board, you know, finding out all the secrets underneath. He's not sure that I'll even be able to stay on."

Momma starts to ask him what he means, but he continues real fast.

"Simon's a really, really interesting man, and not at all what he seems to be, at first, even as positive as that was to me. You gotta spend time talking to him to get to really know what he's about. He's not afraid to change his opinions on something, if he's convinced it's right, even if it goes against the grain. He reminds me of Whalen in a lot of ways." Daddy glances at Momma and waits. When she doesn't add anything, he starts up again.

"One thing I do know now, though, is that Nichols doesn't shy away from keeping what he calls 'the larger perspective' in mind, even when his beliefs are being attacked. So after today, I know, for certain, that he wasn't the one abstaining from me joining the board, you know, as I thought he might have done, knowing us so well, as he does—Shike staying with them and such. It was Wesley. He doesn't have the gumption to go against Simon, and with Classen being his uncle, he didn't think he could out and out vote against me which would've caused trouble, since they had to have consensus. He would've been the one holding everything up. Remember, the other two conservatives—Lewellyn and Yoder—backed me. I would've thought they'd follow Wesley's lead, but they didn't, when it came down to it. They voted for me as a board member and sided with us more liberal members on pacifism. So who coulda guessed?

"Anyway, here's the real dilemma to my mind. Simon talked a lot about wanting me on the board in order to have a more even balance, but he as good as told me that what he and Classen are actually doing is stacking the deck against Wesley and any influence he can gather around him, because they think he's trying to cause a split in the church. So Wesley's followers must count way beyond the board members. Basically, Simon thinks Wesley is his father's plant in our church to help guide those who want to be more conservative away from our church or to help them start expressing more forcefully their point of views, changing church policy. It could be as simple as trying to cause a reformation within these more moderate churches, just like John Holdeman did. And Wesley could use this war issue to do it."

"That makes the most sense to me," Momma says, then adds, "Nice way to get your dad's approval."

"Isn't it? John Holdeman thought the Old Mennonite Church he belonged to needed to be reformed, to the point of starting his own church. His parents had to make a decision to stay with the church they belonged to or leave and go with their son, who'd told them that he'd had a divine revelation to do this breaking away."

"Well, we know how that turned out, don't we?" Momma says. "Mother's spelled it out enough to me. You're supposed to leave the church of your fathers to follow 'the way of the cross.'"

"And we know how that turned out as well, don't we? She didn't follow her own convictions is how! And Ava isn't telling you the whole story if she hasn't told you that Amos Holdeman, John's father, left the Old Mennonite Church immediately upon his son's revelations and establishment of a new reformed church, but his mother didn't."

"I didn't know that. Mother's always made it sound like John Holdeman's parents were his first members."

"Not so, Darlene. Holdeman's mother never left the Old Mennonite Church, even though he wrote her letters attempting to get her to support him by joining his church."

"What was her name?"

"John Holdeman's mother?"

"Yes, isn't that who we're talking about?"

"Nancy Yoder, as I remember. What does that have to do with anything?"

"Just wondered. You ever take a look at any publications put out by the Holdemans? By any of the Mennonite churches, actually. Women are called by their husbands' names, never their own. It's Mrs. Whoever-His-Name-Is. Seems to me it would be nice to say Mrs. Nancy Holdeman, at least."

"Wives, submit to your own husbands, as to the Lord. For the husband is the head of the wife even as Christ is the head of the church—"

"You can stop right there, Vern. I know the scripture well. Ephesians five, twenty-two and twenty-three. I'm not sure this means that women's names can't be voiced though, do you?"

"Well, a-course not. I'm just saying that's probably why there's a Mrs. Whatever-His-Name-Is, instead of hers. It's just the way it is. Look at any church directory."

"Uh-huh. The town telephone directory is the same way. I'm just not so sure I'm in agreement with this practice, wherever it is."

"As long as you keep my last name you can call yourself anything you like besides!" Daddy's teasing her, and she slaps him on his sleeve. He ducks his head like she's going to smack him there, too, and they laugh.

"Watch your driving, you silly idiot."

"By the way, Simon voted Wesley to the board like everybody else. Think about that!

"You can see pretty quick that there's loyalty and friendship, as well as intermarriage between their church and ours. Simon's close to Classen and

Classen's related to Schmidt who wants to keep liberalism from spreading. Classen has clearly drawn his line, and so has Schmidt, which leaves Simon in the middle—his own conscience against his loyalty to Ervin and what they consider to be their church, since they were both part of the founding of it."

"Pretty interesting, huh? You think Wesley could be thinking about enjoying a little bit of freedom, down the road, while doing his father's bidding?"

"Maybe. But he's not likely to stray too far, as you can see. You know, come to think of it, John Holdeman's kids weren't little lambs following in their father's footsteps, by a long shot. One son was excommunicated and never returned to the church. Another one never joined. I don't know if he didn't join any church or just not his father's. Well, you know yourself, how it is with Whalen, and in my own family, with our dads. Neither one joined any church, period. And they both were raised in Holdeman homes."

"You're chockfull of Mennonite history this morning, aren't you, Vernon?"

"I've read a little here and there, but mostly I listen careful to the right people."

"That's good to know," Momma says, laughing. "Dad never interfered with Mother's views, though. And he attended Holdeman revival meetings when I was a kid. He took Mother to church some of the time—to Zion Mennonite in town, of course. But when she could convince him, he'd take her to Cedar Grove. Sometimes, he drove her as far as your mother's church."

"Really? Ava attended Weather Springs?"

"Not often. The drive's forty-five minutes, but when he did take her, he'd even go in with her and hear the sermon."

"I'm amazed. I never knew this. Wonder if Mother ever talked with her—if they ever met?"

"I never thought to ask. But Mom and Dad going as far as Clearview woulda been before the war, probably before we got married."

Momma and Daddy are quiet for a while. We are almost home. My legs are getting tired, but I'm afraid to sit down and miss something important.

"I'm not going to be the only one working out at the Landing Field, maybe. Karl applied for some civil service position out there. It looks like it'll be clerical at first, he told us. He's waiting to hear. And if he gets it, he'll be working for the military very much like I am, as a civilian, but for the army just the same."

"Oh, boy. He'd stop working at Bond Bread? He's worked there for years."

"Yeah. He's a delivery man, but he doesn't see any chance for advancement. He's had some accounting experience, so he's applied for an office job on the base. So there was a discussion about military-based jobs, and we all agreed there needed to be time for a full congregational discussion on this. So Simon said he thought holding a meeting this next Wednesday night instead of prayer meeting would be a good time. That way everybody could have their say. And after that, the board would make a statement about what actually would become church policy."

"I guess I don't understand, Vern. If a person gets to decide according to conscience, it seems like there isn't any limits, is there?"

"Well, that's a good question. I don't think they're thinking about it in quite that way, but you're absolutely right. They're thinking that 1-A status isn't in accordance with conference guidelines, even if each church gets to decide on that. The real question is how to define non-combatance.

"When Harold Mueller wanted to know what the General Conference's stand was on this, Simon told him that the Conference had given out a statement of commitment to non-violence but had left the non-combatant status up for each church to decide. If consensus couldn't be reached in a timely fashion within any church, the Conference suggested that majority rule would then be used by secret ballot. That's kinda interesting to me because the raising of hands is the usual way in our churches. I guess they're trying to keep the chance for church dissension down. This's a really hot issue, so how I'm reading all this is that my place on the board is only temporary—and so is Harold's— until non-combatance is totally defined with congregational input.

"In other words, I can't get kicked out of the church because I'm working at the field, but I may not be able to serve on the board. So all this manipulating that Nichols and Classen think they're doing to save the day might end up blowing up in their faces. But, for now, I'm in."

I open the door when Daddy stops in our driveway and turns off the engine. He tells me to wait a minute. He holds the keys in his hand tight so they don't jiggle, and he tells Momma he thinks most of the men in church aren't

going to give a lot of resistance to him working at the Field because they understand the situation.

"Wesley Schmidt is going to be called up himself. He's young. But he told
us outright that when he's drafted—and he believes he will be soon—his wife
and the baby will move back to her mother's, and he'll go to a CPS camp before he'll do anything for the war effort. But his whole grand standing's moot,
because he'll be exempted on religious and farmer-status grounds. He knows
this. We all know it. I mean, you don't get more Mennonite than his family is.
The history there runs deep. He didn't even go to public school. I do have to
say, they pay taxes—"

"Render to Caesar the things that are Caesar's and to God the things that
are God's. You told me," Momma adds with a sigh.

"Yep. The Amish do, too, most taxes, anyway, just not social security. They
sign away the right to get social security later for not paying into it."

"I didn't know that."

"Oh, yeah, they pay school taxes, even when their kids don't go to public
schools—attend their own. They're property-owners, so they pay on that. But,
for me, the big question isn't whether you pay taxes or not, it's that the payment of them has its complications about where the money goes, doesn't it?
I guess, they justify tax money used for war on the grounds that, just like the
wheat, you give the money or sell the wheat, and what the government decides
to do with it after that is between them and God."

"What was good enough for Caesar is good enough for our government,"
Momma says, patting Daddy's hand.

When we're inside, finally, Momma puts Teddy on the couch with his toy
cars by his side, and she goes into her and Daddy's bedroom to change clothes
for what she calls "kitchen duty," that's on her good days, when she's full of
what Daddy calls "vim-and-vigor" and has a sense of humor. She's having one
of the best days she's had in what feels like forever.

Once I'm in Teddy and my bedroom, I can't hear them talking anymore.

Everything is quiet. I take off my dress, putting it on the bed, spreading it
with my hands carefully before I put on a blouse and my overalls. I'm hoping
Momma won't mind me wearing them while we eat our dinner since there's no

company. I sit down on my bed, and I wonder what living in a real house would be like, and if that ever will happen.